DREAM OF THE RED CHAMBER

CHI-CHEN WANG, the translator, is Professor of Chinese at Columbia University, where he has been teaching language and literature since 1929. Among his other translations from the Chinese are: *Ah Q and Others, Traditional Chinese Tales,* and *Contemporary Chinese Stories. Readings in Traditional Chinese, Readings in Modern Chinese,* and *Current Chinese Readings,* and of *Stories of China at War.* He is also editor of three volumes of Chinese texts.

The present volume is a new translation by Professor Wang. His older translation of *Dream of the Red Chamber* was first published in 1929.

DREAM OF THE RED CHAMBER

Tsao Hsueh-chin

Translated and adapted from the Chinese by Chi-Chen Wang

With a Preface by Mark Van Doren

DOUBLEDAY ANCHOR BOOKS
DOUBLEDAY & COMPANY, INC.
GARDEN CITY, NEW YORK

COVER BY SEONG MOY
TYPOGRAPHY BY EDWARD GOREY

This translation of *Dream of the Red Chamber* was originally published by Twayne Publishers in 1958. The abridged Anchor Books edition is published by arrangement with Twayne Publishers.

Anchor Books edition: 1958

Printed in the United States of America

PREFACE

Dream of the Red Chamber, like any great story of another place and time, is remote and yet familiar, different and yet the same. Much here will strike a Western reader as strange, and naturally so, since a Chinese household of the eighteenth century is about as far away as the imagination can travel. But quite as much will not be strange; indeed, since the story is truly great, its essential features will be recognizable because they are features of the human mind and heart, which neither time nor place ever seems able to alter. Mr. Wang's problem, as he made his selection of chapters to translate, and as he proceeded then to adapt and render those chapters in an English contemporary with himself, was of course not an easy one; at one extreme there was the danger of a literalness that would yield only fantastic results, and at the opposite extreme there was the danger of a freedom that would rob the classic of its ancient flavor. Mr. Wang's solution appears in his admirable style, which is colloquial as that of the original is colloquial, and which does not hesitate to employ modern terms in the faith that their equivalents existed in the matchless novel of manners he translates.

Dream of the Red Chamber is more than a novel of manners, but in its anatomizing of one extensive family it is at least that. The House of Chia is a world in itself, complex and fascinating. Its population consists of those who serve and of those who are served; the maids no less than the mistresses, the messengers no less than the Matriarch. There are hundreds of people altogether, and each of them manages somehow to be an individual at the same time that he (or she, for women dominate the plot) maintains relations with the whole society of which he is a part. The whole society is doubtless what seems most interesting in the end. It is a human organism that must obey the laws of its own survival; and it does so no matter what individual gets in its way. To certain of its members it now and then seems heartless. But to say this is to suggest how far *Dream of the Red Chamber* transcends the ordinary novel of manners. It transcends it, indeed, to the point of tragedy.

Pao-yu and Black Jade are figures of high comedy whose affectations have an infinite charm; yet before the narrative is finished, they are a tragic hero and heroine too. They are Romeo and Juliet: young lovers whose concern for each other is negligible, is nothing compared with the concern their household continues to have for itself. So when Pao-yu must marry there is no thought that he shall marry Black Jade; Phoenix, the female Malvolio who runs the House of Chia with a merciless efficiency and a cold disregard for matters of the heart, decides that he shall marry Precious Virtue; and he does, in a scene reminiscent of Jacob and Leah; and Black Jade does not outlive her disappointment. Meanwhile, however, the courting of the two children—for they are scarcely more than that—has been conducted as high comedy. They are Benedick and Beatrice, they are Mirabell and Millamant: brilliant, proud lovers who quarrel oftener than they confess their feeling. But that has made them all the more attractive to the reader, and all the more convincing as lovers, so that their despair becomes his too, whether he be Western or Eastern. The greatest love stories have no time or place.

Arthur Waley concluded his preface to an earlier and briefer edition of this work by saying: "It only remains to assure the reader that in Mr. Wang's hands he will be perfectly safe. The translation is singularly accurate, and the work of adaptation skillfully performed." It is agreeable to remember now the words of so great an authority and to realize that with the passage of nearly thirty years Mr.

Wang, in addition to doubling the length of his text, has so perfected his style that the inimitable spirit of the original comes to us freely and fully, with neither let nor hindrance nor any least disloyalty of voice.

MARK VAN DOREN

CONTENTS

PART II

Continuation by Kao Ou

INTRODUCTION

Although for more than a century and half the *Hung Lou Meng* or *Dream of the Red Chamber*[1] has been recognized by sophisticated readers in China as the greatest of its novels and its background has been the subject of intensive research, little is known about Tsao Hsueh-chin, its author, even today. All we know definitely about him is that he died on February 1, 1764, at the age of around forty and that he was a grandson by posthumous adoption of Tsao Yin (1658–1712), one of the wealthiest and most eminent men of his time, a patron of literature and something of a poet himself. A few years after Tsao Hsueh-chin was born, however, the family suffered a series of reverses until by around 1742 the author was found living in reduced circumstances in the western suburb of Peking. From a poem written by a friend shortly after his death, we learn that he died "grieving over the death of his son" and that he left behind him a "new wife."

From these known facts, it is clear that Tsao Hsueh-chin had little firsthand knowledge of his family at the height of its prosperity. For artistic purposes he has placed Pao-yu, who is undoubtedly an idealized picture of himself, back in his grandfather's time, so that he would feel more poignantly the vicissitudes of fortune and see more clearly the vanity of life. There is no question, however,

[1] *Hung-lou* or *red chamber* refers to where young ladies live. Since there is more than one heroine in the novel, the English translation is more properly "Dream of Red Chambers," or "Dream of Fair Maidens" if one wishes to make the significance of the title more readily recognizable.

that he was writing about his own family; the parallels between certain incidents in the novel and known facts in his family background are too many and too striking for any doubt on this point. In fact, many puzzling aspects of the novel can be explained only as the result of a conflict between the author's desire to give a faithful account of his family and his wish to respect the feelings and sensibilities of persons directly or indirectly involved.

Tsao Hsueh-chin left eighty chapters of his novel in more or less finished form before his death. Copies of these were made and commented upon by a "Chih Yen Chai" and were circulated among friends. In time some of these fell into the hands of professional copyists and the novel became available to the public in limited numbers.

Two dated copies of this version have come down to us. The first carries the date 1754 and was acquired by Dr. Hu Shih in the winter of 1927–28 and made known to the world in the April 1928 issue of the *Crescent Moon.* It carries the title "The Story of the Stone, Copied and Commented upon for a Second Time by Chih Yen Chai." The other is dated 1760. This is now in the Yenching University Library and was published in a facsimile edition in Peking in 1953. A third copy, undated, was reprinted about 1910.

In the meantime, a 120-chapter version of the novel had appeared in 1792. It carries two prefaces, one by a Cheng Wei-yuan, who evidently financed the publication, and the other by Kao Ou,[2] who "edited" the last forty chapters and thus filled a "long-felt need." In the preface by Cheng, we are told that since the table of contents indicates 120 chapters, the eighty-chapter version is obviously incomplete. Cheng then goes on to say that after painstaking search over a period of years he was at last able to assemble the missing chapters and, with the editorial assistance of

[2] The accepted spelling among so-called sinological circles is O or E. I might add here that I have departed from the accepted system of transliteration in a number of instances in order to avoid confusing the general reader, to whom my translations are addressed.

his friend, Kao Ou, to offer to the public the complete novel for the first time. A second edition, with numerous revisions, was brought out the year following. But unfortunately, for more than a century the reading public knew the novel through reprints of the first edition only.

Kao Ou has been severely criticized on three counts. The first is that he was not telling the truth when he said he did not write but only edited the last forty chapters. This is, however, a question that cannot be categorically answered until new evidence turns up, since there are indications in the Chih Yen Chai comments that there existed at least partially finished chapters beyond the eightieth. The second criticism is that the last forty chapters are poorly written and that they are like "dog's fur sewed unto sable." I am inclined to agree with this judgment, but in fairness to Kao Ou it should be pointed out that for over a hundred years no one saw anything wrong with the sable. The last criticism is that Kao Ou, the chief architect if not the author of the last forty chapters, did not carry out the tragic intent of Tsao Hsueh-chin. He should not have allowed Pao-yu, it is argued, to pass the Provincial Examinations, for a man who achieves the *chü-jen* degree cannot be said to be a complete failure[3] as the author described himself and as he intended Pao-yu to be. Here again, in fairness to Kao Ou, we must not forget that he lived at a time when a *just* and happy ending was almost obligatory and that he should be praised for going so far as to let Black Jade die of a broken heart instead of being criticized for not anticipating and conforming to the standard of values which happens to prevail today. All in all, we should be grateful to Kao Ou. Except for him, the *Dream* would probably not have survived.

Tsao Hsueh-chin left his work unfinished in still another

[3] The author is quoted as so describing himself in a long comment placed at the head of the first chapter of the eighty-chapter versions. In the Kao version this is erroneously printed as part of the text. I made the same mistake in my first translation, published in 1929, as I had only the Kao version to work with.

sense: he never quite finished revising it or reconciling its numerous inconsistencies. In his day the novel was regarded, as it had always been, an outcast of literature and was written or compiled largely by unknown hacks. If a rare self-respecting literocrat should, for one reason or another, undertake to write an original novel, he did so largely for his own amusement, without any idea of publication. He would not even sign his name to his work. It is only by fortuitous circumstance that some of these original novels have come down to us, often not until long after the author's death. For instance, Pu Sung-ling's great novel, *Marriage as Retribution,* was not printed until 1870, 155 years after his death, and the identity of the author was not definitely established until 1933!

Thus, having no deadline to meet, Tsao Hsueh-chin took his time composing his novel. He kept on making changes here and there which only created new inconsistencies and fresh problems. But a novel, more than any other work of art, is to be judged by the total effect it produces, not by the blemishes that loom large only in the microscopic vision of the pedantic scholar and irritate only the translator who has to remove or retouch them.

And judged as a whole, there can be no quarrel with the general if not universal opinion in China that *Dream of the Red Chamber* is the greatest of all Chinese novels.

DREAM OF THE RED CHAMBER

Table of Important Characters Arranged in Genealogical Sequence
(Transliteration of names of female characters given in parentheses)

<table>
<tr><td>Chia Yen, first Lord of the Ningkuofu</td><td>Chia Tai-hua</td><td>Chia Ging</td><td>Chia Gen m. Yu-shih
Compassion Spring (Hsi-chun)</td></tr>
<tr><td rowspan="3">Chia Yuan, first Lord of the Yungkuofu</td><td rowspan="3">Chia Tai-shan m. Mme. Shih, the "Matriarch"</td><td>Chia Sheh m. Mme. Hsing</td><td>Chia Lien, son of Chia Sheh by unnamed spouse or concubine, deceased, m. Phoenix (Hsi-feng), née Wang, niece of Mme. Wang
Maid: Patience (Ping-er)
Welcome Spring (Ying-chun), daughter of unnamed spouse or concubine</td></tr>
<tr><td rowspan="2">Chia Cheng m. Mme. Wang
Chao Yi-niang, his concubine</td><td>Chia Chu, deceased, m. Li Huan</td></tr>
<tr><td>Cardinal Spring, the Imperial Concubine
Pao-yu, son of Chia Cheng and Mme. Wang, hero of the novel
Maids: Pervading Fragrance (Hsi-jen)
Bright Design (Ching-wen)
Musk Moon (Sheh-yueh)
Quest Spring (Tan-chun), daughter of Chao Yi-niang
Chia Huan, son of Chao Yi-niang</td></tr>
<tr><td>Hsueh</td><td>Hsueh</td><td>Hsueh Yi-ma née Wang, sister of Mme. Wang</td><td>Hsueh Pan
Maid: Lotus
Precious Virtue (Pao-chai)
Maid: Oriole</td></tr>
<tr><td>Lin</td><td>Lin</td><td>Lin Ju-hai m. Mme. Chia, daughter of the Matriarch</td><td>Black Jade (Tai-yu), heroine of the novel
Maids: Purple Cuckoo (Tzu-chuan)
Snow Duck</td></tr>
<tr><td>Shih</td><td>Shih</td><td>Shih</td><td>River Mist (Hsiang-yun), grandniece of the Matriarch</td></tr>
</table>

PART I

CHAPTER ONE

In which Chen Shih-yin meets the Stone of Spiritual Understanding
And Chia Yu-tsun encounters a maid of unusual discernment

WHEN the Goddess Nügua undertook to repair the Dome of Heaven, she fashioned at the Great Mythical Mountain under the Nonesuch Bluff 36,501 pieces of stone, each 120 feet high and 240 feet around. Of these she used only 36,500 and left the remaining piece in the shadow of the Green Meadows Peak. However, the divine hands of Nügua had touched off a spark of life in the Stone and endowed it with supernatural powers. It was able to come and go as it pleased and change its size and form at will. But it was not happy because it alone had been rejected by the Goddess, and it was given to sighing over its ill fortune.

As it was thus bemoaning its fate one day, it saw coming toward it a Buddhist monk and a Taoist priest, both of uncommon appearance. They were talking and laughing and, when they reached the shadow of the Peak, they sat down by the side of the Stone and continued their conversation. At first they talked about cloud-wrapped mountains and mist-covered seas and the mysteries of immortal life, but presently they changed the topic of their conversation and spoke of the wealth and luxury and the good things of life in the Red Dust.[1] This stirred the earthly strain in the Stone and aroused in it a desire to experience for itself the pleasures of mortal life. Therefore, it addressed the monk and the priest thus:

"Venerable sirs, forgive me for intruding. I could not help overhearing your conversation and I should like very much to have a taste of the pleasures of the Red Dust of which you spoke. Though I am crude in substance, I am not without some degree of understanding or a sense of gratitude. If you, venerable sirs, would be kind enough to take me for a turn in the Red Dust and let me enjoy for a few years its pleasures and luxuries, I shall be grateful to you for eons to come."

"It is true that the Red Dust has its joys," the two immortals answered with an indulgent smile, "but they are evanescent and illusory. Moreover, there every happiness is spoiled by a certain lack, and all good things are poisoned by the envy and covetousness of other men, so that in the end you will find the pleasure outweighed by sorrow and sadness. We do not advise such a venture."

But the fire of earthly desires, once kindled, could not easily be extinguished. The Stone ignored the warning of the immortals and continued to importune them, until the Buddhist monk said to his companion with a sigh, "We have here another instance of Quiescence giving way to Activity and Non-Existence yielding to Existence." Then turning to the Stone, he said, "We shall take you for a turn in the Red Dust if you insist, but don't blame us if you do not find it to your liking."

"Of course not, of course not," the Stone assured them eagerly.

Then the monk said, "Though you are endowed with some degree of understanding, your substance needs improvement. If we take you into the world the way you are, you will be kicked about and cursed like any ordinary stumbling block. How would you like to be transformed

[1] The mortal world.

into a substance of quality for your sojourn in the Red Dust and then be restored to your original self afterward?"

The Stone agreed, and thereupon the monk exercised the infinite power of the Law and transformed the Stone into a piece of pure translucent jade, oval in shape and about the size of a pendant. The monk held it on his palm and smiled as he said, "You will be treasured now as a precious object, but you still lack real distinguishing marks. A few characters must be engraved upon you so that everyone who sees you will recognize you as something unique. Only then shall we take you down to some prosperous land, where you will enjoy the advantages of a noble and cultured family and all the pleasures that wealth and position can bring."

The Stone was overjoyed on hearing this and asked what characters were to be engraved upon it and where it was to be taken, but the monk only smiled and said, "Don't ask what and where now; you will know when the time comes." So saying, he tucked the Stone in his sleeve and disappeared with the priest to we know not where.

Nor do we know how many generations or epochs it was afterward that the Taoist of the Great Void passed by the Great Mythical Mountain, the Nonesuch Bluff, and the Green Meadows Peak and came upon the Stone, now restored to its original form and substance. Engraved on it was a long, long story. The Taoist read it from beginning to end and found that it was the self-same Stone that was first carried into the Red Dust and then guided to the Other Shore by the Buddhist of Infinite Space and the Taoist of Boundless Time. The story was that of the Stone itself. The land of its descent, the place of its incarnation, the rise and fall of fortunes, the joys and sorrows of reunion and separation—all these were recorded in detail, together with the trivial affairs of the family, the delicate sentiments of the maidens' chambers, and a number of poems and conundrums which one usually finds in such stories. At the end there was this quatrain:

Without merits that would entitle me to a place
in the blue sky,
In vain have I lived in the Red Dust for so many
years.
These are the events before my birth and after my
death—
Who will transcribe them and give the world my
story?

As the material appeared eminently suited for the beguilement of idle moments and the relief of boredom, the Taoist copied it down from beginning to end and gave it the title of *Transcribed by a Priest.* Later, Wu Yü-feng gave it the title of *Dream of the Red Chamber,* while K'ung Mei-ch'i called it *Precious Mirror of Breeze and Moonlight.* Still later, Tsao Hsueh-chin studied it for ten years and revised it five times. He divided it into chapters and then composed an analytical couplet for each. He gave it yet another title, *The Twelve Maidens of Chinling.* He also composed a poem on the novel.

Pages full of unlikely words,
Handfuls of hot, bitter tears.
They call the author a silly fool,
For they know not what he means.

Finally, when "Chih Yen Chai" made still another copy together with a new set of comments in the year *chia-hsu* (1754), he gave it the more appropriate title, *The Story of the Stone.*

Now that the origin of our story has been explained, the reader may turn to what was actually written on the Stone.

In the southeast there was a city named Soochow. The region around Chang-men, one of the city's principal gates, represented one of the foremost centers of wealth and luxury in the Red Dust. Outside Chang-men there was an ancient temple, nicknamed, because of its shape, the Temple of the Gourd. By the side of this temple there lived a member of the gentry by the name of Chen Shih-yin[2] with his wife, Feng-shih.[3] Although not rich, they were one of the well-to-do and respected families of the district.

Shih-yin was a man who cared nothing for fame or fortune. He devoted his time to planting bamboo and watering flowers, sipping wine and writing verses, much after the fashion of the Taoist sages. But unfortunately he lacked one thing to complete his happiness: he was over fifty years of age and had no son. To comfort his old age he had only a three-year-old daughter named Lotus.

One hot summer day, Shih-yin was reading idly in his study. The book dropped from his languid hand and he fell asleep over his desk. He seemed to have traveled far, to some place that he did not recognize. Suddenly he saw a Buddhist monk and a Taoist priest coming in his direction. The Taoist was speaking.

"I am afraid you shouldn't have taken it upon yourself to interfere with the destiny of the Stone. What are you going to do with it?"

"Rest your anxieties," the monk said. "The Stone is, as a matter of fact, involved in a romance that must be enacted on earth. Far from interfering with fate, I am acting as its instrument."

"So another group of spirits have brought upon themselves the curse of incarnation! Where did this drama originate and where is it to be enacted?"

"It is a very amusing story," the monk answered. "As you know, the Stone has been given to wandering about the universe since it acquired supernatural powers. One day it came to the Palace of Vermilion Clouds of the Goddess of Disillusionment. And the Goddess, aware of its unique background and destiny, retained it in her service, conferring upon it the title of the Divine Stone Page. Then one day while roaming along the banks of the Ethereal, it came upon a Crimson Flower growing by the side of the Rock of Three Incarnations. The Stone was struck with the great

[2] Homophone for "true matters concealed."
[3] "Of the Feng family"; cf. *née* Smith.

beauty of the fairy plant and assumed the task of caring for it and feeding it daily with sweet dew. Under this tender care, the Crimson Flower thrived and continued to absorb year after year the cosmic essences of Heaven and Earth until it, too, acquired supernatural qualities and transformed itself into a beautiful fairy goddess. The Goddess manifested, however, a solitary nature and perverse spirit. It was her wont to explore the Realm of Parting Sorrow, to feed upon the Fruit of Unfulfilled Love, and drink from the Fountain of Ineffable Sadness. She was grateful for the care lavished upon her by the Stone and was unhappy because she did not know how to repay it. She used to say to herself, 'I can't pay him back in kind since he has no need of sweet dew. Perhaps I can repay him with my tears, should both of us be sent down to the Red Dust.'

"It was an odd thought but it coincided with the earthly desire of the Stone. The result is that both are to be incarnated, together with a number of other spirits who are in one way or another involved, and all will play their parts in a little drama of the Red Dust."

"It is an odd story indeed," the Taoist said. "I never heard of such a thing as repaying a debt with tears. I imagine the stories of these creatures will be different from the usual 'breeze and moonlight' school."

"Undoubtedly so," the Buddhist answered. "In stories of famous personalities we are usually accorded only the briefest outline of their careers, together with conventional poems by and about them. We are never given any details of their everyday life, what they eat and drink, what they think and say to one another. As to the stories of breeze and moonlight, they all deal with such obvious things as secret meetings and elopements; none venture to describe the real feelings and sentiments that motivate their heroes and heroines. But I have reason to believe that the stories of these creatures will be different, be they good or bad, of subtle sensibilities or gross intemperance."

"I propose," the Taoist said, "that we go down to the

mortal world ourselves when the time comes and save a few that are especially worth saving."

"That is what I am thinking myself," the Buddhist answered. "But we must first take the Stone to the Goddess of Disillusionment and have it registered. We must wait until all the spirits involved have descended before we go ourselves. Only half of them have done so now."

Shih-yin heard every word of the conversation and could not resist the urge to break in at this point. "Greetings, immortal masters. I have heard you speak of things I never heard before and which I only half comprehend. Could you elaborate a bit for the benefit of my obtuse mind and thus point the way to salvation?"

"We cannot, unfortunately, divulge the secrets of Heaven," the two immortals replied. "However, if you remember us when the hour comes, you will be able to escape the fiery pits of Hell."

"If you cannot betray the secrets of Heaven," Shih-yin continued, "perhaps you can show me the Stone of which you spoke?"

"That happens to be within your destiny," the monk replied, as he took the Stone from his sleeve and passed it to Shih-yin. It was the same Stone in the shape of a pendant, clear and translucent, but four characters had been engraved upon it: *T'ung ling pao yü* (Precious Jade of Spiritual Understanding). Before Shih-yin could look at the other side, the monk took it from him, saying, "We have reached the Land of Illusion." Then Shih-yin saw before him a great stone arch, across the top of which were engraved four characters: "Great Void Illusion Land." There was a couplet on the two pillars of the central arch, which read:

> When the unreal is taken for the real, then the
> real becomes unreal;
> Where non-existence is taken for existence, then
> existence becomes non-existence.

The two immortals passed through the archway, but

when Shih-yin tried to follow them, he suddenly heard a crash as if the mountains had collapsed and the earth parted asunder. He woke with a start and saw nothing but the bright sun beating down on the courtyard and the broad leaves of the plantain tree casting a cool shade. He had forgotten most of his dream.

Just then, the nurse came up with his daughter Lotus in her arms, and Shih-yin was filled with joy and pride as he observed how pretty and lovable she had grown to be. He took the child from the nurse and played with her a while and then took her to the gate to watch a procession pass by. As he was about to enter the house, he saw a Buddhist monk and a Taoist priest coming toward him. The monk was barefooted and his head mangy; the priest was lame and his hair disheveled. When they came near and saw Shih-yin with his daughter in his arms, the Buddhist suddenly burst out crying and said, "Kind donor, what are you carrying that ill-fated creature for? She will only bring misfortune upon her parents." Shih-yin ignored him, taking him for a beggar trying to attract attention. The monk continued, "Give her to me as a sacrifice to Buddha. Give her to me!" Shih-yin was annoyed and was about to retreat into the house when the monk as suddenly burst out laughing and, pointing at Shih-yin, recited the following lines:

> Love and tender care will be of no avail;
> The water caltrop will be blighted by snow.
> Rejoice not even though it be the Feast of Lanterns,
> For you may sorrow at what follows in its wake.[4]

As Shih-yin wondered at the significance of the poem and what manner of men the monk and his companion

[4] Example of the kind of conundrum in which the future is forecast. Later, under the name of Fragrant Caltrop, Lotus became the much-abused concubine of the crude and bumptious Hsueh Pan, Hsueh being a homophone for "snow." The significance of the last two lines is made clear in the pages immediately following.

were, he heard the priest say, "We need not go on together from here. Let each go his own way. When the time comes I shall wait for you at Mount Pei Mang and go with you to the Land of Illusion and do what must be done."

"Excellent," the monk replied. And before Shih-yin could speak to them, both had vanished.

Shih-yin realized then that these were not common beggars and regretted that he had not been more attentive to them. His thoughts were interrupted by the appearance of Chia Yu-tsun,[5] a graduate in poor circumstances who lived next door to him in the Temple of the Gourd. A native of Huchow and of a good but impoverished family, he was on his way to the Capital for the Examinations when he found himself stranded in Soochow. He made a precarious living by selling calligraphic scrolls and inscriptions.

"What has brought you to the gate?" Yu-tsun said by way of greeting.

"Nothing," Shih-yin answered. "I was just trying to quiet this crying daughter of mine. You have come at an opportune time. Please come in and help me while away the long summer day." The nurse relieved Shih-yin of Lotus. Tea was served in the study, but presently Shih-yin had to excuse himself because of the arrival of another guest. Yu-tsun amused himself by browsing through the books on the shelves. Suddenly he heard a voice outside the window. It was a maid picking flowers in the courtyard. She was not particularly pretty, but there was something about her features and the way she carried herself that set her apart from the common run of bondmaids, and Yu-tsun found himself staring at her. As she finished her task and was about to leave, she happened to look up and their eyes met.

"This must be Chia Yu-tsun whom the master has often spoken of," the maid thought to herself. "He is evidently in

[5] Homophonous with the first three characters of a four-character phrase meaning "disguised in the idiom of the uncultivated."

poor circumstances, but he does not look like one who would remain poor for very long. The master is right in prophesying a bright future for him." So thinking, she could not help turning her head to steal another glance at Yu-tsun as she walked toward the inner court. On his part, Yu-tsun was pleased with the impression he seemed to have made. "She is not an ordinary maidservant," he said to himself. "She seems to appreciate me when few in the world do."

On the night of the Festival of the Harvest Moon, Yu-tsun found himself alone in his quarters in the Temple of the Gourd. He had not forgotten the maid, and on this festive occasion his thoughts again turned to her. The bright moon stimulated his fancies, and he composed a poem on their meeting. Then he sighed as he thought how far he was from realizing his ambitions and he recited aloud the couplet in which the poet compared himself to a piece of jade waiting to be discovered by someone who recognized its real worth. He was overheard by Shih-yin, who had come in just at the moment.

"I see that you are a man of ambition, Brother Yu-tsun," Shih-yin said.

"Oh, no," Yu-tsun replied with an embarrassed smile. "I was only reciting the lines of a former poet. What has brought you here, Brother Shih-yin?"

"Tonight is the Harvest Moon, the Festival of Reunion," Shih-yin said. "It occurred to me that on this occasion you might feel like honoring me with your company. I have prepared a small measure of wine in my study and should be delighted if you would share it with me."

Yu-tsun readily accepted the invitation and went with Shih-yin to his house. At first, host and guest poured the wine in small cups and sipped it slowly, but as their spirits rose and good cheer mounted, they called for larger cups and drank more freely. The sound of flutes and strings came from every house, and overhead the moon shone in full splendor. Yu-tsun, emboldened by the wine, improvised a poem to the moon, the wonder and admiration of all during its phase of fulfillment.

Shih-yin applauded heartily: "I have always said you are not one to remain in obscurity. Your poem is a portent of better things to come. Let me congratulate you!" He filled another cup for Yu-tsun, and the latter drained it in one draught.

"If you will forgive me for the lack of modesty," Yu-tsun said, "I would like to say that I am not without a degree of competence in the sort of compositions that the Examinations require. I think I have a fair chance of success. But my purse is empty and the Capital far away. I shall never be able to save enough for the journey through the sort of drudgery I have been doing."

"Why have you not spoken of this before?" asked Shih-yin. "I have often thought of this matter but have not presumed to speak of it. The Metropolitan Examinations are coming up next year, and you must go to the Capital to exercise your talents. I shall consider it a great honor if you will allow me to take care of your traveling expenses." He told his servant to go in and get fifty ounces of silver and two suits of winter clothes. "The nineteenth is a propitious day," he said. "You can hire a boat and start your westward journey. Next winter, I am sure I shall have the pleasure of congratulating you on your return."

Yu-tsun accepted the silver and clothes without any pretense at refusing. When Shih-yin sent two letters of introduction to him the next day, the servant brought back the report that Yu-tsun had started on his journey before dawn, leaving word with the temple attendant to thank Shih-yin for his kindness and to tell him that he did not believe in fortunetellers and that he had therefore left without waiting for the nineteenth.

Truly, time passes quickly when the days are uneventful. In a twinkling, the New Year had come and gone, and soon it was the fifteenth of the First Moon, the Feast of Lanterns. As Shih-yin had no inclination for the diversions of the season, he asked his servant Huo Ch'i[6] to take his daughter to see the fireworks and lantern processions. Having to attend to a trivial but necessary call, the hapless servant left Lotus alone for a moment under the shelter of a gate. When he returned, his charge had disappeared. The servant spent most of the night looking for her and when he realized she must have fallen into the hands of a kidnaper, he too disappeared, not having the courage to face his master and mistress. Shih-yin and his wife were deeply stricken by the loss of their only daughter. Crushed by the burden of their grief, first Shih-yin fell sick and then his wife, so that for a time their days were occupied in consulting physicians and fortunetellers.

Blessing seldom comes in two's, and misfortune rarely comes singly. Two months later, on the fifteenth of the third month, a fire broke out in the Temple of the Gourd. Since wood and bamboo were extensively used for hedges and partitions in that region, the fire was soon out of control and spread to the entire street. Shih-yin's house, being next to the temple, was burned to the ground. He talked things over with his wife and decided they should go to live on their farm. But in the years immediately preceding, flood and drought had followed one another, and gangs of bandits sprang up on every hand. Then came the troops, and between their exactions and the depredations of the bandits, life became all but impossible. Under these circumstances, Shih-yin was glad to take his wife's suggestion to sell their farm and go live with her family.

Now Feng Su, Shih-yin's father-in-law, was a small landowner who had done well. He was not of a generous nature and was none too pleased when his daughter and son-in-law came to him as refugees. Fortunately for Shih-yin, he had some money from the sale of his farm and was able to contribute to the household expenses. But he knew little of financial matters, much less how to drive a bargain. So when he asked Feng Su to invest in some property for him,

[6] Homophone for "trouble begins."

the latter took advantage of his ignorance and pocketed a good part of the funds. In a year or two, his money was gone, and his father-in-law began to complain about his improvidence, his laziness, and extravagant ways. Shih-yin realized too late that he had thrown himself on the mercy of the wrong man. The long period of illness and misfortune aged Shih-yin rapidly. He took on the appearance of a man approaching the end of his days. He was walking one day on the street, leaning on a cane, when he saw a lame Taoist in hemp sandals and tattered rags coming toward him, chanting this song:

We all envy the immortals because they are free,
But fame and fortune we cannot forget.
Where are the ministers and generals of the past and the present?
Under neglected graves overgrown with weeds.

We all envy the immortals because they are free,
But gold and silver we cannot forget.
All our lives we save and hoard and wish for more,
When suddenly our eyes are forever closed.

We all envy the immortals because they are free,
But our precious wives we cannot forget.
They speak of love and constancy while we live,
But marry again soon enough after we are dead.

We all envy the immortals because they are free,
But our sons and grandsons we cannot forget.
Many there are, of doting parents, from ancient times—
But how few of the sons are filial and obedient!

After hearing this, Shih-yin went up to the Taoist and asked him, "What are you trying to say? All I can get is 'free' and 'forget.'"

"That's all you need to get," the Taoist answered, laughing. "For if you are free, you'll forget, and if you forget, you'll be free. In other words, to forget is to be free and to be free is to forget. That's why I call my song 'Forget and be free.'"

Now Shih-yin had always been a man of great intuitive understanding. He immediately grasped the purport of the Taoist's enigmatic words. "Would you let me elaborate on your theme?" he asked.

"Please do," the Taoist encouraged, and thereupon Shih-yin recited the following lines:

Dingy rooms and deserted halls
　　Were once filled with insignia of rank.
Fields choked with weeds and blighted trees
　　Were once scenes of dancing and song.
While here spiders weave their webs between carved beams
　　There they replace window mats with silken gauze.
Boast not that you wear your powder and rouge well,
　　But grieve that your temples will soon be covered with frost.
Tonight a pair of cooing doves under red bridal curtains,
　　Tomorrow a heap of bleached bones like those of yesteryear.
Chests filled with gold, chests filled with silver—
　　In a twinkling, beggars despised by all.
One moment we grieve over a short-lived friend,
　　The next we are ourselves overtaken by death.
Careful as we may be with our sons,
　　We cannot be certain they will not turn bandits and thieves.
We would all bring up our daughters to be ladies,
　　But who can say that they will not end up in courtesans' quarters?
Discontent with one's position
　　May bring chains upon one's feet.

Yesterday, 'twas the coat because it was not warm enough;
Today, 'tis the dragon robe because it is too long.
What bustle and confusion, as one set of actors exits and another enters,
Each taking the illusory for the real.
What stupidity; for in the end, in the end
One only wears out one's fingers for someone else's trousseau.

"Wonderful! Wonderful!" the Taoist exclaimed, clapping his hands, and Shih-yin, relieving the Taoist of the sack he was carrying, said, "Let us be on our way!" And so saying, he went off with the priest.

Shih-yin's wife spared no effort in trying to locate her husband, but how can one find a man who wants to be lost? Fortunately she still had the two maids that she had brought with her from Soochow. With their help she was able to contribute to her own support by sewing and embroidering.

CHAPTER TWO

In which Chia Yu-tsun takes a position as tutor to Lin Tai-yu
And Leng Tzu-hsing gives an account of the Yungkuofu

ONE day the older of the two maids was at the gate buying some thread from a peddler, when she suddenly heard heralds shouting to clear the street for some dignitary to pass. From the excited chatter on the street, the maid gathered that it was the new prefect on his way to assume his post. Presently the procession passed by. There were first the insignia of rank and honor carried by soldiers and yamen runners, and then a large sedan chair in which sat an official in a black hat and a red robe. At the sight of the official, the maid started, for she had a feeling that she had seen him before. However, she finished her purchase and went inside without giving the matter further thought.

That evening, just as the Feng household was about to retire for the night, there came a loud knocking at the gate and excited voices saying that messengers had come from the prefect. "Ask Chen Lao-yeh[1] please to come out," the messengers spoke loudly when Feng Su opened the gate.

[1] "His Honor Chen."

"My name is Feng," the latter answered, smiling ingratiatingly. "My son-in-law's name is Chen, but he went off with a Taoist priest a few years back. Could it be my son-in-law that you want?"

"Perhaps," the men answered. "We'll take you, since you are his father-in-law, and let you tell His Honor what you know."

So saying, they escorted Feng Su away, and the Feng household spent many hours of anxious waiting before he returned.

"The new prefect," Feng Su told his family, "is no other than Chia Yu-tsun, an old friend of our son-in-law. He saw our Apricot at the gate this morning and thought that our son-in-law must be living here. That's why he sent messengers to inquire. When I told him what had happened, he was deeply moved. He also asked about our granddaughter and promised that he would order a thorough search for her when he learned that she had been kidnaped. He gave me two ounces of silver at the end of our interview."

That night passed without further incident. The next day, Yu-tsun sent two parcels of silver and four pieces of silk to Shih-yin's wife to repay his debt. He also sent a letter to Feng Su, expressing his wish to have Apricot for his second chamber and asking him to use his good offices with his daughter. Feng Su was, of course, eager to please the new prefect and did his best to persuade Shih-yin's wife to accede to the request. The latter readily gave her consent, since Apricot was of age and had to be married off soon in any case. So in the evening of the same day, the maid was sent to the prefect's yamen in a gaily decorated sedan. Yu-tsun was, needless to say, greatly pleased. To express his gratitude he sent one hundred ounces to Feng Su and many presents for Shih-yin's wife.

Now Apricot was the very same maid who had, a few years earlier, turned back to look at Yu-tsun. Because of that trivial incident, she now became the second wife of a mandarin. Nor was that all, for inside of a year, she bore

Yu-tsun a son, and six months later, when Yu-tsun's first wife died, became the sole mistress of the prefect's yamen.

It will be recalled that Yu-tsun had left for the Capital immediately after receiving Shih-yin's present of silver. He was very successful at the Examinations and received his *Chin-shih* degree. He was assigned to the provinces and after serving a term as magistrate was appointed prefect of Ju-chow. He was a capable administrator but was more than usually corrupt and inclined to be arrogant toward his colleagues and at times insolent to his superiors. In less than a year he was impeached, charged with general malfeasance together with a few specific instances of extortion and miscarriage of justice. The Dragon Countenance became very angry and ordered his immediate removal, much to the satisfaction of everyone under his jurisdiction. Though Yu-tsun was naturally humiliated, he managed not to show it. After turning over the seal of office to his successor, he sent his family and accumulations to his native home and embarked on a tour of the empire.

One day he arrived at Yangchow, one of the principal centers of the government salt monopoly. While there he fell sick and was laid up for more than a month. When he finally recovered, his resources were running low, and he decided to find a post at Yangchow and tarry there for a while before resuming his travels. It was at this juncture that he met some old friends and learned from them that Lin Ju-hai, the commissioner of salt, was looking for a tutor for his only daughter. Through the good offices of these same friends he was able to secure the post.

Now Lin Ju-hai was a native of Soochow and came from a noble family. His great-great-grandfather was a marquis, but under the system of descending succession of the aristocracy, the title passed out of the family on the death of his father, and Ju-hai had to win his own place in the mandarinate through the Examinations. This he did with brilliant success, for he was the *t'an hua*[2] of the previous

[2] Title given to the second highest place in the Imperial Examinations.

Palace Examinations. His family, however, was a small one. He had no brother or sister, and his only son had died the previous year at the age of three. Lin Ju-hai took several concubines, but fate had decreed that he should have no male heir. Now at the age of forty, he had only a daughter by his wife, Madame Chia. The child was named Black Jade and was now about five years old. Both Ju-hai and his wife loved their only daughter dearly and, after the death of their son, decided to give her the advantages of the kind of education usually reserved for boys.

Yu-tsun was delighted with his duties, for Black Jade, his only pupil, was a precocious child and an eager student. Thus more than a year went by. Then Madame Chia died after a siege of illness, and Black Jade was so overcome with grief that for a time she had to abandon her studies. During this time, Yu-tsun would go out into the surrounding countryside and walk in the fields on days when the breeze was gentle and the sun warm. One day in the course of one of these excursions, he dropped into a tavern and there unexpectedly encountered an old friend.

The man's name was Leng Tzu-hsing, a curio dealer whom Yu-tsun had met while attending the Examinations at the Capital. Yu-tsun was impressed with Tzu-hsing's wide connections, while the curio dealer was naturally eager to cultivate a member of the literocracy. The two soon became good friends.

"What news do you have from the Capital?" Yu-tsun asked his friend, after they had exchanged the usual greetings and inquiries about each other.

"Nothing much to tell," Tzu-hsing answered. "However, you might be interested to know about an unusual event that occurred in the house of one of your kinsmen."

"I have no relatives at the Capital," Yu-tsun said.

"They have the same name as yours," Tzu-hsing said.

"Which family are you alluding to?" Yu-tsun asked.

"I am speaking of the Yungkuofu," Tzu-hsing said with a smile. "I hope you are not ashamed to have your name linked with theirs."

"To tell the truth," Yu-tsun replied, "our family is a large one. Since the time of Chia Fa of the Eastern Han dynasty, it has increased and branched out into all the provinces. As to the Yungkuo branch, it happens that we are related, though only remotely. However, I have not tried to cultivate them, since their position is so far above mine."

"You need not be so modest, my friend," Tzu-hsing said. "Besides, the fortunes of the Yungkuofu have suffered a decline; they are no longer what they used to be."

"How is that possible?" Yu-tsun said. "Last year, I was in Chinling and on one of my sightseeing jaunts I passed by the old Chia mansions. They stretched over almost the entire length of the north side of the street, with the Ningkuofu on the east and the Yungkuofu adjoining it on the west. The impression I got was one of great prosperity."

"Haven't you heard the saying that a centipede dies but never falls down?" Tzu-hsing asked. "That applies to the Chia family. Though they still give an appearance of prosperity, their fortunes are far from what they used to be. The whole family is accustomed to luxury and ease, but not one of them ever gives a thought to the necessity of trimming expenditures to their declining income. I understand that those in charge of the family finances are finding it increasingly difficult to make ends meet. But this is to be expected. What is even more regrettable is that the rising generations are deteriorating, each more than the last."

"How can that be?" Yu-tsun said. "I have been told that these two houses have always taken pains to give their children the proper kind of up-bringing."

"But it is as I say," Tzu-hsing insisted. "Now let me tell you something about these two families. The founders of the Ningkuo and Yungkuo houses were brothers. Chia Yen, the first lord of Ningkuo, was the elder. He had four sons, and after his death, Tai-hua, the eldest, succeeded to the title. Tai-hua had two sons. The first died at the age of eight or nine, so that the young son, named Ging, became his heir. But this Ging Lao-yeh became engrossed in Taoist magic and the elixir of life and lost interest in all else. He relinquished the title to his son Chia Gen and went to live in one of the Taoist temples. This Chia Gen never cared anything about books; he dissipates his time and energies in unworthy things and all but turns the Ningkuofu upside down. He has a son named Jung, now sixteen years old.

"So much then for the Ningkuofu. Now let me tell you something about the Yungkuofu, in which this unusual event of which I spoke took place. After the death of Chia Fa, the first lord of Yungkuo, his eldest son Tai-shan succeeded to the title. He married the daughter of Marquis Shih of Chinling and had two sons by her, named Sheh and Cheng. Tai-shan died years ago, but his wife Madame Shih is still living. Chia Sheh inherited his father's title but he is a man of very ordinary abilities and holds no official post and takes no active part in the conduct of family affairs. Chia Cheng, however, is a man of character and ability. From earliest childhood, he manifested a fondness for learning. He was his grandfather's favorite. He intended to make a career for himself through the Examinations, but when his father died, the Emperor, as a special favor to the memory of a faithful courtier, exempted him from the customary requirement and made him an assistant secretary in one of the ministries. By her first labor, his wife, Madame Wang, bore him a son, named Chu. After passing his district Examinations at the age of fourteen, Chu married and had a son but died before he was twenty. By her second labor, Madame Wang had a daughter, born, remarkably enough, on the first day of the year. But even more remarkable is the birth of her second son, for he came into the world with a piece of brilliantly colored jade in his mouth. There is even an inscription on it! Isn't that extraordinary?"

"It is indeed," Yu-tsun agreed. "I imagine he will make a mark in the world."

"That's what everyone says," Tzu-hsing said. "Anyway his grandmother dotes on him and loves him above all her grandchildren. On the first anniversary of his birth, his father, wishing to get an indication of his character, set out all manner of things before him to see what he would reach for. Well, the child ignored everything else and picked up the powder and rouge. Cheng Lao-yeh was displeased and grumbled that the boy would grow up to be a dissolute and licentious sort. Therefore, he does not care much for the son. This makes no difference to the grandmother, who loves him as much as ever and lives only for him. He is now seven or eight years old, full of mischief but so clever that you will not find his equal in a hundred. And he says the strangest things for a mere child—for instance, that girls are made of water while men are made of clay and that's why he feels purified and invigorated in the presence of the one and contaminated and oppressed when in the presence of the other. Isn't that a queer thing for a boy of his age to say? He will undoubtedly grow up to be dissolute and licentious as his father fears."

"I am afraid that you misjudge Pao-yu," Yu-tsun said. "I think he probably represents one of those exceptional beings who are born under a special set of circumstances and who are not generally appreciated and therefore often misunderstood. Generally speaking, Heaven and Earth endow the generality of men with the same mediocre qualities, so that one is hardly distinguishable from another. Not so, however, in the rare instances of the Exceptionally Good and the Exceptionally Evil that flash through the pages of history. The first embodies the Perfect Norm of Heaven and Earth; the second, its Horrid Deviations. The first comes into the world when Harmony is to prevail; the second, when Catastrophe impends. The first ushers in peace and order; the second brings war and strife. Examples of the first are the Emperors Yao, Shun, Yu, and T'ang, the Kings Wen and Wu, the sages Confucius and Mencius, and such philosophers as the Ch'eng brothers and Chu Hsi; examples of the second are the tyrants Ch'ih Yu and Kung Kung, Chieh and Chou and the First Emperor, and such usurpers and traitors as Wang Mang, Huan Wen, and Ch'in K'uai.

"Today, under our divine Sovereign, peace and prosperity reign, and the Perfect Norm is exemplified everywhere. There is, in fact, an overabundance of this Norm which manifests itself in the form of sweet dew and gentle breeze. On the other hand, there is no place under the clear sky and bright sun for the Deviations from the Norm; these had to hide their ugly heads in the abysmal chasms in the bowels of the earth, where they lie inert and powerless. But occasionally, pressed upon by the clouds or wafted by the winds, traces of these evil elements find their way into the upper air and clash with traces of the Norm, causing violent storms and thunder and lightning.

"It is under these special circumstances that the unusual type that I spoke of before comes into being. This represents the embodiment of a new force, the result of a union of traces of the Norm and of its Deviations. Men of this type have neither enough of the one to become sages and wise men nor enough of the other to work havoc and destruction upon the world. Instead, they become romantic figures if born to position and wealth, or poets and hermits if born into bookish families in modest circumstances. Even if born into poverty and lowliness, they achieve distinction as actors or courtesans. In no case could they become menials and servants to be ordered about by vulgar mediocrities in more fortunate circumstances.

"From what you have told me of Pao-yu, I have little doubt that he represents one of these admirable deviations from the Norm. He may be excessively fond of the fair sex and sentimental about them but he will not be a rake or *débauché* in the usual sense of the word."

"Maybe so," Leng Tzu-hsing said noncommittally. "Now let me tell you about the daughters. The eldest is the daughter of Cheng Lao-yeh, named Cardinal Spring, because she was born on New Year's Day, as I have told you. She was chosen as a lady in waiting in the Imperial Palace because of her beauty and virtue. The second, born of the concubine of Sheh Lao-yeh, is named Welcome Spring. The third was also Cheng Lao-yeh's daughter but not by his first wife. She is named Quest Spring. The fourth is the sister of Chia Gen, the head of the Ningkuofu. She is called Compassion Spring. They all study under a private tutor, I have been told, and are well versed in the classics."

"But what common names they have!" Yu-tsun exclaimed. "One would expect them to avoid such trite words as Spring, Crimson, Fragrance, and the like in naming their daughters. Such names are only affected by vulgar and common people."

"You are mistaken in thinking that it was because of bad taste that they used the word 'spring,'" the other answered. "It was chosen because their first daughter happened, as I told you, to be born on the first day of the year, when spring begins. In the preceding generation, the girls all have names analogous to those of the boys. For instance, the name of your pupil's mother is 'Min,' which has the same radical as Sheh and Cheng. You can ask your pupil sometime."

"It must be so," Yu-tsun said. "Now I understand why my pupil always reads the character 'min' as 'mi' and writes it with a stroke missing.[3] But you have said nothing about Sheh Lao-yeh's sons. Doesn't he have any?"

"Yes, but first let me add that Chia Cheng has another son by his concubine. I don't know what kind of boy he is. As to Chia Sheh, he has also two sons,[4] the first being named Lien. He is now over twenty years of age. About two years ago, he married the niece of Madame Wang. He takes no interest in books but he is smooth and soft-spoken, very much a man of the world. He lives with Chia Cheng and has active charge of the affairs of the Yungkuofu. Since he married, however, he has been somewhat eclipsed by his wife, for she is not only a very beautiful woman but also very clever and capable. They all say that she knows

[3] The names of the sovereign and parents were taboo and could not be used except in a "mutilated" form.

[4] I follow here the eighty-chapter version and the first edition of the Kao version; in the revised edition Kao changed the text to read "only one son."

more about what's going on in the two Chia mansions than all the men put together."

"She sounds like another one of those people with an unusual destiny," Yu-tsun said. Then looking out of the window, he remarked, "It's getting late. We had better be starting back if we want to make the city gate before it's locked."

As the two friends paid their bill and were about to go, one of Yu-tsun's former colleagues entered the inn. After the greetings were over, Yu-tsun learned from his friend that the Court had decided to reinstate the officials who had been recently retired. Leng Tzu-hsing immediately suggested that Yu-tsun should speak to his patron and seek his good offices in securing an appointment.

The next day, when Yu-tsun spoke of the matter to Ju-hai, the latter said, "I shall be only too happy to do what I can. It happens that my mother-in-law wishes to have my daughter go and stay in her house so that she can look after her. As a matter of fact, the servants she sent to fetch her were here for some time, but the journey was delayed by my daughter's illness. She is now almost completely recovered, and I have arranged for her to set out on the second of next month. Since you have to go to the Capital yourself, perhaps you would be good enough to make the journey with her?"

Yu-tsun readily agreed. Black Jade was loath to leave her father, but her grandmother insisted. Moreover, her father told her that he had no thought of marrying again and that she would be better off under the loving care of her grandmother and the companionship of her cousins. So she took leave of her father on the appointed day, accompanied by her own nurse and maid, along with several servants whom her grandmother had sent. Yu-tsun followed in another boat.

They reached the Capital in due course. Yu-tsun went immediately to call on Chia Cheng, who welcomed him cordially, for he had already received a letter from Ju-hai commending Yu-tsun. Chia Cheng was favorably impressed by the visitor and did what he could for him. In a few months, Yu-tsun received an appointment as prefect of Yingtienfu.

CHAPTER THREE

In which Black Jade is lovingly welcomed by her grandmother
And Pao-yu is unwittingly upset by his cousin

IN the meantime, Black Jade was met by more servants from the Yungkuofu. She had heard a great deal of the wealth and luxury of her grandmother's family and was much impressed by the costumes of the maidservants who had been sent to escort her to the Capital, though they were ordinary servants of the second or third rank. Being a proud and sensitive child, she told herself that she must watch every step and weigh every word so as not to make any mistakes and be laughed at.

From the windows of her sedan chair, she took in the incomparable wealth and splendor of the Imperial City, which, needless to say, far surpassed that of Yangchow. Suddenly she saw on the north side of a street an imposing entrance, consisting of a great gate and a smaller one on either side. Two huge stone lions flanked the approach, and over the main gate there was a panel bearing the characters "ning kuo fu."[1] The center gate was closed, but one of the side doors was open, and under it there were more than a score of manservants lounging about on long benches. A little farther to the west, there was another entrance of similar proportions, with the inscription "yung

[1] "Ning kuo fu" means "peace to the country mansion."

kuo fu" over the main gate. Black Jade's sedan was carried through the side door to the west. After proceeding a distance of an arrow's flight, the bearers stopped and withdrew, as four well-dressed boys of about seventeen came up and took their places. The maidservants alighted from their carriages and followed the sedan on foot until they reached another gate, covered with overhanging flowers. Here the bearers stopped again and withdrew. The maids raised the curtain of the sedan for Black Jade to descend.

Inside the flower-covered gate two verandas led to a passage hall with a large marble screen in the center. Beyond, there was a large court dominated by the main hall with carved beams and painted pillars. From the rafters of the side chambers hung cages of parrots, thrushes, and other pet birds. The maids sitting on the moon terrace of the main hall rose at the approach of Black Jade. "Lao Tai-tai[2] was just asking about Ku-niang,"[3] they said. Then raising the door curtain, they announced, "Lin Ku-niang is here."

As Black Jade entered the door, a silver-haired lady rose to meet her. Concluding that it must be her grandmother, Black Jade was about to kneel before her, but her grandmother took her in her arms and began to weep, calling her many pet names. The attendants all wept at the touching sight. When the Matriarch[4] finally stopped crying, Black Jade kowtowed and was then introduced to her aunts, Madame Hsing and Madame Wang, and to Li Huan, the wife of the late Chia Chu. Turning to the attendants, the Matriarch said, "Ask your young mistresses to come, and tell them they need not go to school today as there is a guest from far away." Presently the three young ladies entered, escorted by their own nurses and maids.

[2] Honorific designation for the mother of the master of the house.

[3] Designation for unmarried young ladies.

[4] In the original she is referred to as "Chia-mu," or "Mother of the Chias."

Welcome Spring was inclined to plumpness and looked affable. Quest Spring was slender, strong-willed, and independent. Compassion Spring was yet a child.

After the introductions, tea was served. Black Jade answered the endless questions asked by her grandmother and aunts. When did her mother become ill? Who were the doctors called in to attend her? What sort of medicine did they prescribe? When did the funeral take place and who was there? The Matriarch was again in tears as Black Jade told of her mother's illness and death. She said, "Of all my children, I loved your mother best. Now she has preceded me to the grave. And I did not even have a chance to take a last look at her." Again she took Black Jade in her arms and wept.

Though her delicate features were lovely, it was evident that Black Jade was not strong. The Matriarch asked her what medicine she was taking and whether a careful diagnosis had been made.

"I have been like this ever since I can remember," she answered with a wan smile. "Some of the best-known physicians examined me and prescribed all kinds of medicine and pills, but I did not get any better. I remember that when I was about three years old, a mangy old Buddhist monk came to see my parents and asked them to give me away as a sacrifice to Buddha, saying that I would always be sick unless they let him take me away. The only other remedy, he said, was to keep me from weeping and crying and that I must never be allowed to see any of my maternal relatives. No one paid any attention, of course, to such ridiculous and farfetched talk. For the present, I am taking some ginseng pills."

"We are having some pills made," the Matriarch said, "and I will order some of yours for you."

Suddenly Black Jade heard the sound of laughter in the rear courtyard and the rather loud voice of a young woman saying, "I am late in greeting the guest from the south." Who could this be, Black Jade wondered. Everyone else was quiet and demure. This loud laughter was unsuitable to the general atmosphere of dignity and reserve. As Black Jade was thinking thus to herself, a pretty young woman came in. She was tall and slender and carried herself with grace and self-assurance. She was dressed in brighter colors than the granddaughters of the Matriarch and wore an astonishing amount of jewelry; somehow it seemed to suit her well, but there was a certain hardness about her that did not escape the careful observer.

"You wouldn't know who she is, of course," the Matriarch said to Black Jade, as the latter rose to greet the new arrival, "but she has the sharpest and cleverest tongue in this family. She is what they call 'a hot pepper' in Nanking, so you can just call her that."

One of the cousins came to Black Jade's rescue and introduced "Hot Pepper" as Phoenix, the wife of Chia Lien. Phoenix took Black Jade's hands and looked at her admiringly for a long time before returning her to the Matriarch. "What a beautiful girl!" she said. "Positively the most beautiful thing I've ever seen. No wonder Lao Tai-tai is always talking about her. But how cruel of Heaven to deprive such a lovely thing of her mother." She took out a handkerchief and began to wipe her eyes.

"Are you trying to make me cry all over again?" the Matriarch said. "Moreover, your Mei-mei[5] has just come from a long journey and she is not well. We've just succeeded in quieting her. So don't you upset her again."

"Forgive me," Phoenix said, quickly assuming a smile. "I was so overwhelmed with joy and sorrow at meeting Mei-mei that I quite forgot that Lao Tai-tai mustn't grieve too much." Again she took Black Jade's hands and asked her how old she was, whether she had had a tutor, and what medicine she was taking. She enjoined her not to be homesick, to feel perfectly at home, and not hesitate to ask for anything she wanted, and to report to her if any of the maids should be negligent or disrespectful. "You must

[5] "Younger sister."

remember, Mei-mei, that you are not in a stranger's house," she concluded.

Presently Madame Hsing took Black Jade to pay her respects to Chia Sheh. At the flower-covered gate they entered a carriage, which bore them out through the western side gate, east past the main entrance, and then entered a black-lacquered gate. It appeared to Black Jade that this compound must formerly have been a part of the garden of the Yungkuofu. It was built on a less pretentious scale than the Yungkuofu proper but it had its verandas, side chambers, flower plots, artificial rocks, and everything else that goes with a well-planned mansion. A number of maids came out to meet Black Jade and Madame Hsing as they entered the inner court. After they were seated in Madame Hsing's room, a maid was sent to inform Chia Sheh of Black Jade's presence. She said when she returned, "Lao-yeh says he is not feeling well and that, since the meeting will only renew their sorrow, he will not see the guest today. He wants Lin Ku-niang to feel at home and to regard her grandmother's house as her own."

Black Jade rose and listened deferentially while the maid delivered the message from her first uncle. Madame Hsing asked her to stay for dinner, but she declined, as etiquette required her to call on her second uncle without delay.

Madame Wang excused Black Jade from her call on Chia Cheng. "He is busy today," she said. "You will see him some other time. But there is something that I must warn you about. You will have no trouble with your sisters. You will all study and embroider together, and I am sure you will be considerate of one another and have no quarrels. But I have my misgivings about that scourge of mine. He is not home now but he will be back later, and you can see for yourself. You must not pay any attention to him. None of his sisters dare to encourage him in the least."

Black Jade had often heard her mother speak of this cousin of hers, how he was born with a piece of jade in his mouth, how his grandmother doted on him and would not suffer his father to discipline him. Madame Wang must be referring to him now. "I have heard Mother speak of this elder brother," the girl said. "But what is there to fear? Naturally I shall be with my sisters, and he will be with the brothers."

"But he has not been brought up like other children," Madame Wang explained. "He lives with Lao Tai-tai and is a good deal with the girls and maids. He behaves tolerably well if left alone but, if any of the girls encourage him in the least, he becomes quite impossible and may say all sorts of wild things. That's why you must not pay any attention to him or take seriously anything he says."

On their way to dinner at the Matriarch's, they passed by Phoenix's compound. Madame Wang pointed it out to Black Jade and said, "You know now where to go if you want anything." When they arrived in the Matriarch's room, the maids were ready to serve the dinner. There were two chairs on either side of the Matriarch, and Black Jade was ushered by Phoenix to one on the left side nearest to the Matriarch. Black Jade refused the honor, but her grandmother said, "Your aunts and sister-in-law do not dine here. Besides, you are a guest today. So take the seat." Black Jade murmured an apology and obeyed. Madame Wang sat near the table, while Phoenix and Li Huan stood by and waited upon the Matriarch. The three Springs took their places according to age: Welcome Spring sat on the right, nearest the Matriarch; Quest Spring, second on the left; Compassion Spring, second on the right. Out in the courtyard many maids stood by to carry dishes back and forth from the kitchen. After dinner, the Matriarch dismissed Madame Wang, Li Huan, and Phoenix so that she could talk more freely with her granddaughters.

Suddenly there was a sound of footsteps in the courtyard and a maid announced, "Pao-yu has returned." Instead of the slovenly and awkward boy she expected to see, Black Jade looked upon a youth of great beauty and charm. His face was as bright as the harvest moon, his complexion as fresh as flowers of a spring dawn, his hair as neat as if sculptured with a chisel, his eyebrows as black as if painted with ink. He was gracious even in anger and amiable even when he frowned. He wore a purple hat studded with precious stones and a red coat embroidered with butterflies and flowers. His jade was suspended from his neck by a multicolored silk cord.

Black Jade was startled; so familiar were his features that she felt she must have seen him somewhere before. Pao-yu, on his part, was deeply impressed by her delicate and striking features. Her beautifully curved eyebrows seemed, and yet did not seem, knitted; her eyes seemed, and yet did not seem, pleased. Their sparkle suggested tears, and her soft quick breathing indicated how delicately constituted she was. In repose she was like a fragile flower mirrored in the water; in movement she was like a graceful willow swaying in the wind. Her heart had one more aperture than Pi Kan;[6] she was noticeably more fragile than Hsi Shih.

"It seems that I have seen this Mei-mei before," Pao-yu said, with open admiration.

"Nonsense," the Matriarch said. "How could you have seen her?"

"I may not really have seen her," Pao-yu admitted. "Nevertheless, I feel as if I were meeting a friend whom I have not heard from for years."

"I am glad to hear that," the Matriarch said, "for that ought to mean that you will be good friends."

Pao-yu sat by his cousin and asked her all sorts of questions about the south. "Have you any jade?" he asked finally.

"No, I do not have any," Black Jade answered. "It is rare, and not everybody has it as you do."

Pao-yu suddenly flared up with passion. "Rare indeed!" he cried. "I think it is a most stupid thing. I shall have none of it." He took the jade from his neck and dashed it to the floor. The maids rushed forward to pick it up as the Matriarch took Pao-yu in her arms and scolded him

[6] This is another way of saying that Black Jade was supersensitive.

for venting his anger on the precious object upon which his very life depended. Pao-yu said, weeping, "None of my sisters has anything like it. I am the only one who has it. Now this Mei-mei, who is as beautiful as a fairy, doesn't have any either. What do I want this stupid thing for?"

"Your Mei-mei did have a piece of jade," the Matriarch fabricated. "But your aunt was so reluctant to part with your Mei-mei that she took the jade from her as a memento. Your Mei-mei said she had none only because she did not want to appear boastful. As a matter of fact, her jade was even better than yours. Now put it back on before your mother hears of this." Pao-yu appeared to be satisfied with the explanation and made no protest when the Matriarch replaced the jade on his neck.

Black Jade was assigned rooms adjoining Pao-yu's in the Matriarch's apartment. As she had brought with her only her nurse and a very young maid named Snow Duck, the Matriarch gave her Purple Cuckoo, one of her own favorite maids. Besides these, Black Jade was given four matrons and four or five maids-of-all-work, the same as the other granddaughters of the Matriarch.

Pao-yu's nurse was called Li Ma; his handmaid was Pervading Fragrance, who had also been a favorite maid of the Matriarch's. She was a good and conscientious girl and faithful to any person to whom she was assigned. Thus when she was in the Matriarch's service, she took thought for no one else. Now that she was Pao-yu's handmaid, she was entirely devoted to him. Originally she was called Pearl, but Pao-yu, because her family name was Hua (flower), gave her a new name, derived from the line, "By the pervading fragrance of the flowers, one knows that the day is warm." She was given to chiding him for his perverse behavior and was often distressed because he would not listen to her advice.

That evening after Pao-yu and Li Ma had gone to bed, Pervading Fragrance, noticing that Black Jade and Purple Cuckoo were still up, quietly went over for a visit. "Please sit down, Chieh-chieh,"[7] Black Jade said to her, and Pervading Fragrance sat down on the edge of the bed.

"Lin Ku-niang was crying just a while ago because she had unwittingly caused Pao-yu to fly into one of his mad tantrums," Purple Cuckoo said.

"Ku-niang mustn't mind him," Pervading Fragrance said to Black Jade. "You have not seen anything yet of his unpredictable ways. If you let yourself be upset by a little thing like what happened today, you will never have a moment's peace."

The next morning, after presenting herself before the Matriarch, Black Jade went to call on Madame Wang and found her talking with Phoenix and two maidservants from the house of Madame Wang's brother. Not wishing to disturb them, Black Jade joined the three Springs, who were also there for the morning presentation. From Quest Spring she learned that they were discussing what to do to help Hsueh Pan, the son of Madame Wang's sister, against whom a charge of homicide was pending in the yamen of the prefect of Yingtienfu.

It should be remembered that Chia Yu-tsun had been recently appointed prefect of Yingtienfu through the good offices of Chia Cheng. Needless to say, he spared no pains in order to exonerate Hsueh Pan. It should be pointed out also that the case involved Lotus, the lost daughter of Chen Shih-yin, who was sold by her kidnaper first to a certain Feng Yuan and then to Hsueh Pan. It was in a fight over the possession of the ill-fated girl that Feng Yuan was so severely beaten by Hsueh Pan's servants that he died shortly afterward.

Now Hsueh Pan was an only son. His father had died when he was still a child, and as a consequence he was very much spoiled by his mother. He was all but illiterate, though he came from a family about which "there lingers the fragrance of books." He was arrogant and quick-

[7] "Elder sister." Note the courtesy with which some of the more favored bondmaids are treated. The fact that Pervading Fragrance had been the Matriarch's maid adds to her status.

tempered by nature and extravagant and dissolute in his ways. Though ostensibly a merchant and purchasing agent for the Imperial Household, he knew nothing of business and depended entirely upon his managers and trusted servants. His mother was the sister of General Wang Tzu-teng, commander of the metropolitan garrison, and of Madame Wang, the wife of Chia Cheng. She was therefore closely related to the Yungkuofu and was known among the Chias as Hsueh Yi-ma.[8] She was about forty years old and had, besides Hsueh Pan, a daughter named Precious Virtue, who was a few years younger than Hsueh Pan. She was both beautiful and well mannered. Her father had loved her dearly. He gave her a chance to study under a private tutor, and as a scholar she turned out to be ten times better than her brother. But after her father's death, she gave little thought to books; she realized how irresponsible her brother was and decided that she must share her mother's burdens and cares.

There were three reasons why the Hsuehs were going to the Capital. First, Hsueh Yi-ma wanted to present her daughter as a candidate for the honor of lady in waiting in the Imperial Household. Secondly, it was many years since she had seen her sister and brother. Then, Hsueh Pan wanted, ostensibly, to audit the accounts of the various family-owned stores and shops there, though his real reason was the distractions offered by the metropolis.

Shortly before the Hsuehs reached the Capital, they heard that General Wang had been appointed military inspector of nine provinces and was about to leave for his post. The news pleased Hsueh Pan, for if his mother had been able to stay with her brother as planned, he would not have been as free to do as he chose. So he suggested to his mother that they open up one of their houses in the Capital. His mother guessed his reason. "We can go to your aunt's house," she said. "I am sure she will feel offended if we do not. Besides, I have not seen her for many years

[8] "Maternal aunt."

and would like to be with her. If you are afraid you will not be as free as you would like, you can live by yourself, but I and your sister will stay with your aunt."

As Hsueh Yi-ma had expected, Madame Wang urged them to stay in the Yungkuofu. They were installed in Pear Fragrance Court, at the northwestern corner of the mansion. It had its own entrance from the street and was connected to Madame Wang's compound by a passageway, so that Hsueh Yi-ma and her daughter were able to visit the inner apartments of the Yungkuofu without having to go outside the gate. This they did almost every day, sometimes after lunch, sometimes in the evening. The mother would visit with the Matriarch and her own sister, while Precious Virtue visited with the three Springs or Black Jade. Nor did Hsueh Pan have any reason for regret; he soon found among the young men of the Chia clan many boon companions with whom he could carouse, gamble, or visit the courtesans' quarters. In fact, he found that he had a great deal to learn from his new friends. For though Chia Cheng was a strict disciplinarian, he could not possibly know everything that went on in his clan. Moreover, Chia Gen, the nominal head of the clan, was far from being above reproach himself. Thus, Hsueh Pan found himself quite free to follow his own devices and gave up all thought of refurbishing one of his own houses.

CHAPTER FOUR

In which the Divine Stone Page does not recognize his former haunt
And the Goddess of Disillusionment fails to awaken her erstwhile attendant

EVER since Black Jade had arrived in the Yungkuofu, the Matriarch had lavished on her the love and tender solicitude hitherto reserved for Pao-yu. The young girl occupied an even warmer place in the Matriarch's heart than the three Springs, her real granddaughters.[1] She and Pao-yu had also been drawn closer together, not only because they shared the same apartment, but also because of a natural affinity which manifested itself at their first meeting. Now there suddenly appeared on the scene Precious Virtue. Though only a trifle older than Black Jade, she showed a tact and understanding far beyond her years. She was completely unspoiled, always ready to please and enter into the spirit of the occasion and always kind to the servants and bondmaids. In contrast, Black Jade was inclined to haughtiness and held herself aloof. Thus in a short time, Precious Virtue won the hearts of all, and Black Jade could not help feeling a little jealous. Precious Virtue seemed wholly unaware of the situation her presence created.

[1] A daughter's child, having a different surname, is only an "outside" or pseudo grandchild.

As for Pao-yu, he was so simple in nature and so completely guileless that his behavior often struck people as odd, if not mad. He treated everyone alike and never stopped to consider the nearness of kinship of one as compared with that of another. Often he would unwittingly offend Black Jade, sometimes in his very efforts to please her. On such occasions, it was always Pao-yu who made the conciliatory gesture.

One day when the plums in the garden of the Ningkuofu were in full bloom, Yu-shih, the wife of Chia Gen, took the occasion to invite the Matriarch, Madame Wang, Madame Hsing, and other members of the Yungkuofu to a plum-flower feast. Nothing of particular note occurred; it was simply one of these many seasonal family gatherings. After dinner, Pao-yu said he felt tired and wished to take a nap.

"We have a room ready for Uncle Pao," Chin-shih said to the Matriarch. "I'll take him there and see that he has a nice rest."

Now Chin-shih was Chia Jung's wife and the Matriarch's favorite great-granddaughter-in-law. She was a very beautiful young woman, possessed of a slender figure and a most gentle and amiable disposition. The Matriarch felt safe to leave Pao-yu in her hands.

The room to which Chin-shih took Pao-yu was one of the main apartments in the Ningkuofu and was luxuriously furnished, but Pao-yu took objection to the center scroll on the wall, a painting depicting the famous Han scholar Liu Hsiang receiving divine enlightenment. He took an even more violent objection to the scrolls on either side of the painting on which was inscribed the couplet:

> To know through and through the ways of the world is Real Knowledge;
> To conform in every detail the customs of society is True Accomplishment.

"I cannot possibly sleep in this room," he declared.

"If you do not like this room, I am afraid nothing will

suit you," Chin-shih said and then added, "unless perhaps you want to use mine."

Pao-yu smiled assent, but his nurse Li Ma objected, saying, "It is hardly proper for an uncle to sleep in the bedroom of his nephew's wife."

"Don't be ridiculous," Chin-shih said, laughing. "Uncle Pao is just a boy, if he doesn't mind my saying so. Didn't you see my younger brother when he came to visit last month? He is just Uncle Pao's age but he is the taller of the two."

"Where is your brother?" Pao-yu asked, for he wanted to see what the brother of the beautiful Chin-shih was like. "Bring him and let me meet him."

"He is home, many miles from here," she answered. "You will meet him some other time."

Pao-yu detected a subtle and yet intoxicating fragrance as he entered Chin-shih's room. On the wall there was a painting by T'ang Yin, entitled "Lady Taking Nap under Begonia" and a couplet by a Sung poet:

> A gentle chill pervades her dreams because it is spring;
> The fragrance intoxicates one like that of wine.

In the center of the table was a mirror once used by Empress Wu Tse T'ien. At one side there was a golden plate on which the nimble Chao Fei-yen had danced, and on the plate there was a quince that An Lu-shan had playfully thrown at the beautiful Yang Kuei-fei. The carved bed once held the Princess Shou Yang, and the pearl curtains were made for the Princess T'ung Chang.[2]

"I like your room!" Pao-yu exclaimed with delight.

"It is fit for the immortals, if I may say so," Chin-shih said with a smile. She spread out the silk coverlet that was once washed by Hsi Shih and put in place the embroidered cushion that was once embraced by the Red Maid. Pao-yu's nurse withdrew after helping him to bed. Only his four

[2] All famous lovers in Chinese history and legend.

handmaids—Pervading Fragrance, Bright Design, Autumn Sky, and Musk Moon—remained, and they were encouraged by Chin-shih to go outside and watch the kittens play under the eaves.

Pao-yu fell asleep almost as soon as he closed his eyes. In a dream he seemed to follow Chin-shih to some wondrous place where the halls and chambers were of jade and gold and the gardens were filled with exotic blooms. Pao-yu was filled with delight. He thought to himself that he would gladly spend the rest of his life here. Suddenly he heard someone singing on the far side of the hill.

Spring dreams vanish like ever-changing clouds,
Fallen flowers drift downstream never to return.
And so lovers everywhere, heed my words,
'Tis folly to court sorrow and regret.

The song still lingered in Pao-yu's ears when there appeared before him a fairy goddess whose beauty and grace were unlike anything in the mortal world. Pao-yu greeted her and said, "Sister Immortal, where have you come from and where are you going? I have lost my way. Please help me."

She replied, "I am the Goddess of Disillusionment. I inhabit the Realm of Parting Sorrow in the Ocean of Regrets. I am in charge of the plaints of unhappy maidens and sad lovers, their debts of love, and their unfulfilled desires. It is not by accident that I have encountered you. My home is not far from here. I have not much to offer you, but I have some tender tea leaves, which I gathered myself, and a few jars of my own wine. I have several singers trained in exotic dances and have just completed a series of twelve songs which I call 'Dream of the Red Chamber.' Why don't you come with me?"

Chin-shih having now disappeared, Pao-yu followed the Goddess and reached a place dominated by a huge stone arch, across which was written the inscription: "Great Void Illusion Land." On either side this couplet was inscribed:

When the unreal is taken for the real, then the
real becomes unreal;
Where non-existence is taken for existence, then
existence becomes non-existence.

Passing through the arch, Pao-yu found himself standing in front of the gate of a palace, above which was the inscription: "Sea of Passion and Heaven of Love." The couplet read:

Enduring as heaven and earth—no love however
ancient can ever die;
Timeless as light and shadow—no debt of breeze
and moonlight can ever be repaid.

Pao-yu was still too young to understand the meaning of the couplet. He had a vague notion about love but no idea at all of what breeze and moonlight might be. He was naturally curious and said to himself that he must be sure to find out before he left the place. By this innocent thought, Pao-yu became inexplicably involved with the demons of passion.

Entering the second gate, Pao-yu saw long rows of chapels with inscriptions such as "Division of Perverse Sentiments," "Division of Rival Jealousies," "Division of Morning Weeping," "Division of Evening Lament," "Division of Spring Affections," and "Division of Autumn Sorrows."

"Would it be possible for you to take me through these chapels?" Pao-yu asked.

"No," the Goddess answered. "They contain the past, present, and future of the maidens of the entire world. Mortal eyes may not look upon them." As they walked on, Pao-yu continued to importune the Goddess until she finally yielded, saying, "You may see this one." Pao-yu looked up and saw that the chapel was inscribed "Division of the Ill-Fated." There was also this couplet:

Sorrows of spring and sadness of autumn are all
one's own doing;

A face like a flower and features like the moon are
all in vain in the end.

Inside, Pao-yu saw more than ten large cabinets all sealed and labeled with the names of the different provinces. Wishing to find out about his own, he went to the cabinet marked "The Twelve Maidens of the Chinling, File No. 1."

"I have heard that Chinling is a large city. Why is it that there are only twelve maidens? Just in our own family there are several hundred of them."

"We keep records of only the more important ones," the Goddess smiled indulgently.

Pao-yu looked at the next two cabinets and noted that they were marked "The Twelve Maidens of Chinling, File No. 2" and "The Twelve Maidens of Chinling, File No. 3," respectively. He opened the last cabinet and took out a large album. The first page was completely obscured by heavy mist and dark clouds. There was no foreground whatever. Inscribed on the page were the following lines:

Clear days are rarely encountered,
Bright clouds easily scattered.
Her heart was proud as the sky,
But her position was lowly on earth.
Her beauty and accomplishments only invited
jealousy,
Her death was hastened by baseless slander.
And in vain her faithful Prince mourns.[3]

Pao-yu could make nothing of all this. On the next page there was a painting of a bunch of flowers and a broken mat, together with a poem.

Gentle and gracious well she may be,
Like cassia and orchid indeed she is.

[3] Picture and poem forecast the fate of Bright Design, one of Pao-yu's handmaids, who languished and died in disgrace.

But what are these things to the young Prince
When it is the mummer that destiny has favored?[4]

This meant even less to Pao-yu. He replaced the album and took the one in Cabinet 2. The first page was also a picture—this time a sprig of cassia at the top and below it a withered lotus flower on a dried-up pond. The accompanying poem read:

O symbol of purity and innocence,
Your cruel fate is least deserved.
For in two fields one tree will grow
And send your gentle soul to its ancient home.[5]

Again Pao-yu failed to see the significance of the picture or poem. He tried the album in Cabinet 1 and found the pictures and poems equally baffling. He was about to try again when the Goddess, fearing that he might succeed in penetrating the secrets of Heaven if allowed to go on, took the album from him and put it back in the cabinet, saying, "Come and see the rest of the place. What is the use of puzzling over these?"

Pao-yu was led into the inner palace, which was even more splendid than what he had already seen. Several fairies came out at the call of the Goddess, but they seemed to be disappointed when they saw Pao-yu. One of them said rudely, "We thought you were going to bring Sister Crimson. Why this common creature from the mortal world?"

While Pao-yu stood in awkward silence, the Goddess explained to her fairies that she had brought him in order to enlighten him and she begged them to help her in the task. The tea, the wine, and the food were all delicious

[4] The picture represents Pervading Fragrance, whose family name means "flower." She eventually married an actor friend of Pao-yu.

[5] The lotus represents, of course, the daughter of Chen Shih-yin, now a bondmaid in the Hsueh household. She is to suffer great abuse at the hands of Cassia, Hsueh Pan's wife. The character for "cassia" is made up of "two fields and one tree."

beyond anything that Pao-yu had ever tasted. After the feast, the Goddess bade her fairies sing "Dream of the Red Chamber." She gave Pao-yu the manuscript so that he might follow it while it was sung. "For you may not understand this, as you are accustomed only to mortal music," she explained. The singing was exquisite, but Pao-yu could not understand the references and allusions in the lyrics. The Goddess sighed compassionately when she saw that Pao-yu remained unenlightened.

After a while, Pao-yu began to feel sleepy and begged to be excused. The Goddess then took him to a chamber where to his astonishment he found a girl who reminded him of Precious Virtue in graciousness of manner and of Black Jade in beauty of features. He was wondering what was going to happen next when he heard the voice of the Goddess speaking to him. "In the Red Dust," she said, "the embroidered chambers are often desecrated by licentious men and loose women. What is even more deplorable are the attempts to distinguish between love of beauty and licentiousness, forgetting that one always leads to the other. The meetings at Witches' Hill and the transports of cloud and rain invariably climax what is supposedly a pure and chaste love of beauty. I am now, of course, speaking of the generality of men and women. There are rare exceptions, of which you are one. Indeed, I admire you because you are the most licentious of men."

"How could you make such an accusation!" Pao-yu protested. "I have been taken to task for not applying myself to my studies and have been severely reprimanded for it by my parents, but no one has accused me of licentiousness. Besides, I am still young. I hardly know the meaning of the word."

"Do not be alarmed," the Goddess said. "Licentiousness simply means excess, and there are all kinds of excesses. The most common kind is an insatiable greed of the flesh. We are all familiar with those coarse creatures who cannot think of beautiful women except as means for gratifying their animal desires. They are a constant danger and threat to womankind. Your licentiousness, however, is of a more subtle kind, one that can only be apprehended but not described. Nevertheless, it is just as excessive and insatiable as the kind the world is familiar with, but whereas the latter constitutes a constant danger to womankind, your licentiousness makes you a most welcome companion in the maidens' chambers. But what makes you desirable in the maidens' chambers also makes you appear strange and unnatural in the eyes of the world. It is necessary for you to experience what most men experience, so that you may know its nature and limitations. I have, therefore, arranged that you should marry my sister Chien-mei.[6] This is the night for you to consummate your union. After you have seen for yourself that the pleasures of fairyland are but thus and so, you may perhaps realize their vanity and turn your mind to the teachings of Confucius and Mencius and devote your efforts to the welfare of mankind."

She whispered in Pao-yu's ears the secrets of cloud and rain and pushed him toward her sister Chien-mei. Then she left them, closing the door after her. Pao-yu followed the instructions of the Goddess and disported himself with his bride in ways that may well be imagined but may not be detailed here. The next day Pao-yu went out for a walk with his bride. Suddenly he found himself in a field overgrown with thorn and bramble and overrun with tigers and wolves. In front of him an expanse of water blocked the way of escape. As he tried desperately to think of what to do, the Goddess' voice spoke to him from behind, "Stop and turn back before it is too late!" As she spoke, a deafening roar issued from the water, and a horde of monsters rushed toward Pao-yu. Frantically he cried out, "Help me, Chien-mei! Help! Help!"

Thereupon he awoke, bathed in a cold sweat, as Pervading Fragrance and the other maids rushed to his bedside, saying, "Don't be afraid Pao-yu. We are all here with you."

[6] Meaning "combining the best features of both," that is, Precious Virtue and Black Jade.

Chin-shih, who had heard Pao-yu calling Chien-mei, wondered, "How did he happen to know my child's name?"

As Pervading Fragrance helped Pao-yu to adjust his clothes, her hand came in contact with something cold and clammy. Quickly withdrawing her hand, she asked Pao-yu what it was. Pao-yu did not answer but only blushed and gave her hand a gentle squeeze. Being a clever maid and a year or two older than Pao-yu, she too blushed and said no more. Later that evening, when she was alone with him in the apartment, she brought Pao-yu a change of clothing.

"Please don't tell anyone," Pao-yu said embarrassedly. Then he confided to her his dream. When he came to what happened in the bridal chamber, the maid blushed and laughed and covered her face with her hands. Now Pao-yu had always been very fond of the maid, so he proposed to demonstrate what the Goddess had taught him. At first Pervading Fragrance refused but in the end she acquiesced, since she knew that she would eventually be Pao-yu's concubine. Thenceforward, Pao-yu treated her with more tenderness than ever, and the maid on her part ministered to the comforts of her young master even more faithfully than before.

CHAPTER FIVE

In which Liu Lao-lao for the first time visits the Yungkuofu
And Madame Wang once again helps one of her poor relations

ALTHOUGH the Yungkuofu was not unduly large, there were over three hundred mouths, from master to servant and mistress to maid. Although the household duties were not unduly burdensome, there occurred daily at least scores of things to be attended to. For one who attempts to unravel the story, the problems are as perplexing as a mass of hemp with a thousand loose ends. Just at the point when we were at a loss as to what to use for the further development of our story, there came to the Yungkuofu a visitor from a poor family only remotely related to the Chias. This family, then, will serve our purpose.

The surname of this family was Wang. The grandfather, a petty official in the Capital, was acquainted with Phoenix's grandfather. Impressed by the wealth and influence of the more fortunate Wangs, this petty official had "joined family" with them as a "nephew" of Phoenix's grandfather. After his death, his son Wang Cheng went back to the country to live. Then Wang Cheng died, leaving a son by the name of Kou-er.[1] Kou-er married a Liu-shih, who bore

[1] Er is a diminutive suffix.

him a son named Pan-er and a daughter named Tsing-er. Liu Lao-lao, Liu-shih's widowed mother, also lived with them.

The family was now in poor circumstances. In a good year, they were able to manage on the produce of their small farm, but this year found Kou-er unprepared for the winter. One day he drank some wine in order to forget his troubles and, having nothing better to do, amused himself by baiting his wife and children. Liu-shih did not dare talk back to him, but Liu Lao-lao at last intervened. "Son-in-law," she said, "I hope you don't mind my butting in, but we poor folks must know our place and eat according to the size of our bowl. The trouble with you is that you have been spoiled. When you lay your hand on some money, you spend it like water. Then when you have nothing to spend, you become quarrelsome and pick on your wife and children. That's no way for a man to behave. There is plenty of money to be made in the Capital for those who know how. It doesn't help things any to pick quarrels at home."

"Of course it is easy for you to jabber nonsense, sitting there on the k'ang,"[2] Kou-er retorted. "How is money to be gotten so easily in the Capital? Do you suggest that I should go out and commit robbery?"

"I suggest nothing of the kind," Liu Lao-lao answered. "But we ought to be able to think of something. It is certain that pieces of silver will not come hopping into our house by themselves."

"I wouldn't be sitting around here doing nothing if there was anything for me to do," Kou-er said. "I have no relatives who are tax collectors or friends who are officials. If I did, they probably would not have anything to do with me anyhow."

"One can never tell," Liu Lao-lao said. "If we did our

[2] A large bed built of brick or earth and so constructed that it can be heated either by a fire underneath or by acting as a sort of chimney for a stove built in front of it. It was largely used in North China.

part, Heaven might take pity on us and give us a chance. Now this is what I have in mind. Your grandfather once joined family with the Wangs of Chinling. Twenty years ago, they used to take good care of your family, but since then, your family and theirs have drifted apart because your people have been too proud in their poverty. I visited them once with my daughter. I found them very nice people, especially their second daughter who is now the wife of Cheng Lao-yeh of the Yungkuofu. The Wangs are not in the Capital now, but why don't you go to see Madame Wang? She may still remember us. I understand that she has become even more generous and charitable with age. There's certainly no harm in trying."

"Mother is right," Liu-shih said, "but I am afraid we shall have trouble getting past the gatekeepers."

But Kou-er was now anxious to explore the possibilities of such a visit. So he said, "Since Mother was there once before, why doesn't she go now and see how the wind blows?"

"I?" Liu Lao-lao protested. "It would not do any good for me to go. The servants do not know me."

"That does not matter," Kou-er encouraged her. "Supposing you go with your grandson and call on Chou Jui, Madame Wang's pei-fang.[3] My father once did him a favor and I am sure he will try to help us."

"I know," Liu Lao-lao said. "But that was a long time ago, and we have not seen them since. Who knows how they will react? But we'll have to take a chance. I suppose I shall have to go, since you are a man and cannot risk losing your self-respect, and Daughter is still too young to be going about calling on strangers. I am old and more thick-skinned, and it won't hurt as much if my face gets slapped."

Thus, things were decided. The next morning, Liu Lao-lao got up before dawn, combed her hair and washed her face, and coached Pan-er, who was to accompany her, in what he was to say. She went into the city and inquired

[3] A bondservant who accompanies his or her mistress to her husband's house.

her way to the Yungkuofu. After waiting a while by one of the stone lions, she went timidly to the side gate and greeted in very humble terms the servants sitting around there. They surveyed grandmother and child from head to foot, then asked what she wanted. "I have come to see Chou Ta-yeh,[4] Tai-tai's pei-fang," Liu Lao-lao answered with a smile. "Would one of you gentlemen be kind enough to ask him please to come out?"

It was some time before one of them answered, "Go over there in the corner and wait. He may come out by and by."

Liu Lao-lao was about to comply when an older man admonished the first speaker, saying, "You shouldn't make her waste her time like that," and then turning to Liu Lao-lao, he added, "Chou Ta-yeh is on a trip to the south. But his wife is at home. If you want to see her, you can go to the back street and inquire at the gate there."

Liu Lao-lao thanked the man and made her way with Pan-er to the back gate. She saw there a number of peddlers, some selling food and some selling toys and other things, and a score or so of servant boys. She caught hold of one of the latter and asked, "Would you tell me, little brother, where I can find Chou Ta-niang?"[5]

"Which Chou Ta-niang?" the boy asked impatiently. "We have several of them here."

"I want the one who is Tai-tai's pei-fang," Liu Lao-lao said.

"That's easy," the boy said. "You come along with me." He led Liu Lao-lao inside and, pointing to one of the small compounds, said to her, "That's where she lives." Then he called, "Chou Ta-niang, someone is here to see you."

When Chou Jui's wife finally recognized her caller, she said, "So it is you, Liu Lao-lao. I am sorry I did not recognize you immediately. It is so long since we saw each other. Please come in."

[4] Ta-yeh ("big father," or "uncle older than one's father") is here used merely as an honorific.

[5] Ta-niang ("big mother," or "wife of an uncle older than one's father") is here used as an honorific for a married woman.

After exchanging polite inquiries, Chou Jui's wife asked Liu Lao-lao whether she was just passing by or had come on some special business. "I have come just to see you," the latter answered. "But I would like to present my greetings to our Ku Tai-tai [Madame Wang] as long as I am here. If Sao-sao[6] can arrange an interview for me, it would be a great honor, but if it is not convenient, just mention my visit when you have the opportunity."

Chou Jui's wife was, of course, not deceived as to Liu Lao-lao's real purpose. She recalled how Kou-er's father had been of some assistance to her husband in a lawsuit and felt obliged to do what she could for Liu Lao-lao. Besides, she wanted to prove that she herself was somebody in the Yungkuofu. So she said, "Rest assured, Lao-lao. After you have come all the way from the country, I would not think of letting you go away without seeing the Buddha herself. Strictly speaking, this falls outside our regular duties, but since you are Tai-tai's relative and you have come to us as if we were somebody, I shall make this an exception and arrange something for you. But I must tell you that things are different here from what they were five or six years ago. Then Tai-tai was in active charge, but now it is Lien Er[7] Nai-nai. And who do you think this Lien Er Nai-nai is? Well, she is no other than Tai-tai's own niece, whose child name, you will remember, is Feng-ko [Phoenix]."

"Is that so?" Liu Lao-lao said. "I hope I shall get a chance to see her."

"Of course," Chou Jui's wife said. "She is the one who entertains all the visitors. As a matter of fact, you can afford not to see Tai-tai, but you must see Er Nai-nai if you are not to go away empty-handed."

"*Amitofo!*" Liu Lao-lao said. "I am greatly obliged to

[6] "Wife of an older brother."

[7] Ordinal prefix meaning "Number Two." For readers who may wonder why there should be three Number Two's (Chia Lien, Pao-yu, and Chia Huan) in the Yungkuofu, the answer is that this is one of many unexplained mysteries of the novel.

you for telling me this and I leave everything to your kindness of heart."

"It's nothing," Chou Jui's wife said. "Besides, who knows but that some day you will be in a position to do me a good turn?"

So saying, she sent a bondmaid to find out if breakfast had been served in the Matriarch's apartment. In the meantime, she continued to chat with the visitor. "I imagine our Feng Ku-niang[8] cannot be more than twenty at the most," Liu Lao-lao said. "It is remarkable that she should be put in charge of things when she is still so young."

"She is indeed a remarkable person," Chou Jui's wife said. "She handles things much more capably than anyone else in the house. And clever. When it comes to making a point, ten eloquent men cannot match her. You will see for yourself when you meet her later. The only trouble with her is that she is a bit too strict with the servants."

Presently the maid returned and reported that the Matriarch had finished breakfast and that Phoenix had gone to Madame Wang's apartment. Thereupon, Chou Jui's wife got up, saying, "Let us go now. She always waits on Lao Tai-tai at meals. She'll be back in her own apartment soon now. We'll go and wait for her, for later she may be busy with other matters." So saying, she led Liu Lao-lao to Chia Lien's compound and bade her visitor wait in the hall while she went inside. Seeking out Patience, Phoenix's confidential maid, she told her about the visitors, reminding her that Liu Lao-lao had called in the past and that Madame Wang had always received her. On being told to bring the visitors in, Chou Jui's wife went out to fetch Liu Lao-lao and Pan-er.

First, Liu Lao-lao passed through Phoenix's sitting room. There her nostrils were assailed by a perfume the like of which she had never smelled before, while her eyes were

[8] Ku-niang ("paternal aunt") is an honorific for unmarried young ladies. Liu Lao-lao is thinking of Phoenix as a young girl she used to know, hence she uses Ku-niang.

dazzled by a variety of furnishings the like of which they had never seen, so that she felt dizzy and light as if treading on clouds. She was ushered into a chamber to the east, where she discovered, sitting on the k'ang, a young lady, pretty as a flower and dressed in satin and brocade. Assuming that this was Phoenix, Liu Lao-lao was about to address her as Ku Nai-nai, when she heard Chou Jui's wife call her Ping Ku-niang and thus realized that she was only one of the more favored maids.

After seating herself at Patience's invitation, Liu Lao-lao became conscious of a slow, rhythmic sound, as of a sieve pushed back and forth on runners. She looked around and discovered that the sound came from a boxlike object hanging on a pillar in the outer room and that it was synchronized with the movement of something suspended from the bottom of the box. She wondered what the thing could be for and was about to ask, when the maids announced from the yard that Phoenix was returning to her apartment. Thereupon, Chou Jui's wife and Patience got up and, bidding Liu Lao-lao to wait, went out to meet their mistress.

Liu Lao-lao heard voices and laughter approaching from the distance and then saw some ten or fifteen women pass through the sitting room into another room on the other side. Presently most of the women came out again and left. Next, several servants entered with trays of food. There followed a long silence. Then two of the servants carried from the other room a low table set with dishes of various delicacies which had hardly been touched. They placed the table on the k'ang beside Liu Lao-lao. At this, Pan-er reached out and clamored for some meat, but Liu Lao-lao slapped his hand and told him to be quiet. Presently Chou Jui's wife came to the door and beckoned to her, smiling, whereupon Liu Lao-lao got up and, leading Pan-er by the hand, followed her into Phoenix's room.

Phoenix was stirring the charcoal in her hand warmer with a pair of tongs, while Patience stood by with tea on a tray. As Liu Lao-lao entered, she said, without looking up, "Ask the guest please to come in." She seemed surprised when she looked up and saw Liu Lao-lao and made a motion as if to rise, but before she could do so, Liu Lao-lao knelt and kowtowed several times. "Chou Chieh-chieh," Phoenix said to Chou Jui's wife, "don't let the guest do me such honor. Why didn't you tell me that she has been waiting? I am young and do not know the proper form of address to use."[9]

Pan-er had hidden behind his grandmother's back and would not come out to say his lines. Phoenix smiled at this and said, "The relatives have all drifted away from us. People who know say that they neglect us, but those who don't say that we have forgotten them."

"*Amitofo!*" Liu Lao-lao murmured. "The only reason we have not come to see Ku Nai-nai is that we have been having a hard time of it and did not want to humiliate Ku Nai-nai. I am afraid we are not very presentable, even before the servants."

"Don't say such ridiculous things," Phoenix protested. "It is said that even the Emperor has poor relations, so how it must be with you and me. Besides, we are merely an empty show, trying to keep up appearances."

Then turning to Chou Jui's wife, Phoenix said, "Have you told Tai-tai that we have a guest?"

"Not yet," Chou Jui's wife answered. "We are waiting for Nai-nai's instructions."

"Please go and see what Tai-tai is doing. Do not disturb her if she is busy; but if she is not, tell her of our visitor and see what she says."

After Chou Jui's wife left, Phoenix had some sweetmeats given to Pan-er. Presently Chou Jui's wife returned and reported, "Tai-tai says she is busy today and that Nai-nai should entertain the guest. She says to thank the guest for coming and to tell Nai-nai if she has come on some special business."

At this, Liu Lao-lao said, "I have not come for any spe-

[9] That is, she is not sure whether she is "inferior" or "superior" to Liu Lao-lao with regard to family relationship.

cial reason. We just wanted to pay our respects to Ku Tai-tai and Ku Nai-nai, being relatives as we are."

But Chou Jui's wife, seeing that Liu Lao-lao was letting politeness get the better of her, said, "Be sure you have nothing special in mind. If you do have, there is no need to feel embarrassed about it before Er Nai-nai."

Thus encouraged, Liu Lao-lao finally managed to say, blushing a little, "I should not mention such a thing on this my first visit in many years, but since I have come a long way, I guess there is no helping it. Well, the truth is times have been hard for your nephew's parents. They are so poor that they have hardly anything to eat. Now winter is coming on, making things worse. So I have come here with your nephew to seek your help." Pushing Pan-er forward she admonished him, "Tell Ku Nai-nai what your father said, what we have come for. Do not stand there and act dumb."

Phoenix did not wait for the boy to recite his lines. "There is no need for him to speak. I understand." Then she asked Liu Lao-lao if she had had breakfast and on being answered no, she gave orders to have the visitor served.

Later while Liu Lao-lao was eating in the east room, she sent for Chou Jui's wife and asked her what Madame Wang had actually said. "Tai-tai said that they are related to us only by joining families," Chou Jui's wife answered. "They used to come some years ago and were never sent away empty-handed. Tai-tai says that if they need help now, Nai-nai should use her own judgment as to how much to give them."

"I wondered why it was that I knew nothing about them," Phoenix said. "So they are not real relatives."

Liu Lao-lao had finished her dinner and came in with Pan-er to thank Phoenix. Phoenix said to her, smiling, "I understand perfectly what you said a little while ago. Among relatives, we should take care of those who are in need before they open their mouths. But it is impossible for Tai-tai to remember everyone. Besides, I have been taking care of things lately. You must appreciate the fact that although we seem prosperous, actually it is not at all easy for us to manage. That is the truth, though few would believe it. But today you have come a long distance, and this is the first time you ask us for help. We cannot possibly let you go away empty-handed. Fortunately, today Tai-tai gave me twenty ounces of silver for making clothing for the maids. If you do not mind the insignificance of the amount, please accept it."

Liu Lao-lao's countenance sank during the first part of Phoenix's speech but she brightened when she heard the unbelievable sum of twenty ounces of silver. "Ah!" she exclaimed, "I know that times are hard and that it is difficult to manage, but it is said, 'A camel that dies of starvation is larger than a fat horse.' A hair from Ku Nai-nai's body is larger than our waist . . ."

Chou Jui's wife tried to cut short these homely remarks, but Phoenix did not seem to mind them. Patience brought the parcel of silver and in addition a string of *cash*.

"Take this silver and make some clothes for the children," Phoenix said. "Come often when you have nothing to do, as relatives should. I shall not try to detain you, as it is growing late and you have a long way to go. Give my best wishes to everyone whom I should be remembered to." She stood up as she finished these words. Liu Lao-lao thanked her profusely and left with Chou Jui's wife. She offered a small piece of silver to her guide, but the latter declined it, as such small sums were nothing to her.

CHAPTER SIX

In which Precious Virtue describes a complicated prescription
And Pao-yu hears some unmentionable secrets

AFTER Liu Lao-lao left, Chou Jui's wife went to report to Madame Wang. On being told by the maids that her mistress was visiting Hsueh Yi-ma, she went to the Pear Fragrance Court. There on the veranda she saw Golden Bracelet, one of Madame Wang's handmaids, playing with another little girl who had just let her hair grow. Chou Jui's wife went quietly inside and found Madame Wang busy talking with Hsueh Yi-ma. Not daring to disturb them, she went into the inner room, where Precious Virtue was copying embroidery patterns with her maid Oriole. Precious Virtue put down her brush and asked Chou Jui's wife to sit down.

"How have you been, Ku-niang?" the latter asked as she sat down on the edge of the k'ang. "You have not been over to the other side for many a day. What has happened? Did Pao-yu say something to offend you?"

"Oh, no," Precious Virtue answered. "I have had to stay home because an old ailment has been troubling me again."

"There is nothing like a good rest," Chou Jui's wife said. "But what is the trouble? You should call in a physician and get to the bottom of it. It may become serious one of these days."

"We have gone to enough trouble and expense," Precious Virtue said, "but none of the physicians could do anything for me. Finally, a monk who claimed to specialize in diseases that regular medicine fails to diagnose gave us a prescription, together with a package of wonderfully aromatic powders. It's the only thing that gives me relief."

"What is the prescription?" Chou Jui's wife asked. "Won't you tell me so that I can give it to those who need it? It would be a good deed."

"It is a most bothersome thing to fill," Precious Virtue answered. "The ingredients are common enough, but they take time to assemble. For instance, you have to gather twelve ounces of white peony flowers which bloom in the spring, twelve ounces of white lotus which bloom in the summer, twelve ounces of white lilies which bloom in the autumn, and twelve ounces of plum flowers which bloom in the winter. These flowers must be dried and ground up on the following vernal equinox and mixed with the powder that the monk left with us. For this purpose one must have twelve *ch'ien*[1] of rain water that falls on the day of Rain Begins—"

"*Ai-ya!*" Chou Jui's wife exclaimed. "That means about three years. And what if there is no rain on the day of Rain Begins?"

"Then you simply will have to wait," Precious Virtue answered. "But this is not all. It further requires twelve *ch'ien* of dew gathered on the day of White Dew, twelve *ch'ien* of frost gathered on the day of Frost Falls, and twelve *ch'ien* of snow gathered on the day of Light Snow. These four kinds of water are added to the powders and mixed thoroughly. The mixture is then made into pills, and these must be kept buried in an old porcelain jar under some flowering tree and taken out as they are needed."

"*Amitofo!*" Chou Jui's wife gasped. "That means about ten years to prepare it, if you are lucky."

"It did not take us that long, fortunately," Precious Virtue said. "By a series of happy coincidences, we got every-

[1] A *ch'ien* is one tenth of a Chinese ounce.

thing together in about two years and made a supply of the pills. They are buried under one of the pear trees now."

"Does this pill have any special name?" Chou Jui's wife asked.

"It has," Precious Virtue answered. "The monk called it the Cold Perfume Pill."

"What are the symptoms of your ailment?" Chou Jui's wife again asked.

"Nothing very serious," Precious Virtue answered. "I just feel weak and short of breath, and a pill gives immediate relief."

Chou Jui's wife was about to say something more when Madame Wang asked who was there. Chou Jui's wife hastened out and reported to her about Liu Lao-lao. As she started to leave the room, Hsueh Yi-ma stopped her, saying, "Wait just a moment. I have something for you to take back." Then she called for Lotus, and the little girl whom Chou Jui's wife had seen on the veranda came in. At the command of her mistress, she brought out a brocaded box containing twelve flower coronets made of silk according to patterns then in vogue in the Imperial Palace.

"These have been lying around for some time," Hsueh Yi-ma said. "It occurred to me yesterday that your young mistresses might like them. I was going to have them sent over but forgot about it. You might as well take them with you. Give two each to your three Ku-niang. Of the remaining six, give two to Lin Ku-niang and the rest to your Nai-nai."

Chou Jui's wife took the box and left the room. Finding Golden Bracelet still outside, Chou Jui's wife asked her, "Is that the girl whom they have been talking about? I mean the maid whose purchase involved a life?"

"That's she, all right," Golden Bracelet answered.

Just then, Lotus herself came out. Chou Jui's wife took her by the hand and looked at her closely. "She reminds me of Jung Nai-nai[2] of the East Mansion," she said to Golden Bracelet.

[2] That is, Chin-shih, Chia Jung's wife.

The latter agreed, "That's what I've been saying."

Chou Jui's wife asked Lotus how old she was, where her parents were, and similar questions, but Lotus only shook her head, saying that she didn't know.

The next day, Phoenix went to the Ningkuofu at Yu-shih's invitation, and Pao-yu coaxed her into taking him along. Chin Chung, Chin-shih's brother whom Pao-yu had expressed a desire to meet, happened to be visiting his sister. He was about Pao-yu's age, of slender build with delicate features. He was even handsomer than Pao-yu but a bit too shy and effeminate. After dinner, the boys chatted while the ladies played mahjong. Pao-yu was greatly taken with his new friend and indulged in many silly thoughts, as was his habit.

"I never thought that there were such lovely persons in the world," he said to himself. "Compared to him, I am but a pig wallowing in the mud and a mongrel afflicted with sores. What a pity that I should be born in a rich family and be kept from intimate associations with such a lovable person!" Chin Chung felt much the same about Pao-yu, only he was sorry that he himself was poor. When Pao-yu asked him whether he was going to school and what book he was studying, Chin Chung told him that he was out of school just then because his tutor had recently resigned. His father was, in fact, thinking of asking Chia Cheng to let him attend the Chias' family school. Pao-yu gladly offered to do what he could to get Chin Chung into his family school. It would be an easy matter, he said, for all he had to do was speak to the Matriarch and tell her that he wanted a congenial companion. All afternoon, the boys talked and planned what they would do in the future, and they became fast friends before they parted.

The mahjong game was over. When the chips were counted, Yu-shih and Chin-shih proved to be the losers. They had agreed that the forfeit for the losers would be a feast with theatricals, to be held at the Ningkuofu a few days later.

After supper, Chin Chung was sent off first, as he lived

at some distance. Chiao Ta, the old servant detailed by the steward to take Chin Chung home, resented the assignment and was busy cursing the steward when Pao-yu and Phoenix reached the gate where their carriages were waiting. "You son of a turtle!" he was shouting. "What kind of a steward are you? You wretch without a heart, you are always trying to pass on to me jobs that no one else wants. Who do you think your grandfather Chiao is? Not only do I have nothing but contempt for such bastards as you, but . . ."

Chia Jung tried to silence him, but Chiao Ta was not to be cowed. He was an old family servant who had served under Chia Jung's great-grandfather and had once saved his master's life on the battlefield. Because of this and his advanced age, no one ever thought of disciplining him and he had become quite insolent. Instead of heeding Chia Jung, he called him familiarly by name and told him that he could not play the master before him. "Jung Ko-er," he shouted, "not even your daddy or granddaddy can try that I-am-the-master stuff on Chiao Ta." Then pointing his finger deprecatingly at Chia Jung, he continued, "Where would you be today if not for Chiao Ta? Now instead of repaying me the debt that you all owe me, you all try to impose on an old man. So shut up, or I'll bury a white blade in you and pull out a red one."

Phoenix thought that the old servant had gone too far, so she said to Chia Jung, "Why don't you teach the impudent wretch some manners? It is a disgrace to a family like ours to have him act like this."

The other servants came forward at the command of Chia Jung and dragged Chiao Ta away. The old servant became more profane at this unaccustomed treatment. He cried and begged to be taken to the ancestral hall so that he could tell his grievances to the spirit of his master. "I shall tell Tai Lao-yeh what beasts his children have turned out to be. Do you think that Chiao Ta is blind? He is not, I assure you. He knows who is carrying on with her younger brother-in-law and who is crawling in ashes.[3] You cannot hide a broken arm in your sleeves. It will come out . . ."

Phoenix and Yu-shih pretended not to hear, but Pao-yu asked innocently what the old servant meant by some of the things he said. "Don't you dare repeat the words of a drunken man!" Phoenix said to him in a stern tone. "I shall tell Tai-tai if you ever mention it again to anyone."

Pao-yu was frightened, for Phoenix had never spoken to him like that before. He pleaded, "I won't say it again, ever! Please don't tell Tai-tai." Phoenix relented and promised Pao-yu that she would try to persuade the Matriarch to let Chin Chung attend the Chias' family school.

[3] *P'a hui,* a slang term applied to adultery with one's daughter-in-law. Commentators generally agree that the author here intends to suggest that Chia Gen and Chin-shih had adulterous relations.

CHAPTER SEVEN

In which Pao-yu, by a strange destiny, meets the golden locket
And Precious Virtue, by a happy coincidence, sees the "Spiritual Understanding"

AFTER returning to the Yungkuofu, Pao-yu spoke to the Matriarch the first chance he had about letting Chin Chung attend their own family school. He said that with a congenial companion in school, he would be able to work harder and make better progress. He also gave the Matriarch a glowing description of Chin Chung's character and his winning ways. She was bound to like him, he assured her. Phoenix did her part, too, and said that Chin Chung would be calling on the Matriarch soon. The latter was greatly pleased and readily gave her consent.

Later in the day, Pao-yu went to see Precious Virtue. Arriving at the Pear Fragrance Court, Pao-yu found Hsueh Yi-ma preparing some sewing for the maids. She took Pao-yu in her arms and said, hugging him, "It is good of you to come over to see me on such a cold day, my son. Come, sit on the k'ang and get warmed up." She asked the maids to make some very hot tea. Pao-yu asked if Hsueh Pan was home, and his aunt said with a sigh, "He is always out somewhere. You'll never catch him home."

"I hope Chieh-chieh is much better," Pao-yu then said.

"A little," Hsueh Yi-ma said. "She is in there now," she

continued, indicating the inner room. "Why don't you go visit with her? It is warmer there. I shall join you as soon as I have finished with the maids."

Pao-yu quickly left the k'ang and went into the inner room, where he found Precious Virtue sewing, seated on the k'ang. Her lacquer-black hair was done up in a plain knot and she wore clothes that were neither too old nor too new. A quiet, simple elegance characterized everything about her.

"Is Chieh-chieh feeling better?" Pao-yu asked, as he eyed her appreciatively.

"Yes, I feel much better," she answered. She invited Pao-yu to sit down and asked about the Matriarch, Madame Wang, and the others. Then noticing the jade he always wore around his neck, she said to him, "I have heard so much about your jade but never had a chance to get a good look at it. I should like to do so today."

Pao-yu took the jade off and handed it to her. She held it in the palm of her hand and examined it closely. She found that it was about the size of a sparrow's egg, iridescent like an opal, and brilliant like a sun-fringed cloud. This was, of course, the same Stone that the Taoist of the Great Void saw under the Green Meadows Peak of the Great Mythical Mountain, but now in its contracted phase. It now bore the inscriptions engraved upon it by the Buddhist of Infinite Space. The obverse side read:

Precious Jade of Spiritual Understanding
Never Lose Never Forget
Immortal Life Everlasting

The reverse side:

1 Destroys Evil Spirits
2 Cures Malignant Maladies
3 Foretells Blessings and Calamities

After having examined both sides, Precious Virtue looked again at the obverse and read the inscription aloud.

Noticing Oriole standing beside her and listening intently, she said to her, "Why haven't you gone to get the tea?"

Oriole answered, laughing, "What Ku-niang has just read sounds very much like the words engraved on Ku-niang's locket."

"So there is an inscription on your locket, too, Chieh-chieh?" Pao-yu said. "Please let me see it."

"Don't listen to her," Precious Virtue said. "There isn't anything on it."

But Pao-yu would not be put off. "Please let me see it," he insisted. "I let you see mine."

"It does have a lucky motto engraved on it," Precious Virtue conceded. "That's why Mother insists on my wearing it. It's sort of heavy around the neck." Then taking the locket off, she gave it to Pao-yu. The latter took it and read on the obverse:

Never Relinquish, Never Abandon

On the reverse:

Long Life, Forever Enduring

Pao-yu also recited the mottoes aloud and then his own, remarking, "It is indeed like mine."

"It was suggested by a monk," Oriole said. "And he said that it must be engraved on some gold ornament." Before she could finish, Precious Virtue scolded her for not going to get the tea and sent her out of the room.

As Pao-yu was sitting beside Precious Virtue, he became conscious of an unfamiliar perfume. "What kind of incense do you use? I never smelled anything like it before."

"I hate incense," Precious Virtue said. "I don't see why one should want to scent one's clothes."

"What is it then?" Pao-yu asked.

"Ah," Precious Virtue answered, after a moment's reflection. "It must be the Cold Perfume Pill I took this morning."

"What Cold Perfume Pill?" Pao-yu said, laughing. "What a nice smell. Let me have one, too."

"Don't be silly," Precious Virtue smiled. "You don't take medicine just for the fun of it."

Just then, Black Jade was announced. She exclaimed on seeing Pao-yu, "*Ai-ya!* I have come at an inopportune moment."

"Why do you say that?" Precious Virtue asked.

"I mean I wouldn't have come if I had known he was here," Black Jade answered.

"I still do not understand."

"Isn't it pretty obvious?" Black Jade said. "It's no good to have everyone come at once. If your visitors took turns, there would always be someone around; you'd never have too many and never be alone."

Noticing that Black Jade was wearing a cape, Pao-yu asked the maids if it was snowing outside. "It has been for some time," they answered.

"Then go and get my cape," Pao-yu said.

Hearing this, Black Jade said, laughing, "Didn't I say so? Now that I've come, it's time for him to go."

"I didn't say I was going," Pao-yu said. "I only want to be ready when I do go."

In the meantime, Hsueh Yi-ma had had tea and refreshments set out. Pao-yu happened to mention the delicious salted goose feet and duck gizzards served by Yu-shih the day before. Whereupon, Hsueh Yi-ma sent for some of her own for Pao-yu to try. When he commented that the delicacies went best with wine, Hsueh Yi-ma immediately ordered wine. But Pao-yu's old nurse Li Ma intervened, saying, "Yi Tai-tai had better let the wine go."

"Just one cup," Pao-yu pleaded.

"It won't do," Li Ma said. "When you are with Lao Tai-tai or Tai-tai, I don't care if you drink a whole jug. But I haven't forgotten the scolding I got from Lao Tai-tai the other day when some irresponsible wretch tried to please you and gave you some wine when I was not looking." Turning to Hsueh Yi-ma, she continued, "Yi Tai-tai has no idea how naughty he can be when he's had some wine. One never knows about Lao Tai-tai. Some days she lets him drink all he wants; other days she would not let him have a drop. I don't want to be held responsible."

"Don't worry, you old thing," Hsueh Yi-ma said, laughing. "You go and have something to drink yourself. I won't let him drink too much. And if Lao Tai-tai asks about it, I'll take the responsibility." After this, there was nothing for Li Ma to do except join the other servants and drink with them.

"Don't bother to warm the wine," said Pao-yu. "I like it cold."

"You mustn't do that," Hsueh Yi-ma said. "Cold wine will make your hand shake when you write."

"Mother is right," Precious Virtue said. "I am surprised you are not aware that the nature of wine is hot and must be drunk hot, so it will evaporate readily from the system. When you drink it cold, it stays in your system and draws the heat from your vital organs. That is most harmful."

Convinced by the argument, Pao-yu put down the cold wine and waited for the maid to heat it. In the meantime, Black Jade was watching Pao-yu with an amused smile. Just then, Snow Duck, one of her maids, came in with a hand warmer for her. "Who told you to bring this?" Black Jade asked. When the maid said that Purple Cuckoo had asked her to bring it, her mistress said, "So there is *someone* whom you listen to! How is it that whatever I say goes right through one ear and comes out the other, while you obey promptly everything *she* says as if it were an Imperial edict?"

Pao-yu knew that in chiding Snow Duck, Black Jade really had him in mind, but he said nothing. Nor did Precious Virtue, for she, too, was used to these veiled sarcasms. But Hsueh Yi-ma did not see the point and commented, "You should be pleased when a maid is thoughtful, instead of scolding her."

Black Jade replied, "You don't understand, Yi-ma. It happens that I am here at your house. If it were elsewhere and a maid turned up with a hand warmer, what would my host think? They would take it as an indelicate hint that they had neglected my comfort."

At this, Hsueh Yi-ma laughed and said, "You are entirely too sensitive. I would never have thought of that."

By this time, Pao-yu had had three cups of wine, and Li Ma again came in to remonstrate. "You had better be careful," she said. "Lao-yeh is home today and may want to see you and ask you about your studies." The reference to his father immediately dampened Pao-yu's spirits. He put down the cup and fell into an embarrassed silence.

Black Jade tried to cheer him, saying, "Never mind her. If Uncle should send for you, Yi-ma can say she wants to keep you for a while."

Li Ma was acquainted with Black Jade's perverse ways. She said, smiling, "Lin Ku-niang should not encourage him to drink. She should try to dissuade him, for she is the one person that he listens to."

Black Jade smiled coldly and said, "Why should I encourage him or discourage him? You are a little too officious. He often drinks when he is with Lao Tai-tai. It wouldn't hurt him to drink a cup or two more. Maybe you think this is a stranger's house and that Pao-yu should not drink here too freely?"

Li Ma was so distressed by this remark that she slapped her own face, as she said, "How cruel Lin Ku-niang can be. She can say things that cut worse than a knife. How would I dare to think such a thing?"

Precious Virtue merely laughed and, pinching Black Jade's cheeks, commented, "This one has indeed a sharp tongue. It can cut so many ways that one never knows what to make of it."

"Don't be afraid, my son," Hsueh Yi-ma said to Pao-yu. "Go ahead and drink all you want. You might as well stay for supper. And you can sleep here if the wine makes you drunk." Thus, Li Ma was forced to let Pao-yu have his way. She went home, leaving word with the other maids to see that he did not drink too much. Pao-yu and Black Jade stayed all afternoon, returning to their rooms after supper. The Matriarch did not scold Pao-yu but told him to rest and not to go out again that evening. Noticing that Li Ma was not with Pao-yu, she asked where she was. The other maids, afraid to say that she had gone home, answered that she had been with Pao-yu all the time and must have gone out for a moment.

Back in his own room Pao-yu suddenly remembered something as he chatted with his maids. "By the way," he asked Bright Design, "where are the bean-curd paotzu I sent back this morning? I was having breakfast on the other side and remembered that you liked them. I told Gen Sao-sao that I would like to have some for supper. They were really for you."

"Don't ask," Bright Design said. "I knew you must have got them for me the minute I saw them, but I had just had my dinner, so I put them away. Li Ma-ma saw them and said, 'I don't think Pao-yu is going to eat these. I'll take them home for my grandson.' And take them she did."

Pao-yu frowned but said nothing. Another maid brought a cup of tea. After drinking half the cup, Pao-yu remembered the tea he had in the morning. He asked the maid, "Why did you bring this tea? I had some maple-dew tea this morning. I told you to save it as it is at its best after two or three seepings."

"I did save it," the maid said, "but Li Ma-ma came along and drank it up."

This was too much for Pao-yu. He dashed the cup to the floor and said, "Who is she that you all cater to her the way you do? Just because I had a few mouthfuls of her milk when I was little, she thinks that she is more important than Lao Tai-tai herself! I have had enough of this and shall go now and tell Lao Tai-tai to send her away."

He rose to go at once to the Matriarch, but Pervading Fragrance, who was not really asleep but listening to the conversation, got up and managed to quiet him down. The Matriarch heard the sound of the broken cup and sent someone to inquire what had happened. Pervading Fragrance hastily said that she had carelessly broken a cup.

She induced Pao-yu to go to bed, after carefully taking his jade off and tucking it under the pillow so that it would not be cold to the touch when he put it on the next morning. In the meantime, Li Ma had come back and had some anxious moments. When she found that Pao-yu had at last gone to bed, she sighed with relief and went home.

CHAPTER EIGHT

In which Chin Chung receives consideration through Pao-yu's friendship
And Kin Zung suffers humiliation because of his lack of influence

UPON waking early the next morning, Pao-yu was told that Chia Jung had brought Chin Chung to call. He hastened to greet his friend and took him to the Matriarch's apartment to introduce him. With his handsome appearance and ingratiating ways, Chin Chung immediately won the Matriarch's approval as a worthy companion for her favorite grandson. She asked him to stay for dinner and had him meet Madame Wang and others. She urged him to make himself at home in the Yungkuofu, saying, "You live quite a distance away. If the weather is bad, don't hesitate to stay overnight with us. Try to be with your Uncle Pao as much as you can, instead of getting into mischief with the other boys."

Now Chin Yeh, Chin Chung's father, was a minor official in one of the ministries. He was close to seventy years old. As he had no children after he was past his middle years, he adopted a boy and a girl from a foundling home. The boy died, leaving only the girl, named Chien-mei.[1] She grew up to be a very beautiful and gracious young woman and became Chia Jung's wife, the two families being re-

[1] This refers, of course, to Chin-shih.

motely related in some fashion. Chin Chung was born when Chin Yeh was already over fifty. Because Chin Chung's teacher had returned to the south and the boy was doing no more than review his lessons at home, his father was thinking of approaching the Chias himself about entering his son in their school. He was therefore overjoyed at the opportunity that now presented itself.

The school was established by ancestors of the Chia clan and was supported by its wealthier members. At this time, it was presided over by Chia Tai-ju, an old scholar of Pao-yu's grandfather's generation.

Pao-yu and Chin Chung soon became inseparable companions. Always impetuous and disregardful of the conventions, Pao-yu insisted that Chin Chung should treat him as one of his own generation rather than as an "uncle." Chin Chung protested at first but finally yielded.

The proverb says well, "The dragon sires a brood of nine—each different from the rest." And so the boys in the school were of all sorts and varieties, though they were all members or relatives of the Chia clan. Hsueh Pan, for instance, became a student there soon after his arrival in the Capital. He went there, of course, not because of his thirst for learning but because of the prospects of finding a few Prince Lung-yangs among the students. Nor was he disappointed. He soon succeeded in corrupting not a few boys with his money and his lavish presents. For a time, his favorites were two boys nicknamed Lovely Jade and Adorable Perfume. Many other students also had their eyes on these two youths, but they were afraid of Hsueh Pan and left them more or less alone.

In this sort of atmosphere, it was not surprising that the intimacy between Pao-yu and Chin Chung should become the object of evil gossip and base suspicion. Later when it became evident that they, too, had come under the spell of Lovely Jade and Adorable Perfume and that the latter were far from indifferent to their well-guarded advances, the more jealous of their other admirers began to resort to less and less subtle ways of embarrassing the four friends.

One day it happened that Chia Tai-ju had business to attend to and left his grandson Chia Jui in charge of the school. It also happened that Chin Chung and Adorable Perfume had left the schoolroom together on the customary excuse and were chatting together in the rear courtyard. Suddenly someone coughed loudly behind them. They turned and found Kin Zung, one of the students, sniggering at them. "Why did you cough?" Adorable Perfume demanded, blushing all over. "Can't we talk if we want to?"

Kin Zung laughed and answered, "If you can talk when you want to, then why can't I cough if I feel like it? Why couldn't you two talk like honest people, anyway? Why should you be so sneaky about it? I know what you have been up to and I have caught you at last. There is no use denying it. Let me get my share and I won't say a word about it. Otherwise I shall shout and expose you."

Chin Chung and Adorable Perfume asked, "What have you caught us at? What are you going to expose? What do you mean?" Kin Zung enjoyed their discomfiture. He clapped his hands in glee and danced around them, shouting that they knew what he meant, that they had been caught at last.

Chin Chung and Adorable Perfume went into the schoolroom and complained to Chia Jui. Now Chia Jui was an unscrupulous sort and had often taken advantage of his position to extract things from the students. He not only did not try to curb Hsueh Pan's corrupting influence but actually helped him, for Hsueh Pan could be very generous when he chose. But Hsueh Pan was also very fickle. He had just now acquired a new interest and cast aside Lovely Jade and Adorable Perfume, to say nothing of Kin Zung whom they had replaced. Since Chia Jui was no longer of use to him, Hsueh Pan ceased to give him money and presents. Chia Jui did not know this but thought that Jade and Perfume were not trying to exert the right kind of influence on Hsueh Pan. So he was not inclined to feel sympathetic when Chin Chung and Adorable Perfume complained to him about Kin Zung. Because of Pao-yu, he did not dare reprimand Chin Chung and he therefore made a scapegoat of Perfume and gave him a sound scolding.

Kin Zung was elated by his triumph and repeated his accusations to all who would listen, improving his story each time with more elaborate details. Things might have stopped there if the story had not happened to offend still another person. And who do you think this was? Well, his name was Chia Chiang, a "great-grandson" of the Matriarch as was Chia Jung. He was orphaned early and brought up under Chia Gen. He was now sixteen years old and even more handsome than Chia Jung, with whom he was on the best of terms. Now, "more people, more talk," especially when disgruntled servants are concerned. And so there was quite a lot of wicked talk about Chia Gen's interest in this nephew of his. These evil rumors finally reached Chia Gen's ears, and he decided to put an end to them by providing Chia Chiang with a house of his own.

It goes without saying that Chia Chiang, being intimate with Chia Jung, did not like to see Chin Chung, the latter's brother-in-law, thus humiliated. His first impulse was to fight Kin Zung in the open, but he later thought better of it, as he was on good terms with Hsueh Pan and did not want to take sides against his friends. A scheme suggested itself to him. After making the customary excuse for leaving the schoolroom, he went out, summoned Ming-yen, Pao-yu's faithful page, and told him that his master's good friends had been picked on by Kin Zung thus and so and that even Pao-yu's name had been dragged in the mud. Now Ming-yen had a doglike devotion to Pao-yu and not much sense. Immediately on hearing the story, he rushed into the schoolroom to look for Kin Zung, while Chia Chiang, expecting trouble and wanting no part of it, slipped away. Ming-yen went up to Kin Zung and shouted to him, "Hey, you son of the Kin clan, what business is it of yours whatever we choose to do? You should be glad we haven't violated your own father. Come on out and have a round with your Master Ming if you aren't a coward!"

The whole school was dumbfounded by this unheard-of

behavior on the part of a servant. Chia Jui shouted, "How dare you, Ming-yen!"

Kin Zung was livid with rage. "This is treason," he shouted. "I shall not degrade myself by arguing with you but shall take your master to account for this." So saying, he made for Pao-yu. Someone threw an inkstone at Chin Chung. He dodged just in time, and the missile fell with a crash on the desk occupied by Chia Lung and Chia Chun, both great-grandsons of the Matriarch. Chia Lung was inclined to overlook the matter, as he knew that the missile was not aimed at them, but Chia Chun was more pugnacious. He picked up his stationery box and hurled it at the offender. It fell short, but Chia Chun followed it up by falling upon the boy who had thrown the inkstone.

Kin Zung had now armed himself with a bamboo stick and was whirling it around. Ming-yen's head received the first blow. He stood stunned for a moment. Then he shouted to the other pages, "Come to the rescue, all of you. What are you waiting for?" The pages rushed in at the signal, as they liked nothing better than a good fight. They armed themselves with door latches and whips and joined in the fray.

The schoolroom was soon a bedlam of confused yelling and screaming. Chia Jui pleaded and threatened, but no one heeded him. Some, either because they loved a fight for its own sake or because they had private scores to settle, took advantage of the general confusion to put in a blow here and there; others stood on chairs and desks and cheered the active belligerents; still others, who were more timid or peaceable, hid under the tables and in safe corners.

Chin Chung had been hit on the head by Kin Zung, and Pao-yu was rubbing the lump when Li Kuei and the other older servants came in and stopped the fight. Pao-yu told Li Kuei to gather up his books and get his horse, saying, "I am going to tell Tai-yeh about this. We were picked on, and yet Jui Ta-yeh said it was our fault."

Li Kuei begged him not to be hasty. "We must not trouble Tai-yeh," he said. "It would seem inconsiderate of us to go to him when he is busy. We must settle this among ourselves." Turning to Chia Jui, he said, "If you will forgive my boldness, Jui Ta-yeh, I will venture to say that you are responsible. You are in charge of the school during Tai-yeh's absence. If anyone misbehaves you should, as the master here, deal with the case promptly and justly. You should not have let it come to this."

"I tried to stop them," Chia Jui said helplessly, "but they would not listen to me."

"If you will forgive me," Li Kuei said, "I must say that it is your own fault. If you had been fair, you would have been able to command more respect. It will go hard with you if this gets to Tai-yeh. You had better think of some way to settle this."

"What is there to settle?" Pao-yu said. "It is very clear who were the offenders. I am going to report this to Tai-yeh."

"I am not going to remain here," Chin Chung said, weeping, "if Kin Zung is allowed to stay in the school."

"Nothing of the sort," Pao-yu said. Turning to Li Kuei, he asked, "Tell me, who is this Kin Zung?"

Li Kuei hesitated for a moment and then said, "It is better not to ask. It will only cause ill feeling among relatives."

"He is the nephew of Huang Ta Nai-nai on the east side," Ming-yen volunteered from the courtyard. "He would never have gotten in here if his aunt had not——"

"Shut up, you dog!" Li Kuei shouted at him.

"I wondered whose relative he was," Pao-yu smiled darkly. "I shall go and speak to her myself. Come, Ming-yen, and get my books ready."

Ming-yen was elated when he came in to gather Pao-yu's books. He said, "You need not go to that trouble. It will save you a trip if I just go and tell her that Lao Tai-tai wants her. You can then speak to her and tell her what her nephew has been up to."

"Do you want to die?" Li Kuei shook him fiercely. "If you don't shut up right away, I shall give you a sound thrashing and then tell Lao-yeh that you stirred up the whole trouble here."

Chia Jui, fearing that word of the fight might reach his grandfather, begged Kin Zung to apologize to Chin Chung and Pao-yu. This Kin Zung did reluctantly, but Pao-yu was not satisfied and insisted upon the more abject kowtow. Kin Zung refused at first but eventually gave in to Pao-yu's terms, and the affair was settled without an appeal to the aged tutor.

Kin-shih, Chia Huang's wife, was indignant when she heard about the incident. "Our Zung-er is just as much a relative of the Chia clan as that bastard Chin Chung," she said angrily to Kin Zung's mother. "They have no right to treat him like this, especially after the other has been caught at such an indecent thing. I'll go to the East Mansion and see what Chin Chung's sister has to say about it!"

By the time Kin-shih arrived at the Ningkuofu and saw Yu-shih, however, she was neither so angry nor so sure that she wanted to have it out with Chin Chung's sister. She greeted Yu-shih with a servile solicitude and, after chatting for a while, asked casually, "How is it that Jung Ta Nai-nai is not around today?"

"She hasn't been well lately," Yu-shih answered. "She has not had her period for two months in a row. The physicians who examined her all say that it does not indicate a blessed event. She feels weak by afternoon and has dizzy spells. I have told her not to bother about presenting herself mornings and evenings and that I would make apologies for her to relatives who come to visit. I have even told Jung-er to take care not to provoke her in any way. 'You'll never find another wife like her,' I said to him, 'so take good care of her. Let her have all the rest she can and get well.' So you see how worried I have been about her condition. Then her brother had to upset her this morning with his petty grievances! He told her that he had been picked upon by one of the boys, not one of our own but only a relative, and that there had been a fight because of it. He even repeated some of the filthy things that some of the boys have been saying about one another. Sao-sao, you know how she is. She may not show anything but she is terribly sensitive and would worry over the least little thing for days on end. That probably accounts for her illness more than anything else. So you can imagine how upset she was by her brother's tale. She did not even touch any breakfast. I wish I knew what to do. Does Sao-sao know of a good doctor by any chance?"

"No, I don't know of any," Chia Huang's wife answered. Long before Yu-shih had finished, she had decided that this was not the time to complain to Chin-shih. "From what you have said, it might be pregnancy after all. In that case, indiscriminate doctoring would only make things worse."

"That's what I have been thinking, too," Yu-shih said.

Just then, Chia Gen came in. Seeing Kin-shih, he made a few polite remarks and went on into the next room. He returned after Kin-shih left and asked what she had to say.

"She did not say," Yu-shih answered. "She seemed to be very angry when she came in but calmed down on hearing that our daughter-in-law is ill. Now about daughter-in-law, you must try to get a good doctor. These people that have been attending her are of no use. All they do is listen to the symptoms we tell them and then repeat them in their medical jargon."

"I was just going to tell you," Chia Gen said. "This morning, Feng Tzu-ying came to see me and, noticing that I looked worried, asked me what the trouble was. I told him of our daughter-in-law's illness and how no one has been able to make a clear diagnosis. Feng Tzu-ying recommended a Chang Yu-shih, a very learned man and an excellent diagnostician, though he does not practice professionally. I have written asking him to come, which he undoubtedly will do as a favor to Feng Tzu-ying."

Chang Yu-shih came the following day and was ushered into Chin-shih's room by Chia Jung. The latter proposed to tell the physician of his wife's symptoms, but the physician said, "I should like to feel her pulse first and see for myself the cause of the illness. We can then compare our observations and devise a prescription."

The physician first took Chin-shih's right hand and then her left, taking more than a quarter of an hour for each. Then he retired with Chia Jung to the outer room.

"How do you find the patient's pulse?" Chia Jung asked, after tea had been served.

"This is what I found," the physician answered. "The pulse on her left hand is deep and agitated under my forefinger; it is deep and faint under the second finger. On her right hand it is vague and lacks vitality under the forefinger. The first indicates a febrile state arising from a weak action of the heart; the second, a sluggishness of the liver. The vague and spiritless forefinger pulse of the right hand suggests a disturbance in the lung humors, while the vague second finger pulse bespeaks a wood element in the liver too strong for the earth element in the spleen. The symptoms of the first disturbance should be pain in the ribs, tardy menses, and a burning sensation around the heart. Disturbance of the lung humors generally leads to giddiness and perspiration in the early morning hours during sleep. The prevalence of the wood element in the liver over the earth element in the spleen should lead to lack of appetite, general fatigue, and soreness of the limbs. If I am correct in reading the action of the pulse, these symptoms should be present. Some may confuse this pulse with one indicating pregnancy, but I am afraid that I cannot agree with such a diagnosis."

A maidservant who had been attending Chin-shih said, "The doctor is right in every detail. None of the other doctors have described the symptoms so correctly. Some say that the young mistress is blessed; others, that it is something else. Some say that it is no consequence; others say that there will be serious danger at about the Winter Solstice."

"I do not want to minimize the skill and knowledge of the other doctors," Chang Yu-shih said, after looking over the old prescriptions, "but the patient has suffered from their ignorance. There is still hope. After taking my prescribed medicine, there will be more hope if the patient can sleep. Judging from the pulse, the patient is proud, haughty, and sensitive to the extreme. Because of these traits, she is often hurt and irritated by little things. Her spleen has been thus affected, causing enlarged liver and other symptoms. If medicine had been used to nurture the heart and regulate the humors, her illness would not have reached the present stage, which is clearly a case of lack of water and a superabundance of fire." Then he wrote a prescription and gave it to Chia Jung.

When Chia Jung questioned the doctor about the patient's chances for recovery, the latter answered, "You are a sensible man and ought to know that at this stage it is impossible to tell how soon the patient will recover. Medicine will do its part, but more depends upon the will of Heaven. In my opinion, there is no danger this winter. The crisis will come in the spring. She will get well if she can manage through the spring."

After the doctor left, Chia Jung showed the prescription to Chia Gen and told him and Yu-shih what the doctor had said.

"No one has diagnosed her condition so accurately," Yu-shih said. "His prescription ought to do some good."

"He is not an ordinary physician," Chia Gen said. "Let's hope that our daughter-in-law will be cured by him." Then turning to Chia Jung, he said, "I see ginseng is called for. You can weigh out the required quantity from the new supply we bought the other day. It is better than anything the medicine stores can readily provide." So saying, he gave the prescription to his son, who in turn gave it to a servant to have it filled.

CHAPTER NINE

In which Phoenix proves herself an able strategist
And Chia Jui shows himself a ready dupe

CHIA Ging's birthday occurred a few days later. When Chia Gen went to see him at his retreat in the Taoist temple and asked if he would come home for a few days to celebrate with the family, he refused, saying that he had no desire to become entangled again in the snares of the Red Dust. The only thing he wanted Chia Gen to do for him was to print and distribute ten thousand copies of his annotated version of the Taoist tract *Rewards and Punishments.*

On the day of the celebration, there were the usual feasts and theatricals at the Ningkuofu for friends and relatives. With the exception of the Matriarch, who was indisposed, everyone from the Yungkuofu was there, including, of course, Phoenix and Pao-yu. They all asked about Chin-shih, and Phoenix and Pao-yu went to see her, while the rest of the party went to the garden for the theatrical performance.

As they entered the room, Chin-shih made an effort to get up, but Phoenix hastened to her, saying, "Don't. It will make you faint." Then, taking her hand, she said, "How thin you have become in the last few days!" She sat down beside Chin-shih, while Pao-yu sat in a chair opposite them.

"I suppose I am not meant for such happiness as I have

enjoyed here," Chin-shih said, forcing a smile. "Both father and mother treat me as if I were their own daughter, and your nephew never had a cross word for me. Everyone has been most kind to me, you above all. I want so much to be worthy of all this kindness, but there is so little time left. I am afraid I'll not live to see the new year."

Pao-yu was looking at the painting by T'ang Yin and recalling the time he took a nap in this room and the wonderful dream he had. Now hearing what Chin-shih said, his heart felt as if pierced by ten thousand arrows, and his tears began to flow. Phoenix, too, was on the verge of tears but, reminding herself that she had come to cheer up Chin-shih, not to sadden her, she forced back her tears and said to Pao-yu in the most lighthearted manner she could assume, "Pao-yu, you are behaving like an old woman. It's not as bad as the patient would have us believe. She is young yet and will get well soon enough." Then turning to Chin-shih, she said, "You must not have such silly ideas. It will only make things worse." So saying, she persuaded Pao-yu to go back to the party, while she stayed with Chin-shih and continued to exhort her to take courage. She did not leave her until Yu-shih, for a third time, sent word for her to rejoin the party.

On the way Phoenix lingered here and there to take in the autumn scene. Suddenly a man appeared from behind the artificial mountain and greeted her. Phoenix was startled but recovered herself immediately and said, "Are you not perhaps Jui Ta-yeh?"

"Don't tell me that you don't know who I am, Sao-sao!" Chia Jui said.

"Of course I do," Phoenix said. "But you appeared very suddenly, and I did not expect to see you here."

"It's destiny," Chia Jui said, leering at Phoenix. "I just happened to sneak off from the banquet for a stroll, and here you are, too. What's this if not destiny!"

Chia Jui's veiled declaration was not lost on Phoenix. "You are very kind," she said with a smile. "No wonder your brother has such good things to say about you. It is easy to see how clever and understanding you are. I cannot talk to you now, for I must get back to the banquet. But I hope to see you some time."

"I have often wanted to come to see Sao-sao," Chia Jui said, "but Sao-sao is still very young, and it may not seem right for me to call."

"What nonsense!" Phoenix said. "Aren't we of the same flesh and blood?"

Chia Jui was happy beyond words at this encouragement. "What luck!" he said to himself as he stood and gazed greedily at Phoenix.

"Don't let them catch you absent from the banquet and make you drink forfeits," Phoenix said, as if she were very much concerned for him. "Better run back to them."

Chia Jui obeyed but turned around to look at Phoenix every other step. She also slowed her steps as if reluctant to leave him. But to herself she thought, "You never can tell what these men will be up to next. I shall teach him not to trifle with me, the beast."

For the next month or two, Phoenix was a frequent visitor at the Ningkuofu. The patient did not get worse but she did not improve either. On the second day of the Twelfth Moon, when Phoenix again went to see her at the bidding of the Matriarch, Chin-shih was thinner than ever and seemed despondent. "It is only a question of time," she said with resignation. "We shall know by spring."

When Phoenix was alone with Yu-shih, the latter asked, "Frankly, what do you think of the chances of the patient?"

Phoenix bowed her head and said after a long silence, "There seems to be little hope. If I were you I would attend to her afterlife things. This might propitiate the evil spirits."

"I have thought of this, too, and have quietly made preparations."

Phoenix did not tell the Matriarch the seriousness of Chin-shih's condition, for she did not want to alarm her. The Matriarch, however, sensed the danger from Phoenix's manner.

On returning to her room, Phoenix asked Patience what had come up during her absence. "Nothing much," Patience answered. "Lai Wang Sao-sao came with the interest she finally collected on the three hundred ounces. Then Jui Ta-yeh sent someone to ask if Nai-nai was home and whether he could come over. I don't know what he wants, but he has been here almost every day for the last month." When Phoenix confided to her about the encounter with him, Patience said, "A case of 'a toad hankering for a taste of the swan's flesh.' He should be made to suffer for this."

"You need not worry about that," Phoenix said darkly. "I shall take care of him."

Just then, Chia Jui was announced. He came in and greeted Phoenix with broad smiles. Phoenix tried her best to conceal her distaste.

"Why isn't Er-ko home yet?" Chia Jui asked.

"I wouldn't know," Phoenix answered.

"Perhaps he has been detained by someone from whom he cannot tear himself away?" Chia Jui ventured.

"Perhaps so," Phoenix said. "Men are like that. They are bewitched by every pretty face they see."

"Sao-sao is wrong," Chia Jui said with a smile. "Not all men. I for one am not like that."

"But unfortunately there are not many like you. One does not find one like you in a thousand," Phoenix said.

Chia Jui simpered and scratched his ears and cheeks in embarrassment. After a while, he ventured again, "Is Sao-sao lonely and bored sometimes?"

"Yes, and I was just hoping that someone would come and keep me company."

"I have nothing to do, Sao-sao. Would you like to have me come and amuse you?"

"You are trying to flatter me. I know you wouldn't want to waste your time here with me."

"May thunder strike me if I dare to deceive Sao-sao," Chia Jui said. "I have not come before because I was told that Sao-sao is cold and aloof. If I had known that she is so kind, I would have come long, long ago, even if I were to die for it."

"You are indeed very understanding," Phoenix further encouraged him. "Not like Jung-er and Chiang-er. They are really very stupid, though they look intelligent and understanding."

Chia Jui drew closer to Phoenix and professed an interest in her rings.

"Take care," Phoenix cautioned. "Don't let the maids see us." Chia Jui hastily drew back at the command. "It is time for you to go now," Phoenix said to him in low tones, as if she regretted the necessity.

"How cruel you are, Sao-sao!" Chia Jui said. "Let me stay a while longer."

"But this is neither the time nor the place for us," Phoenix whispered. "Go now but return tonight at the beginning of the watchman's rounds and wait for me at the western passageway."

Chia Jui was overjoyed to hear this. Then a doubt crossed his mind. "Sao-sao must be teasing me," he said to Phoenix. "The passageway is hardly a good place; people are always passing back and forth."

"But I shall dismiss the night attendants," Phoenix reassured him. "It will be nice and quiet there with the doors on either side closed."

At nightfall, Chia Jui made his way to the appointed place. The gate leading to the Matriarch's courtyard was already locked. There was no one in the passageway. As he waited, he began to grow apprehensive. A maidservant appeared in the court and locked the gate on the east, leaving him no exit. The walls were too high to scale.

It was the Twelfth Moon, and a biting wind blew through the passageway. Chia Jui shivered through the interminable winter night and almost froze to death. Finally, dawn came and a maidservant opened the east gate. He managed to slip out as she went to knock on the other gate.

Chia Jui's parents had died when he was an infant. He

was brought up by his grandfather, Chia Tai-ju, who was very strict with him and made him account for every hour, so that there could be no time to squander in gambling houses and such wicked places. The grandfather was scandalized when Chia Jui did not return that night. He did not believe Chia Jui's story that he was with his maternal uncle. "I have told you many times you are not to leave the house without my permission. You ought to be punished for your disobedience, to say nothing about your lying to me just now." He gave Chia Jui a sound thrashing and bade him kneel in the courtyard all day and study his lessons. He would not let him have any food the whole day.

One would think this lesson would have been enough, but a person in love is blind, and so Chia Jui went to see Phoenix again the first chance he had. He accepted the blame readily when Phoenix told him he had misunderstood about the meeting place. "Come again tonight," she said to him, "and wait for me in the vacant room to the northwest of the passageway. It would be better there than the passageway itself. But be sure you don't make another mistake."

"I won't, but make sure that you are there, too," Chia Jui said.

"Don't come if you don't believe me," Phoenix said, as if hurt by Chia Jui's doubt.

"I'll come," Chia Jui answered hastily. "I'll come even though I should die for it."

He went away and waited impatiently for the night, while Phoenix set about laying another trap for him.

"Is she going to make a fool of me again?" Chia Jui thought to himself as he paced the empty room restlessly, like an ant on a hot stove. The silence oppressed him.

Suddenly someone appeared in the doorway. It was too dark to see, but Chia Jui sprang toward the figure and embraced it, like a hungry tiger leaping upon its prey, and said passionately, "Dearest Sao-sao, I have been waiting for ages. I have been dying of longing for you." He carried the yielding figure to the k'ang at one end of the room and showered on it passionate kisses. Suddenly a lantern shone at the doorway and lit up the room. The man carrying the lantern asked, "Who is there?"

The figure that Chia Jui was embracing spoke for the first time. "Uncle Jui is trying to make love to me."

In the light Chia Jui recognized Chia Jung. He rushed for the door, but his way was blocked by the man with the lantern. It was Chia Chiang, who caught hold of him and said, "You can't go. Lien Er-shen[1] has told Tai-tai what you have been up to. Tai-tai is very angry. She asked me to catch you and take you to her."

"Please cover up for me this once, my good nephew," Chia Jui pleaded. "Tell Tai-tai that you did not find me here. I'll pay you well for it tomorrow."

"I suppose I could do that," Chia Chiang relented, "but how much could you pay? It will have to be in writing."

Fifty ounces of silver was finally agreed upon, and Chia Jui drew up two notes in the form of gambling debts and gave them to his captors.

"Now you can go," Chia Chiang said. "But wait, let me find out which is the safest way. You can't wait here, for I know that someone is coming soon. Come with me." He put out the lantern and took Chia Jui to the foot of a flight of steps, where he told Chia Jui to wait while he went off to reconnoiter.

Chia Jui meekly submitted. As he waited and shivered in the cold and wondered what was going to happen next, he heard a splash over him and, before he knew it, he was drenched in a most foul-smelling mixture of filth. Then Chia Chiang came running and said to him, "Come with me. The rear gate is open." Chia Jui followed him and bolted into the darkness.

When he thought of Phoenix's treachery, Chia Jui resolved never to have anything to do with her again but then he would see Phoenix's image before him, lovelier than ever and all the more desirable now that he knew she had

[1] "Shen" means "the wife of an uncle younger than one's father."

never cared for him. He told himself that he would gladly die if he could have her in his arms for one brief moment. He knew better, though, than to let himself be seen again at the Yungkuofu.

This proved only the beginning of his real troubles. Chia Jung and Chia Chiang pressed him for the payment of the notes, and his grandfather imposed on him more severe tasks as a punishment for his recent escapades. His desire stimulated by the constant image of Phoenix, he gave way to evil habits and slept but poorly. The two nights of exposure produced their effects, and he soon took to bed. Of such tonic medicines as cinnamon, aconitum seeds, turtle shell, and the like, he took several tens of pounds but he got no better. The doctors later prescribed the sole use of the best grade of ginseng, something that Tai-ju could not afford. Madame Wang was appealed to, but as Phoenix was acting for Madame Wang, the supply of ginseng thus obtained was both meager and poor in quality.

One day a lame Taoist priest came asking for alms and claimed that he specialized in curing sickness of the soul. Chia Jui heard him and begged his family to let the Taoist come in to see him. The latter looked at him and said, "Your affliction is not something to be remedied by medicine. I have a magic mirror here which will cure you if you follow my directions." He took from his sleeve a mirror polished on both sides and bearing the inscription, "Precious Mirror for Breeze and Moonlight." He said to Chia Jui, "This mirror was made by the Goddess of Disillusionment and is designed to cure diseases resulting from impure thoughts and self-destructive habits. It is intended for youths such as you. But do not look into the right side. Use only the reverse side of the mirror. I shall be back for it in three days and congratulate you on your recovery." He went away, refusing to accept any money.

Chia Jui took the mirror and looked into the reverse side as the Taoist had directed. He threw it down in horror, for he saw a gruesome skeleton staring at him through its hollow eyes. He cursed the Taoist for playing such a crude joke upon him. Then he thought he would see what was on the right side. When he did so, he saw Phoenix standing there and beckoning to him. Chia Jui felt himself wafted into a mirror world, wherein he fulfilled his desire. He woke up from his trance and found the mirror lying wrong side up, revealing the horrible skeleton. He felt exhausted from the experience that the more deceptive side of the mirror gave him, but it was so delicious that he could not resist the temptation of looking into the right side again. Again he saw Phoenix beckoning to him and again he yielded to the temptation. This happened three or four times. When he was about to leave the mirror on his last visit, he was seized by two men and put in chains.

"Just a moment, officers," Chia Jui pleaded. "Let me take my mirror with me." These were his last words.

CHAPTER TEN

In which Black Jade returns to Yangchow to attend her father's illness
And Phoenix goes to the Ningkuofu to take charge of Chin-shih's funeral

TOWARD the end of the year, a letter came from Lin Ju-hai in Yangchow, saying that he was seriously ill and would like to see his daughter. The Matriarch immediately made preparations for Black Jade's journey. Pao-yu was reluctant to have her go but he could say nothing, as it was her duty to be at her father's side in his illness. So, shortly after the New Year, Black Jade set out for Yangchow, escorted, at the Matriarch's insistence, by Chia Lien.

One evening Phoenix lay awake long after Patience had fallen asleep. She was thinking of Chia Lien and counting off the days it would take him to return. It was not until after midnight that she began to feel sleepy. Suddenly through her drowsy eyes, she saw Chin-shih standing before her.

"What a time to be sleeping, Shen-shen," Chin-shih said with a smile. "I am going away, and you do not even get up to see me off. But I cannot go without saying good-by to you. Besides, there is something I can confide to no one but you."

"What is it that you wish to tell me?" Phoenix asked sleepily.

"You are a very unusual woman, Shen-shen," Chin-shih said. "In many ways you have more intelligence and foresight than many men who wear caps and gowns. So surely you know the meaning of the saying that the moon waxes only to wane and the cup fills only to overflow, or the saying that the higher the climb the harder the fall. Our family has prospered for over a hundred years. If one day misfortune should overtake us, would it not be laughable if we were as unprepared for it as the proverbial monkeys when their tree home falls from under them?"

Phoenix shuddered at the ominous words. "What can we do to prevent possible reverses?" she asked.

"How naïve you are, Shen-shen," Chin-shih answered a little sadly. "Reverses follow prosperity, and disgrace comes after honor. One cannot prevent it; one can only provide for famine in times of plenty. There are two things that should be done." When Phoenix asked what they were, Chin-shih answered, "We must first make provision for perpetuating ancestral offerings and then for the family school. We should buy large tracts of land around the cemetery. The rental will take care of the offerings and the maintenance of the school. In this way the future will be assured; for even in case of Imperial disfavor and confiscation, this consecrated land will be exempted. Just now the family fortune is in the ascendancy—an event is to occur that will bring new honors to the family—but reverses always come when least expected."

"What event?" Phoenix asked.

"I dare not betray the secrets of Heaven," Chin-shih answered.

Phoenix was about to question her further, when she was roused by Patience, who told her that a messenger from the Ningkuofu had just brought word of Chin-shih's death. Phoenix dressed hastily and went over to Madame Wang's apartment. By that time, the news had reached every courtyard and every apartment. Everyone was shocked by the suddenness of Chin-shih's death, and all were mystified as to its possible cause.[1] But all wept and cried over the loss, for Chin-shih was beloved by all.

Pao-yu had gone to bed in the dejected mood that had become habitual since Black Jade's departure. He was awakened by the general stir in the house. The news that Chin-shih had died was a knife plunged into his heart. He uttered a sharp cry and spat out a mouthful of blood. Despite the Matriarch's objections, he insisted on going over to the Ningkuofu.

The main gate of the East Mansion was wide open and ablaze with light. The mourners had gathered, and soon the sound of weeping and wailing shook the whole mansion. Pao-yu rushed into the room where the body lay and wept inconsolably. In the outer hall he found Chia Gen surrounded by the close relatives of the Chia clan. Chia Gen was bathed in tears and, between fits of sobbing and wailing, was telling everyone how wonderful his daughter-in-law was and what a great loss the Ningkuofu had suffered.

A member from the Imperial Astrological Institute selected the day for the funeral. The body was to lie in the house for forty-nine days, during which time one hundred and eight Buddhist monks were to pray for the dead in the main hall, while ninety-nine Taoist priests conducted services in another part of the Mansion.

Chia Ging, Chia Gen's father, was the only one who seemed unconcerned. He refused to leave the monastery for the Red Dust and thus negate all the years spent in solitude and contemplation. Chia Gen was therefore free to indulge in as extravagant a funeral as he wished.

Suddenly it was reported from the inner apartments that one of Chin-shih's maids, Jui-chu, had killed herself so that

[1] Since the author has prepared the reader for Chin-shih's death by elaborately describing her illness, there should be no shock or mystery about it. Commentators are agreed that this is the author's way of hinting that Chin-shih had committed suicide because her adulterous relations with Chia Gen had been discovered.

she could serve her mistress in death.[2] This extraordinary devotion deeply moved the assembled mourners. Chia Gen ordered that the maid be buried as if she were his granddaughter. Another maid, Pao-chu, volunteered to be the posthumously adopted daughter of her mistress, as Chin-shih had left no children. The idea pleased Chia Gen, who gave orders to the servants that Pao-chu should henceforth be addressed as Ku-niang.

The mourning ceremonies went smoothly, but Chia Gen was not satisfied: Chia Jung was only a district graduate and had no official rank. The problem was solved by the arrival of an influential eunuch. To him Chia Gen confided his wish to purchase a title for his son.

"This is a very lucky coincidence," the eunuch said. "It happens that there have been two vacancies in the Imperial Guards. One of them is now filled, but the other is still open, as I have been too busy to attend to an application from the Viceroy of Yung-hsing. If your boy wants this post, all you have to do is to give me his application."

The application was duly written, with the name and native place of Chia Jung and the names and titles of his great-grandfather, grandfather, and father. The eunuch handed it to one of his attendants and said, "Give this to old Chao of the Ministry of Civil Service and tell him to fill out a decree in accordance with it. I shall see him about it tomorrow."

"Where shall I send the money?" Chia Gen asked as he escorted the eunuch to the gate. "You had better send it to me, as the people in the ministry might try to hold you up if you send it to them," the eunuch answered.

How much of the thousand ounces of silver sent by Chia Gen to the eunuch actually reached the Ministry of Civil Service we do not know, but Chia Jung did get his appointment. Immediately, among the many banners on

[2] It is suggested that Jui-chu was the maid who had unwittingly surprised Chin-shih and Chia Gen at their last secret meeting. She committed suicide for fear of Chia Gen's vengeance.

the funeral tower there appeared a large one bearing the legend "The funeral of Lady Chin-shih of the House of Chia, the wife of the Cavalier of the Imperial Dragon Guards, Defenders of the Inner Palace, and the granddaughter-in-law of the Lord of Ningkuo." In the days following, mourning guests arrived and departed in constant procession. All people of any consequence in the Capital were there, including many dukes and marquises and numerous officials of the highest rank.

The management of the Ningkuofu was no easy task in ordinary circumstances. Yu-shih was never quite equal to it, and the Ningkuofu was known as the less ably managed of the two Chia mansions. One can imagine, therefore, Chia Gen's anxiety when Yu-shih was suddenly taken ill at the time of her daughter-in-law's death. He was afraid that something might go wrong and spoil the perfect funeral he was resolved upon. Pao-yu noticed his anxiety and, on being told the cause of it, said, "I'll recommend someone to you. If you can get her to help you, everything will go perfectly."

The person whom Pao-yu recommended was, as one may well guess, Phoenix. Chia Gen heartily agreed and immediately went to see Madame Wang and Madame Hsing to secure their permission. The decision rested with Madame Wang, for though Phoenix was Madame Hsing's daughter-in-law, she was actually the chief aide of Madame Wang, the real mistress of the Yungkuofu. She hesitated, for it was a difficult assignment and Phoenix, capable though she was, had no experience with funerals. But Phoenix was eager for the opportunity. When Madame Wang turned to her and searched her face for an indication of her reactions, Phoenix said, "Tai-tai might as well give her consent since Ta-ko really seems to need help."

When Lai Sheng, chief steward of the Ningkuofu, heard that Phoenix had been asked to take charge of the inner affairs, he summoned his colleagues and said to them, "The master has asked Lien Er Nai-nai to take charge inside. We'll be getting orders and instructions from her. We must be very careful, indeed, if we do not want to lose face. You know how she is."

All the servants agreed with their chief and one of them remarked, "Frankly, it is time someone came along and cleaned up this mess. Conditions are getting a bit impossible."

At the appointed hour the next day, all the maidservants gathered before the hall that Phoenix had made her headquarters. "Since your master has asked me to take charge here," Phoenix said to Lai Sheng's wife in the hearing of all, "I am afraid you will all have to put up with me and my way of doing things for a while. I am not like your mistress, who is kind and good-natured and lets you have your own way. Don't tell me, ever, that such and such is the custom of this house; just do as I bid you. Those who dare to neglect their duties will receive due punishment, no matter what prestige they have with your master and mistress, for I don't care who are favorites and who are not."

One of her maids called the roll, and Phoenix inspected the servants, one by one, as they came in.

"These twenty," she said when the roll call was over, "will be divided into groups of ten each and will take charge of serving tea to the guests. These twenty, also divided into two groups, will take charge of tea and dinner for relatives. These forty will wait in and around the spirit hall, keeping the incense and candles burning and the offering of rice and tea fresh, and will help with the mourning. These four will be responsible for the teapots and cups, and these four for the dinnerware and wine pots. These eight will receive and record all the funeral presents. These eight will take charge of the distribution of candles, oil, and paper to the various places according to a list that will be furnished them. These twenty will keep watch at night and see to it that the courts are kept clean and free from fire hazards. The rest will supervise and be responsible for the various apartments and halls and will have to replace any loss or theft that occurs in their respective areas. Lai Sheng's wife will supervise generally. I shall expect you to see that everything is done according to schedule and report to me any negligence, evasion, gambling, drinking, and other misdemeanors. Failure to do this because of favoritism or for any other reason will not only bring immediate punishment upon the culprit but also disgrace upon the family name. I warn you all in advance so that no one can plead ignorance."

With every servant and maid assigned her special duty, order was restored to the Ningkuofu. Throughout the trying period of the funeral, the household was better managed than when Yu-shih herself was in charge. There were no thefts; there were no complaints and quarrels among the servants because some thought they were worked harder than others. Thus the days went by until the fifth day of the Fifth Seven.

Phoenix arrived at the Ningkuofu at the appointed hour but, instead of going to her headquarters, she went to the spirit hall of Chin-shih in the Garden of Ningkuofu. In the courtyard several attendants stood silently with spirit paper ready, and in the hall others were ready with the various offerings. Tears started to flow from Phoenix's eyes as she saw the coffin. Gongs were struck, and the musicians played their mournful number in a shed near by. Phoenix wept without restraint and was joined by the attendants and others, until heaven and earth resounded with their grief. Presently Chia Gen and Yu-shih sent someone to beg Phoenix to restrain her grief, and gradually the mourning ceased.

Everyone was in attendance at the roll call in the council hall except one among those whose duty was to usher in and out the guests and relatives. The tardy servant was later summoned.

"So you consider yourself above the rest and think that you do not have to answer the roll call!" Phoenix said sternly.

"I have been on time every day," the hapless servant

answered, trembling with fear, "I beg Nai-nai to forgive me this first offense."

At this point, a maidservant from the Yungkuofu came for authorization to issue from the storehouse threads for making tassels for the carriages. She presented a list to Phoenix's attendant, who read it aloud to her mistress. There were two large sedans, three small ones, and four carriages. So many tassels were needed in all, and so many beads, and so many pounds of thread. Finding the figures correct, Phoenix gave her approval. Four more servants from the Yungkuofu appeared, each with requests of various kinds. Of these two were approved and two rejected because of some error in the figures. Still others appeared, some from the Yungkuofu and others from the Ningkuofu. When everything was disposed of, Phoenix said, without looking at the guilty servant, "Today you are late and tomorrow it will be someone else. Soon there won't be anyone here to carry on. I would like to spare you, but I am afraid that I shall not be able to carry on the duties here if I do." Then she commanded sternly, "Take her out and give her twenty lashes." None of the servants dared to intercede, as Phoenix's countenance discouraged any such intentions. They dragged the guilty servant out and gave her the prescribed number of lashes. As a further punishment, she was deprived of one month's wages.

CHAPTER ELEVEN

In which Phoenix satisfies her greed at the Iron Sill Temple
And Chin Chung fulfills his hunger at the Water Moon Convent

A few days before the funeral, Chia Gen went to the Iron Sill Temple to supervise personally the extensive preparations for the reception of the mourning guests and to arrange for the numerous services and prayers to be conducted there. On the day of the funeral, sixty-four bearers for the elaborate hearse arrived, and the body of Chin-shih was moved from the Garden of the Ningkuofu. Innumerable insignia of rank were carried by men in proper costumes, as were streamers, banners, umbrellas of various colors, and placards of wood, lacquered, painted, and inscribed in gold. Pao-chu, the daughter of Chin-shih by posthumous adoption, acted as chief mourner.

We cannot give a complete roster of the notables present at the funeral. The sedans bearing the women guests alone numbered over a hundred and with the conveyances of the Chias formed a line over four li in length. At frequent intervals along the road to the temple were the decorative tents of the mourning guests, in which were spread offerings to the spirit of the departed. The tents of four princes came first; they were followed in proper order by those of notables of lesser rank.

Prince Peace of the North waited at his tent for the procession to approach. As the procession neared the Prince's tent, it stopped, and Chia Gen hastened forward to the Prince's tent with Chia Cheng and Chia Sheh. Chia Gen expressed his gratitude to the Prince and his own unworthiness of the great honor bestowed by the Prince upon him.

The Prince had heard about Pao-yu. He asked Chia Cheng to present him and seemed to take a great liking to him. He asked to see Pao-yu's jade and gave him a string of beads which were a present from the Emperor. After thanking the Prince again, Chia Sheh and others urged him to return home, but the Prince insisted on waiting for the procession to pass, saying that though he was a prince, Chin-shih had now joined the ranks of the immortals and must therefore take precedence. Chia Gen ordered the cessation of the music, and the cortege passed the tent of the Prince in silence.

It was not until late in the morning that the procession finally reached the temple. There the Taoists and Buddhists were in readiness. Various services were conducted, and banquets were given for the mourning guests. By late afternoon, the majority of the guests had departed, and only the close friends and relatives remained for the three-day services. Madame Wang and Madame Hsing returned to the Capital, while Phoenix remained to continue her supervision. Pao-yu and Chin Chung also stayed, because they were delighted with the countryside. All three had accommodations at the Water Moon Convent, while the rest stayed at the temple.

After the day's ceremonies were over, Phoenix went to the convent accompanied by Pao-yu and Chin Chung. While Phoenix was entertained by the old nun in charge, the two youths walked around the grounds. In the front hall they ran into Chih-neng, a pretty nun in her late teens. She was a frequent visitor at the Yungkuofu, and both Pao-yu and Chin Chung had met her before. Pao-yu nudged Chin Chung and said, "There goes Neng-er."

"What of it?" Chin Chung said, pretending innocence.

"What of it!" Pao-yu exclaimed. "Don't pretend. Tell me what you were doing with her the other day when you two were alone in Lao Tai-tai's room. I saw her in your arms, so don't tell me differently."

"Don't tell tales," Chin Chung protested.

"We'll not argue about that," Pao-yu said, "but speak to her and tell her to bring us some tea."

"Can't you do it yourself?" Chin Chung asked. "She would do it for you just as she would for me, since that is one of her duties."

"But it would not be for love if she did it for me. For you, it would be."

Unable to put off Pao-yu's insistence, Chin Chung turned to the nun and said, "Bring us some tea, Neng-er."

When the nun brought the tea, Chin Chung said to her, "Give it to me."

Pao-yu said also, "Give it to me."

The nun said, giggling a little, "Do I have honey on my hands that you must fight over even a cup of tea?"

The appearance of another nun interrupted them, and Chih-neng went back to her work. The two boys joined Phoenix and the old nun for refreshments but were off again as soon as they could leave.

The old nun said to Phoenix, "I have something that I want to speak about to Tai-tai, but I would like Nai-nai's advice and permission first." Phoenix asked her what it was, and the old nun continued, "*Amitofo*. When I was at the Convent of our Goddess of Mercy at Chang-an, we had a rich patron by the name of Chang. One day the Changs came with their daughter, named Kin-kuo, to make offerings to the Goddess. It so happened that the brother-in-law of the prefect was also visiting the temple. He saw Kin-kuo, fell in love with her, and almost immediately sent someone to the girl's parents with a marriage proposal. Unfortunately the girl was already engaged to the son of the garrison commander. The rumor of the proposal reached the commander who, without inquiring into the facts, accused the Chang family of attempting to break the engagement in favor of a better match. He would not let the Changs return the engagement presents and brought suit against them. Now the Changs feel outraged and are determined to break the engagement if only to spite the commander. They are in the Capital trying to secure the assistance of their influential friends. The viceroy of Chang-an, I understand, is a friend of your noble house. If you could persuade the viceroy to say a word to the garrison commander, the latter would surely drop the suit and return the engagement presents. If this should happen, the Changs would willingly bankrupt themselves to show their gratitude."

"It is a trifle that could easily be arranged," Phoenix said, "but Tai-tai does not like to meddle in such affairs."

"Then perhaps Nai-nai would attend to it?" the old nun suggested hopefully.

"Why should I?" Phoenix said. "The Changs mean nothing to me."

The old nun sighed and was silent for a while. Then she said, half to herself, "I suppose there is nothing to be done since Nai-nai does not want to be bothered. But the Changs know that I am going to speak to you. When I tell them that you don't want to be bothered, they may think that you are unable to do anything for them."

Her words produced the desired effect, for the wily old nun knew of Phoenix's love of power and that she could not bear to have others think there was anything she couldn't do. She said to the nun, "You know I never cared what the superstitious say about the final reckoning. I do what I please, and what I please I can always do. If the Changs are willing to put up three thousand taels, I will help them vindicate themselves."

The old nun assured her that the Changs would be more than glad to pay the sum. Phoenix concluded by telling the nun that the three thousand taels was nothing to her and that it was for the messenger she would have to dispatch. "Do not think that I am doing this for the trifling sum of money," she said. "My resources are such that even thirty thousand is nothing to me." The old nun voiced her agreement, though she knew well what three thousand taels meant to Phoenix. She said many things to flatter Phoenix, and the two talked far into the night.

In the meantime, Chin Chung had slipped into Chih-neng's room where she was doing some work. He tiptoed up to her and put his arms around her waist. The nun stamped her feet and threatened to call for help. But Chin Chung pleaded with her, whispering passionate words into her ears.

"What do you want of me?" the nun said resignedly. "You should think of rescuing me from this living death. Then we can be united and live together."

"Yes, yes," Chin Chung said, "I have thought of it often and I am sure that it can be arranged. But 'distant water cannot quench a nearby fire.' You must have pity on me tonight, for I am dying for you." He blew out the lamp and carried the nun to the k'ang. The latter struggled to free herself, but in vain. She could have called out for help, but she did not want an open scandal. Besides, she was very fond of Chin Chung. Gradually her struggles ceased.

Suddenly someone laid hands on Chin Chung and the nun without a word of warning. The lovers were scared to death, but the laughter which the intruder was unable to suppress reassured them, for it was only Pao-yu. The nun slipped away.

"You have a very perverted sense of humor," Chin Chung said dryly. "What do you mean by this?"

"Now that I have caught you in the act," Pao-yu said laughing, "do you still insist she is nothing to you?"

"All right," Chin Chung said. "I promise anything you want if you won't tell."

"We'll not talk about it now," Pao-yu said. "I'll settle with you later, after we go to bed."

Pao-yu, Chin Chung, and Phoenix occupied one suite of two rooms in the convent. Phoenix, who occupied the inner room, took Pao-yu's jade before they said good night and put it under her own pillow for safekeeping. It is not known what settlement Pao-yu made with his friend that night nor how, and we shall not venture any speculations.

The Matriarch, ever solicitous over the comfort and safety of her favorite grandson, sent for Pao-yu the next day, but he was enjoying the excursion too well to obey. Besides, Chin Chung could not bear to part with the nun and begged Pao-yu to stay with him. Phoenix, too, wanted to stay another day in order to fulfill her promise to the old nun. The three therefore spent another night at the convent. Before they finally left, Chih-neng begged Chin Chung to send for her as soon as possible, and the latter swore again and again that he would do his utmost.

In the meantime, Phoenix had sent Lai Wang, one of her confidential servants, to the viceroy of Chang-an, with a letter in the name of Chia Lien. The viceroy's hint to the commander caused the latter to drop the suit and return the engagement presents. The affair would have ended there, if it had not happened that Kin-kuo was in character quite different from her unscrupulous parents. When she learned of the broken engagement, she quietly committed suicide rather than be unfaithful to her first betrothed. And the commander's son, whose constancy was equal to that of his fiancée, drowned himself when he learned of her suicide. Thus, the Changs lost all around by their faithlessness, while Phoenix was enriched by three thousand ounces of good silver. This affair was never discovered by Madame Wang or Chia Lien. Emboldened by this success, Phoenix perpetrated many similar evil deeds which we shall not record in detail.

CHAPTER TWELVE

In which Cardinal Spring is advanced in the Imperial Palace
And Chin Chung is taken to the Other World

It was Chia Cheng's birthday, and the Ningkuo and Yungkuo mansions were celebrating it with the usual festivities, when the chief eunuch was suddenly announced. The festivities were immediately suspended, the main gate of the Yungkuofu was thrown open, and the central hall was hastily made ready to receive the Imperial Messenger in state. The eunuch marched into the central hall with a retinue of eunuchs, turned, and faced south, while Chia Sheh and Chia Cheng knelt before him to hear the Imperial will. The eunuch carried no written edict. He merely said, "By special edict, Chia Cheng is hereby ordered to present himself at once at the Lin-ching Hall for an audience." Then he left as suddenly as he had come, without even stopping for a sip of tea.

Chia Cheng quickly changed into court costume and set out for the Palace. No one had any inkling of the purpose of the unexpected summons, and since the Dragon Countenance was noted for its uncertain aspects, anxiety cast a shadow over everyone. Lai Ta, chief steward of the Yungkuofu, was sent to the Palace to ascertain the nature of the summons and report back at the earliest possible moment. Finally after three or four hours, Lai Ta returned and reported that Chia Cheng had been summoned to be informed of his daughter's promotion to the rank of an Imperial consort of the second degree. Anxiety immediately gave way to joy, and exultation was written on every face from the Matriarch to the humblest bondmaid.

Pao-yu alone seemed insensible of the great honor that had come to the family. The reason for his distraction was because a few days earlier the nun Chih-neng had secretly visited Chin Chung in his home. Chin Chung's father discovered this; he drove the nun away and gave Chin Chung a sound thrashing. The mortification brought on a recurrence of an old ailment, and four or five days later, the old man died. Chin Chung had never been strong. Now, what with the beating, his grief over his father's death, and his worry for the nun, he, too, fell seriously ill and had to take to bed. That was why Pao-yu appeared preoccupied and evinced no interest in the festivities that attended the new honor the Emperor had conferred upon the family. But no one knew of the cause of his preoccupation; it was taken simply as another example of his queerness.

Fortunately a messenger came from Chia Lien one day and reported that he and Black Jade would arrive the following day. Now Black Jade's father had died, and after his funeral, she set out for the Capital once more with Chia Lien, this time to live permanently with her grandmother.

Pao-yu was cheered by Black Jade's return. She had grown more beautiful than ever, for girls of her age have a way of blossoming almost under one's eyes. She brought back gifts for all her cousins—books, writing brushes, inkstones, and decorated paper. On his part, Pao-yu offered her the string of beads given him by Prince Peace of the North, but she refused, saying she would not touch anything that had been handled by unknown men.

After presenting himself to his father, Chia Cheng, and others, Chia Lien went back to his own compound, where he was greeted by Phoenix with exaggerated politeness. She congratulated him, addressing him, half in jest and half seriously, as "His Excellency the Imperial Relative." When

Chia Lien complimented her on having handled the funeral so splendidly, she professed abasement at her failure, her clumsiness, and lack of tact and insisted that she accepted the assignment only because a refusal might have offended Madame Wang. Her professions deceived no one and were not even intended to deceive.

As she went on to tell Chia Lien of the events during his absence, she heard Patience talking with someone in the outer room. Phoenix asked who was there, and Patience entered to tell her that Hsueh Yi-ma had sent Lotus on an errand and that she had taken care of it.

"That Lotus is quite nice looking," Chia Lien remarked. "When I was over at Yi-ma's a while back, I happened to run into her and wondered who she was. I asked Yi-ma and only then did I realize that she was the girl involved in the homocide case. What a pity that such a nice-looking morsel should fall into the imbecile Hsueh's mouth. He is unworthy of her."

"Humph," Phoenix said disapprovingly. "I should think you would be somewhat less susceptible since you've just come back from Soochow where they say all the women are beautiful. But apparently you are as greedy as ever. If you like her, how about my exchanging Patience for her? I am sure it will be all right with Hsueh Lao-ta, for he, like you, always has his eyes on the pot while he is eating out of his bowl. For a whole year, he pestered Yi-ma because he could not have Lotus, but in less than a month after he got her, he lost interest in her . . ."

Just then, word was brought in that Chia Cheng wanted Chia Lien immediately. The latter was glad of the opportunity to drop the subject of Lotus. After he left the room, Phoenix asked Patience what Lotus wanted, and Patience said, "She was never here. It was Lai Wang Sao-sao, who stupidly chose just this time to come in with the interest that is long overdue. Luckily I happened to run into her. Otherwise she would have come in and blurted her errand before Er-yeh. You know how careless he is with money. If he knew that Nai-nai has some of her own, he would spend even more freely. So I scolded her a little for bringing the interest in when Er-yeh was around."

"So that's it," Phoenix said, laughing. "I was wondering what Yi-ma should want so urgently that she had to send Lotus."

Presently Chia Lien returned. When Phoenix asked him what Chia Cheng wanted, he told her it was about the Imperial Visit which the Capital had been full of for the past few days.

Now the reigning Emperor was a benevolent sovereign. Shortly after the favor conferred upon Cardinal Spring, it occurred to His Imperial Majesty that it would contribute to the cultivation and fulfillment of the cardinal virtue of filial piety if the families of the Imperial Concubines were allowed to visit their daughters in the Palace. Therefore, after consulting Their Most High Majesties the ex-Emperor and Empress, His Majesty decreed that the female members of their immediate families might visit their daughters in the Palace on days wherein the numerals two and six occur.[1] Their Most High Majesties were pleased at the thoughtfulness of the Emperor and suggested that, since Court formalities might prevent parents and daughters from deriving the fullest possible benefits from these visits, it should be further decreed that families in a position to receive the Imperial Concubines might ask permission to do so. His Majesty complied, and the families of the Imperial Concubines Chou and Wu and the Yungkuo itself all began to build palaces worthy of Imperial patronage.

The Takuanyuan,[2] the name later given to the palace by Cardinal Spring, was built on the site of the Garden of the Ningkuofu and the eastern portion of the Yungkuofu. It was about three-and-a-half li in circumference and was

[1] That is, the second, sixth, twelfth, etc., days of the month. The seven-day division was not the custom in traditional China. China.

[2] Though "ta kuan" literally means "great view, sight, or spectacle," it suggests here the idea of completeness; hence, "Takuanyuan" may be translated "Complete Garden."

crossed by a brook which separated the two Chia mansions. The wall between the two mansions was torn down, and a new one was built around the Takuanyuan. The labor and expense was great, but not as great as if they had had to start from nothing, if every rock had to be sought out and brought down from the hills and every tree and shrub especially planted. The original scheme of the Ningkuo garden lent itself to the new one, and the landscape talents among the secretaries of Chia Cheng were able to draw up a plan whereby the original pavilions, towers, artificial mountains, halls, and verandas were utilized.

The work of supervision fell chiefly upon Chia Gen and Chia Lien, with the advice of the large staff of secretaries; for Chia Cheng had neither the time nor inclination for such details. As the construction work progressed, craftsmen in gold and silver, in brass and pewter, and in other materials necessary for the outfitting of the new palace, were assembled and set to work. The task of recruiting and outfitting a troupe of young actresses and of purchasing large quantities of silks was assigned to Chia Chiang, a favorite of Chia Gen. Chia Jung was put in charge of the goldsmiths and silversmiths.

Because of these activities in the Yungkuofu, Pao-yu was left very much to himself by his father, who had been in the habit of inquiring into his studies and thus necessitating a certain amount of preparation. He would have been happy because of this freedom if not for the fact that his friend Chin Chung died during this period.

CHAPTER THIRTEEN

In which Pao-yu is made to suffer because of the perversity of Black Jade
And Cardinal Spring is allowed to visit her family by the magnanimity of the Son of Heaven

THE Takuanyuan was at last finished. One day Chia Cheng, accompanied by his secretaries and companions, went to inspect it and to think up the names that must be inscribed on the plaques over the entrances to the buildings and compounds and to compose the couplets that must go on either side. The names were only tentative, to be inscribed on paper lanterns made in the shape of the plaques and hung in front of them; the ultimate choice of names was properly a prerogative of the Imperial Concubine.

It happened that Pao-yu was in the Garden that day. He was still mourning the death of Chin Chung, and to distract him from his grief, the Matriarch had encouraged him to go into the Garden. Warned of the approach of his father, he hastened out to avoid an encounter, but Chia Cheng saw him and bade him join his party. Pao-yu felt uneasy, not knowing what was in store. It turned out to be a pleasant surprise. His father had heard the tutor praise Pao-yu's skill at composing antithetical couplets, and this seemed a good time for a test. Pao-yu acquitted himself well. Many of his compositions were accepted and even won some qualified approval from his exacting father. Chia Cheng was secretly pleased with his son's accomplishment, though he sternly told him that he should not waste his time in such idle occupations but should apply himself to the type of essays required in the Examinations.

When Pao-yu was finally dismissed, his pages swarmed around him and congratulated him for the good showing he had made. "It's something to celebrate to win praise from Lao-yeh," they said. "Lao Tai-tai knows that you were with Lao-yeh and asked how you were doing. We told her you were doing very well indeed. If it had been otherwise, she would have sent for you and rescued you from any further embarrassment. They say your couplets are even better than those of the old scholars. So you must give us something to mark the occasion."

"All right," Pao-yu said, smiling with gratification, "I'll give you a string of *cash* each."

"Who cares for that?" one of the pages said. "What we want is a more personal memento from you." And so saying, he helped himself to the ornamental pouch on Pao-yu's sash. His example was followed by the others, and soon Pao-yu's sash was stripped of all its ornaments. Only then did they escort him back to the Matriarch, who, needless to say, was pleased that for once Chia Cheng found no fault with his son.

Apparently this was not the first time that Pao-yu returned without his ornaments, for Pervading Fragrance noticed the loss as soon as he entered the room and remarked, "So you have let those shameless wretches take everything away from you again."

Black Jade, overhearing this, said to Pao-yu, "I suppose you gave away the pouch I made for you, too. Never, never again expect me to make another one for you." So saying and before Pao-yu had a chance to explain, she went to her room and began to cut up the pouch she was working on. Pao-yu was annoyed in his turn. He unbuttoned his robe and revealed the pouch Black Jade had made for him, saying, "There is your pouch! You should know I would not let anyone take that."

Black Jade was ashamed of her impetuous behavior but was too proud to admit it or to say anything to placate Pao-yu. He now took off the pouch and threw it to her, saying, "Perhaps you are sorry you gave me this. If so, you might as well have it back." At this, Black Jade started to cry and would have destroyed that one, too, if Pao-yu had not rescued it just in time. Always ready to forgive and assume all blame where Black Jade was concerned, he tried his best now to soothe her.

Finally, Black Jade threw down her scissors and said, wiping off her tears, "You needn't tease me like this. We can leave each other alone from now on." She lay down on the bed and turned her face toward the wall. Pao-yu was not easily rebuffed and continued to plead and coax until Black Jade relented. She got up and said, "I shall leave this room, since you will not let me have a moment's peace."

"I shall follow you wherever you go," Pao-yu replied with an apologetic smile. Black Jade could not suppress her amusement at his repentant and anxious look. She laughed gratifyingly, and peace was restored between the two lovers, who seemed destined for such endless quarrels and complaints.

Now Chia Chiang had returned from Soochow with quantities of silks and a fully equipped troupe of twelve young actresses and their master. They were put to rehearsing their parts in the Pear Fragrance Court, which had in the meantime been vacated by Hsueh Yi-ma. Twelve Buddhist nuns and twelve Taoist nuns were recruited to fill the convent in the Takuanyuan so that they could say prayers for the Imperial Concubine. Miao-yu, an accomplished nun, was invited to take charge.

By New Year's, all the preparations were completed. On receiving Chia Cheng's memorial, the Emperor chose the fifteenth of the First Moon, the Feast of Lanterns, for the Imperial Concubine's visit. As early as the eighth, eunuchs arrived from the Palace to inspect the Takuanyuan and to supervise the final arrangements. On the eve of the visit, no one in the Yungkuofu slept, so great was the excitement. The next morning before dawn, all the members of the Yungkuofu put on their court costumes and waited for the arrival of the Imperial Concubine—Chia Sheh and Chia Cheng at the head of the street, and the Matriarch and others outside the Yungkuo gate. The morning wore on. They were all beginning to tire when a eunuch arrived from the Palace to announce that the Imperial Concubine was not expected to leave the Imperial Palace much before seven in the evening. On hearing this, the Matriarch and the others retired into the Yungkuofu and rested until they heard the sound of the heralds in the streets. Then they all hurried out and took their positions as before.

As they waited silently, two eunuchs came riding slowly into the street. The eunuchs dismounted and stood facing the west, the direction from which the Imperial Concubine's procession was coming. Presently another pair appeared, and yet another, until there were ten or more. A band was heard in the distance, and soon a procession of eunuchs appeared, carrying dragon banners, phoenix umbrellas, and ceremonial fans made of pheasants' plumes. From a pair of gold incense burners suspended by chains, wreaths of fragrant smoke curled up. Then a large yellow state umbrella embroidered with seven phoenixes came into view. Under it were eunuchs carrying the court costumes of the Imperial Concubine, and it was followed by other eunuchs carrying the various articles for the use of the Imperial Concubine during her visit. Finally, there appeared a seven-phoenix state sedan chair surmounted by a gold crown and carried by eight eunuchs. The Matriarch knelt with the others, but the Imperial Concubine commanded some of the eunuchs to help her rise. At the second gate of the Takuanyuan, Cardinal Spring descended from her sedan and entered a hall, whence, after a brief rest, she embarked on a boat to survey the splendors of the Garden. Although it was midwinter and the peach and apricot trees were bare, the boughs had been trimmed with artificial flowers and leaves, so that, illumined by countless lanterns, they gave the illusion of full bloom. Cardinal Spring was delighted; she regretted only that her visit had occasioned such extravagant display.

The eunuch in charge of ceremonies now requested her to ascend her seat in the main reception hall. First to be ushered in were Chia Sheh, Chia Cheng, and the male members of the Chia mansions, and after them the Matriarch and the female members.

After tea was offered three times, the Imperial Concubine left the Takuanyuan and proceeded to the Yungkuofu where, in the Matriarch's apartment, she expressed her wish to salute the Matriarch, Madame Wang, and the others according to family precedence. The Matriarch, however, would not let her.

So much was to be said on every side that no one knew where to begin. Moreover, there was the barrier of exalted position which, try as they would, they could not overcome. For a while, there was nothing to be heard in the room but the sound of weeping. Finally, the Imperial Concubine forced a smile and said, "This is my first visit home since you sent me to that place where I can see none of you. We should rejoice instead of weeping! I don't know when, if ever, I will be permitted to visit you again."

Then, with the Imperial Concubine's permission, Hsueh Yi-ma, Black Jade, and Precious Virtue were presented, and finally Pao-yu because he was, although a male without official position, his sister's favorite.

It was now announced that the feast was ready at the Takuanyuan. Accompanied by the Matriarch and the others, the Imperial Concubine returned to the main hall in the Garden, where for a little time she was able to experience once again the joys of family life. She retained most of the names proposed by Pao-yu for the various courts and pavilions, partly because her brother's inventions were good and partly out of affection for him. She asked her cousins and Pao-yu to compose verses to celebrate the occasion and awarded the highest honors to Precious Virtue and Black Jade.

After the feast and the theatrical presentation, the Imperial Concubine went to the convent to offer incense and prayers. Again Cardinal Spring wept. She could hardly bear to tear herself away, but she dared not tarry, as the rules of the Court were strict.

CHAPTER FOURTEEN

In which a cup of custard sets aflame a smoldering jealousy
And a handful of pennies brings to surface a characteristic meanness

AFTER recovering from the strenuous activities attendant upon the visit of the Imperial Concubine, the Chia mansions settled down to a more leisurely enjoyment of the festivities of the New Year season. There were theatrical performances, lantern shows and conundrum-guessing games, banquets, friends to visit, and leaves for some of the more favored maidservants. Among these was Pervading Fragrance, who was given permission to spend a day with her family.

During her absence, Pao-yu's maids had given themselves over entirely to games and play. It so happened that Pao-yu's old nurse Li Ma had come to visit him. She was displeased to see how untidy the room was, the floors littered with melon seed shells, and the maids all absorbed in their games. "You girls have become very spoiled since I left the service," she complained. "Pao-yu is like a tall lamp which lights up everything except itself. He is always complaining about other people's untidiness but he doesn't seem to notice the mess in his own rooms."

The maids paid no attention to her, for she had retired from active service and had no authority over them. They were used to her grumbling. The old woman kept on asking about Pao-yu, about his appetite, and when he went to bed, and so on. The maids answered her in desultory fashion, some of the more impatient muttering, "What a nuisance the old witch makes of herself."

Presently Li Ma discovered a custard that Pao-yu had saved for Pervading Fragrance. "What a nice custard!" she said. "Why didn't you girls offer it to me?"

But as she took up the bowl, Bright Design warned her, saying, "Leave that alone. Pao-yu said to save it for Hsi-jen;[1] so don't touch it, unless you are ready to take the blame."

This made Li Ma feel humiliated and angry. She said, "I don't think Pao-yu can be so ungrateful as to begrudge me this. Not just a bowl of custard. He could hardly say anything if it was something worth a hundred times as much. For surely he cannot so soon forget that he sucked at my breast and think more of Hsi-jen than me. I'll show you!" So saying, she proceeded to help herself to the custard.

Musk Moon, more tactful, tried to placate her. "Ma-ma is right, of course. Pao-yu wouldn't mind. If he realized that you liked it, I am sure he would have sent it over to you."

"Don't try to jolly me," the nurse said. "Don't think that I don't know that he threatened to tell Lao Tai-tai about the tea. But I don't mind. Just tell him I ate the custard. I'll be responsible for the consequences." She finished the custard defiantly and then left.

Presently Pao-yu returned and immediately sent someone to fetch Pervading Fragrance. Noticing Bright Design lying in bed, he asked, "Is she sick or has she lost money?"

Autumn Sky said, "She was ahead until the Grand Dowager Li came and distracted everyone with her complaints. She lost steadily after that and is very unhappy about it."

"You mustn't mind her," Pao-yu said, laughing.

When Pervading Fragrance returned, Pao-yu asked for

[1] Pervading Fragrance.

the custard. The maids told him what had happened. He was about to say something, but Pervading Fragrance said hastily, "So that's what you have been saving for me. It is very good of you to do that, but I have been eating too many sweets and have had an attack of indigestion. I am glad she ate it, since otherwise it would have been wasted."

The next morning, Pervading Fragrance woke up with a headache accompanied by fever. At first, she tried to go about her tasks as usual but later found it necessary to lie down. Pao-yu told the Matriarch about it, and a physician was sent for. He said it was only a cold and that she would be all right after a few doses of the medicine he prescribed. Pao-yu supervised the preparation of the medicine and watched the maid take it. After making sure that she had covers enough to induce perspiration, he went to see Black Jade. After he chatted with her a while, Precious Virtue came in. But she had hardly sat down when they heard a commotion in Pao-yu's room.

"It sounds like your nurse Li Ma scolding Hsi-jen," Black Jade said. "The maid is courteous enough to her, but Li Ma always seems to pick on her. Old people do get difficult sometimes."

As Pao-yu started to go to his own room and find out what the trouble was, Precious Virtue cautioned him, saying, "Don't argue with her. You must humor her, since she is getting on in years."

"I understand," Pao-yu said, realizing that he must not take the maid's part against his nurse.

When Pao-yu got to his room, Li Ma was still berating Pervading Fragrance. "You ungrateful little prostitute," she was saying, "now you have come to ignore me completely. You don't even get up to greet me when I come in. I know you have been saying things against me to Pao-yu and setting him against me. He now only listens to you. Who do you think you are? You are only a bondmaid bought for a few taels of silver. If you don't behave, I'll have you thrown out and married off. See if you can bewitch Pao-yu then!"

At first, Pervading Fragrance thought that Li Ma was offended because she had not risen to greet her, so she explained, "I am not well and have been trying to sweat. I couldn't see you come in with my head covered." But later when Li Ma accused her of bewitching Pao-yu and turning him against her, she felt deeply humiliated and began to cry.

Although Pao-yu tried not to side with Pervading Fragrance, he couldn't help putting in a word for her. He told his nurse that the maid was really not well and that she had had to take medicine. "If you do not believe it, you can ask the other maids," he said.

This only made Li Ma more angry. She said, "You are always siding with these foxes. You have forgotten all about what I have done for you. What good does it do for me to ask the other maids? They will say anything to help you and Hsi-jen. I know your tricks. I'd like to go with you before Lao Tai-tai and tell her what has been going on. I have brought you up with my own milk, and now that you don't need me any more, you cast me aside in favor of these shameless foxes." She, too, began to cry.

Now Black Jade and Precious Virtue had also come into the room. They tried to placate her, saying that she, being older and wiser, should overlook these little things. Thereupon, Li Ma began to enumerate her grievances; she told them about the tea and the custard and other petty incidents.

It happened that Phoenix was in the Matriarch's room counting up the losses and winnings. When she heard the commotion in Pao-yu's room, she guessed that Li Ma was again on a rampage, probably because she had lost some money at cards and was in a bad humor. Phoenix hastened over and, taking Li Ma's hand, said, "Don't let yourself be upset, Ma-ma. It's New Year's time, you know, and Lao Tai-tai is in a very good humor. Instead of losing your own temper, you should try to be a peacemaker when others quarrel. You don't want to spoil Lao Tai-tai's day, do you? If anyone has offended you, tell me, and I'll see that she is properly punished. I have some nice stewed pheasant, so come along with me and have some." There was a sigh of relief as Phoenix hustled Li Ma off.

"A good thing Phoenix came along," Pao-yu said, "otherwise there's no telling how long the old woman would have carried on. Someone has probably offended her. She was just taking it out on Hsi-jen."

But Bright Design, a little jealous at the sympathy the other maid was getting, said, "I can't think of anyone else who could have offended her. If it had been me who got her started, I would have assumed the full responsibility instead of letting her drag others in."

Pervading Fragrance made no retort, as she did not want to cause Pao-yu any further annoyance. By that time, the medicine was ready, and Pao-yu personally gave it to Pervading Fragrance.

"You had better show yourself in Lao Tai-tai's room whether or not you are hungry," Pervading Fragrance said to him. "I can have a nice rest while you are away."

Pao-yu did so but returned immediately after dinner, as he was concerned with how Pervading Fragrance was getting along. He was relieved to find her sleeping comfortably.

At this time, Bright Design and the other maids had gone off to play cards and otherwise amuse themselves. Only Musk Moon was in the outside room, playing solitaire.

"Why didn't you go with them?" Pao-yu asked.

"I have no money," Musk Moon answered.

"How about that pile of *cash* under your bed?" Pao-yu said. "Isn't that enough for you?"

"Someone has to stay and watch over things," Musk Moon answered.

"She sounds just like another Hsi-jen," Pao-yu thought. "I'll stay here," he said aloud, "so you can go and play."

"Well, since you are here I might as well stay and keep you company."

"What shall we do?" Pao-yu said. "Suppose I comb your hair for you? Didn't you say that your head itched this morning?"

"All right," Musk Moon said. She brought over her toilet box and took down her hair.

Pao-yu had hardly begun to comb it when Bright Design came in for more money. When she saw what Pao-yu was doing, she said with a sneer, "What! Combing her hair already when you haven't even exchanged wedding cups?"

"You come here, too, and I'll comb yours for you," Pao-yu said, laughing.

"I am not worthy of such honor," Bright Design said, as she took some money and walked out again.

Pao-yu and Musk Moon looked at each other in the mirror and laughed. "She certainly has a sharp tongue," Pao-yu said.

He caught Musk Moon gesturing to him to say nothing, but it was too late. Bright Design rushed back into the room and said, "What do you mean by saying that I have a sharp tongue? What makes you say that, I would like to know?"

"Go back to your game," Musk Moon said. "Don't mind him."

"Trying to protect him, eh?" Bright Design said. "You can't fool me with your little tricks. I'll see you two later after I have won back my money."

Pervading Fragrance felt much better the next day after a good sweat during the night. Pao-yu was relieved and after lunch went to visit Hsueh Yi-ma.

At that time, Precious Virtue, Oriole, and Lotus were playing a game of checkers with Chia Huan, Pao-yu's half brother by Chia Cheng's concubine, Chao Yi-niang. Precious Virtue had always treated Chia Huan with consideration, so when he came in and wanted to join the game, she readily made room for him. They had agreed on ten *cash* for each game. Chia Huan won the first game and was very happy about it, but later he lost several games in succession and began to be disagreeable. At this particular point, he would win if he threw a seven or a six but would lose if he threw a three, so he took up the pair of dice and threw it with all his might. The first die settled down and turned up a two while the other was still spinning. Oriole shouted for a one, while Chia Huan yelled for a four or five, but the die turned up a one.

Chia Huan was desperate. He grabbed the die and insisted that it was a four.

"It was clearly one," Oriole said.

But Precious Virtue, noticing Chia Huan's desperation, gave Oriole a look of warning and said, "You are forgetting yourself. Could it be that a young master would try to cheat you out of a few *cash*?"

Oriole relinquished the money but mumbled to herself that she never thought one of the masters would try to beat a maid out of a few *cash*. "Pao-yu," she said, "would never do such a thing. He never minded losing and always gave the maids whatever money he had left at the end of the game."

"How can I compare with Pao-yu?" Chia Huan said, beginning to blubber. "You all side with him and pick on me because I am not Tai-tai's own son." So saying, he began to cry in earnest.

It was at this point that Pao-yu entered the room. He asked what the trouble was. Chia Huan wiped his eyes and said nothing, for it was a strict rule with the Chia family that the younger brother must obey and respect the older. Pao-yu, however, was not in the habit of exerting his authority and demanding obedience. He had always treated Chia Huan with consideration, because he did not want his half brother to feel that he was in a less fortunate position than he. Today, however, he was vexed by Chia Huan's behavior. He knew how diplomatic Precious Virtue was. She could not have given Chia Huan cause for his behavior; so he gave his half brother a scolding and sent him away.

When Chia Huan returned to his mother's room, she noticed at once the injured look on his face and asked him, "Who stepped on you this time?" Chia Huan gave his version of the incident, whereupon Chao Yi-niang uttered an exclamation of disgust and continued, "Who told you to climb up high? Disgraceful and thick-skinned thing! Must you go where you are not welcome and get smeared on the nose?"

It happened that Phoenix was walking by outside the window at this moment and heard what Chao Yi-niang said. "That is no way to talk in the First Month of the year," she stopped and spoke through the window. "He is only a child. You should try to admonish him gently if he does anything wrong instead of talking to him like that. You must remember that after all he is Lao-yeh and Tai-tai's son and that it is for them to discipline him. What is it to you, whatever he does? Come with me, Brother Huan." Chia Huan obeyed, as he had always stood in awe of Phoenix, even more than of Madame Wang. Nor did Chao Yi-niang dare to say a word.

"I have told you again and again to behave yourself," Phoenix said to Chia Huan on the way to her room. "How can you expect people to respect you when you do nothing but degrade yourself? How much money did you lose?"

"About two hundred *cash*," Chia Huan answered.

"Such a fuss over two hundred *cash!*" Phoenix said in a tone of disgust. "And you a master, too! Feng-er!" she called to one of her maids, "go and get a thousand *cash*." She gave the string of coins to Chia Huan and sent him off with the warning that she would see that he got a good spanking if he did not mend his ways.

In the meantime, Pao-yu and Precious Virtue received word that River Mist, one of the Matriarch's grandnieces, had come for a visit.[2] They went together to the Matriarch's room to greet the visitor. There they found River Mist laughing and talking away as was her habit. She had been a tomboy, delighting everyone with her candid, open ways and her pranks. She was now older and slightly more reserved but still exhibited a more lively spirit than the other young ladies in the Yungkuofu.

[2] This is exactly how River Mist (or Hsiang-yun), one of the "Twelve Maidens of Chinling," is introduced. Some of the "Chih-yen Chai" comments clearly suggest that in an earlier draft the author did touch upon River Mist before this.

Black Jade was already there and, when she saw Pao-yu, asked where he had been.

"I was at Pao Chieh-chieh's," he answered.

"So that's it," Black Jade said acidly. "Otherwise I am sure you'd have been here long before this."

"Don't be like that," Pao-yu said. "You don't want me to neglect everyone, do you? There is no need to be sarcastic just because I happened to stay with her a little while."

"I don't know what you are talking about," Black Jade said. "What is it to me where you go? I expect nothing from you. I don't care if you never come to see me again." So saying, she went back to her own room.

Pao-yu followed her and said coaxingly, "Why get mad all of a sudden? Even if I said something to offend you, you shouldn't have left so abruptly when a visitor was in the room."

"It's none of your business," Black Jade said.

"Of course not," Pao-yu placated, "but I didn't want you to upset yourself and get sick again."

"What is it to you if I do get sick? It's none of your affair even if I die."

"Must you talk like that?" Pao-yu said. "It is the First Month of the year, after all, and you talk about death."

"I can say what I please. Die, die, die!" Black Jade said defiantly.

Precious Virtue came in at this point and told Pao-yu that River Mist was asking what had become of him. "So come along now," she said and dragged Pao-yu off by the hand. At that, Black Jade became even more angry and began to weep. In no time, Pao-yu was back again and, seeing her weep, tried his best to soothe her.

"What made you come back?" Black Jade said. "What do you care whether I live or die! You have plenty of people to play with, people cleverer and more accomplished than I, people who are so much more solicitous about you, who know when to come to rescue you from an unpleasant situation."

Finally, Pao-yu said to her with a serious air, "Please now, could it be that you don't know the saying that a distant relative can't come between near relatives and that new friends can't come between old ones? For, after all, you are my cousin on my father's side, while Pao Chieh-chieh is only a cousin on my mother's side. You came long before she did. We practically grew up together, eating at the same table and sleeping in the same room. How could I feel closer to her than to you?"

"Did you really think that it made me angry because you were paying attention to her? I am not that simple. The reason is in my heart."

"It's the same with me," Pao-yu said. "You should also understand what is in my heart."

Black Jade was silent for a moment and then said, "But you are always doing things to provoke me. Today, for instance, it is definitely cold, but you won't wear your cape."

"I was wearing it," Pao-yu said, smiling, "but I got excited when I saw you mad and so took it off."

"And you'll catch cold and upset everyone else."

Just then, River Mist, who always stayed[3] with Black Jade on her visits, came in and, seeing Pao-yu there, teased them, saying that she deserved a little attention at least on the first day of her visit. Black Jade, in her turn, made fun of River Mist's habit of lisping. Then Precious Virtue came in, and they talked and laughed until summoned to dinner at the Matriarch's.

[3] Another indication that River Mist is mentioned previously in a now-lost version of the novel.

CHAPTER FIFTEEN

In which Pao-yu betrays a peculiar habit of his own
And Chia Lien exhibits the common failing of his kind

PAO-YU rose early the next morning and hurried over to Black Jade's apartment, where he found her and River Mist in bed, still sleeping peacefully. The covers were snugly tucked in above Black Jade's shoulders, but River Mist's shoulders were bare. "She couldn't even sleep quietly," Pao-yu said to himself. "If there's a draft, she'll complain of her aching shoulders again." As he pulled the covers up over her, Black Jade awoke and asked Pao-yu what he was doing there so early in the morning.

"Early! Get up and see for yourself what time it is," Pao-yu said.

"Leave the room then," Black Jade said, "and let us get dressed."

Pao-yu went into the sitting room, while Black Jade awakened River Mist. As soon as the two were dressed, Pao-yu rejoined them and sat by the dressing table watching as they washed their faces and arranged their hair. When River Mist finished washing and the maid was about to throw out the water, Pao-yu stopped her, saying, "I might as well wash myself with the same water. There's no use wasting water, and it will save me a trip to my own room."

Pao-yu's ostentatious excuses did not deceive the maid, who shook her head, saying, "Still the same Pao-yu. When are you going to turn over a new leaf?"

After River Mist finished doing her hair, Pao-yu begged her to do his, and after some coaxing, she did. While River Mist was thus engaged, Pao-yu played with the various toilet articles. Finally he picked up the box of rouge and was wondering whether he could have a taste of it without River Mist's knowledge, when she saw in the mirror what he was about to do and knocked the box out of his hands, saying, "What a disgusting habit! Can't you ever change your ways?"

Just then, Pervading Fragrance entered the room and, concluding that Pao-yu had no need of her services, went back to his apartment to perform her own morning toilet. Soon Precious Virtue dropped in. When she asked the maid where Pao-yu was, Pervading Fragrance answered with a bitter smile, "He is hardly ever home these days." Precious Virtue understood and said nothing. The maid continued, "There's nothing wrong for cousins to be good friends, but there is a limit to everything. Such intimacy day and night is hardly proper. But there's no use talking to Pao-yu about it. That kind of advice has about as much effect on him as a breath of wind passing his ears." Precious Virtue was impressed with Pervading Fragrance's remarks and sat down for a long chat with her, asking her about her family and sounding out her views on various subjects. She became more and more impressed with her tact and thoughtfulness as she learned more about her. She did not leave until Pao-yu came back some time later, when she rose and left without exchanging more than a bare greeting with him.

"Why did Pao Chieh-chieh leave so abruptly?" Pao-yu asked. "You were having such a nice chat."

Pervading Fragrance did not answer until he repeated the question. Then she replied coldly, "Why ask me? How do I know what goes on between you two?"

Noticing the tone of her voice, Pao-yu said with a conciliating smile, "What has made you angry again?"

"How dare I presume to be angry?" Pervading Fragrance answered, unmollified. "Don't ever come back here again. You have others to wait on you now and have no more need of me. I'll go back to Lao Tai-tai and serve her as I used to do." So saying, she lay down on the k'ang and closed her eyes, refusing to pay any further attention to Pao-yu. Finally, he wearied of trying to placate her and went to his own bed and lay down himself. Later, when Pervading Fragrance, thinking he had fallen asleep, went to throw a cover on him, he brushed it aside and ignored her. "You don't have to be angry," Pervading Fragrance said. "From now on I'll play dumb and never say a word, if that's what you want."

"But what have I done?" Pao-yu said. "I don't mind your advice but I don't like to be kept guessing. You never told me what it is."

"You know perfectly well what it is," the maid said.

Again the Matriarch's summons to dinner interrupted their exchange. When he returned to his own apartment, Pervading Fragrance was lying down, and Musk Moon was playing solitaire. He ignored both of them, as he knew that they were on especially good terms, and went into his own room. Musk Moon got up and followed him to see if he wanted anything, but he pushed her out, saying, "Don't bother. I wouldn't think of troubling you." He decided he must be firm, so as not to be constantly upset by the well-meant advice and admonitions of his chief maid. If he could not bring himself to act as a master and tell her to shut up, he could at least ignore her for the moment and let her and the others know that he was displeased. So all evening he read and paid no attention to Pervading Fragrance or Musk Moon.

Pao-yu, however, was not one to bear a grudge for long. When he woke up the next morning, he had forgotten completely his tiff with Pervading Fragrance of the previous evening. The maid, however, was uneasy and had slept in her clothes on top of the cover. Pao-yu's immediate reaction was to awaken her and make her undress and get under the covers. "Don't mind me," the maid said, "but hurry over there and get washed before it is too late." It then dawned upon Pao-yu why Pervading Fragrance was angry with him. He realized, of course, that the maid remonstrated with him out of loyalty, and it seemed to him that she was more lovely than ever in her peevishness. So he took up a jade hair pin and broke it in two, saying, "May I be like this pin if I should ever again give you reason to complain."

"Must you make such terrible oaths? And the first thing in the morning, too!" the maid said, picking up the broken pieces.

"You have no idea how it upsets me to see you angry," Pao-yu said.

"So you are upset!" Pervading Fragrance retorted. "How about me? You had better get dressed now. It's time for you to go over to Lao Tai-tai's."

At the Matriarch's Pao-yu learned that Chia-chieh, Phoenix's daughter, had come down with smallpox. Phoenix was busy supervising the necessary measures and precautions taken in such cases. A tablet to the Goddess of Pox was set up, and offerings were made before it; the servants and maids attached to Phoenix's apartment were instructed to observe the prescribed taboos. A room was set aside for the two physicians in attendance, while Chia Lien moved into his study in the outer compound.

Now Chia Lien was not in the habit of sleeping alone; he was given to looking for diversions when he was not under the watchful eyes of his wife. For the first two nights, he made use of one or two of the more handsome of his pages but he soon found something much better. It happened that in the Yungkuofu there was a cook who had a pretty wife. His name was To, and he was referred to as Hun-chung, or Besotted Worm, because he cared about nothing so long as he had wine. So it came about that his wife, known as To Ku-niang, had more freedom of action than was good for her. Chia Lien had had his eyes on her for some time but had been unable to share in her favors because of the vigilance of his wife. To Ku-niang, on her part, had aspirations along the same lines, knowing well that he would reward her more generously than the servants could afford to do. So she found all kinds of pretexts to go to Chia Lien's study and flaunt her charms before him.

Chia Lien decided that this was his chance. He had no trouble in making arrangements for her to come to the study, as more than one of his servants had been intimate with her. To Hun-chung was encouraged to drink and was soon lost to the world and the doings of his wife. To Kuniang then went to Chia Lien's study, and the two wasted no time. The woman was as wanton and seductive as the best of professionals and soon had Chia Lien completely in thrall. "You had better not come near me," she said. "You have smallpox in the family and you mustn't make yourself unclean and offend the Goddess of Pox."

To which Chia Lien could only answer, a bit breathlessly, "You are *my* goddess. What do I care whether *she* takes offense or not."

Thus, Chia Lien came at last to know To Ku-niang. He made the most of the twelve days during which he stayed in his study and afterward continued to meet her whenever he had the opportunity.

When Chia Lien moved back to his own apartment, "the long separation had made for another honeymoon," and he was more than usually appreciative of Phoenix's favors. The next morning after Phoenix had gone to Madame Wang's apartment to attend to the affairs of the day, Patience proceeded to tidy up the bedding Chia Lien had used in his study. In the course of this task, she found a strand of hair on the pillowcase. She picked it up and went into Chia Lien's room and, holding it up to him, said, with a knowing smile, "What is this?"

Chia Lien rushed up and tried to take it away from her. He held her against the bed and threatened to twist her arm if she did not give it to him.

"How ungrateful you are," she said, giggling. "I tried to conceal it from her, and now you try to take it from me by force. What would happen to you if I told her?"

Thereupon, Chia Lien released her, saying, "All right then, my good-hearted one. I won't try to use force, but please be good and give it to me."

Just then, Phoenix came back into the room and asked Patience to look for some patterns for Madame Wang. Then suddenly recalling Chia Lien's bedding, she asked if it had been brought in.

"It has," Patience answered.

"Anything missing?" Phoenix asked.

"No, everything is all right," Patience answered.

"Is anything there that shouldn't be there?" Phoenix continued.

"What do you mean?" Patience asked, pretending innocence. "I should think we'd be concerned only with what might be missing."

"You never can tell about a man," Phoenix said. "Maybe someone inadvertently left a ring, or a handkerchief, or perhaps a strand of hair."

At this, Chia Lien's face became livid and he made pleading gestures to Patience. Patience pretended not to see him but she did cover up for him by answering, "I thought of that, as a matter of fact. I looked through everything carefully but found nothing. Nai-nai can look and see for herself."

"Don't be silly," Phoenix said, laughing. "Do you think he'd leave some telltale things for us to find?" So saying, she left the room with the patterns Patience had got out for her.

"How are you going to thank me for this?" Patience said to Chia Lien. Chia Lien put his arms around the maid and called her many a pet name. "I'll have this on you for the rest of my life," the maid said, smiling and dangling the strand of hair before him. "Everything will be all right if all goes well between us. Otherwise I'll drag this out and show it to her."

"Put it away carefully and don't ever let her find it,"

Chia Lien importuned. Then catching Patience off guard, he snatched the hair from her, saying, "It's safest out of your hands and destroyed."

"Ungrateful brute," Patience said with a pretty pout. "Don't ever expect me to lie for you again."

In his tussle with Patience Chia Lien began to feel the fire of passion burn within him. Patience now looked prettier than ever with her pouted lips and her provocative scolding. He tried again to put his arms around her and make love to her, but Patience wriggled free and fled from the room. "You shameless little wanton," Chia Lien said. "You get one all excited and then run away."

Standing outside the window, Patience retorted, "Who's trying to get you excited? You only think of your pleasure. What's going to happen to me when she finds out?"

"Don't be afraid of her," Chia Lien said. "One of these days I'll get good and mad and give that jealous vinegar jar a good and proper beating and teach her who is master. She spies on me as if I were a thief. It's all right for her to talk and laugh with the men of the family, but she grows suspicious if she sees me so much as look at another woman."

"It's all right for her, because that's what she has to do," Patience said in defense of her mistress. "If she didn't try to be nice to everyone, how could she run the house? But you—you are always thinking things you have no business thinking. Even I do not trust you."

As they were thus talking through the window, Phoenix entered the court. "Why are you standing outside and talking through the window?" she asked Patience. "Can't you go inside and talk?"

"That's what I say," Chia Lien said from the room. "She acts as if I were a tiger about to devour her."

"I don't want to be in the room with him when there is no one else around," Patience said.

"I should think that would be the best time," Phoenix said, with a sly smile.

"Was that remark meant for me?" Patience said.

"Who else could it be for?" Phoenix said.

"Don't make me say things that would be unpleasant to hear," Patience said and walked off without even holding up the door curtain for her mistress. Phoenix lifted the curtain herself and entered the room, saying, "The girl has gone mad! She is actually trying to have the last word with me. You had better look out for your skin."

Chia Lien was greatly amused by the exchange between Phoenix and her maid. He said, clapping his hands and laughing, "I didn't know that Patience was so brave. She's actually gotten the better of you."

"It's all your fault that she's so spoiled," Phoenix said. "I'll hold you accountable."

"I won't stand here and let you blame everything on me," Chia Lien said and started toward the door.

But Phoenix stopped him, saying, "Wait a minute. I want you to tell me what to do about Hsueh Mei-mei's birthday. It's on the twenty-first, you know."

"Why ask me about that?" Chia Lien said. "You have handled many big birthday celebrations before."

"That's just it," Phoenix said. "With big birthdays there are the usual precedents to follow. But this is different."

"Why not do the same thing as was done for Lin Mei-mei's last birthday?" Chia Lien said, after reflecting a moment.

"That's what I thought at first," Phoenix said. "But Lao Tai-tai was asking about the girls' birthdays and when she learned that Hsueh Mei-mei will be fifteen, she said that, though it did not make a round number of years, it did mark the beginning of the 'engagement years' and that she wanted to give her a special party."

"Spend a little more then," Chia Lien said.

"That's what I have been thinking," Phoenix said, "but I want to make sure that it's all right with you so you won't be finding fault with me afterwards."

"Why so thoughtful all of a sudden?" Chia Lien said as he went out. "I'll be satisfied if you don't find fault with me."

CHAPTER SIXTEEN

In which Pao-yu is aggrieved by two instances of misunderstanding
And Chia Cheng is saddened by four conundrums of ill omen

ON the twenty-first, a small stage was set up in the Matriarch's court and a troupe of actresses was hired for the occasion. It was entirely a family affair, and no guests were present except for Hsueh Yi-ma, Precious Virtue, and River Mist. When Precious Virtue was asked to name what she wished to see, she refused the honor at first but yielded at the Matriarch's insistence and named a scene from *Monkey Sun,* as she knew that the Matriarch liked plays with plenty of action and acrobatics. The Matriarch was naturally delighted with the performance. She then asked Hsueh Yi-ma what she would like, but the latter steadfastly refused because her daughter had just had the privilege of choosing. Finally, Phoenix also named something that she knew would please the Matriarch. After that came Black Jade's turn, followed by Pao-yu, River Mist, Welcome Spring, and the others.

The Matriarch was in high spirits all evening. She was especially taken with the child who acted the part of the heroines and the one who took the part of clowns. At the end of the evening's performance, she called the two actresses to her and talked to them. She found that the heroine was only eleven and the other nine. Their tender ages moved her deeply. She gave them money and some delicacies from her table.

Looking at the older actress, Phoenix suddenly remarked, "That child reminds me of someone. Guess who?"

The answer came immediately to Precious Virtue, but she said nothing. Pao-yu also knew but he would not say anything either. River Mist, however, was not so discreet. "Yes," she said, "she does look like Lin Mei-mei." Pao-yu tried to stop her with his eyes, but it was too late. Now that River Mist had pointed out the resemblance, everyone laughed and agreed that the actress was indeed the very image of Black Jade.

When River Mist returned to her room, she told her maid to pack up. "What is the hurry?" the maid said. "We aren't going yet for a few days, are we?"

Pao-yu, who had followed her into the room, said, "You misjudge me, Mei-mei. Lin Mei-mei is very sensitive. Everyone knew whom the actress resembled, but no one would say it for fear of offending Lin Mei-mei. I tried to stop you because I especially don't want you to offend her. I wouldn't care a bit if it had been someone else."

"Don't try to flatter me," River Mist said. "I know what you had in mind. You thought that I am unworthy of saying anything about your Lin Mei-mei. And you are right, for they are grand ladies while I am nobody."

"What injustice!" Pao-yu said desperately. "I was only thinking of you. If I had any such ideas as you attribute to me, let me turn into ashes and be trampled upon by ten thousand feet."

"You don't have to make such oaths before me," River Mist said. "Save them for more sensitive souls." So saying, she went out of the room, leaving Pao-yu feeling hurt and misused.

Pao-yu then went to look for Black Jade, but the latter pushed him out of the room and shut the door against him. He was perplexed. He pleaded with her but was ignored. After a while, Black Jade opened the door, thinking that he had gone away. Pao-yu went in and again pleaded with her to tell him what he had done to offend her.

"You have the brazenness to ask!" Black Jade said. "I suppose I am meant to be the butt of your jokes, to be compared with an actress!"

"You know I didn't make the comparison," Pao-yu said. "Why should you be angry with me?"

"You didn't say anything, it is true, but you were making eyes at your Yun Mei-mei and secretly laughing at me. That's even worse than laughing openly. Moreover, what do you care whether she offends me or not? Is it because you think that she would demean herself by joking about me? Too bad she doesn't seem to appreciate your thoughtfulness, while I do mind being criticized behind my back. What is it to you if I am sensitive and cannot take a joke?"

Pao-yu realized then that Black Jade had overheard his conversation with River Mist. He had thought only of their feelings, and yet this was all the thanks he got. Why should he try to be a peacemaker if this was his reward? So thinking, he turned around and went off without a word. This was so unlike the usual Pao-yu that Black Jade was in turn annoyed, and she shouted after him that he need never come back or speak to her again.

Back in his own room Pao-yu lay down and brooded over his grievances. Pervading Fragrance tried to cheer him. "Today's party will be followed by another," she said. "Hsueh Ku-niang is bound to return the courtesy and invite us to her home."

"What do I care whether she does or not?" Pao-yu said.

"What makes you say that?" Pervading Fragrance remonstrated. "This is the First Month of the year, when everyone ought to feel happy."

"But I am not everyone," Pao-yu said coldly. "Everyone else may have reasons for rejoicing, but I have none. I am alone in this world." Saddened by his own words, he burst out into an inconsolable fit of sobbing. Then he got up and went to his desk and composed a poem in which he denied the validity of all human passions and relationships, parodying the enigmatic verbiage of the Buddhist poets. He felt calmer after this. He went back to bed and was soon fast asleep.

Pervading Fragrance was, however, worried about Pao-yu. The next morning, she showed his composition to Precious Virtue who was very much amused by it and showed it, in turn, to Black Jade and River Mist. Then they confronted Pao-yu with it, and in the lighthearted pleasantries that followed, the misunderstandings of the previous day were soon forgotten.

Just then, word came from the Matriarch that the Imperial Concubine had sent a conundrum for them to solve. They all went to the Matriarch's room and found there a eunuch with a square lantern of white silk, especially designed for exhibiting conundrums during the season. The conundrum composed by the Imperial Concubine was pasted on the lantern. The eunuch cautioned them not to announce their solutions but to write them out and send them in together with their own compositions. Precious Virtue examined the four-line poem and found it neither difficult nor original but she praised its ingenuity politely and pretended to have difficulty in guessing the correct solution. Presently the solutions and original conundrums were finished and the riddles pasted on the lantern brought by the eunuch.

In the evening, the eunuch returned to announce that the solutions were correct, except for those of Welcome Spring and Chia Huan. Most of Her Highness' solutions were also correct. Prizes were distributed to the winners. Welcome Spring did not mind being left out, but Chia Huan took it very much to heart. Moreover, the eunuch said that Her Highness did not attempt to solve the conundrum that he composed because it did not seem to make sense to her. She asked Chia Huan to explain it. This was Chia Huan's riddle:

> First brother has corners eight,
> Second brother has horns two.[1]

[1] The words "corners" and "horns" are represented by the same characters in Chinese.

First brother sits all day long on the bed,
Second brother likes to squat on the roof.

Everyone laughed at this, while Chia Huan sheepishly explained that the first brother was a square pillow and the second brother a decorative "animal head."

The interest of the Imperial Concubine in the traditional pastime of the season made the Matriarch decide to conduct a contest of her own. She ordered a fine lantern and had it placed in her drawing room. Conundrums were composed by her grandchildren and pasted on it, and prizes were prepared for the winners. Noting his mother's high spirits, Chia Cheng also decided to be present and do what he could to please the Matriarch. However, his presence had the effect of discouraging everyone's gaiety and conversation, especially Pao-yu's, who usually enlivened the Matriarch's dinner table. Therefore, after three rounds of wine, the Matriarch suggested that Chia Cheng should retire early.

"I have come to take part in the contest of conundrums," he protested with a smile. "I know that I cannot compete with the grandchildren for Lao Tai-tai's affections, but surely Lao Tai-tai can spare a little of her love for her son?"

"None of them will talk and laugh with you here," the Matriarch said, "and I want talk and laughter around me. If you want to solve conundrums, I'll give you one. But remember the forfeits if you don't give the correct answer."

"Of course," Chia Cheng said, laughing, "and I expect prizes, too, if I guess right."

"That goes without saying," the Matriarch said and recited the following:

"The Monkey, being light of body, stands far out
on the limb.
—The name of a fruit."

Chia Cheng knew immediately that the lichee[2] was meant but he kept on giving the wrong answers and for-

[2] Homophone for "stand on branch."

feiting things to the Matriarch before he gave the correct solution and claimed his prize. Then he proposed the following:

Its body upright and square,
Its substance firm and hard.
Though it cannot speak,
It enables others to do so.
—An article of utility.

He whispered the correct answer to Pao-yu, and the latter whispered it to the Matriarch, who reflected a moment and decided that Pao-yu was right. So she said, "It's the inkstone."

"Lao Tai-tai would get it right on the first try," Chia Cheng said, laughing. Then turning to the maidservants standing outside, he said, "Bring the prizes," whereupon they brought a procession of trays and boxes containing all sorts of novel and ingenious articles. The Matriarch examined them one by one and was greatly pleased.

"Pour a cup of wine for Lao-yeh," she said, whereupon Pao-yu and Welcome Spring stood up, one pouring the wine and the other presenting it to Chia Cheng.

"Try some of the children's compositions," the Matriarch then said. Chia Cheng went to the lantern and read aloud the first one, by Cardinal Spring.

It puts to flight all manners of evil spirits,
For though silken-bodied, it has a voice like thunder.
But before its sound has ceased ringing in one's ears,
It has already turned into ash.

"It must be firecrackers," Chia Cheng said, and Pao-yu said that was correct. The next one was by Welcome Spring.

Destiny and human effort both play their part,
But without destiny all efforts are vain.

And so all day long it calculates without cease,
Though it'll never arrive at the figures decreed
by fate.

Chia Cheng named the abacus, and Welcome Spring said that was right. The next one was composed by Quest Spring.

'Tis the season when children's faces are turned
toward the sky,
Where it forms a fitting decoration.
But when the gossamer thread breaks and lets it
drift
It must not complain of its uncertain fate.

Chia Cheng correctly named the kite. By this time, however, Chia Cheng began to feel depressed because of the unlucky significance of the compositions. To him the firecracker, which explodes and dissipates into nothingness at the very moment of fulfillment, suggested the brevity of life; the abacus was a symbol of ceaseless activity which leads to nothing in the end; the kite with its broken string suggested lack of security and unknown destination. He became even more depressed when he came to Compassion Spring's conundrum on the votive lamp doomed to shine in the ghostly dark of a Buddhist temple.[3]

Noticing her son's mood, the Matriarch said, "You must be tired. You had better go back to your own rooms and let the rest of the conundrums go. We won't be staying up very much longer."

Chia Cheng obeyed but, saddened by his experience, he was unable to fall asleep for a long while.

"You can all relax and have some fun now," the Matriarch said after Chia Cheng's departure. Pao-yu needed no encouragement. The minute his father left, he ran up to

[3] The Imperial Concubine died young; Quest Spring married into a family in a remote part of the country; Welcome Spring's marriage turned out to be an unhappy one; and Compassion Spring became a nun.

the lantern and began to criticize this and that, like a monkey freed from its chain.

"You need to have Lao-yeh around to make you behave," Phoenix said laughing. "We should have suggested that you compose some conundrums while he was still here. You'd be sweating yourself instead of criticizing others' work."

CHAPTER SEVENTEEN

In which Pao-yu, with the maidens, moves into the Takuanyuan
And Black Jade, with her usual supersensitivity, takes offense at Pao-yu

SHORTLY after her return to the Palace, it occurred to the Imperial Concubine that Chia Cheng, in deference to her, would probably close the Takuanyuan. She gave him permission, therefore, to use the Garden in any way he pleased and suggested that her sisters might move in there to live. Remembering how Pao-yu loved the Garden, she expressed the wish that he be permitted to move there, too.

Pao-yu was in raptures at this special favor. He was in the Matriarch's room discussing the allotment of the various courtyards and apartments, when Chia Cheng sent for him. He clung to the Matriarch for some word of assurance.

"Go, my treasure," the Matriarch said to him. "Don't be afraid. I shall not let him be severe with you. I think he wants to say a few words to you, to tell you to mind your studies, that's all. There is nothing to fear." She summoned two of her older maidservants and said to them, "Go with Pao-yu and do not let his father frighten him."

Pao-yu went reluctantly, with slow, painful steps. On reaching his father's compound, he found the maids standing silently under the eaves. They all grinned at him, because he looked frightened and upset. One of them, Golden Bracelet, held her face up to him and said, "I have some very nice perfumed paint on my lips. Don't you want to try it?"

Another maid pushed Golden Bracelet aside and said to her, "Don't taunt him when he is in such trouble." Then she said to Pao-yu, "Go in while he is still in a good humor."

Pao-yu edged into the apartment. Chia Cheng and Madame Wang were in the inner room. Chao Yi-niang drew the curtain back for Pao-yu. His parents were sitting on the k'ang. Opposite them were Welcome Spring, Quest Spring, Compassion Spring, and Chia Huan. All but Welcome Spring stood up as Pao-yu entered.

Chia Cheng's eyes rested on him for a moment and then wandered toward Chia Huan; the comparison was to Pao-yu's advantage. The father then recalled his eldest son who was now dead. Pao-yu was his only son by his first wife. Chia Cheng's beard was turning from gray to white. "If anything should happen to Pao-yu . . ." His heart softened with these thoughts and, when he finally broke the silence, he did not speak harshly.

"Her Gracious Highness says that you should be allowed to live in the Garden so that you can study without any outside distraction. You may move in with your sisters but mind that you apply yourself to your studies from now on."

Pao-yu answered, "*shih, shih,*"[1] without daring to look up. Madame Wang made him sit by her side. The two younger sisters and Chia Huan sat down after him. Madame Wang patted Pao-yu gently and asked whether he had finished the pills he was taking. Pao-yu answered that there was only one left. "Get ten more," Madame Wang said, "and tell Hsi-jen to remember to give you one every night before you go to bed."

"Who is Hsi-jen?" Chia Cheng asked.

"It is the name of a maid," Madame Wang answered.

[1] Though roughly equivalent to the English word "yes," *shih* is used in contexts such as this only when one wishes to show fear, reverence, or servility.

"A maid?" Chia Cheng said, frowning. "How does she come to have such an odd name?"[2]

"It was given her by Lao Tai-tai," Madame Wang said, trying to shield Pao-yu.

"How would Lao Tai-tai think of such a name?" Chia Cheng said. "It must have been Pao-yu."

Realizing that he could not deceive his father, Pao-yu rose and explained why he had given the maid the name.

Madame Wang said hastily, anticipating her husband's displeasure, "You can call her something else. Don't make your father angry over such a little matter."

"It doesn't really matter," Chia Cheng said, "and the name needn't be changed. But it shows that Pao-yu does not apply himself to the necessary studies but wastes his time on things that get him nowhere in the Examinations." Then he said, by way of dismissing his son, "What are you waiting for, evildoer?"

"Go now," Madame Wang also said. "Lao Tai-tai must be waiting for you."

Pao-yu walked slowly out of the room. Passing Golden Bracelet in the court, he made a face at her, as much as to say he had had a narrow escape. At the passage he found Pervading Fragrance waiting.

"Why did Lao-yeh send for you?" she asked anxiously.

"Nothing at all," Pao-yu answered. "He just wants me to mind my studies, that's all."

Back in the Matriarch's room he recounted to her what had happened. As Black Jade and Precious Virtue were there, the matter of the allotment of the quarters in the Garden was again discussed.

"I am thinking of the Bamboo Retreat," Black Jade said. "It is quieter than elsewhere with its nice grove of bamboos and its winding veranda."

"I was thinking of the same thing," Pao-yu said. "I shall live in the Peony Court. We will be near each other."

The twenty-second of the Second Moon, being propi-

[2] These two characters, which I have translated as "Pervading Fragrance," literally mean "to assail people." See page 34.

tious, was chosen for the moving day. Black Jade took the Bamboo Retreat; Welcome Spring, the Brocade Chamber; Quest Spring, the Autumn Study; Compassion Spring, the Plantain Breeze; Li Huan, the Rice Village; Pao-yu, the Peony Court; Precious Virtue, the Wistaria Arbor. Each had two older women servants and four maids, not counting those who did the sweeping and cleaning exclusively.

Pao-yu found life in the Takuanyuan all that he could wish. He studied a little and did exercises in calligraphy, but for the most part, his days were spent with his sisters and cousins and in the company of his favorite maids, playing chess or some musical instrument, painting or composing verses, sometimes even taking a hand at embroidering or assisting the young ladies in their toilet.

Some of his poems found their way outside of the Yungkuofu. They were not exceptional poems but they had spontaneity and genuineness of feeling. However, those who judged a person's achievement by his status were impressed by Pao-yu's verses (or said they were) because they were written by the young lord of the Yungkuofu only in his teens. The poems were copied, circulated, and praised in various circles. Some of his admirers even paid Pao-yu the compliment of requesting him to write scrolls for them or inscribe their fans. He was very much pleased and spent a good deal of time in fulfilling the requests.

After a time, Pao-yu began to feel restless and discontented. He did not know exactly what he wanted, but something was clamoring within him, undefined and yet insistent. Ming-yen sought to relieve his boredom, securing for his master some novels based on the lives of the Empress Wu Tse-t'ien and of the incomparable Yang Kuei-fei of the T'ang Dynasty, and plays such as *Record of the Western Chamber*. To Pao-yu these were great discoveries. Ming-yen asked him not to take the books into the Takuanyuan, where they might be discovered and traced to him. But what use were the books if Pao-yu, who lived in the Takuanyuan, could not take them with him? So he selected a safe corner in his room and, when no one was around, he would take them out and pore over them.

One day about the middle of the Third Moon, Pao-yu sat reading *Record of the Western Chamber* in a peach grove by the brook that wound its way through the Takuanyuan. As he reached the passage containing the line "petals falling into patterns of red," a gust of wind seemed to respond to the words and scattered the peach blossoms all around him, covering his lap and the book. He hesitated to shake them on the ground lest he trample on them. Instead, he carefully gathered them in the broad folds of his garment and shook them into the brook. They eddied near him for a moment and then were caught in the current and carried out through the opening in the wall. He returned to the place where he had been sitting and was wondering what to do about the rest of the flowers when someone asked what he was doing there.

It was Black Jade, with a flower hoe on her shoulder, a muslin bag hanging from the handle of the hoe, and a broom in her other hand.

"You have come at an opportune moment," Pao-yu said. "Let us sweep up the flowers and throw them into the water. I have just disposed of some."

"Not into the water," Black Jade said. "It seems clean to you but you don't know what may be on the other side of the wall to contaminate the flowers. There over the hill is my flowers' burial mound. I am going to sweep these up, put them into this bag, and bury them there."

"Let me help you. But first I must put away my book," Pao-yu said, enchanted by Black Jade's beautiful sentiment.

"What have you there?" Black Jade asked.

Pao-yu did not have time to hide the book, as Black Jade came quite suddenly. He tried to appear nonchalant. "Oh, nothing worth reading. Just the *Doctrine of the Golden Mean* and the *Great Learning*."

"Don't try to fib," Black Jade said. "You might as well show it to me."

"Well," Pao-yu said apologetically as he passed her the

book, "I do not mind letting you see it, but you mustn't tell anyone. This is a true masterpiece. You won't be able to put it down once you start reading it."

Black Jade put down her flower-burial things and took the book. It caught her interest from the start, and she became more and more absorbed in it as she read on. She was especially struck by the beauty of the verses, which "left a lingering fragrance in the mouth."

"What do you think of it?" Pao-yu said, smiling. "Isn't it wonderful?" Black Jade did not stop to answer him; she only smiled and nodded.

"What are you thinking about, Mei-mei?" Pao-yu asked. "Don't you think it is exquisite?"

"It is very interesting indeed," Black Jade agreed.

Without realizing the context of what he was quoting, Pao-yu said, "I am one 'laden with sorrow and maladies,' and you are 'a beauty that ruins cities and nations.'"

Black Jade blushed violently, for she never failed to catch the subtlest innuendo, whether intended or not. She shook her finger at Pao-yu and said, "How dare you read such improper books and then insult me by quoting from them. I am going to tell Uncle and Aunt about this." She turned to go as if to make good her threat.

Thinking that Black Jade was in earnest, Pao-yu jumped up and blocked her way, saying, "Please forgive me this once, Mei-mei. I did not know what I was saying. If I had any intention of insulting you, may I fall into the pond and be swallowed by a loathsome tortoise, and be changed into a big tortoise myself, and be condemned to bear the weight of your tombstone when you have become a lady of the first rank and returned to Paradise."

At this elaborate oath, Black Jade burst into laughter in spite of herself. She said, wiping off her tears, "What a coward! I was only fooling. So you are nothing but 'a wax spearhead that merely looks like silver.'"

"Now you are quoting from that improper book," Pao-yu said. "It is my turn now to tell on you."

"You are not the only one who can recite from memory,"

Black Jade said, laughing. "Now let us get to the flowers."

As they were finishing with the burial of the flowers, Pervading Fragrance arrived on the scene. "Here you are," she said to Pao-yu. "I have been looking all over for you. Ta Lao-yeh is indisposed, and the young mistresses have all gone over to call on him. Lao Tai-tai told me to see that you do not forget to go. So come along and change."

CHAPTER EIGHTEEN

In which, because of evil spells cast over them,
Pao-yu and Phoenix are brought near death
But, by the efficacy of the precious jade, find
their way back to life

ONE day after Chia Huan came home from school, Madame Wang asked him to make a copy of the *Diamond Sutra* for her. This made him feel very important. He ordered Rainbow to bring him tea and Jade Bracelet to trim the wick and he complained to Golden Bracelet that she was blocking his light. Since he was thoroughly disliked by all the maids, no one paid any attention to him except Rainbow, who happened to be on good terms with him. She brought him the tea and whispered to him, "Don't make such a fuss. You only make a nuisance of yourself."

Chia Huan gave her a contemptuous look and said, "Don't try to appear solicitous. I know you have attached yourself to Pao-yu and that I mean nothing to you."

At this groundless accusation, Rainbow ground her teeth and said resentfully, "So this is what I get for being good to you, like the dog that would bite Lu Tung-pin that you are!"

Just then, Madame Wang came back with Phoenix, followed shortly by Pao-yu. After removing his outer garments, Pao-yu settled himself in his mother's lap. She stroked his head tenderly and asked him what he had been doing that day. "You have been drinking again, my son," she said. "You had better lie down and rest a while."

Pao-yu did so and then, complaining of soreness in the legs, asked Rainbow to massage them for him. The maid obeyed but she was listless and frequently glanced in the direction of Chia Huan. Noticing this, Pao-yu whispered to her, "*Hao* Chieh-chieh, why don't you pay a little attention to me, too?" He tried to take her hand, but the maid pulled away from him and threatened to call out if he did not leave her alone.

Chia Huan overheard them and could not suppress his anger and jealousy. Pretending inadvertence, he swept his hand across the table and pushed the candle in Pao-yu's face. Pao-yu gave a sharp cry of pain as the hot wax spilled on his face. Phoenix hastened to him and, as she wiped the wax from his face, she said to Chia Huan, "Won't you ever learn to be more careful? I have always said that you can't be trusted for a moment. I should think that Chao Yi-niang would have drilled some sense into you by this time."

The reference to Chia Huan's natural mother had its desired effect. Madame Wang summoned Chao Yi-niang and berated her thus, "Why don't you teach that black-hearted offspring of yours to be a little more careful? I have overlooked things like this again and again, but it only seems to make him more careless."

Chao Yi-niang suppressed her resentment at the fuss over Pao-yu and said nothing, while she hovered over him and did what she could. Fortunately Pao-yu suffered nothing worse than a blister or two; his eyes had not been touched.

But Madame Wang's concern was not relieved. She was especially worried that the Matriarch would ask about it. "It is nothing," Pao-yu assured her. "If Lao Tai-tai asks about it, I'll say that I upset the candle myself."

"But even then she will scold us for not watching over you," Phoenix said.

After some lotion had been applied to the burns, Pao-yu went back to his own rooms, where the mishap caused another flutter of excitement. Black Jade came over to look at him, but he covered his face and would not let her see it, for he knew how fastidious she was and did not want to distress her.

Two days later, a certain Ma Tao-po, an old woman who dealt in charms and remedies, happened to visit the Yungkuofu. When told of Pao-yu's accident, she went to see him and made certain motions over him with her hand and uttered some unintelligible words, declaring that he would be all right after a few days. She explained to the Matriarch that the children of the rich were always haunted by wicked, jealous spirits, who would pinch their victims and cause them to drop their rice bowls or to stumble and fall. When asked how these evil spirits might be prevented from doing harm, she said that the spirits were controlled by a certain Buddha to whom prayers must be said and offerings made. She accepted a donation of five pounds of oil a month to keep the eternal light burning before the Buddha and promised to say prayers for Pao-yu.

After leaving the Matriarch, the woman visited the other compounds, hoping to secure more donations. She came at last to Chao Yi-niang's room and there found her making slippers. A pile of small pieces of material lay on the k'ang at her side. When Ma Tao-po asked if she might have a few pieces, Chao Yi-niang said with a sigh, "You won't find anything decent in that pile, for I only get what no one else wants. However, you are welcome to anything you care to have." From this she went on to pour out her grievances to the witch woman—the favoritism shown to Pao-yu, the injustices to her son, and especially her resentment of Phoenix.

"Why don't you do something about it?" the old woman asked her.

"What can I do? All I can hope is that they do not pick on me."

"There are ways and means," the other said. "The question is whether you want to resort to them."

The hint was not lost on Chao Yi-niang, and after some parrying back and forth, the two came to an agreement.

Chao Yi-niang gave Ma Tao-po what cash she had on hand and a note for fifty taels to be paid when results were obtained. After this, the old woman cut two figures out of a piece of paper and wrote on them the year, month, day, and hour of the birth of Pao-yu and Phoenix. Then, with a piece of black paper, she cut out the forms of five evil spirits and pinned these against the effigies of the victims. She told Chao Yi-niang to put these away and said, "I shall incant the spells, and in a few days you will see results."

Just then, a maid came from Madame Wang's room and said, "Tai-tai would like to see Yi-niang," whereupon the two conspirators took leave of each other and went their separate ways.

Because of the accident, Pao-yu was confined to his room. During this time, he was frequently visited by the young ladies in the Garden. One day when Black Jade went to see him, she found Phoenix, Li Huan, and Precious Virtue already there.

"Here comes another," they said when Black Jade entered the room.

"It is as if invitations had been sent out," Black Jade said, surveying the company.

"How did you like the tea I sent over the other day?" Phoenix asked her.

"Quite well," Black Jade answered. "I was just going to thank you for it."

"I didn't care much for it," Pao-yu said. "I wonder how it seems to others."

"It has a nice bouquet," Precious Virtue said, "but the color does not seem quite right."

"It is from the Palace," Phoenix said. "A tribute from Siam, I am told, but frankly I don't think it is as good as what we usually use."

"I liked it very much," Black Jade said. "I don't see why you people don't."

"In that case, you can have mine, too," Pao-yu offered.

"You don't have to do that, for I have plenty more left," Phoenix said.

Just then, Chao Yi-niang and Chia Shen's concubine, Chou Yi-niang, came in to see Pao-yu. Everyone rose to greet them except Phoenix, who went on talking as if unaware of their presence. After a while, the visitors all left except Black Jade, whom Pao-yu had asked to stay behind. When they were alone, he took her hand and smiled but said nothing. Black Jade blushed and was trying to pull away her hand and leave when Pao-yu complained that his head ached.

"It serves you right," Black Jade said jokingly. Suddenly, with a piercing cry, Pao-yu leaped three or four feet into the air and began to jabber words that no one could understand. Black Jade and the maids were frightened and sent for Madame Wang and the Matriarch. By the time they arrived at the Peony Court, Pao-yu was even worse. He dashed about wildly, uttering unintelligible sounds and apparently bent on self-destruction.

The Matriarch and Madame Wang began to wail and appeal piteously to Pao-yu. Soon the news spread throughout both mansions. Chia Sheh, Chia Cheng, and Chia Gen arrived with other male members just as Madame Hsing and the other ladies appeared. In the midst of the confusion Phoenix suddenly entered, brandishing a knife and threatening everybody. Fortunately Chou Jui's wife, aided by some of the more husky maidservants, managed to disarm her before any damage was done. Phoenix was carried protesting back to her own room.

There was no end of suggestions as to what to do for the afflicted persons, and many things were tried, but to no avail. They grew progressively worse until they became too much for the young bondmaids to handle. So they were both moved to a room in Madame Wang's compound, where the Matriarch, Madame Wang, Madame Hsing, and Hsueh Yi-ma, together with the older servants, could watch over them.

After three days, Phoenix and Pao-yu grew weak from their ravings. They lay quietly in bed with only faint signs of life. As hope faded, quiet preparations were made for their afterlife things.

On the morning of the fourth day, Pao-yu suddenly opened his eyes and said to the Matriarch, "I am not going to be here much longer. It is time to send me off on my way."

The Matriarch sobbed as if something tore at her heart. Chao Yi-niang tried to calm her, saying, "Obviously there is no hope for him. It is best to change his clothes and let him go. To detain him would only cause him unnecessary suffering."

But the Matriarch spat in her face and said to her, "May your tongue rot, you evil woman. What makes you think that there is no hope for him? Perhaps you think you will benefit by his death. But you are wrong, for if anything happens to him, I shall hold you responsible. It is all your fault. You turned his father against him and made him persecute him until he was frightened out of his wits. It is all your fault, and you will suffer if he should die, I promise you."

Chia Cheng was aghast at the Matriarch's accusation. He bade Chao Yi-niang to be gone and tried to calm his mother. Just then, one of the servants from the outside came in and reported that the coffins were ready. This threw the Matriarch into another outburst. "Who ordered the coffins?" she demanded. "Seize him and beat him to death!"

Suddenly there came from the street the sound of a wooden rattle and a chant promising relief from the possession of evil spirits. The Matriarch sent a servant to investigate. Presently he came back, escorting a Buddhist monk with a mangy head and a Taoist priest lame in one leg. Chia Cheng asked where they were from, but they brushed the question aside, saying, "There is no need to inquire into that. Suffice it that you know we have come to bring help to the sick ones in your mansion."

When Chia Cheng asked what remedies they had, the monk said, "You have a miraculous remedy right at hand, only you did not know enough to make use of it."

Chia Cheng guessed immediately what the monk alluded to. He said, "It is true that my son was born with a piece of jade in his mouth, and on this jade are some words to the effect that it has the power to ward off evil. But it has not lived up to its promise, as you see."

"That's because of something you fail to understand," the monk replied. "The jade was endowed with miraculous powers, but the things of this world with which it has come into contact have robbed it of its powers. Give it to me, and I will restore them."

Chia Cheng took the jade from Pao-yu's neck and gave it to the monk. The latter took it and, looking at it, said with a long sigh, "It is now thirteen years since I saw you under the Green Meadows Peak. How the things of the Red Dust have obscured your understanding, and what a pity that you must remain here a while longer!" He spoke these queer words to the jade and other words that were even harder to understand, while stroking and fondling it. After a while, he returned it to Chia Cheng, saying, "Now its powers have been restored. Hang it over the door of the sickroom, and it will work its magic. In thirty-three days, the sick ones will have completely recovered."

With this, the monk and priest went away, refusing to stay for tea. The jade was hung over the door as directed, and surely enough, Phoenix and Pao-yu presently recovered consciousness and, for the first time in many days, asked for food. After that, they improved rapidly and, by the end of thirty-three days, had fully recovered as predicted.

CHAPTER NINETEEN

In which Golden Bracelet is disgraced because of Pao-yu's attentions to her
And Black Jade is deeply moved because of Pao-yu's declaration of his love

ONE day after a visit at Black Jade's, Pao-yu wandered about the courtyards. The summer days were hot and long, and the courts were quiet, as most people were taking their noon naps. Finally, he entered his mother's room. She was resting on a bamboo couch as Golden Bracelet sat by, gently massaging her legs for her. The maid was dozing, too, her eyes closed. Pao-yu pulled her by an earring and said in a low voice, "How sleepy you are!"

The maid opened her eyes lazily and closed them again after motioning him to leave her alone. He peeped over Madame Wang's shoulders and saw that she was apparently asleep. He decided to talk with the maid, who was not unattractive. He took a perfumed tablet from his pocket and put it into the maid's mouth. She accepted it, without opening her eyes. Pao-yu took her hands and whispered, "I shall ask Tai-tai for you so that we can be together." When the maid did not answer, Pao-yu continued, "Well, I shall go now but I shall ask Tai-tai when she wakes."

"What is your hurry?" Golden Bracelet said. "Let me tell you a secret. If you go to the little courtyard to the east, you will catch Huan-ko and Rainbow."

"I don't care what they do," Pao-yu said. "I just want to stay here with you."

Suddenly Madame Wang sat up and slapped the maid's face, saying, "Degraded little prostitute! Such as you are responsible for the corruption of the boys."

Madame Wang summoned Golden Bracelet's sister, Jade Bracelet, and said to her, "Go tell your mother to come and take your sister away."

Hearing this, Golden Bracelet knelt down before Madame Wang and pleaded, "Tai-tai, I shall never let such a thing happen again. Tai-tai can punish me any way she wants to, but please do not send me away. I have served Tai-tai more than ten years now, and Tai-tai has always been kind to me. How can I face the disgrace if Tai-tai sends me away?"

Madame Wang had always been kind to her maids and had never been known to strike any of them. But she was very strict when it came to offenses such as Golden Bracelet was apparently guilty of. So, in spite of the maid's pleas, she sent for her mother and had her taken away in disgrace. Pao-yu had slipped away and so did not know what happened to the unlucky maid. Though he was sorry and ashamed for having got Golden Bracelet into trouble, he was not particularly concerned over it, thinking that Madame Wang would do no more than give the maid a scolding and then forget the episode. Moreover, River Mist arrived just then for a visit, and in the excitement of seeing her again, he thought nothing more of the incident.

One day while Pao-yu was having a visit from River Mist and Precious Virtue in the Peony Court, he was sent for by his father and was told that Chia Yu-tsun was in the guest hall, having asked to see him. Pao-yu had met Yu-tsun and did not like him. He mumbled as he changed his clothes, "I don't know why he asks to see me every time he comes."

River Mist said, fanning herself, "It must be because Lao-yeh thinks you are a good host. Otherwise he would not send for you."

"But it is not Lao-yeh," Pao-yu said. "It is he himself who asks to see me."

"It is said that when the host is worthy, the guests become innumerable. Yu-tsun must consider you a worthy host. You ought to feel flattered."

"Enough," Pao-yu said impatiently. "I do not pretend to be worthy and I don't care to associate with such worthy people as he."

"Still the same Pao-yu," River Mist commented. "I should think you would be interested in the Examinations now that you are older and are ambitious to get a degree. Failing that, you ought to associate with officials, so as to learn something of the official world and acquire some friends to help you in the future. You will get nowhere if you spend your life among us."

"Ku-niang will please go somewhere else," Pao-yu said with mock dignity. "I am afraid I am not worthy of one as wise as you are."

Pervading Fragrance said to River Mist, "Ku-niang, don't talk to him like that. The last time Pao Ku-niang brought up the subject, he got up and left the room without a word. I felt very embarrassed, but Pao Ku-niang did not seem to take offense. If it had been Lin Ku-niang, there would have been another scene. But Pao Ku-niang is a rare person, so good-natured, so forgiving, and so generous. Yet this one seems to stand aloof from her. When Lin Ku-niang is offended, whether it is his fault or not, he goes to her and makes the most abject apologies."

"But Lin Ku-niang never made such vulgar suggestions. If she did, I would feel the same toward her," Pao-yu said.

River Mist and Pervading Fragrance said derisively, "Yes, of course, it is vulgar to speak of such matters."

It happened that Black Jade came into the Peony Court at this point and heard Pao-yu's last remark. She was both pleased and surprised: pleased because she had not misjudged him; surprised that he should be so indiscreet as to betray his feelings toward her before other people. Then she felt sad as she recalled the talk about the destiny of the gold and jade. Why the constant reference to this destiny if she and Pao-yu loved each other, if they were meant for each other? Why didn't she possess the symbol of gold, instead of Precious Virtue?

Then she reflected on the fact that her parents were dead, that she had no mother to confide in and to speak for her, and must wait upon the whims of fate. Moreover, she had never been well, and more recently, the physicians had warned her that her blood was thin and her vitality low and that consumption would set in unless she built up her strength. "Though I appreciate your love," she thought to herself, "I may not be able to wait for you long; and though you appreciate me, you may find me gone before my time." As these thoughts plagued her, her tears began again to flow, and she turned away without making her presence known.

But Pao-yu saw her when at last he set out for the guest hall. He recognized her and thought he could see traces of tears on her face.

"Where are you going, Mei-mei?" he asked. "And why have you been crying?"

"I haven't been crying," Black Jade said. "Why should I?"

"Look, there are still tears in your eyes. How can you deny it?"

Pao-yu tried to wipe away her tears, but Black Jade drew back and said, "You are forgetting yourself again."

"Your tears make me forget everything, even death itself," Pao-yu said.

"Death doesn't mean anything," Black Jade replied, "but what are you going to do about the golden locket if you die?"

Pao-yu was annoyed. He said, "Just what do you mean by constantly referring to those things?"

Remembering their recent quarrels and what her maid had said about them, Black Jade was for once contrite. She said, "Forgive me. It was my mistake, but you need not be so angry. Your veins are fairly bursting on your forehead." And she, too, forgot herself and reached out her hand to wipe the perspiration from Pao-yu's forehead.

Pao-yu stood meditatively and then said, "You may rest assured."

Black Jade was taken aback by the sudden reassuring words which seemed to be apropos of nothing. "What am I to be assured of?" she asked. "I do not know what you are talking about."

"Don't you really understand?" Pao-yu said. "Then I must have been mistaken in what I think of you, and small wonder that I have caused you so much irritation."

"I really don't understand what you mean by rest assured or not rest assured," Black Jade said.

"*Hao* Mei-mei," Pao-yu said earnestly. "Don't pretend that you do not understand. Have I then been mistaken all this time, and have my thoughts of you been all in vain? If that is the case, I have wronged you, too. You are now burdened with illness largely because you worry too much. If you had not worn yourself out with worry, your illness would not have become more serious every day."

These words struck Black Jade with the force of thunder and lightning, for they were as close to her innermost thoughts as if they had been wrung from her own heart. There were a thousand things that she wanted to say, but she could not find suitable words for a single sentence. So she merely stared at Pao-yu in silence. Pao-yu felt the same and he, too, stared at her vacantly. Tears again came to her eyes as she turned away to hide her emotion. Pao-yu stopped her and said, "*Hao* Mei-mei, don't go until I have spoken of something else that is on my mind."

"There is no need," Black Jade said, "for I know it already."

Pao-yu had forgotten his fan, and Pervading Fragrance came after him with it. She came up to Pao-yu after Black Jade had gone and said, "You have forgotten your fan. Fortunately I saw it. Here it is."

Pao-yu was still thinking about Black Jade and did not realize that she was not there, nor did he recognize his maid. He took her hands and said passionately, "*Hao* Meimei, I never dared to speak the secrets of my heart to you. I'll be bold today and I care not if I die as a consequence. I am also sick because I am constantly thinking of you. I dare not tell anyone. I won't be well until you are well again. I cannot forget you even in my dreams."

The astonished maid stopped him, saying, "Are you mad? Better go immediately to Lao-yeh. He'll get impatient and angry with you if you don't hurry."

Realizing what he had done, Pao-yu blushed violently and hurried off, leaving Pervading Fragrance standing under the hot sun and wondering to herself what had been going on between Pao-yu and Black Jade. Just then Precious Virtue appeared on the scene and asked her what she was thinking about so intently. "Nothing," she answered. "I was only watching the birds."

"What was Pao-yu in such a hurry about?" Precious Virtue asked. "He was in such a hurry that he did not even stop to speak to me."

"Lao-yeh sent for him," Pervading Fragrance said.

"No wonder," Precious Virtue said. "What could it be? I hope he has not suddenly thought of something that he wants to scold Pao-yu for."

"It's nothing like that fortunately," Pervading Fragrance said. "I understand that it's because a visitor wants to see him."

"I should think any sensible person would stay home on a hot day like this instead of going around making calls. It's a stupid thing to do."

"Isn't it, though?" Pervading Fragrance agreed.

"What's Shih Ku-niang doing?"

"We were just chatting," the maid answered. "I was making a pair of shoes, but she is so much better at it. I am thinking of asking her to make a pair for me."

When Precious Virtue heard this, she looked about to make sure that no one was near and then said to Pervading Fragrance in a lowered voice, "Haven't you noticed, thoughtful as you are? I am afraid that she has her hands full at home. She hasn't said anything to me exactly, but I gather that her people do not have all the hands they need and that they have to do a lot of their own sewing. How do you expect her to have time to sew anything for you, flattering as your request might be?"

"Ku-niang must be right," Pervading Fragrance said. "Last month, I asked her to make some butterfly knots. She did not send them for quite a long time. She apologized for not having taken as much care in making them, saying that she would try to make something much nicer when she came to visit us. It must be because she has no time at home. How thoughtless of me. But you know how Pao-yu is; he is so particular, about not only the work but also the person who does it."

Just then an old maidservant came on the scene. "Have you heard?" she asked them. "Golden Bracelet has jumped into the well and drowned herself!"

"Which Golden Bracelet?" Pervading Fragrance asked in astonishment.

"There is only one," the maidservant answered. "The one in Tai-tai's room. For some reason or other, Tai-tai was displeased with her and sent her back to her own family. She cried most of the time after she got home, but no one paid much attention to her. Then yesterday she disappeared, and the next thing you know, someone discovered a corpse in the well. It was her all right, when they dragged it up."

Precious Virtue hastened to Madame Wang's apartment and there found her weeping in her own room. Not wishing to bring up the subject herself, she sat down without speaking.

"Where were you just now?" Madame Wang asked her.

"In the Garden," she answered.

"Did you see Pao-yu?"

"I did. He was dressed up and was on his way out. He seemed to be in a great hurry."

"Did you know that Golden Bracelet had drowned herself in a well?"

"Not really! Why should she drown herself?"

"A few days ago, she broke something. Nothing of any consequence, but I was feeling out of sorts and gave her a slap and sent her home. I felt sorry afterward and meant to send for her. Who could guess she would take it so much to heart and drown herself! How can I ever forgive myself for having caused her death."

"Naturally Tai-tai would blame herself, being so kind-hearted," Precious Virtue said. "But I don't think Golden Bracelet would have taken it so much to heart. It must have been an accident. If not, it shows how little she appreciated Tai-tai's kindness and how undeserving she is of Tai-tai's grief."

"I hope you are right, my child," Madame Wang said gratefully. "But, still, how I wish I had not been so harsh with her."

"You should not blame yourself so much," Precious Virtue said. "There is nothing you can do now except to treat her family generously."

"I have given her mother fifty taels," Madame Wang said. "I was thinking of giving her a new dress for the burial, but it happens there isn't anything new except a couple of dresses made for your Lin Mei-mei for her coming birthday. I can't ask your Lin Mei-mei. She is such a sensitive child and not well, and very likely she would be superstitious about such a matter. I am asking the tailors to rush out a dress. If it had been some other maid, I wouldn't have bothered, but Golden Bracelet was always like a daughter to me." So saying, she began to weep again.

"There is no need of having one made," Precious Virtue said. "I had a few new dresses made the other day. It happens that we wear the same size, too."

"Aren't you superstitious about such things?" Madame Wang asked.

"Not at all," Precious Virtue said, as she went off to fetch the dress. When Precious Virtue returned a few moments later, she found Pao-yu sitting at his mother's side, weeping. Apparently he had learned of the death of Golden Bracelet and had received a scolding from Madame Wang.

CHAPTER TWENTY

In which Chia Cheng discovers the escapades of his erring son
And Pao-yu suffers the chastisement of his severe father

WHEN Pao-yu learned of the suicide of Golden Bracelet, his heart burned with grief and, when Madame Wang scolded him, he was too full of self-reproach to try to justify himself. He was relieved when Precious Virtue's entrance interrupted the ordeal. He went outside and wandered about the courtyards, aimless and distracted, until he found himself in the front hall. As he turned the wall screen, he ran into someone without recognizing who it was.

"Stand there!" he heard the man cry. He looked up to discover his father glaring at him. He gasped involuntarily and stood aside reverently, as he was bidden.

"What are you sighing and moaning about?" his father asked. "It took you a long time to come out when Yu-tsun asked to see you. When you did appear, you had nothing to say. You looked dissipated and seemed restless and ill at ease. What are you unhappy about now? What cause can you possibly have for discontentment?"

Ordinarily Pao-yu was quick of wit and eloquent. But now his mind was occupied with Golden Bracelet's death, and he wished that he could follow her to the other world. He did not hear what his father said but only stood as if he had lost the power of speech. Chia Cheng was annoyed by his silence and evident confusion. He had not been angry at first but he was now. He was about to say a few more words of admonition to his son, when an officer from the palace of the Prince of Loyalty and Obedience was announced. Chia Cheng was puzzled, for he had no connections with the Prince. He hurriedly put on his court robes to meet the emissary.

"I have presumed to intrude," the officer said, "because of a delicate matter which concerns the Prince and a member of your house. The Prince would like Your Excellency's intercession. I hope Your Excellency will pardon the presumption and give the matter your kind consideration."

Chia Cheng was more mystified than ever. He rose and said, "Since Your Excellency has come with a command from the Prince, would not Your Excellency be explicit so that your humble student can obey?"

"It is a very simple matter, if only Your Excellency would say the word," the officer continued. "There is an actor in the Prince's palace by the name of Chi-kuan who has not been seen for many days. Upon inquiry in the various resorts of the Capital, eight out of ten persons seem to be of the opinion that he is intimately connected with your noble heir. When we heard this, we did not dare come here to search for the actor as in the case of an ordinary family. So we informed the Prince, who said that he would not think of troubling Your Excellency for a hundred other actors in his palace, but Chi-kuan is different. He is quite essential to the happiness and health of the Prince in his old age. We implore you, therefore, to ask your noble heir to relinquish Chi-kuan, so as to quiet the anxiety of the Prince and to spare this humble officer the necessity of searching further." The aide from the palace bowed reverently as he concluded.

Chia Cheng was astounded. He summoned Pao-yu and said to him, "You death-deserving knave! Is it not enough for you to neglect your studies? Must you also commit treasonable crimes? Chi-kuan is an attendant of the Prince.

How dare you conceal him and bring calamity upon me?"

Pao-yu had recently met Chi-kuan, whose real name was Chiang Yu-han, at the birthday party of Hsueh Pan. He became attached to the actor, and the actor to him. The two had exchanged presents on the occasion and doubtless had been in communication with one another. Pao-yu was surprised at the turn of events but denied the charges and any knowledge of what the two words "Chi-kuan" meant. But the palace emissary was not to be put off so easily. He said with a sardonic smile, "Please don't try to conceal him. If he is hidden in the mansion or if you know his whereabouts, be kind enough to enlighten us. It will save us futile search."

"I really don't know anything about it," Pao-yu persisted. "You must have been misinformed."

"We have proof," the aide from the palace smiled, "but we did not want to show it in front of your reverend father lest we make it too unpleasant for you. Since you force us to it then, if you do not know who Chi-kuan is, may we ask you how it happens that you have his red handkerchief hanging from your inner belt?"

Pao-yu realized the futility of further denials. He said, "If they know everything, how could they have overlooked the most important detail? I seem to have heard someone say that he bought a house about twenty li from the Capital in a village with a name something like Purple Tower. I should think you might find him there."

The aide from the palace smiled and said, "He must be there if you say so. We shall go and investigate. If we do not find him, we are afraid that we shall have to come back to seek further enlightenment."

With these words he took his leave. Chia Cheng was speechless with astonishment. He escorted the aide to the gate, telling Pao-yu not to stir from where he was. On his way back, he saw Chia Huan running in the opposite direction. "Stop there!" Chia Cheng shouted to him. Chia Huan stopped in his tracks and awaited his fate.

"What are you running like a wild horse for?" Chia Cheng asked. "Aren't you supposed to be at school?"

Chia Huan saw his chance. He whispered to his father, "I did not mean to run but I was so frightened by the corpse of the maid, her face and body all swollen, that I ran away from the well as fast as I could."

"Who has jumped into the well?" Chia Cheng asked. "Such a thing has never happened in this house. Since the time of our ancestors, we have always treated our servants with kindness. Because of my negligence in recent years, those in charge of affairs must have been persecuting the more helpless of the servants. What a disgrace to the memory of our ancestors!"

Chia Huan pulled at his sleeves and whispered, "No one knows anything about this except those in Tai-tai's room. I heard my mother say . . ." He stopped and looked around. Chia Cheng motioned the attendants to withdraw. Chia Huan continued, "My mother says that brother Pao-yu was attempting to rape Golden Bracelet, a maid in Tai-tai's room. The maid resisted and was tortured. Then she committed suicide."

"Seize Pao-yu and bring him here!" Chia Cheng thundered, his face yellow with anger. He went to his study and said to his secretaries and companions, "If anyone tries to stop me today, I shall give him my official insignia and my house and property and tell him to serve Pao-yu. I shall cut off these few remaining hairs and find an unsoiled place to live, so that I may not degrade my ancestors above and be held responsible for the crimes of my treasonable son below." Chia Cheng's companions had saved Pao-yu from his father's wrath on many previous occasions but now they realized that Chia Cheng would not countenance any interference. They all withdrew in silence.

Chia Cheng shouted to his servants, "Bring him at once. Bring a heavy bamboo. Bind him. Lock the gates. I shall kill anyone who dares to inform the inner apartments."

The servants obeyed; some of them went to get Pao-yu, who was pacing anxiously in the guest hall. The Chi-kuan affair was serious enough without Chia Huan adding more fuel to his father's anger. Pao-yu was looking for someone to take a message to the Matriarch but he found no one around. At last, an old maidservant appeared, and Pao-yu seized upon her as heaven-sent. "Lao-yeh is going to beat me to death," he told her. "Go in and tell them. Hurry. It is urgent, most urgent [*yao-chin*]."

The old woman was hard of hearing, and Pao-yu, in his haste and terror, did not pronounce the words distinctly. She thought he had said, "*tiao ching* [jump into well]."

"Let him jump into the well," she said to herself. "What does it matter to you?"

Before he had a chance to explain to her, Pao-yu was taken to the study. Chia Cheng was mad with rage at the sight of his erring son. Without bothering to enumerate his many crimes, he simply shouted to the attendants, "Gag his mouth and beat him to death!"

The attendants did not dare disobey. They laid Pao-yu on a bench and tied him to it. Then at Chia Cheng's command, they began to beat him with a heavy bamboo rod. Chia Cheng was not satisfied. He thrust aside the man with the rod, seized it himself, and beat Pao-yu more than ten strokes with all his might.

At first, Pao-yu wept and cried out, but gradually his voice grew weak as each stroke of the heavy rod took effect. The companions came in to intervene, seeing that Chia Cheng was almost murderous in his rage. But he seared them with these words, "Ask yourselves if such conduct as his can be forgiven. It is all because of you that he has been so spoiled. I suppose you would still intercede for him even if he murdered his own father and his Sovereign?"

The companions realized the futility of reasoning with Chia Cheng. They managed to smuggle a message to the inner apartments. Madame Wang was the first to answer the call. All the companions hurried away as she appeared. Chia Cheng's frenzy was aggravated at this interference, and his heavy rod came down upon Pao-yu even more furiously.

As the two attendants released their hold, Pao-yu lay motionless. Chia Cheng raised his rod again, but Madame Wang stopped it with her arms. She cried, "Though Pao-yu deserves punishment, Lao-yeh must also consider his own health and not overexert himself. Besides, Lao Tai-tai is not feeling well these warm days. It would matter little if Pao-yu perished under your punishment, but what if Lao Tai-tai should suffer?"

Chia Cheng smiled with scorn and said, "I am guilty of impiety by the very birth of this monster. Whenever I tried to discipline him, everyone interceded for him. It is best that I strangle him to death today before he involves us in greater crimes." He took a piece of rope and was about to strangle Pao-yu.

Madame Wang held him back, crying, "It is true that it is Lao-yeh's duty to discipline and punish his son, but he must also consider his wife. I am now over fifty years of age and have only this one evil thing. Your determination to kill him is the same as wishing me not to live. Strangle me first and then do away with him! It would be better if we died together, so that we could be together when we reach the other world." She put her arms around Pao-yu and wept piteously.

Chia Cheng was silent. He sighed and sat down on a chair, his eyes also moist with tears. Pao-yu's face was white and his breathing faint. His blood-stained clothes clung to his body. From his legs to his shoulders he was covered with bruises, some blue, some purple. There was not a single inch of uninjured flesh. Madame Wang moaned, "Pao-yu, Pao-yu," more piteously than ever. Then she remembered Chia Chu, her firstborn, and cried, apostrophizing him, "Chu-er, if you were alive, I would not care if a hundred Pao-yus perished by the rod!"

By this time, everyone in the inner apartments had heard the news. Li Huan, Phoenix, and the three Springs all came to see Pao-yu. When Madame Wang cried out "Chia Chu," Li Huan's old sorrow was awakened, and she, too, burst out crying.

Suddenly a maid announced, "Lao Tai-tai is coming!" Before this electric announcement ceased ringing in their ears, the Matriarch's voice was heard.

"Kill me first and then you can kill him!"

Chia Cheng hurried out to meet his mother. He tried to smile as he said, "Mother should not have come out on a warm day like this. If she wishes anything, she should send for her son and command him."

The Matriarch said sternly, "Are you speaking to me? Yes, I have many things to say but I have borne no obedient son to command."

Chia Cheng was hurt deeply by his mother's words. He fell on his knees and said, "Your son disciplined his son because he has the honor of the family at heart. These words of Mother's—how is a son to bear them?"

"You cannot bear just a few words from me?" the Matriarch said coldly. "Then how could you expect Pao-yu to bear your cruel beating? You say you are trying to bring honor to the family. Have you forgotten, then, how your father brought you up?" The Matriarch's eyes began to fill with tears.

Again Chia Cheng tried to smile. "Please do not grieve, Mother. It is all your son's fault. He could not control himself. He will never touch his son again."

"You need not try to spite me," the Matriarch said. "You can beat him if you want to, since he is your son. Now you must be getting tired of us. It would be best to leave you alone." She commanded the attendants to get her sedan ready. "I want to return to Chinling immediately with your Tai-tai and Pao-yu," she said. The attendants obeyed. Then she said to Madame Wang, "Don't cry any more. While Pao-yu is young, you love him and suffer for him. But when he grows up, he will forget that you are his mother. It is better not to love him now; then you will be spared future regret."

Chia Cheng kowtowed again and said, "Mother is saying things that make a son wish he were dead."

"It is clear that you are the one who wants me out of

the way," the Matriarch said. "I shall leave you so that no one will be here to interfere when you want to beat him." She renewed her order to have the sedan ready. Then she went into the study to see Pao-yu. She had never seen him suffer such severe punishment. Once more she burst into tears, and it was some time before she stopped. As Pao-yu was carried back to his room, Chia Cheng did not dare retire to his own apartment but followed the procession. He realized he had gone too far. Then Madame Wang, still crying piteously, said to Pao-yu, "You should have died for Chu-er long before this. If you had, my life would not have been in vain, for he would have known how to please your father. If you die now, whom am I to lean upon the rest of my life?"

Finally, the Matriarch dismissed Chia Cheng, saying, "Of course a son should be disciplined when he misbehaves, but you should know where to stop. You can leave now. Have you not done enough? Must you go on until he dies?" Chia Cheng left the room.

With Madame Wang and the others hovering over Pao-yu and the Matriarch watching over them all, Pervading Fragrance, who ordinarily attended to Pao-yu's every need, had no chance to wait on him now. So she slipped out of the room and sent for Ming-yen. She asked him how Chia Cheng came to give Pao-yu such a beating and why he did not try to get word to the Matriarch.

"It all happened when I was not there," Ming-yen said. "I did not learn about it until Lao-yeh had already started on him. I have made inquiries and found that it was because of the actor Chi-kuan and Golden Bracelet."

"How did Lao-yeh find out?"

"As to the Chi-kuan affair, Hsueh Ta-yeh is most likely responsible. He is jealous of Pao Er-yeh over Chi-kuan and must have instigated someone to tell on him. As to Golden Bracelet's death, the men around Lao-yeh say that he heard it from San-yeh [Chia Huan]."

When Pervading Fragrance returned to Pao-yu's room, the Matriarch and the others were still there. After a while, they left, bidding the maid to take good care of Pao-yu.

CHAPTER TWENTY-ONE

In which Pervading Fragrance gives a candid appraisal to Madame Wang
And Pao-yu sends a subtle hint to Black Jade

AFTER the Matriarch and the others left the room, Pervading Fragrance proceeded to undress Pao-yu. It was not an easy task, for Pao-yu groaned every time she touched him. Finally, she succeeded in getting his clothes off, revealing large bruises from the waist down.

"Dear Mother!" the maid exclaimed. "How could he have been so cruel? But you would never have suffered this if you had listened to advice. Fortunately the bones aren't damaged. You might have been crippled."

Precious Virtue was announced. Pervading Fragrance hastily threw the covers over Pao-yu, as she had not had time to dress him. Precious Virtue held in her hand a pill which she told the maid to dissolve in wine and apply over the wounds at night.

"Are you feeling better now?" she asked Pao-yu.

"Yes," Pao-yu answered, "I feel much better. Please sit down."

"If you had listened to advice," she said, "this would not have happened today. It not only breaks Lao Tai-tai's heart to see you in this condition, but even we——"

She stopped abruptly with embarrassment, for she realized that in her anxiety she had forgotten her maidenly reserve. Pao-yu was touched by her evident concern. He was even more grateful when he saw how embarrassed she was, how she played with her sash, her head bent and her face red. He forgot his pain and thought to himself, "How they pity me and suffer for me just for the little beating I have had! How dear of them and how they deserve my affection! And how they would mourn and grieve for me if I should die! Death would be sweet if people cared for you and mourned for you like this."

"What was it that caused Lao-yeh's displeasure?" Precious Virtue asked Pervading Fragrance. Without realizing that it would embarrass Precious Virtue, the maid repeated the story she had heard from Ming-yen.

"I am sure Brother Hsueh wouldn't do a thing like that," Pao-yu said, trying to spare Precious Virtue's feelings. "It's nothing but a wild guess."

"How thoughtful he is," Precious Virtue said to herself. "Even while suffering so much pain, he is only concerned with the feelings of others. If he had only given one tenth as much attention to his father's wishes, he would not have undergone what he did today. But I know my own brother; he behaves very badly over Chin Chung, and it would be just like him to let his jealousy get the better of him today." Then she said aloud, "There is no use in blaming this one or that. The main thing is that Brother Pao should not have associated with such people and thus have incurred Lao-yeh's displeasure. My brother might very well have been indiscreet and blurted out Brother Pao's name, but it is unlikely, as Brother Pao says, that he did it intentionally. Very few men are as thoughtful as Brother Pao."

Pao-yu dozed off after Precious Virtue left. He dreamed that Chiang Yu-han, the actor, came to tell him of his capture by the Prince; and he dreamed of Golden Bracelet, who told him that she had died for him and had forgiven him. Someone was gently shaking him. He opened his eyes and found Black Jade weeping over him. Pao-yu was afraid that he was still dreaming. To reassure himself, he leaned forward to look at her more closely. Her eyes were swollen as big as peaches, and her face was streaked by the tears she had shed. It was indeed Black Jade.

"You should not have come," he said. "Though the sun has set, the heat reflected from the ground is still in the air and you might be affected by it. I do not suffer very much from the beating. I am only pretending, so that Lao-yeh will think I have been seriously injured. So please do not worry on my account."

Black Jade did not cry aloud, but her silent sobbing was more eloquent than the most articulate grief. On hearing Pao-yu's thoughtful reassurance, she could find no words to express herself. Finally, she managed to say, "You must mend your ways from now on."

Just then, Phoenix was announced.

"I shall leave by the back door," Black Jade said, as she stood up hurriedly. "I will come back later."

Pao-yu said, "Why should you go because she is coming? What is there to be afraid of?"

"But look at my eyes," Black Jade said. "She will make fun of me if she sees me like this."

After Phoenix left, Hsueh Yi-ma came and then someone from the Matriarch's room. In the evening after Pao-yu had fallen asleep, word was received that Madame Wang wanted to speak to someone from his room. After reflecting a moment, Pervading Fragrance decided to go herself.

Madame Wang was sitting on a bamboo couch fanning herself when the maid entered. "You needn't have come yourself," she said to the maid. "Who's to take care of Pao-yu?"

"Er-yeh has gone to sleep," Pervading Fragrance replied. "I thought Tai-tai might have instructions for us and was afraid that if I sent someone else, she might not get them right."

"I have nothing especially in mind," Madame Wang said. "I just want to know how Pao-yu is. Is the pain any better?"

"Pao Ku-niang brought over some medicine," the maid answered. "It has relieved the pain considerably."

"Did he eat anything?"

"Lao Tai-tai sent over some soup, but he did not drink much of it. He complained of thirst and wished to have some sour-plum drink. But I did not let him have it. It is repressive in nature and may bring complications. I persuaded him to have some rose syrup with water, but he did not like it much."

"You should have told me," Madame Wang said. "A few days ago, someone gave me a few bottles of fruit concentrate made especially for the Palace. You can take a couple of bottles with you. You don't need much, just a teaspoonful with a cup of water."

As Pervading Fragrance was on the point of going, Madame Wang suddenly thought of something. "Just a minute," she said and, dismissing the other attendants, she continued in a low voice, "I seem to have heard someone say that Huan-er was responsible for Pao-yu's beating today. Have you heard anything?"

"I have not heard anything about that," Pervading Fragrance answered. "I was told that it was because of some actor that Er-yeh has been going around with."

"That's not the only thing," Madame Wang said, shaking her head.

Pervading Fragrance hesitated a moment and then said, "I think——" But she stopped short.

"Go on," Madame Wang said.

"I am afraid that Tai-tai will be angry."

"I won't be," Madame Wang assured her. "Go ahead and say it."

"I think Pao Er-yeh needed the lesson," Pervading Fragrance said very deliberately. "If Lao-yeh had let matters pass today, there is no telling what Er-yeh might do next."

On hearing this, Madame Wang nodded appreciatively and said with a sigh, "My child, you are quite right. It shows how understanding you are. I realize as you do that Pao-yu needs discipline. You know how strict I was with your Chu Ta-yeh when he was living. But I am now fifty years old and have only this one son. Not only that, he is

Lao Tai-tai's favorite. That's why I have not been as strict with him as I might. Moreover, Pao-yu is not strong. What if anything should happen to him as a result of the beating he has received?"

She began to weep, and seeing her, Pervading Fragrance wept, too. "It is not difficult to realize how Tai-tai must feel," she said. "Even we his servants feel the same way. Never a day passes but I try to urge Er-yeh to mend his ways. But it has been no use. Moreover, it is difficult for him to keep away from such people as the actor Chi-kuan, when they all take to him so readily and flatter him so much. I have thought a great deal about Pao-yu's position and have often thought of speaking to Tai-tai about it; but I hesitated to do so because I was afraid that it would only worry Tai-tai without doing any real good."

Madame Wang was even more impressed by this thoughtful speech. She said, again using the endearing term, "My child, tell me everything without reserve. I have been hearing good things about you but I had thought it was just because you were attentive to Pao-yu's comfort and considerate in little things. But what you have just said shows that your loyalty to Pao-yu goes beyond little things. You think of him as I do. So go ahead and tell me everything."

"I have nothing to tell in particular," Pervading Fragrance said. "I was only thinking that it may be wise to have Er-yeh move out of the Garden on some pretext."

Madame Wang was astonished. She took the maid by the hand and asked anxiously, "Has Pao-yu done anything to make you say that?"

"No," Pervading Fragrance hastily assured her. "But Er-yeh is growing up, as the young mistresses are. Though they are brother and sisters, yet there is no telling what evil tongues might say. If Er-yeh becomes the subject of evil gossip, we whose duty it is to wait upon him will have to answer for it. That is a small matter, for we should gladly die for our master, but what is more important is Er-yeh's reputation. I know it is presumptuous of me to say such things, but Lao Tai-tai and Tai-tai have shown great confidence in me by giving me the privilege of serving him; I would be guilty of something much more serious if I did not tell Tai-tai what has occurred to my mind."

As Pervading Fragrance spoke Madame Wang could not help thinking of the Golden Bracelet incident and appreciated even more the thoughtfulness of the maid. "My child, you have thought of everything! I'll think the matter over and act accordingly. I am glad you told me all this, and I feel relieved now that I know I have someone to share my worries with. You may go now. Take good care of Pao-yu, and you may be sure that I won't forget your goodness."

Pao-yu had just awakened when Pervading Fragrance returned to Peony Court. He tried some of the fruit concentrate with water and found it to be indeed different from anything he had had before. But his thoughts were with Black Jade. He wanted to find out how she was but, not wishing to have Pervading Fragrance know about it and remonstrate with him, he sent her to the Wistaria Arbor to borrow some books from Precious Virtue. Then he called Bright Design to him and said to her, "Go and see what Lin Ku-niang is doing. If she asks about me, just say that I am quite all right now."

"You'll have to think of a better excuse than that," Bright Design said. "Isn't there anything that you can send or want to borrow? I don't want to go there and feel like a fool without anything to say."

Pao-yu thought for a moment and then took two handkerchiefs from under his pillow and gave them to the maid, saying, "Well then, tell her that I sent you with these."

"What a strange present to send," the maid smiled. "What does she want two old handkerchiefs for? She will be angry again and say that you are trying to make fun of her."

"Don't worry," Pao-yu assured her. "She will understand."

Black Jade had already retired when Bright Design arrived at the Bamboo Retreat. "What brought you at this hour?" Black Jade asked.

"Er-yeh asked me to bring these handkerchiefs for Ku-niang."

For a moment Black Jade was at a loss to see why Pao-yu should send her such a present at that particular moment. She said, "I suppose they must be something unusual that somebody gave him. Tell him to keep them himself or give them to someone who will appreciate them. I have no need of them."

"They are nothing unusual," Bright Design said, "just two ordinary handkerchiefs that he happened to have around." Black Jade was even more puzzled, and then it suddenly dawned upon her: Pao-yu knew that she would weep for him and so sent two old handkerchiefs of his own.

"You can leave them then," she said to Bright Design, who in turn was surprised that Black Jade did not take offense at what seemed to her a crude joke.

As Black Jade thought over the significance of the handkerchiefs she was happy and sad by turns: happy because Pao-yu read her innermost thoughts and sad because she wondered if what was uppermost in her thoughts would ever be fulfilled. Thinking thus to herself of the future and of the past, she could not fall asleep. Despite Purple Cuckoo's remonstrances, she had her lamp relit and began to compose a series of quatrains, writing them directly on the handkerchiefs that Pao-yu had sent. After writing three stanzas, she began to feel exhausted and feverish. Going to her mirror, she found her cheeks flushed as if they were afire. She thought nothing of it, but from that moment on, her illness entered a more critical stage.

CHAPTER TWENTY-TWO

In which Precious Virtue confesses her suspicion of Hsueh Pan
And Pao-yu declares his preference for Black Jade

IN the meantime, Pervading Fragrance had gone to the Wistaria Arbor. It happened that Precious Virtue was not in the Garden but had gone home to see her mother, and Pervading Fragrance, not wishing to go back to Pao-yu empty-handed, decided to wait for her. It was not until some time later that Precious Virtue returned.

She was not in a happy mood, for she had just had a scene at home with her brother over Pao-yu. Knowing her brother as she did, she couldn't help believing the accusations made against him. But ironically enough, Hsueh Pan was innocent this time and knew nothing of the suspicion he was under. Neither Precious Virtue nor Hsueh Yi-ma mentioned the subject when he got home that evening, for he had been drinking and they did not want to upset him, but Hsueh Pan brought up the subject himself as he was about to retire to his own room.

"By the way," he said, "I heard Pao-yu got a beating today. Do you know what brought it on?"

"You have the brazenness to ask, you thoughtless fool!" Hsueh Yi-ma said, pointing angrily at him. "You know perfectly well you are responsible for it all."

"Why should I be responsible for it?" Hsueh Pan said in astonishment.

"Don't pretend innocence," Hsueh Yi-ma said. "Everyone says that it was you who told on Pao-yu."

"I suppose you'd believe it if they accused me of murder," Hsueh Pan said.

"Even your Mei-mei knows that it was you," Hsueh Yi-ma said.

"Let's not talk about it now," Precious Virtue said, trying to restore peace between her mother and her brother. "The truth will come out one of these days." Then turning to Hsueh Pan, she said, "It makes little difference whether it was you who told or not. What is past cannot be undone. But I urge you to be more careful in the future and try not to interfere in other people's business. If you do that, people won't be suspecting you."

Now Hsueh Pan was a straightforward man and nothing aroused him more than such roundabout innuendoes. He flew into a rage and began to shout threats against his unknown accusers. "I'll find out who that convict-begotten liar is and knock out all his teeth for him," he fumed. "It must be someone who tries to curry favor with Lao Tai-tai. But why must he pick on me? And who is Pao-yu anyway? You'd think he was a god the way everyone carries on every time his father gives him a beating. The last time, they blamed it on Gen Ta-ko, and what a bawling-out he got from Lao Tai-tai. Now they try to blame me for it. But I won't take it. I'll go and beat Pao-yu to death and then answer for it with my own life."

So saying, he pulled out the big wooden latch from the back door and started to go. Hsueh Yi-ma hastened toward him and held him back, saying, "You trouble-making monster! You might as well kill me first if you are going to make trouble like that."

"You mustn't behave like that," Precious Virtue said to him. "Mother was upset enough without your trying to irritate her."

"You are the one who upset her in the first place with

your tales," Hsueh Pan retorted. "Pao-yu is not as innocent as you think. Let me just tell you what happened the other day with that actor Chi-kuan. I have seen that boy dozens of times, but he never said anything nice to me. But the first time Pao-yu met him, he gave Pao-yu a handkerchief. Pao-yu must be an old hand at such things to get on such intimate terms with him the first time they meet."

"Now you have as much as confessed it yourself," Hsueh Yi-ma said. "It was exactly because of Chi-kuan that Pao-yu was beaten."

"You are driving me mad," Hsueh Pan cried. Then trying to get even with his sister, he said, "Don't think I don't know why you are siding with Pao-yu against me. It's because of that nonsense about the destiny of the gold and jade."

Precious Virtue burst out crying and said, turning to her mother, "Listen to what Brother is saying, Mother."

Hsueh Pan realized that he had said too much. He felt helpless and so turned around and went to his own room. Precious Virtue, not wishing to distress her mother any more, suppressed her tears and went back to the Garden. But she was deeply hurt by her brother's innuendoes and cried most of the night. The next morning, she hurried through her toilet and went to her mother again. On her way she encountered Black Jade, and the latter, noticing her swollen eyes, said to her, "Better take care of yourself and not grieve too much. Tears won't do the bruises any good." But Precious Virtue was too busy with her own thoughts to retort.

Black Jade stood under the shade of some trees and looked toward the Peony Court. She saw Li Huan, Welcome Spring, and others enter and depart from their calls. She wondered why Phoenix had not appeared. Surely, however busy she might be, she would put in an appearance to please Lao Tai-tai, she thought to herself. Then looking up, she found the answer. Another group of callers was approaching the Peony Court; Phoenix and the Matriarch were among them. How lucky Pao-yu was to have so many people care for him, she reflected; then she thought of her own position and her parents and suddenly felt sad.

Just then, Purple Cuckoo came and said to her, "It is time for Ku-niang to take her medicine. The water is getting cold." Black Jade lingered a little, then turned toward her compound, leaning upon her maid.

The Matriarch was pleased with Pao-yu's visible progress toward recovery but, to make sure that Chia Cheng would not give more trouble, she sent for one of his attendants and said, "If your Lao-yeh should ask for Pao-yu, just tell him that I want Pao-yu to take a good long rest. Moreover, the fortuneteller says that he is going through a critical period and must not see any strangers until after the Eighth Month."

Thus, Pao-yu was given even more freedom than before. He spent most of his time playing the willing slave to the young ladies and his favored maids. Occasionally Pervading Fragrance or Precious Virtue would remonstrate with him and advise him to give some thought to his studies and his future career, but such advice only irritated him and brought the retort that he was surprised to see in them the same worldliness that he only associated with the more vulgar sex. Black Jade, alone, never gave him occasion for such remarks.

Now since the death of Golden Bracelet, Phoenix began to receive presents from some of the maidservants. She did not think anything of it at first but one day, after receiving another such present, she couldn't help remarking about it to Patience.

"I am surprised that it has not occurred to Nai-nai," Patience said. "The presents all come from those who have daughters in Tai-tai's room. As Nai-nai knows, Tai-tai has four personal maids with a monthly allowance of one tael each. The rest get only a few hundred *cash* apiece. Needless to say, each one is hoping that Nai-nai will suggest her own daughter to fill the vacancy."

"Of course," Phoenix said, laughing. "I should have known that before. People are never satisfied. They get more than they deserve already but they must have more. Let them come with presents, but I have my own ideas on the subject."

Then one day she went to Madame Wang and asked for instructions. Hsueh Yi-ma, Precious Virtue, and Black Jade were with her, eating watermelon.

"Since Jade Bracelet's sister died," Phoenix said, "there has been a vacancy among Tai-tai's personal maids. Would Tai-tai please select one from among the others so that the next monthly allowance will be issued to her accordingly?"

Madame Wang thought for a while and then said, "I think there is no need to fill the vacancy. I don't have to have four personal maids."

"Tai-tai is right, of course," Phoenix said, "but it is the established rule. It would not seem right for Tai-tai to have fewer personal maids than others."

Madame Wang said, after another moment's reflection, "Let Jade Bracelet have her sister's allowance in addition to her own. Her sister was a good girl and died such a tragic death."

Phoenix turned to the lucky maid and congratulated her. The maid kowtowed to her mistress and thanked her. Then Madame Wang asked Phoenix, "What are the amounts allowed for Chou Yi-niang and Chao Yi-niang?"

"The established allowance is two taels each," Phoenix answered. "However, Chao Yi-niang actually receives four taels as she takes care of Huan Hsiung-ti's allowance also. They also receive four strings of *cash* for the maids."

"Have the allowances been paid regularly?"

"Of course they have been," Phoenix answered. "Why does Tai-tai ask?"

"I thought I heard someone complain about being short of a string of *cash*."

"Oh, that!" Phoenix said with relief. "The original allowance set for Yi-niang's maids was a string of *cash* each, but last year they decided to reduce it by half. Since they each have two maids, naturally they get a string less than before. I have nothing to do with the amount; I only pass it out. I have tried to persuade them to restore the original amount, but they would not do it."

"How many in Lao Tai-tai's room get one tael each?" Madame Wang again asked after a moment's pause.

"Eight," Phoenix answered. "But only seven of them are actually in Lao Tai-tai's room. The eighth one is Hsi-jen [Pervading Fragrance]."

"Yes, of course," Madame Wang said. "Your Pao Hsiung-ti[1] is not entitled to a maid with such an allowance. Hsi-jen is still nominally Lao Tai-tai's."

"That's right," Phoenix said. "If Pao Hsiung-ti is allowed to have a maid with such an allowance, Huan Hsiung-ti will have to have one too to make it right. Now there are seven maids in Pao Hsiung-ti's room who draw one string of *cash* each and eight who draw only half the amount. It's all Lao Tai-tai's orders."

"Listen to her rattling it off like a walnut crusher," Hsueh Yi-ma remarked, laughing. "She remembers everything and knows all the answers."

"Did I say anything wrong, Yi-ma?" Phoenix said, laughing also.

"Not at all," Hsueh Yi-ma said, "but you can save some energy by going more slowly."

Then Madame Wang said, after another pause, "Tomorrow you can pick out another maid to take the place of Hsi-jen in Lao Tai-tai's room and stop paying her allowance out of regular funds, except for the one string of *cash* to which she is entitled. But I want you to pay her, in addition, two taels out of my own allowance of twenty taels. From now on, whenever there is any special distribution, she should receive the same share as Chou Yi-niang and Chao Yi-niang."

"Did you hear that, Yi-ma?" Phoenix said. "Didn't I say that Hsi-jen would be rewarded for her faithfulness one of these days?"

"It's time that the child got her deserts," Hsueh Yi-ma

[1] "Hsiung-ti" means "younger brother."

said. "She is not only pretty but so good and conducts herself so well."

"You do not begin to know her real worth," Madame Wang said. "Pao-yu is really lucky to have her wait upon him."

When the watermelon party broke up at Madame Wang's, Precious Virtue went to Peony Court to see Pao-yu and to tell Pervading Fragrance of the good fortune that had come upon her. She found Pao-yu taking a nap and the maid sitting by him working on some embroidery and occasionally waving a fan over her master. Precious Virtue chatted with her for a while and later when the maid had to go out for something, she took up her embroidery, sat where Pervading Fragrance had been sitting, and began to work on it.

In the meantime, Black Jade and River Mist had also come to congratulate Pervading Fragrance. River Mist went directly to look for her, while Black Jade went over to Pao-yu's room and peeped through the window. Suppressing her laughter, she beckoned to River Mist to come and see the picture of domesticity Precious Virtue presented. River Mist was on the point of laughing aloud; then remembering how good Precious Virtue had always been to her, she decided to spare her the embarrassment. She said to Black Jade, "Pervading Fragrance is not in her room. They tell me that she has gone to the pond to do some washing, so let us go and look for her there."

Precious Virtue went on with her embroidering, not realizing that she had been observed. Suddenly she heard Pao-yu exclaim in his dream, "How can you believe the words of monks and priests? The destiny of gold and jade! All nonsense. I insist on saying, instead, the destiny of wood and stone!"

Precious Virtue was startled by the vehemence with which Pao-yu expressed these sentiments.

CHAPTER TWENTY-THREE

In which the Matriarch twice feasts in the Takuanyuan
And Liu Lao-lao again visits the Yungkuofu

A FEW days later, River Mist's family sent for her, and she had to go home. She was reluctant to leave her cousins and the Garden but she tried not to show it, for fear that the maids sent to fetch her might tell her aunt and cause the latter to complain that she preferred her relatives to her own family. Before she left, she managed to whisper to Pao-yu, "If Lao Tai-tai should forget to send for me, be sure to remind her."

Then Chia Cheng was appointed Grand Examiner for one of the provinces and left the Capital on the twentieth of the Eighth Month, giving Pao-yu even greater freedom to indulge in his whims and fancies.

One day Pao-yu received a formal note of invitation from Quest Spring proposing the formation of a poetry club. When he arrived at the Autumn Study, he found Black Jade, Precious Virtue, and the others already there. Everyone was delighted with the idea, and it was decided that meetings should be held on the second and sixteenth of the month. Each was to play host in turn and to provide refreshments for the occasion. Li Huan, who was not given to writing verses but was by general consent a fair and discriminating critic, was made chairman. At Black Jade's suggestion, the first meeting was held on that very day, and the *hai-tang,* or begonia flower, was chosen as the theme.

Quest Spring was the first to finish, followed by Precious Virtue and Pao-yu. Only then did Black Jade proceed to compose her verse, which, however, she dashed off as fast as she could write the characters. Li Huan awarded the prize to Precious Virtue for the depth of her sentiment, though she and the others all agreed that Black Jade's poems showed the most originality.

At the next meeting, River Mist was added to the membership, as Pao-yu, suddenly remembering her, pestered the Matriarch to send for her immediately. The theme was the chrysanthemum, and River Mist was to act as hostess, assisted by Precious Virtue, with whom she always stayed during her visits. As River Mist's family circumstances were not comparable to the Chias, Precious Virtue suggested that she might use the occasion to entertain the Matriarch and the rest of the family. Precious Virtue secured through her brother several baskets of crabs, which were inexpensive and at the same time different from what the sophisticated palates of the members of the Yungkuofu were used to.

The feast was a great success, for the Matriarch was in a good mood and responded well to Phoenix's efforts to entertain her. After the feast, the Matriarch, Madame Wang, and others departed, and the members of the poetry club proceeded with their contest. On this occasion, Black Jade won all the three prizes.

As the respective merits of the compositions were being discussed, Patience came in and said that Phoenix would like to have some more crabs. "Nai-nai was so busy waiting upon Lao Tai-tai that she did not have a chance to eat any herself," she explained.

"There are plenty left," River Mist said, as she picked out ten big ones and laid them out on a tray.

They invited Patience to join them. The maid said she couldn't, but Li Huan dragged her to a chair and made her sit down, saying, "Tell your mistress that I insisted." The crabs were sent by another maid.

Pao-yu and the young ladies took turns in offering Patience wine. "Such a lovely girl," Li Huan said as she patted the maid affectionately. "She carries herself with such dignity and grace. No one would ever take her for a maid. But there's no arguing with fate."

"You tickle me, Nai-nai," Patience said, giggling.

"*Ai-ya!* what's this hard lump?" Li Huan asked.

"It's a bunch of keys," Patience answered.

"What valuables does your Nai-nai have that she has to keep things locked?" Li Huan said. "I have often remarked that it is just as impossible to imagine the T'ang Pilgrim without his white horse as to imagine Feng-chieh without her faithful Patience. What use does she have for keys when she has you, her master key?"

"Nai-nai is making fun of me again," Patience said, laughing.

"She is only telling the truth," Precious Virtue said. "We have often spoken of you among ourselves and we all agree that you are one among hundreds. We all recognize your Nai-nai's abilities, but we are convinced that without you she would be like a bird without wings."

Presently the party broke up. Pervading Fragrance invited Patience to her room, and the two chatted a while. As Patience got up to go, Pervading Fragrance asked what had become of the allowance for the month. "No one seems to have received it yet," she said. "Not even Lao Tai-tai and Tai-tai."

Patience looked to make sure that no one was within hearing before she answered, saying, "Don't go to Nai-nai and ask about it. It will be coming along in a few days."

"What's wrong?" Pervading Fragrance said. "You look so mysterious."

"The fact is," Patience whispered, "that the allowance for the month was received from the outside long ago, but Nai-nai let it out on short-term loans. She expects to collect in a few days. I wouldn't tell anyone but you, so make sure that you keep it to yourself."

"Why should she want to do that?" Pervading Fragrance

said. "Surely she couldn't be short of funds. One would think her hands were full enough without this additional worry."

"That's what I think, too, but that's the way she is. During the last few years, she must have made close to a thousand taels a year in interest, what with the money passing through her hands and the money she has been saving out of her own allowance."

"So that's why we have to wait for our money!"

"What do you care if you have to wait a few days?" Patience said. "It is not as if you needed it to buy rice."

"I do not need it myself," Pervading Fragrance explained, "but you know how free Pao-yu is with money. That's why I always like to have some cash on hand."

"If you really need anything now, I can lend you some and deduct it from the allowance," Patience said, getting up to go.

"Not now," Pervading Fragrance said. "But I shall remember your offer if I am ever in need."

Arriving at Phoenix's apartment, Patience found Liu Lao-lao and her grandson Pan-er, distant relatives of Madame Wang who had visited the Yungkuofu three years ago, waiting there for her mistress. Chou Jui's wife was with them, as on their first visit. On the floor there were sacks containing jujubes, carrots, and pumpkins and other farm produce.

Everyone stood up as Patience entered the room, including Liu Lao-lao, who also understood the important position occupied by the maid in the Chia mansion. "How is Ku-niang?" she said, beaming at Patience. "Everyone home sends their greetings. We have been wanting to come to see our Ku Nai-nai, but it's busy on the farm. Luckily we have had a good harvest this year, and the fruits and vegetables are especially good. These are our first pickings. They are nothing in themselves but they are the best we have to offer and different from the rich delicacies that you live on."

"Have you seen Nai-nai yet?" Patience asked her.

"Yes, but she asked us to wait for her." Then looking out at the sky, she continued, "It's getting late. We had better be going or we may not get to the city gate before it's closed."

"Just wait a while longer while I go and see what Nai-nai is doing," Chou Jui's wife said.

Presently she returned and said to Liu Lao-lao, "Luck must be with you today. Nai-nai was with Lao Tai-tai. I told her that you wanted to go home before it got dark, but Nai-nai said, 'It's so kind of her to come from such a long distance and to bring so many things. Ask her to spend the night with us.' And that's not all. Lao Tai-tai heard us and asked who you were. When Nai-nai told her, she asked to see you. See how lucky you are?"

"But how can I present myself before Lao Tai-tai?" Liu Lao-lao protested.

"Don't be so bashful," Patience said. "Our Lao Tai-tai is most kind and doesn't put on airs as some people do. So come along. Chou Ta-niang and I will take you there."

Pao-yu and the young ladies of the Takuanyuan were all in the Matriarch's room when Patience entered with Liu Lao-lao. The latter was dazzled by the bright jewels and gorgeous costumes of the young ladies but she was able to make out an aged lady lying on a couch with a beautiful maid massaging her legs and concluded that it must be the Matriarch. She curtsied profoundly and said, "Greetings to the ancient goddess of longevity." The Matriarch returned the greeting and asked her to sit down.

"How old are you?" the Matriarch asked, addressing her as an old relative.

"Seventy-five," Liu Lao-lao stood up to reply.

"See how strong she is," the Matriarch said to those present, "and yet she is older than I am.[1] I don't know how useless and dependent I shall be when I am her age."

"But we are born to labor while Lao Tai-tai is born to enjoy the blessings of Heaven," Liu Lao-lao said. "What

[1] Two years later, in Chapter 32, the Matriarch celebrates her eightieth birthday.

would become of all the farm work if we were like Lao Tai-tai?"

"Are your eyes and all your teeth in good condition?" the Matriarch asked.

"Yes, they are all in good condition," Liu Lao-lao answered, "except that my left molar is getting a bit loose."

"I am getting quite old and useless," the Matriarch said regretfully. "My eyes are dim, my ears deaf, and my memory unreliable. I do not see many visitors now for fear of betraying my infirmities. All I do is eat whatever my teeth can chew, sleep when I can, and amuse myself with my children and grandchildren when I need diversion."

"That is Lao Tai-tai's blessing from Heaven," Liu Lao-lao said. "I would like to do those things but I can't."

The Matriarch was pleased with her rustic visitor and with her simplicity. She asked her to stay for a few days. Phoenix, seeing that the Matriarch had taken a liking to Liu Lao-lao, also urged her to stay, saying that though the Yungkuofu was not as large and spacious as her farm, there were a few vacant rooms in which she could stay.

The following day, the Matriarch, accompanied by her daughters-in-law and grandchildren, visited the Takuanyuan and showed Liu Lao-lao the sights. The visitor was impressed by everything. "We used to get pictures for the walls at New Year time," she said, "—pictures of palaces and great mansions. We always thought that such houses as those in the pictures did not exist, but now I see your garden is much prettier than the pictures. How wonderful it would be if you could get someone to make a picture of the garden and let the country folk improve their knowledge!"

Dinner was served in the Autumn Study, Quest Spring's apartment. In the meantime, Faith had, after a whispered consultation with Phoenix, taken Liu Lao-lao aside and told her how she should behave at the table. "This is the custom in this house," she concluded. "You must observe it carefully if you do not want them to laugh at you." Liu Lao-lao assured her that she would do exactly as she was told.

The visitor was placed near the Matriarch at a small table. Ordinarily Faith did not do the menial tasks, such as passing towels and wafting the fly brush, but on this occasion, she stood behind the Matriarch so that she could direct operations. She winked at Liu Lao-lao to remind her, and the latter said, "Do not worry, Ku-niang, I shall do everything as you told me."

After seating herself, Liu Lao-lao was confronted with a pair of old-fashioned ivory chopsticks covered with gold. They were heavy and difficult to manage. "These implements," she said ruefully, looking at the chopsticks, "are heavier than our iron prongs. How can I handle them?" After serving the Matriarch, Phoenix selected a bowl of pigeon eggs and placed it in front of Liu Lao-lao. When the Matriarch picked up her chopsticks and invited her guest to help herself, Liu Lao-lao stood up and said with great solemnity:

> Liu the old dame, the old dame,
> Her appetite's given her well-earned fame,
> She'll eat a whole cow as easily as you say her
> name.

She then sat down as if she had performed a sacred ritual. At first, everyone was astounded and did not know what to make of it but in the next instant, they all burst into laughter. River Mist spilled the tea as Black Jade choked with laughter, leaning upon the table, crying and groaning. Pao-yu fell convulsively into the arms of the Matriarch, who was hysterically calling him all sorts of pet names. Even Madame Wang could not maintain her dignity. Some had to leave the table.

Phoenix and Faith were the only ones to maintain their gravity. They stood by Liu Lao-lao and urged her to eat.

She surveyed the pigeon eggs and said, "Well, well, even your chickens are more elegant and delicate than ours. See what tiny eggs they lay." This caused a fresh outburst of laughter.

"The rascal Feng Ya-tou must be up to her tricks again," the Matriarch said. "Don't take her advice, Lao-lao."

Phoenix continued to urge Liu Lao-lao to help herself. "Go ahead and eat," she said. "These eggs cost a tael each and won't be good cold."

But the pigeon eggs were hard to manage, especially with the unwieldy chopsticks that Phoenix had purposely given her. After chasing the eggs in the bowl with her chopsticks for some time, Liu Lao-lao finally succeeded in capturing one. As she brought her mouth toward the egg and the egg toward her mouth, and the two were about to meet, the egg slipped and fell to the floor. Again everyone laughed. The Matriarch then ordered the maids to have another pair of chopsticks brought for Liu Lao-lao. The new pair was made of ebony, covered on both ends with silver. Liu Lao-lao remarked that, after all, plain wooden chopsticks were the best for practical purposes.

"But the silver serves a purpose," Phoenix said, "for if the food is poisoned, the silver will show it."

"Poison!" Liu Lao-lao exclaimed. "If this is poison, then our food is all arsenic. Even if it is poison, I will die without regret. It will be a pleasant death."

The Matriarch, whose pampered appetite was none too good, was delighted to see how much Liu Lao-lao enjoyed her food.

The old woman, it turned out, was not as unconscious of what she was doing as the maid had imagined, for when Faith apologized for making fun of her, she said, "There is no need of apologizing. I am glad that I succeeded in furnishing Lao Tai-tai some amusement."

In the afternoon after visiting the various courts in the Takuanyuan, the Matriarch took Liu Lao-lao to the convent in one corner of the Takuanyuan where Exquisite Jade lived. The nun asked the Matriarch and her train to go into the inner hall, but the Matriarch declined, saying that she had just eaten meat and did not want to desecrate the holy ground.

Pao-yu, who was acquainted with the fastidious habits of the nun, watched her closely to see how she entertained her guests. The nun poured tea in a cup made in the Ch'eng Hua period (A.D. 1665–88) and presented it to the Matriarch on a tray of carved lacquer. The Matriarch asked her what water she used, and the nun answered that it was rain water saved from the year before. The Matriarch drank half the cup and gave the rest to Liu Lao-lao, saying, "You taste this tea, too." Liu Lao-lao did so. When asked how she liked it, she said it was too light.

After the others had been served, the nun tugged Black Jade and Precious Virtue by their dresses and took them into another room. Pao-yu followed, curious to see what the nun had to say or offer to them. He found that Exquisite Jade was making some special tea for them. He went in, saying that he must have his share of the special treat. The nun poured the tea into two cups of different patterns, of the rare Sung period (A.D. 960–1225) and gave them to Black Jade and Precious Virtue. For Pao-yu she used her own cup of white jade.

"Is this also last year's rain water?" Black Jade asked, sipping her tea.

"I am surprised to hear you say that," the nun said. "Can't you tell the difference? This water was snow that I gathered from the plum trees five years ago. It filled that blue jar there, and I have saved it all this time. It was buried under the earth and was opened only this last summer. This is the second time I have used it. How could you expect rain water to possess such lightness and clarity?"

Black Jade also knew the nun's fastidiousness and perversity, so she said nothing. One of the maids came in with the cups that the visitors in the outer hall had used, but the nun stopped her and told her not to put away the cup used by Liu Lao-lao.

Reading the nun's thoughts, Pao-yu said, "It would be a pity to throw that cup away. Why don't you give it to her? She can sell it and get a good price for it."

"Give it to her yourself if you want to," the nun said. "Fortunately I have never used the cup myself. If I had, I would break it before I would give it to her."

"Of course," Pao-yu agreed. "Tomorrow I will send someone with a few buckets of river water for you to wash the floor where she stood."

"That will be excellent," the nun said. "But tell your men to leave the buckets outside the gate. I will have the maids bring them in."

At supper there were games of impromptu verse, and Liu Lao-lao again amused everyone by her crude compositions. It had been a full day and a strenuous one for the Matriarch, who seldom visited more than one or two places in the Takuanyuan at a time. As a result, she was ill the next day. Chia-chieh, Phoenix's daughter, was also ill. Liu Lao-lao offered advice on how to avoid malign spirits. It was because they disregarded certain elementary taboos, she said, that people got sick.

Liu Lao-lao left with many presents of clothing, family remedies, food, and money from the various members of the Yungkuofu. She was invited to return whenever she chose. After this, she visited the Chias frequently, bringing them simple gifts from the farm and taking with her valuable things in return.

CHAPTER TWENTY-FOUR

In which it is proved that human events are as uncertain as the weather
And that a man would sooner apologize to his concubine than to his wife

It was the second of the Ninth Month, and the Yungkuofu was celebrating Phoenix's birthday in the Matriarch's courtyard, where an elaborate party was in progress in recognition of her faithful and capable management of the affairs of the mansion. After a while, the Matriarch retired to her own room so that the younger generation could enjoy themselves without restraint. She bade Yu-shih to made sure that Phoenix had a good time. Yu-shih obeyed but presently said that Phoenix was not used to sitting down at table and that she wouldn't drink anything.

"You do not know how to urge her," the Matriarch said in her own room. "I shall come out myself if you do not have better success."

Phoenix hurried in and said, "Lao Tai-tai mustn't believe her. I have drunk several cups already."

"Take her back," the Matriarch said to Yu-shih. "Let everyone offer her a birthday cup. If she still refuses to drink, I shall come out and urge her myself."

Yu-shih dragged Phoenix back to the table, filled a cup and offered it to her, saying, "You have been very faithful to Lao Tai-tai, Tai-tai, and myself. I now offer you a cup of wine with my own hands."

"Before accepting it I should make you offer it to me on your knees," Phoenix said laughingly as she drank. Next, Pao-yu and the young ladies presented cups to Phoenix, and after them, the more important of the stewards' wives and maids. She began to feel the effect of the wine and made some excuse to escape.

Accompanied by Patience, she walked toward her own apartment. One of her maids was standing at the head of the veranda. Suddenly she turned around and, as soon as she saw Phoenix, started to run away. Phoenix became suspicious. She called to the maid, who at first pretended not to hear her but came forward reluctantly when called by name. Phoenix sat on the moon terrace and bade the maid kneel. Then she said to Patience, "Go and summon two attendants to come with whips and flog this impudent wretch until there is no skin left on her back."

The maid trembled and begged for mercy.

"I am not a monster," Phoenix said. "Why did you not stand by as I came in? Why did you run away when I called you?"

"I did not see Nai-nai," the maid cried. "I ran because I suddenly remembered that there was no one in the room to look after things."

"If there was no one in the room," Phoenix said, "then why did you come here in the first place? Even if you did not see me, you must have heard Patience and myself calling you at the top of our voices. You are not deaf." She slapped the maid first on one cheek and then on the other. In an instant, the maid's face began to swell. Patience interceded for her, saying that her mistress must not hurt her own hands.

"Strike her," Phoenix commanded, "and ask her why she ran. If she still won't tell, tear open her cheeks!"

The maid held steadfastly to her story, until Phoenix threatened to burn her cheeks with hot iron. Then she said, weeping, "Er-yeh is home. He told me to watch out for

Nai-nai and let him know as soon as Nai-nai left the banquet. I did not think that Nai-nai would return so soon."

Phoenix saw that her suspicion was not unfounded. She said to the maid, "Why did he ask you to do that? Why should he be afraid of my return? There must be a reason. Tell me and I will be good to you, but if you won't tell me everything, I shall have you sliced to pieces." She took a hairpin and threatened to jab the maid with it.

"I will tell Nai-nai," the maid cringed and cried, "but please do not tell Er-yeh that I said it. Er-yeh came home a while back and took out two large pieces of silver, two hairpins, and two pieces of silk. He told me to give these to Pao-er's wife and ask her to come in. Pao-er's wife took the things and came. Then Er-yeh told me to watch out for Nai-nai. I do not know what happened after that."

Phoenix hurried toward her compound. At the gate another maid was stationed. As soon as she saw Phoenix, she too started to run. Phoenix called to her by name, and the maid, with more presence of mind than the first, turned around immediately and came running toward her instead.

"I was going to see Nai-nai," she said. "How fortunate that Nai-nai has come!" She gave a recital similar to that of the first maid.

"Where have you been all this time?" Phoenix asked her. "It's only because I saw you that you came and told me. I know your tricks."

As she drew near her room, she heard a woman's voice saying, "It will be easier for us when that monster of yours dies."

"There will be another one, and she will be the same," answered Chia Lien's voice.

"You can make Patience your wife," the woman said. "She will be easier to manage."

"She won't even let me touch Patience," Chia Lien said. "And Patience doesn't dare complain, though she doesn't like her vigilance either. I wonder what I have done to deserve such a wife."

Phoenix shook with rage. Thinking that Patience must

have complained behind her back, she turned to her and slapped her face. She then burst into the room, seized Pao-er's wife and struck her repeatedly. Fearing that Chia Lien would bolt from the room, she planted herself at the door while she denounced the woman. "Prostitute!" she cried, "you seduce your mistress's husband and then plot to murder her! And you," she turned to Patience, "you prostitutes are all in conspiracy against me, though you pretend to be on my side." She struck Patience again.

Patience was outraged. She cried, "You two—is it not enough for you to do this shameful thing without dragging me in?" She also made for Pao-er's wife.

Chia Lien, who had until now stood helplessly watching Phoenix beat Pao-er's wife, took the opportunity to hide his own embarrassment by beating Patience. "Who are you to raise your hand against her?" he said to the maid.

Patience retreated and said, weeping, "But why did you drag me into it?"

Phoenix's anger mounted when she saw that Patience was afraid of Chia Lien and commanded her to ignore him and beat Pao-er's wife. The maid, outraged and helpless, ran out of the room, crying and threatening to kill herself.

Phoenix now threw herself at Chia Lien, crying that he might as well kill her then and there since he wanted to get rid of her. Chia Lien grew desperate. He seized a sword from the wall and said he would gladly oblige if she insisted.

Yu-shih and others arrived on the scene. "What is the matter now?" she asked. "Everything was going well a moment ago."

Emboldened by the presence of the newcomers, Chia Lien became more menacing. Phoenix, on the other hand, quieted herself and left the scene to seek the protection of the Matriarch. She threw herself sobbing into the Matriarch's arms and said, "Save me, Lao Tai-tai. Lien Er-yeh wants to kill me."

The Matriarch, Madame Wang, and Madame Hsing asked her what had happened, and she sobbed out her story. "I went home to change my clothes," she said. "But Lien Er-yeh was talking with someone inside. I did not dare intrude, thinking that he might be entertaining some guest, but I overheard some of the conversation and found that it was Pao-er's wife, who was plotting with him to poison me and put Patience in my place. I did not dare quarrel with him. I only gave Patience a few slaps and asked her why she wanted to murder me. He became embarrassed and threatened to kill me."

The Matriarch took Phoenix's words literally and ordered the attendants to seize Chia Lien and bring him before her. But he voluntarily came in, sword in hand, emboldened by his intoxicated state and relying on the Matriarch's usual indulgence.

Madame Hsing and Madame Wang stopped him and said to him sternly, "Have you gone mad, you wretch? How dare you behave like this in Lao Tai-tai's presence?"

"It is all Lao Tai-tai's fault that she is so spoiled," Chia Lien said. Madame Hsing took the sword from him and ordered him to leave. Chia Lien continued to mumble until the Matriarch threatened to send for his father. Only then did he stagger off.

The Matriarch said to Phoenix, "This is much ado about nothing. Children will be children and kittens will steal fish. It is all my fault. I should not have made you drink so much wine, which undoubtedly gave you a desire for vinegar." Everyone laughed at this reference to Phoenix's jealousy. The Matriarch continued, "Don't cry now. Tomorrow I will tell him to apologize to you. You had better not go over today to shame him. As for Patience, I have always thought her a good girl. I didn't realize that she would be like this."

Yu-shih said, laughing, "Patience hasn't done anything at all. They are just making a scapegoat of her, that's all. They always do that when they have a quarrel."

"Of course," the Matriarch said. "I should have known better. I was wondering how she could be capable of such a thing." Then she turned to Amber, one of her maids, and said, "Go tell Patience that I know everything and that I will have her mistress apologize to her tomorrow. But she mustn't carry on any more today, since it's her mistress's birthday."

In the meantime, Li Huan and the young ladies escorted Patience into the Takuanyuan and tried to comfort her. "You are an understanding person," Precious Virtue said to her. "I needn't remind you how your mistress has always treated you. Today she is not herself. She feels closest to you; who else is there to vent her anger on? If you do not stop weeping, it will get around, and people will laugh at your mistress. Surely you do not want that."

Amber came in just then to deliver the Matriarch's message. Patience felt vindicated and gradually stopped weeping. She did not go back to Phoenix's apartment that night but stayed with Li Huan. Phoenix stayed at the Matriarch's.

The following morning, Madame Hsing took Chia Lien to the Matriarch. "What have you to say for yourself?" she asked, as Chia Lien knelt down before her. He smiled apologetically and said, "It was because I had drunk too much that I came in to disturb Lao Tai-tai. I've come to beg Lao Tai-tai's pardon."

"If you really have any consideration for me," the Matriarch said, "apologize graciously to your wife there, and I will forgive you. Otherwise, leave me; I want none of your apologies."

Phoenix was standing behind the Matriarch, her eyes swollen with weeping and her face bare of powder; she looked pitiful and lovely. Chia Lien felt more inclined to apologize than on the day before. Besides, there was nothing else he could do with the Matriarch on his wife's side. He said sheepishly, "How dare I disobey Lao Tai-tai, but I am afraid Lao Tai-tai is spoiling her."

"Spoiling her!" the Matriarch exclaimed. "Don't be so shameless! She is not a shrew; she knows how to conduct herself properly. If she ever offends you unjustly, I will permit you to punish her."

Chia Lien rose and bowed to Phoenix, saying, "It was

my fault, Nai-nai. Please do not be angry with me any more."

Amid the merriment caused by this humility, the Matriarch continued, "Feng Ya-tou must not feel offended any more. I shall be angry if she continues to sulk."

Then calling Patience, she bade Chia Lien and Phoenix apologize to her. Chia Lien was even readier to apologize to his maid than to his wife. He went up to her and said, "Please do not be angry any more, Ku-niang. It was my fault. Even if Nai-nai offended you, it was because of me."

Before Phoenix said anything to Patience, the latter went to her and said, kneeling down, "I deserve death to have given Nai-nai occasion to be angry on her birthday."

Phoenix was ashamed at having humiliated Patience so unjustly. Now seeing her beg forgiveness instead of complaining, she could not refrain from tears. She helped the maid to her feet, as Patience continued, "I have served Nai-nai for several years, and Nai-nai has never raised a finger against me. I know that it was all the fault of that woman." She wept also.

The Matriarch sent the three back to their own apartment, with the warning that she would personally administer a spanking to anyone who dared to mention the subject again.

Alone with her husband, Phoenix asked, "Just why am I a monster? Am I less to you than that prostitute?" She began to cry.

"What more do you want?" Chia Lien said. "I'll not say who made more fuss yesterday, but is it not enough that I apologized before everyone? Do you want me to go down on my knees and beg your forgiveness? One should know where to stop."

They were interrupted by a maidservant who came with the news that Pao-er's wife had hanged herself. Chia Lien and Phoenix were both astounded, but Phoenix recovered herself quickly and said, "What if she did? Why should you be so excited over it?"

The maidservant was followed by Lin Chih-hsiao's wife,

one of the stewards of the Yungkuofu. She said to Phoenix, "Pao-er's wife has committed suicide. Her people are threatening to bring suit."

Phoenix smiled coldly and said, "That is all right with me. I am thinking of bringing suit myself."

Lin Chih-hsiao's wife said, "We have been trying to pacify them, and they seemed willing to listen to reason after we promised them some money."

"Money?" Phoenix said. "I have no money to throw away. Even if I had, I wouldn't squander it like that. Let them bring suit. After they lose, I will myself bring suit against them for blackmail."

This embarrassed Lin Chih-hsiao's wife, who did not know what to make of it. Then she caught a sign from Chia Lien and withdrew. Chia Lien told Phoenix he would go see what could be done. She told him not to give them any money, but Chia Lien knew better what must be done in such cases. He bought off the family of the suicide with two hundred taels and charged the amount to miscellaneous expenses.

CHAPTER TWENTY-FIVE

In which one would expect such unbecoming behavior from such a person as Chia Sheh
Nor is one surprised at such admirable resolution from a girl like Faith

MADAME Hsing seemed mysterious when Phoenix went to her at her request. She dismissed the maids and said to Phoenix, "There is something that I want to speak to you about. Lao-yeh [referring to Chia Sheh] has given me a difficult problem, and I want your opinion before I do anything about it. Lao-yeh has taken a fancy to Lao Tai-tai's maid Yuan-yang [Faith] and wants to take her for his room. He asked me to ask Lao Tai-tai for her. There is nothing extraordinary about this, but I am afraid that Lao Tai-tai may refuse. What would you advise me to do?"

"If I were Tai-tai," Phoenix said, "I would not knock my head against this big nail. Lao Tai-tai cannot get along without Yuan-yang and will not part with her. Besides, Lao Tai-tai has often expressed her disapproval of Lao-yeh's large number of concubines. 'What does he keep them for?' she has often said. 'He is only keeping them from marrying while they are of the marriageable age. He is getting old but he still dissipates his vitality, neglects his duties, and spends his days with his concubines.' From this Tai-tai can see what Lao Tai-tai thinks of Lao-yeh. I should think that Lao-yeh ought to think of how to avoid the further displeasure of Lao Tai-tai, instead of tickling the tiger's nose with a straw. Tai-tai ought to dissuade him from this, it seems to me."

"It is not unusual for a man in Lao-yeh's position to have three or four concubines," Madame Hsing said in a displeased tone. "Besides, there is no dissuading him once he has his mind set on something. It will only turn him against me if I advise him against it."

Phoenix realized the futility of reasoning with Madame Hsing, who was always in fear of her husband and did whatever he told her to. "Tai-tai is right, I am sure," she said. "What can I know, young as I am? I suppose a son will always have what he wants from his parents. I was silly to have taken what Lao Tai-tai said seriously. Even with Pao-yu, for instance, she acts as if she were going to beat him to death when he displeases her. But when she sees him, she loves him as much as ever and gives him everything he wants. It must be so with Lao-yeh. Lao Tai-tai is in a good humor today. I shall go and prepare her. When Tai-tai comes, I shall leave her and take everyone with me so that you can speak to her in private."

Madame Hsing was mollified. "In my opinion," she said, "it is better that we do not speak to Lao Tai-tai now. I shall approach Yuan-yang herself first. If she consents, Lao Tai-tai will find it difficult to refuse, even though she does not want to part with her."

"After all," Phoenix said ingratiatingly, "Tai-tai knows best. Who doesn't want to climb to the top? She will be happy to become half a mistress instead of marrying a common servant or peasant."

"That is what I think, too," Madame Hsing said. "She ought to feel flattered. You can go to the other side now, but do not let what we have just discussed get out. I shall come over after breakfast."

"Yuan-yang is a girl with a mind of her own," Phoenix thought. "If I go back first, all will be well if she accepts Tai-tai's proposal. But if she refuses, Tai-tai may think that

I let the secret out. It would be safer to wait and go with Tai-tai, so no blame will fall on me." With this in mind, Phoenix arranged things so that Madame Hsing was the first to arrive at the Matriarch's and the first to have the opportunity to speak with Faith.

After waiting on the Matriarch for a few moments, Madame Hsing went into Faith's room. She watched the maid embroider and praised her skill. Under her continued scrutiny, the maid had the uneasy feeling that the visitor was up to something.

"Why did Tai-tai come over so early today?" the maid asked.

Madame Hsing signaled the other maids to withdraw and then taking Faith by the hand said, "I have come to congratulate Ku-niang." Faith guessed her intention but said nothing, while Madame Hsing went on to say that her husband needed someone whom he could trust, that he had chosen Faith from the scores of eager candidates, and that one day the maid would be looked upon as her own equal after she had borne Chia Sheh a son. "Come," she concluded, "we'll go and speak to Lao Tai-tai."

Faith withdrew her hand rudely and would not answer.

"You need not be bashful," Madame Hsing said. "You do not have to say anything to Lao Tai-tai. All you have to do is to come with me."

Faith still hung her head in silence.

"Do you mean to say that you really do not wish it? If so, you are a simpleton indeed! How can you refuse to be a mistress and choose instead to remain a servant. After a few years, you will marry one of the servants and you will still be a slave. Come with me. You know that I am good-tempered and will be good to you."

Faith remained silent.

"I suppose you feel that your parents ought to arrange these things for you," Madame Hsing said. "Well, I will speak to your people and ask them to speak to you. You can tell them what you have in mind without feeling shy."

After learning of the failure of his wife's mission, Chia Sheh thought for a moment and then summoned Chia Lien.

"There is more than one caretaker at Chinling," he said. "Send someone to Chinling at once and bring Chin Tsai, Yuan-yang's father."

Chia Lien tried to evade his father. He said, "The last report from Chinling is that he is very ill and that the coffin money has already been issued to him. If he is still living, he is probably delirious and won't be of any use. His wife is deaf—"

"Unfilial beast," Chia Sheh interrupted him, "you seem to know everything. Get out."

Chia Lien hastily withdrew and waited anxiously in his study for developments. Chia Sheh then summoned Chin Wen-hsiang, Faith's brother, and told him to use his influence with his sister. When the maid was summoned by her brother, she hesitated to rouse the Matriarch's displeasure by telling her about it but she clenched her teeth and refused all her brother's pleas. The latter went timidly to report to Chia Sheh on the maid's stubbornness.

"Tell your wife to tell her I know what she is thinking," Chia Sheh said. "Since the beginning of time, maidens have preferred youth to age. She must think I am too old for her. She has her heart set on the next generation, I should think—Pao-yu, for instance. If that is what she has in mind, tell her to forget it! Who would dare take her knowing that I wanted her? This is the first thing she must know. The second is that, if she has ambitions of becoming the wife of someone outside, let her consider well; for no matter whom she marries, she won't get out of my reach. Unless she decides to die or remain unmarried all her life, she had better change her mind. I shall forgive her and be good to her."

There was nothing for Chin Wen-hsiang to do except to say aye to everything and to promise to bring whatever pressure he could on his sister.

"Don't try to hoodwink me," Chia Sheh continued. "Tomorrow I am going to send your Tai-tai to her again. If she consents after you have told me that she won't change her mind, then watch out for your scalp."

Faith was stupefied at Chia Sheh's unbecoming conduct. After hearing her brother's words, she considered for a moment and then said, "Even if I were willing to go to him, it would be necessary for me to speak to Lao Tai-tai."

Her brother was overjoyed, for he thought it meant that she had changed her mind. Her sister-in-law took her to the Matriarch, who was talking with Madame Wang, Hsueh Yi-ma, Li Huan, Phoenix, Pao-yu, and others. Faith knelt before her and, between weeping and sobbing, told her story.

"Ta Lao-yeh says that I have set my heart on Pao-yu or have ambitions of becoming the wife of someone outside. He says that I will never escape his hands even if I mount Heaven itself. I am resolved, and I say it here before everyone, that, be it Pao-yu or anybody else, I will never marry in my life. Even if Lao Tai-tai tried to force me to, I would die before I would obey. After I have seen Lao Tai-tai return west, I will not go back to my parents or to my brother. I will either die or become a nun. If I do not speak from the heart, let Heaven and Earth and the Sun and Moon and all the deities and demons bear witness and afflict me with chronic sores in my throat . . ."

Before coming to see the Matriarch, Faith had concealed a pair of scissors in her sleeve. She took the scissors out and began to cut her hair. A few strands had already been cut off when everyone rushed toward her and took the scissors from her.

The Matriarch shook with rage when she heard the maid's story. "I have only one maid that I can rely upon, and they want to take her away from me," she said in a trembling voice. She turned to Madame Wang and said, "So you all try to deceive me. Ostensibly you are filial and obedient but you all plot against me in secret. When I have anything good, you ask me for it. Now I have only one maid left, and you are jealous of her because I am kind to her. You want to get her out of the way so you can plot against me."

Madame Wang stood up and listened in silence, as it was not becoming for a daughter-in-law to defend herself when accused by her mother-in-law. Hsueh Yi-ma, of course, could not say anything, as Madame Wang was her sister. Li Huan and the others had left the room as soon as Faith began her recital of the story unfit for maidenly ears. Madame Wang, guiltless as she was, stood and listened in silence.

Quest Spring comprehended Madame Wang's difficult position. She realized that it was not for her to defend herself, nor for Hsueh Yi-ma to defend her sister, nor for Precious Virtue to defend her aunt. It was also not fitting for Li Huan or Phoenix or Pao-yu to speak. This was a time when daughters were needed. But Welcome Spring lacked courage and Compassion Spring was too young. It was for her to speak out. She entered the room and smiled at the Matriarch.

"What does this have to do with Tai-tai?" she said. "Think for a moment, Lao Tai-tai, how could a younger sister-in-law know the affairs of her elder brother-in-law?"

"Of course," the Matriarch smiled, realizing her mistake. "I must be losing my senses with age." She said to Hsueh Yi-ma, "You must not laugh at me, Yi Tai-tai. Your sister is very filial and obedient to me, not like our Ta Tai-tai who knows only her husband. I have been unjust to your good sister."

Hsueh Yi-ma said that perhaps the Matriarch was partial to the wife of her younger son.

"No," said the Matriarch, "I am not partial. I am only speaking the truth. And Pao-yu," turning to her grandson, "why did you not point out my mistake to me and so prevent my scolding your mother unjustly?"

"But how could I defend Mother against Uncle and Aunt? I would like to take the blame but I was afraid that Lao Tai-tai would not believe it."

"That sounds reasonable also," the Matriarch smiled.

"Now kowtow to your mother and ask her not to be angry, to consider the infirmities of my old age, and to forget the injustice for the sake of Pao-yu." He was about to do so when Madame Wang stopped him, saying, "This is absurd, Pao-yu. How can you apologize for Lao Tai-tai?"

Pao-yu rose, understanding that to apologize as he was bid would be to admit that his grandmother was wrong.

"And Feng Ya-tou would not remind me!" the Matriarch said, turning toward Phoenix.

"Well, well," Phoenix said. "I have refrained from scolding Lao Tai-tai, but Lao Tai-tai now tries to find fault with me." At this, the Matriarch laughed as did everyone else.

Just then, Madame Hsing was announced, and Madame Wang went out to meet her. The former had just learned from the maids what had happened, but it was too late to retreat. She went in with Madame Wang and greeted the Matriarch as usual. The latter was silent. Phoenix excused herself and was followed by the others, as they did not want to be present to embarrass Madame Hsing.

"I understand you have been trying to act as matchmaker for your Lao-yeh," the Matriarch said to Madame Hsing when they were alone. "You are indeed a virtuous and obedient wife, but I think you are a bit too obedient. You now have sons and grandsons, yet you are still afraid of him and let him have his way in everything."

"I have often remonstrated with him," Madame Hsing said, "but Lao Tai-tai knows what good that does. I cannot help it——"

"Would you commit murder if he asked you to?" the Matriarch said. She went on to explain how she could not part with her maid and concluded, "You tell your Lao-yeh that I have money here with which he can buy someone he likes. I don't care if it costs ten thousand taels. But I must have this maid to wait on me. If he would let me keep this maid, it would be better than if he came and waited on me himself."

Then turning to one of the attendants, the Matriarch

said, "Ask Yi Tai-tai and others to come back. Why have they all disappeared?"

The others returned, and a game of mahjong was started. As the Matriarch's sight was not good, Faith sat by her and watched her tiles for her. When she saw that the Matriarch needed only a "two of circles" to complete an all-circle hand, she signaled to Phoenix the tile wanted. Phoenix's turn came. She pretended to hesitate and then said, "Yi Tai-tai has the piece I want, but she is trying to hold out. I must play this so that she will have to relinquish the piece I want."

"I am sure that I don't have anything you want," Hsueh Yi-ma said.

"I won't believe it until I have seen your hand," Phoenix said.

"If you find later that I have been holding your piece, you can penalize me," Hsueh Yi-ma said. "In the meantime, please play and do not delay the game."

Phoenix played the "two of circles" and pushed it in front of Hsueh Yi-ma as if she were sure that the latter would take it.

"I do not want it," Hsueh Yi-ma said, "but I am afraid that Lao Tai-tai is going to score the limit with it."

Phoenix made a gesture to recapture the piece, but the Matriarch had laid down her hand and cried, "Too late!"

"Did I not say that I was bound to lose with Lao Tai-tai's spies stationed all around me?" Phoenix said. "But this time it was really my own fault."

"Indeed you have no one else to blame," the Matriarch said, pleased to have scored one of the highest hands possible. "You should slap your own face and ask yourself why you played that, when I have not played a single circle all through the game." Then she said to Hsueh Yi-ma, "I do not care for the money, but it does give me pleasure to win a hand once in a while."

Phoenix was counting out her money. At the Matriarch's words, she stopped and said, "Since Lao Tai-tai plays only for the fun of it, then there is no use of my paying."

Faith, who usually made the tiles for the Matriarch, did not stir. The Matriarch asked her what the trouble was, and the maid said that Phoenix wouldn't pay.

"So she won't pay!" the Matriarch exclaimed. "She will know enough to pay promptly the next time." So saying, she told a maid who was standing by to take the whole string of *cash* in front of Phoenix and put it by her pile.

Phoenix pleaded, "Please give it back to me, and I shall pay according to the points."

"Phoenix is so miserly," Hsueh Yi-ma said. "It is only for fun. She takes a string of *cash* so seriously."

"But," Phoenix said, pointing to the wooden chest in a corner of the room, "look at that. I don't know how much of my money is in there. It is only half an hour since we began, and the coins in the box have been beckoning to mine so hard that my string is pretty nearly all gone. Well, soon I shall have lost all, Lao Tai-tai's good humor will have been restored, and I shall go back to attend to my duties."

Just then, Patience came with another string of money, thinking that Phoenix might not have enough. "Put that money with Lao Tai-tai's pile," she said to her maid, smiling. "It will save the coins in the chest the effort of beckoning to it." The Matriarch laughed and threw the tiles all over the table. She told Faith to go and tear Phoenix's mouth.

Patience put the money down and left after a moment. In the courtyard she met Chia Lien, sent by Chia Sheh to find out what luck Madame Hsing had. Patience advised Chia Lien not to go in, saying, "I would not go in if I were you. Lao Tai-tai was very angry. You would only be knocking your head against a hard nail if you went in. She has just recovered somewhat after Nai-nai took so much trouble to amuse her."

"Since she is no longer angry, I don't think I have anything to worry about," Chia Lien said. "Lao-yeh asked me to come and will be angry with me if he finds out that I did not."

Chia Lien slowed his footsteps as he neared the Matriarch's room. Phoenix caught sight of him and signaled him not to come in and then whispered to Madame Hsing. The latter was afraid to leave immediately. She poured a cup of tea for the Matriarch, hoping to catch her attention and be dismissed. But as the Matriarch turned to take the cup, she caught sight of the retreating Chia Lien.

"Who is that?" she asked.

Realizing that it was impossible to sneak away, Chia Lien edged into the room and said, "I came to inquire if Lao Tai-tai is going to Lai Ta's house so that I can have her sedan ready."

"Why did you not come in instead of sneaking around like a spy?" the Matriarch asked.

Chia Lien smiled ingratiatingly and said, "I was afraid to disturb Lao Tai-tai in her game and was trying to signal my wife to come out so that I could tell her."

"I do not believe that you are in any such hurry over the sedan," the Matriarch said. "You have all the time you need to speak to your wife when she returns. From the way you acted, I think you were trying to spy on me and tell someone about my movements. It annoys me. Since I want to keep your wife a while yet, you can go now and plot with Chao-er's wife against her."

Everyone laughed at the Matriarch's joke. Faith said, "It is Pao-er's wife. Why does Lao Tai-tai drag in Chao-er's wife?"

"I don't care whether it is Chao-er or Pao-er," the Matriarch said. "How would I remember such shameful matters? I cannot help being angry when I think of them. I came into this house as a great-granddaughter-in-law, and after fifty-four years, I myself have great-granddaughters-in-law; but I have never heard of such a thing in all these years. And what are you waiting for now?" Chia Lien withdrew sheepishly at the curt dismissal.

Patience, who was waiting outside to see what happened, said, "Did I not tell you?"

Madame Hsing also came out. Chia Lien said to her,

"It is all because of Lao-yeh that Lao Tai-tai has humiliated us like this."

"You unfilial son," Madame Hsing scolded. "Others would gladly die for their fathers. Now you complain just because Lao Tai-tai said a few words to you. If you do not mind how you behave, Lao-yeh may break your legs one of these days."

Chia Sheh felt keenly the shame and humiliation caused by his own imprudence. He feigned illness and excused himself from his morning and evening inquiries at the Matriarch's apartment. Nevertheless, he bought, for eight hundred taels, a pretty girl of seventeen to take the place of Faith.

CHAPTER TWENTY-SIX

In which the glory of the master is reflected in the prosperity of the servant
And the honor of the profession is vindicated by the actor Liu Hsiang-lien

THE fourteenth soon came around, the day set for the celebration of the appointment of Lai Shang-jung, Lai Ta's son, to a magistracy. The Lais had been stewards of the Yungkuofu for generations and, by this time, they had prospered to such an extent that they were able to purchase an office for the most promising member of the family. Lai Ta's mother, an aged woman who had long since been exempted from service, had persuaded the Matriarch and others to honor her house by their presence.

While the Matriarch and the female members of the Yungkuo and Ningkuo mansions were entertained in the inner apartments, Lai Shang-jung entertained Chia Chen, Chia Lien, Pao-yu, Hsueh Pan, and others in the outer courtyards. The Lais also invited some of their more presentable friends to help entertain their masters. Among them was a Liu Hsiang-lien, a friend of Pao-yu and of the late Chin Chung.

Hsueh Pan had met Liu Hsiang-lien before and had taken a great liking to him. He learned that the youth liked acting and that he had appeared on the amateur stage as a female impersonator. Hsueh Pan hoped that he might corrupt Liu Hsiang-lien, as he had so many other youths, but he was mistaken. Hsiang-lien was of good family but was erratic and unconventional, doing what he pleased and caring little what others said about him. His parents died when he was still a child. He was fond of acting, playing with sword and spear, gambling, and similar pastimes that gay youths indulged in. As he was extremely handsome and agreeable, those who did not know him took him to be of the usual actor type with an actor's morals. He resented the attentions of Hsueh Pan and was about to leave, but Lai Shang-jung told him that Pao-yu had asked him to wait for him. "Be patient a while yet," Lai Shang-jung said. "I will send for Pao Er-yeh now."

Pao-yu had known Liu Hsiang-lien for some time. They were both friends of Chin Chung. On this occasion, Pao-yu wanted to ask Liu Hsiang-lien to look after Chin Chung's tomb and to make regular offerings there, as he was not always free to go himself. When Pao-yu asked why he was leaving the banquet so soon, Liu Hsiang-lien said that Hsueh Pan was annoying him. He also spoke of a long journey. He did not know just where he was going but would let Pao-yu know later if Pao-yu would not betray his whereabouts to others.

He bade Pao-yu good-by and walked toward the gate. There he saw Hsueh Pan asking excitedly who had dared to let that "little Liu person" go. Sparks of fire flew from Liu Hsiang-lien's eyes when he heard Hsueh Pan's insulting words. He would have killed him on the spot if it had not been for the fact that they were both guests at Lai Shang-jung's house. Hsueh Pan was obviously overjoyed to see him. He took his hand and said, "Where are you going, my own brother?"

Liu Hsiang-lien tried to evade him, saying, "I won't be gone long but I must go and attend to something."

"Don't go," Hsueh Pan urged. "Stay a while longer to show that you like your brother Hsueh, who would do anything for you."

Liu Hsiang-lien burned with rage and hatred. A scheme

came to his mind. He took Hsueh Pan aside and said to him, "Are you really eager to be a friend or are you pretending?"

"My good brother," Hsueh Pan said, beaming, "how can you ask such a question? Let me perish right this instant if my heart is not true."

"In that case," Liu Hsiang-lien said, "you come with me, for this is not a convenient place to talk. Come to my place and we will drink all night. Don't bring anyone with you, as I have attendants who will take care of everything."

"Really?" Hsueh Pan asked, hardly believing his ears.

"You seem to doubt one the minute one speaks from his heart," Liu Hsiang-lien said.

"Of course, I believe you," Hsueh Pan said hastily. "But I don't know where you live. How am I to find you if you are to leave the banquet before I do?"

"My place is outside of the Northern Gate," Liu Hsiang-lien said. "I will wait for you on the bridge immediately beyond the gate. But let us return to the banquet now. I will leave first, for we must not let people see us leave together."

At the banquet Hsueh Pan looked admiringly at Liu Hsiang-lien and became more and more pleased with his unexpected good fortune. Without urging, he drank cup after cup until he was more drunk than sober. He followed Liu Hsiang-lien shortly after the latter had slipped away.

Liu Hsiang-lien dismissed his servant and rode alone to the appointed bridge and waited for Hsueh Pan. Presently the latter appeared through the city gate, swaying from side to side on his horse. He passed by without noticing Hsiang-lien. The latter followed, his hatred giving place to amusement at the sight of the awkward Hsueh Pan.

"I knew that you would keep a promise," he said when he saw Hsiang-lien.

"Ride on," Hsiang-lien said. "We must not let anyone see us." He spurred his horse and was followed by Hsueh Pan, who tried his best to hold on to his saddle. They rode on for several li north until they reached a deserted marsh far from any village or temple. Hsiang-lien alighted and bade Hsueh Pan to do likewise.

"Let us take an oath," Hsiang-lien said, "so that whoever changes his heart and betrays the secret will suffer the proper curse."

"Good," Hsueh Pan agreed, as he got down from his horse. He knelt on the ground and said, "If I, Hsueh Pan, should ever change my heart and tell other people, I—"

Suddenly he heard a crash as if an iron hammer had been brought down upon his back. A thousand golden stars seemed to dance before him in a total darkness. He fell to the ground. Hsiang-lien turned him over and struck him in the face until it was red and purple like a fruit stand. He struggled to rise, but Hsiang-lien gave him a push with his foot and down he went again.

"No one was trying to force you into anything," Hsueh Pan said. "If you didn't wish to have me, you could have said so instead of doing this to me." He began cursing Liu Hsiang-lien and calling him names.

"Look at your Liu Ta-yeh and see who he is, you blind son of a clumsy turtle," Liu Hsiang-lien cursed. "And even now you dare insult me! I am not going to kill you, but I shall let you know who I am." He took his whip and began to lay it upon Hsueh Pan. As the latter began to groan, Hsiang-lien taunted him, saying, "I thought you were an iron man who could take it." He dragged his victim through the bushes to the edge of the swamp. "Now do you know who I am?"

Hsueh Pan was stubborn. He groaned but would not say a word. Hsiang-lien threw aside his whip and began pounding his victim with his fist, until Hsueh Pan could bear it no longer.

"I know that you are an honorable person," he said. "It was because I believed the gossip about you."

"Don't drag anyone else into this," Hsiang-lien said, kicking him in the ribs.

"What more do you want me to say," Hsueh Pan moaned, "besides that I am mistaken about you?"

"You will have to be more humble than that," Hsiang-lien said, kicking him again.

Hsueh Pan groaned and began again, "*Hao* Ko-ko—" Hsiang-lien became impatient and struck him repeatedly.

"*Ai-ya!*" Hsueh Pan groaned more piteously. "*Hao* Lao-yeh, forgive this blind idiot who does not know an honorable man when he sees one. I shall respect Lao-yeh and fear Lao-yeh from now on."

Hsiang-lien seemed satisfied with this but said, indicating the foul swamp, "Now drink some of this water."

Hsueh Pan winced. "Have mercy, Lao-yeh," he begged. "How can one drink that?" Then hastily, as Hsiang-lien struck him again, "Stop, stop, I'll drink it. I'll drink it." He reached his head down to the roots of the weeds and drank a mouthful. The foul odor nauseated him, and he vomited, water, wine, and all.

"This foul stuff," Hsiang-lien said, holding his nose and indicating the puddle, "eat this up and I'll let you off."

At this Hsueh Pan balked. He kowtowed and begged but said that he would not eat it even though Hsiang-lien killed him.

"I can't stay any longer," Hsiang-lien said. "This stuff is nauseating me." He gave Hsueh Pan a final kick and rode away.

Hsueh Pan tried to struggle to his feet, but his bruises hurt him at the least exertion. He lay back and cried for help.

Chia Chen, noticing Hsueh Pan's absence, finally sent his son Chia Jung to look for him. Two li beyond the Northern Gate they sighted his horse wandering by itself and, as they drew near the swamp, they heard groans. Hsueh Pan was covered with mud, his face disfigured and bleeding. Chia Jung guessed what must have happened and teased him, saying, "How does it happen that Hsueh Ta-shu has chosen such a place for a rendezvous? Has he been favored by the Dragon King?"

Hsueh Pan's wounds made it impossible for him to ride, and a sedan was hired. Chia Jung at first insisted mockingly on taking him back to the banquet, but Hsueh Pan pleaded with him and was taken home. His mother cried and wept when she saw him and thought of bringing charges against Liu Hsiang-lien. Precious Virtue was more discreet, however, and pointed out to her mother that it would only cause a scandal and expose Hsueh Pan to ridicule among his friends.

After recovering from his wounds, Hsueh Pan left the Capital, partly to give his friends in the Capital time to forget his disgrace and partly because he felt that he ought to do something to redeem his useless life of the past. At first, Hsueh Yi-ma opposed the journey, as she could not trust him by himself, but Precious Virtue encouraged it, saying that it might be a good thing for him. He was accompanied by a manager of one of his stores on what was to be a business journey.

Hsueh Pan's absence made it possible for Precious Virtue to take Lotus into the Takuanyuan to stay with her in the Wistaria Arbor. Her father had taught her to read and write, and now under the tutelage of Black Jade, she soon learned to write verse, for which accomplishment she was accepted by the young ladies as one of themselves.

In the meantime, the Garden was enlivened by the arrival of more young maidens destined to forgather there. There were Li Huan's two cousins, Li Wen and Li Chi, and their widowed mother. There were Hsueh Pao-chin (Precious Harp) and her brother Hsueh Kuo, cousins of Precious Virtue. There was Madame Hsing's elder sister-in-law, with her daughter Hsin Ti-yen (Mountain Wreath). On their way to the Capital from the south they had met and, discovering that they were all related and all bound for the same destination, they had continued the journey together.

The Matriarch, who loved company, was happy at the unexpected visitors and insisted that they must stay with her in the Yungkuofu and the Takuanyuan. The young ladies, too, were happy at the prospect of so many more companions, for the newcomers were beautiful and accomplished maidens. Li Huan, Precious Virtue, and Welcome Spring, who were closely related to the new guests, were, of course, more pleased than the rest.

Precious Harp, more than anyone else, captured the hearts of the Matriarch and others. The Matriarch asked Madame Wang to take her as foster daughter and even considered her as a suitable match for Pao-yu. She asked her age and the hour, day, and month of her birth. Hsueh Yi-ma, guessing the Matriarch's intention, remarked that Precious Harp was already engaged to a family by the name of Mei and had, in fact, come to the Capital in anticipation of her wedding.

Precious Harp lived with Precious Virtue. She and Black Jade soon became fast friends, for she was an exceptionally gifted girl and, having discovered Black Jade's talents, did not hide her preference for her.

Li Huan's two cousins lived with her at the Rice Village, and Mountain Wreath shared the Brocade Chamber with Welcome Spring. Mountain Wreath was unlike Madame Hsing, and all wondered at her refinement. Phoenix took a liking to her and, knowing that the Hsings were not rich, took every opportunity to help her.

It happened also at about this time that River Mist's uncle was appointed to some provincial post, and the family left the Capital. The Matriarch did not want to see her go and arranged with her family to have her stay at the Yungkuofu. The Matriarch offered her an apartment, but River Mist preferred to stay with Precious Virtue. Altogether, there were now living in the Takuanyuan, or closely identified with it, thirteen young people, including Phoenix and Pao-yu. Li Huan was eldest, and next was Phoenix. The others—Welcome Spring, Quest Spring, Compassion Spring, Precious Virtue, Black Jade, River Mist, Li Wen, Li Chi, Precious Harp, and Mountain Wreath—were all about the same age, between fifteen and seventeen, with different birthdays. They themselves often confused their ages and addressed one another incorrectly.

CHAPTER TWENTY-SEVEN

In which capable Quest Spring takes charge of affairs because of Phoenix's illness
And blundering Chao Yi-niang causes humiliation to her own daughter

PHOENIX had been with child for some months but, being of an active nature, she would not relinquish any of the multitudinous duties she had taken upon herself. The New Year season just passed had been a particularly trying one, and despite her condition, Phoenix had not spared herself. The result was a miscarriage shortly after the Lantern Festival. Complications developed, and she was forced to stay in bed. This was no less than a calamity for Phoenix, who loved to lead an active life and to feel the sense of her own importance and indispensability. She fretted under the inactivity and wished that she could get well shortly and attend to things again, but she was not as strong as she thought and did not completely recover until late in the Third Month.

Without Phoenix, Madame Wang felt as helpless as if she had lost her right arm. She tried to take care of the more important affairs herself as best she could but entrusted lesser matters to Li Huan. The latter, however, was known more for her virtues than her abilities and she inevitably spoiled the servants and maids. Madame Wang, therefore, asked Quest Spring to assist her. Later when it became evident that Phoenix's illness would be a long one, she also enlisted the help of Precious Virtue.

The servants were at first secretly glad of this turn of events, for they knew how kind and indulgent Li Huan was. Quest Spring was an unknown quantity, but they did not give much thought to her. She was still an unmarried maiden whose modesty and shyness would probably make her an easy mistress to serve. They were all pleased with the prospect of easier times ahead. After a few days, however, they discovered that they were mistaken about Quest Spring. Her manners were less severe and her tongue less sharp than was true of Phoenix, but in her attention to detail and in her uncanny ability to detect irregularities, she even surpassed Phoenix.

An incident that occurred one day gave Quest Spring an opportunity to show the maids she was not to be trifled with. As usual, she and Li Huan were sitting in the council hall, when Wu Hsin-teng's wife came in to inform them that Chao Kuo-chi, the brother of Chao Yi-niang, had died. "I have reported the matter to Lao Tai-tai," Wu's wife said, "and she said that I should tell Ku-niang."

After this, she stood by quietly and waited for the comment and decision of Quest Spring. Others, too, were waiting in the courtyard to hear what Quest Spring would say. If she disposed of the matter in a fitting way, they would respect her. If not, they would be justified in making light of her judgment. Ordinarily Wu's wife would have reminded Phoenix of what the custom had been in such cases and what might be done in view of the precedents, leaving her to choose from the suggestions what she deemed best. She said nothing to help Quest Spring.

The latter turned to Li Huan and asked what should be done. Li Huan thought for a moment and then said that since Pervading Fragrance received forty taels when her mother died, the same amount might be paid to the Chao family. Wu's wife answered yes and was about to go when Quest Spring stopped her.

"Do not go yet," she said. "Let me ask you a few questions. In Lao Tai-tai's room there are several Lao Yi Tai-tai.[1] Some of them are our own people and some came from the outside. Would you tell me what the custom has been in the case of deaths in the families of those of our own people and those of the outside?"

Wu's wife could not recall the precedents. She evaded the question and answered, smiling, "It does not matter. Ku-niang can use her own judgment. Who will dare to complain that it is too much or too little?"

"That would hardly do," Quest Spring said, smiling but firm. "I would just as soon give a hundred taels. But if it is not done according to the established custom, not only would you people laugh at me, but I would be ashamed to face your Er Nai-nai for whom I am acting."

"In that case," Wu's wife said, "I will go and look up the records, for I cannot recall just what the precedents are."

Quest Spring smiled again, a little sardonically, and said, "You have been entrusted with affairs for years and yet you do not remember? Would you plead forgetfulness to your Er Nai-nai? I thought she was an exacting mistress, but if she tolerated such incompetence, I think she has been too lenient. Now go immediately and bring back the records."

Wu's wife blushed and withdrew in confusion. The servants waiting outside were all open-mouthed with surprise.

The records showed that of the concubines of the late Chia Tai-shan, two were daughters of the family servants and two were from the outside. In the first instance, the amount paid for funeral expenses was twenty-four taels each, and in the second instance, forty. Two others from the outside received a hundred taels and sixty taels respectively, but there were special reasons for the extra amount. Since there was no reason for special consideration in the present case, Quest Spring authorized only twenty-four taels to the family of Chao Kuo-chi, as they were family servants.

[1] Concubines of Pao-yu's late grandfather.

Shortly after Wu's wife left, Chao Yi-niang came in and said in a dissatisfied tone, "Everyone is trampling on my head. I should think that Ku-niang at least would stand up for me." She began to cry as she was speaking.

Quest Spring said, "Who has dared to trample on Yi-niang's head? What does Yi-niang mean? Tell me and I will do what I can to vindicate you."

"It is Ku-niang herself," Chao Yi-niang said.

Quest Spring stood up and said, "What does Yi-niang refer to? I never dreamed of doing such a thing."

Li Huan also stood up and tried to calm Chao Yi-niang.

"I have served Lao-yeh for years," Chao Yi-niang said, "and now you have a brother, too. But it seems that I am not as important as Hsi-jen. It is a humiliation not only to me, but to Ku-niang herself."

"Is that then Yi-niang's complaint?" Quest Spring said, smiling. She took the records and showed them to Chao Yi-niang, saying, "You see I have not dared to break the precedents that have been handed down by the ancestors. If Huan-er should some day take a maid of outside parents, her people will get as much as Hsi-jen's. This is all a matter of custom; it has nothing to do with honor or humiliation. Chao Kuo-chi is Tai-tai's servant. What difference does it make to me if his family received a thousand from Tai-tai or nothing at all? And I might advise Yi-niang to retire and rest herself and not let such things trouble her. Tai-tai is very kind to me, but on more than one occasion I have been humiliated and made unhappy by Yi-niang. If I were a boy, I would have left this house and vindicated myself through some accomplishment. Unfortunately I am only a girl and am bound to the inner apartments. Tai-tai has been thoughtful enough to understand my position and has honored me by asking me to take charge of things. Now Yi-niang has come to make things difficult for me. If Tai-tai should learn of this and, not wishing to see me placed in a difficult position, should relieve me of my duties, it would be a real disgrace to me as well as to Yi-niang."

Quest Spring began to weep, too, as she spoke. Chao Yi-niang could not think of anything to say. So she touched upon the delicate theme. "Ku-niang should help us since she has so much influence with Tai-tai. You seem to have forgotten us in your eagerness to curry favor with Tai-tai."

"No," Quest Spring said, "I have not forgotten. But I do not see why I should take these things upon my shoulders. Masters all reward their faithful and deserving servants. They do not need the good offices of others."

Li Huan tried to make peace between Quest Spring and her natural mother. She said, "Yi-niang, do not be angry. I am sure that Ku-niang would like to help you, but she cannot say so openly."

"Do not be ridiculous, Sao-sao," Quest Spring replied. "Who ever heard of a mistress who got herself involved in the affairs of servants? What are their affairs to me?"

Chao Yi-niang resented the formal tone of her daughter. She said, "I did not ask you to get mixed with the affairs of other servants. But you are now in charge of things. If you say one it is one, and if you say two it is two. For your uncle's funeral allowance, I am sure Tai-tai would not protest if you gave an extra twenty or thirty taels. Tai-tai is kind and generous, but you seem to be otherwise. Why should Ku-niang be so thrifty? It is not your own money. I have always hoped you would remember the family of Chao, even after you married. But it seems that you have forgotten your nest before you have even grown feathers."

Quest Spring's face was white with anger. She said, weeping, "Who is my uncle? My uncle is the man who has just been appointed military inspector of the Nine Provinces. Where does this other uncle you mention come from? I have been considerate, but it has only brought me unheard-of and unknown relatives. If what you say is true, why did Chao Kuo-chi rise and stand reverently whenever Huan-er went out and then follow him to school, instead of acting like an uncle? Yi-niang, do not be absurd. Who does not know that you gave me birth? What is the use of proclaiming this obvious fact every time you have a chance? You say that I am humiliating you, but it is evident that you are the one who is continually insulting and humiliating me."

Li Huan tried to pacify Chao Yi-niang, but the latter kept on grumbling and did not stop until Patience came in with a message from Phoenix. "Er Nai-nai thought that Ta Nai-nai and San Ku-niang might not know what the usual allowance would be in connection with the death of Chao Yi-niang's brother," Patience said. "She said that the rule is twenty-four taels, but in this case, San Ku-niang may authorize a larger amount if she wishes."

"Why make an exception in this case?" Quest Spring asked. "Do we have here a man who took twenty-four months to be born or who saved his master's life, as Chiao Ta in the other mansion did? How clever your Nai-nai is, trying to put the responsibility of breaking the rules on me and at the same time getting for herself the reputation of generosity! Tell your Nai-nai that I would not dare assume this responsibility. If she wants to be generous, she will have to wait until she is back in charge again."

Patience had sensed that something was wrong when she came in; now she guessed the cause. She listened in respectful silence as Quest Spring spoke, though ordinarily she was more like a sister and companion than a servant to members of the Yungkuofu of Pao-yu's generation.

At this point, Precious Virtue came in from Madame Wang's and joined Quest Spring and Li Huan. Some maid-of-all-work now brought a basin of water for Quest Spring to wash her tear-stained face. As she bent over the basin, another servant came in and, without waiting for her to finish, began speaking. "The school has sent someone for the allowance for Huan-yeh and Lan-ko," she said.

"What's your hurry?" Patience spoke to her sharply. "Can't you see that Ku-niang is busy? Would you dare be so lax with Er Nai-nai? Ku-niang may be lenient, but don't blame me if Er Nai-nai hears about this and gives you what you deserve for your lack of manners."

"How stupid of me!" the servant said, smiling ingratiatingly as she withdrew.

"If you had come a moment earlier," Quest Spring said to Patience as she powdered her face, "you would have seen something even more ridiculous. It was Wu Chieh-chieh. Experienced as she is, she came for instructions without first looking into the precedents involved in the case. I did not know that your Nai-nai was so patient with carelessness and incompetence."

"She wouldn't tolerate it," Patience said. "They are only taking advantage of Ta Nai-nai and Ku-niang." Then turning toward the door, she spoke loud enough for the servants waiting outside to hear, "Go on and play your tricks all you want to but wait and see what happens to you when Er Nai-nai gets well."

Quest Spring called in the servant who had come for the school allowance and asked, "What is this annual allowance for?"

"It's for refreshments and stationery," the woman answered. "Each is allowed eight taels a year."

"Why do they need it when they already have their monthly allowance?" Quest Spring remarked and ordered the expense abolished. Then turning to Patience, "You go back and tell your Nai-nai what I have done. I do not see why this expense should be necessary."

Quest Spring also introduced a number of other measures calculated to reduce expenses and prevent irregularities on the part of the stewards in charge of purchases. One of these was to put the flower beds, the shrubs and trees, the lotus pond, the bamboo groves, and other productive resources of the Takuanyuan under the supervision of various qualified and deserving servants. They were charged with keeping things in good condition and providing the family with a certain portion of the produce according to season. Many of the servants would have liked to make cash bids to secure the concessions (for the Takuanyuan was large, and there was a good profit to be realized from selling the flowers, bamboo shoots, lotus roots, apples, and so on), but Quest Spring appointed only the older maidservants with good records. She waived the money that they offered but suggested that they distribute part of their profits to their colleagues in the Garden, so that the latter would not be jealous and try to damage the products through spite.

Phoenix was pleased when she heard of the reforms introduced by Quest Spring. She said to Patience, "I have always said that our San Ku-niang is an excellent assistant. She is doing well. But how unfortunate that she was not born of Tai-tai!"

"What difference should that make?" Patience asked. "Who dares to look down upon her? Is she not a daughter of Lao-yeh?"

"That is true, theoretically," Phoenix answered. "And practically she is no different from the other Ku-niang as long as she remains in our house. But she will marry eventually. There are people who prefer the daughters of the first wife to those of concubines. This is a very silly notion, and someone is going to lose an excellent daughter-in-law because of it. But the notion persists, nevertheless."

CHAPTER TWENTY-EIGHT

In which Purple Cuckoo shows how concerned she is over the future of her mistress
And Pao-yu gives new evidence that he cannot live without Black Jade

ONE day Pao-yu went to the Bamboo Retreat to see Black Jade. She was taking a nap and, not wishing to disturb her, he joined Purple Cuckoo, who was sitting on the balustrade sewing.

"Was her cough better last night?" he asked.

"A little better," the maid answered.

"*Amitofo!* I wish she would get well once and for all."

"It is news indeed when you invoke the name of Buddha," Purple Cuckoo smiled. She was wearing an ink-black silk coat padded with a thin layer of cotton and a green satin vest.

Pao-yu felt her clothes and said, "You should not sit in the wind so lightly dressed. The weather is very uncertain. It will add to my anxiety if you also get sick."

Purple Cuckoo pulled herself away and said distantly, "From now on, let us talk all we want to, but please do not touch me. One grows older every year. There are people who love to gossip. We must not act as if we were still children. Ku-niang has often told us not to talk to you. Don't you see that she herself is trying to keep as far away from you as possible?" So saying, she got up and walked away.

Pao-yu was hurt. He stood a while staring at the bamboo grove and then sat down on a rock, his tears beginning to flow. After about the space of a meal, Snow Duck saw him on returning from an errand and asked why he was sitting there like a stone.

"What do you want to speak to me for?" Pao-yu said. "Are you not also a girl? Wouldn't they gossip if they saw us? Go away before anyone sees you."

Snow Duck assumed that he had quarreled with Black Jade again. She left him and told Purple Cuckoo what she saw. "Who has offended him again?" she asked. "He is sitting there weeping all by himself."

Purple Cuckoo hurried to him. "I was only thinking of the best for all of us," she said. "You must not take offense and sit here in the wind. What if you should catch cold?"

"I did not take offense," Pao-yu replied. "What you said was perfectly true. But if everyone thinks and talks the way you do, then it won't be long before no one will speak to me at all. That is why I feel sad." As Purple Cuckoo sat down beside him, he continued, "Just a little while ago, you left me abruptly when I was only standing opposite you. Now you sit right beside me! Are you not afraid that people will gossip?"

"You seem to have forgotten all about it," Purple Cuckoo said, ignoring Pao-yu's remark. "A few days ago, you and our Ku-niang were talking when you were interrupted by Chao Yi-niang. I heard you say something about bird's nest——"

"Oh, yes," Pao-yu said. "I was thinking that we ought not impose too much upon Pao Chieh-chieh, especially since Lin Mei-mei must take bird's nest every day. So I was going to tell her that I would speak to Lao Tai-tai about it. I have already done so. I understand that she has been sending over one ounce every day, so I have said nothing more about it."

"So that's the reason. Thank you very much. We have

been wondering how it happened that Lao Tai-tai suddenly remembered us."

"Well," Pao-yu said, "if she would only take it every day, maybe she would get well after two or three years."

"Yes, but where would the money for this come from next year when she returns home?"

Pao-yu was startled. "What home?" he asked.

"Soochow, of course. Ku-niang is going back to Soochow."

"Nonsense," Pao-yu said. "Although Soochow is her native place, her parents are no longer living. That is why she came to live with us in the first place. Whom is she going back to? This proves that you are talking nonsense about returning to Soochow."

"You think too little of others," Purple Cuckoo said, smiling coldly. "Do you think that no one but you has any relatives? Lao Tai-tai sent for her because Lao Tai-tai wanted to have her near. But soon she will be of marriageable age, and Lao Tai-tai will send her back to Soochow to be married. And if Lao Tai-tai did not do so, the Lins would come to get her, for it would be very improper to have her stay all her life with relatives. Ku-niang was telling me the other evening that you are to return everything that she gave you. She has all your things together and will return them to you."

Pao-yu was thunderstruck. Purple Cuckoo waited for him to say something, but no words came. She was about to speak again, when Bright Design came to fetch him. Back in his own apartment he remained silent, but drops of perspiration now covered his brow. Pervading Fragrance was frightened, but what alarmed her most was Pao-yu's stony stare and his apparent unawareness. He would lie down when a pillow was handed him, would sit up if pulled, and drink tea if it were brought to him, but he did all this like an automaton.

Pervading Fragrance and the other maids did not know what to do. They did not want to report to the Matriarch without being sure of the gravity of Pao-yu's strange behavior. So Li Ma-ma was sent for. She looked at Pao-yu, felt his pulse, pinched his cheeks with her nails, but he seemed to feel nothing. Thereupon, Li Ma-ma uttered one heartbreaking *Ai-ya!* and burst out crying, declaring that she had nursed Pao-yu in vain. Pervading Fragrance was frightened and thought the world must be coming to an end. She, too, began to cry. She asked Bright Design where she had found Pao-yu, under what circumstances, and to whom he was speaking. She flew to the Bamboo Retreat when Bright Design told her that he was with Purple Cuckoo.

Purple Cuckoo was giving Black Jade her medicine.

"What did you say to Pao-yu?" Pervading Fragrance asked her. "You can go and tell Lao Tai-tai that I am through!" She sat down in a chair unceremoniously, contrary to her usual rectitude. Black Jade was astonished at Pervading Fragrance's strange conduct. "What has happened?" she asked.

"I don't know what her ladyship told the simpleton," Pervading Fragrance said vehemently, "but his eyes have become stony, his hands and feet cold. He does not speak and he feels no pain when he is pinched. A greater part of him is dead already. Even Li Ma-ma says that there is no hope. Everyone was crying when I left. He may be dead now for all I know."

At this, Black Jade threw up all the medicine she had just taken and much more besides. She coughed until it seemed that her lungs would burst; her face was flushed and her hair disheveled. Purple Cuckoo hurried to her and began to pound her back to relieve her, but Black Jade pushed her away, saying, "Don't pound my back. I don't want to trouble you. Go get a rope and strangle me. It will suit your purpose better."

"I did not say anything," Purple Cuckoo said. "I only said a few words to him in jest, but it seems he took them to heart."

"Don't you know he is a simpleton and that he takes everything seriously?" Pervading Fragrance said.

"What did you say to him?" Black Jade asked. "Go to

him and explain that it was only a joke. Maybe it will bring him back."

The Matriarch, Madame Wang, and others were all in the Peony Court when Pervading Fragrance returned with Purple Cuckoo. The Matriarch's eyes flashed when she saw the latter. "What did you say to him, you little wretch?" she asked sternly.

Pao-yu cried out at the sight of Purple Cuckoo. Everyone was relieved, for it was the first sound he had uttered since his attack. The Matriarch thought Purple Cuckoo had offended him and told her to apologize. But Pao-yu took Purple Cuckoo's hands and said, "If you go, you must take me with you." No one understood what he meant until the maid explained that she had told him Black Jade was going back to Soochow.

"You have always been a discreet child," the Matriarch said to Purple Cuckoo. "I would have expected you to know better than to say such a thing to him."

As she was speaking, Lin Chih-hsiao's wife and others came to inquire after Pao-yu. The Matriarch was pleased with their thoughtfulness and bade them come in and see Pao-yu. But as soon as he heard the name "Lin," he became frantic again. "Help! help!" he shouted. "The Lins have come to get Lin Mei-mei!" The Matriarch assured him that the Lins had all died and this was not a Lin related to Black Jade.

"I don't care whether they are related or not," Pao-yu said. "No one but Lin Mei-mei should have the name Lin."

"All right," the Matriarch said. "There are no Lins here now. They have all been thrown out." She whispered to the attendants not to mention the name again and to tell Lin Chih-hsiao's wife not to come in. The attendants suppressed their laughter and obeyed. Then Pao-yu noticed a toy ship on the shelf of antiques. "Look!" he shouted, pointing to the ship. "Look! There is the ship that has come to get them! Give it to me." He tucked the toy under the covers and said that now they could not leave. He still held onto Purple Cuckoo.

After taking some soothing medicine prescribed by the doctor, Pao-yu improved rapidly. By the next day, he had recovered his senses. However, he now pretended to be still slightly unsettled in his mind, so that he could keep Purple Cuckoo at his bedside.

"Why did you try to frighten me?" he asked her, when they were alone.

"I was only joking with you," the maid said.

"But it sounded so plausible. How could it be just a joke?"

"I really made it all up," the maid answered. "The Lins are not a large family. What Lins there are left are all very distantly related to Ku-niang's family and they are scattered all over the different provinces. Even if they came to get us, Lao Tai-tai probably would not let us go."

"Even if Lao Tai-tai would let you go, I wouldn't."

"You wouldn't?" Purple Cuckoo said. "That is all flattery, I am afraid. You are growing up and are already engaged. After you get me married off in two or three years, you will have forgotten everything."

"Who is engaged?" Pao-yu asked. "And to whom?"

"I hear that Lao Tai-tai has engaged Chin Ku-niang [Precious Harp] for you," Purple Cuckoo said. "Lao Tai-tai would not be so good to her if it weren't for that."

Pao-yu was relieved and said, "They say I am a simpleton, but you are worse than I am. Don't you know that she is already engaged to the Mei family? They were just joking about it. And did you think that I would consent to it if it were true? Have you forgotten the many scenes we have had because of this? I wish," he said earnestly, "I wish I could take out my heart and show it to you. Then I would gladly die, be turned to ashes and smoke, and be dissipated by the wind."

Purple Cuckoo put her hand to his mouth and said, "Don't get excited. It is because of my anxiety that I tested you like this."

"What anxiety?" Pao-yu asked.

"You know that I am not originally Lin Ku-niang's maid.

I was like Yuan-yang and Hsi-jen. But since Lao Tai-tai gave me to Lin Ku-niang, I have become very much attached to her. She is very good to me, too, and treats me better than the maid that she brought from Soochow. We are together all the time, and I cannot bear the thought of leaving her. I was afraid that the time would come when she would have to leave. Then what would I do? If I did not go with her, it would mean that all these years would come to nothing. If I went with her, I would be separated from my own people. So I tried to find out how you felt. I did not think you would take it so hard."

"You are a simpleton indeed," Pao-yu said, "to worry about this. Rest your heart. Let me say this: if we live we shall live together, and if we die we shall turn to ashes and smoke together."

Purple Cuckoo grew thoughtful but she was interrupted by the arrival of Chia Huan and Chia Lan, who had come to inquire after Pao-yu.

Purple Cuckoo said to Pao-yu, "I ought to go back to the other one and see how she is today. You do not need me now."

"I was thinking about that myself last night," Pao-yu said, "but forgot about it today. You can go back to her now."

Because of what happened to Pao-yu, Black Jade had suffered a relapse and had shed a good many tears. She was relieved when Purple Cuckoo returned and told her that Pao-yu had recovered. At night after they had gone to bed, the maid said to her, "Pao-yu's heart is loyal. He simply went out of his mind when he heard that we were going away!" Black Jade did not answer, and the maid went on, half to herself, "You two would make a perfect match. You were brought up together and know each other's disposition."

"Are you not tired after these last few days?" Black Jade said, as if disgusted. "Why don't you go to sleep instead of chewing maggots?"

Purple Cuckoo went on, however, remarking that it was

advisable for Black Jade to keep "the most important thing in life" constantly in mind, and that it should be brought about before the Matriarch died. "Don't you know," she said, "the proverb that says that it is easier to get ten thousand ounces of gold than a real understanding heart?"

"This maid has gone mad," Black Jade said. "How could you change so much in a few days? I shall tell Lao Tai-tai that I no longer dare to keep you."

"I am only saying this for the sake of Ku-niang," Purple Cuckoo said, a little injured. She turned around and went to sleep. But Black Jade stayed awake, thinking about what her loyal maid had told her and crying most of the night.

CHAPTER TWENTY-NINE

In which Chia Lien secretly marries Yu Er-chieh as his concubine
And San-chieh openly demands Liu Hsiang-lien for her husband

ONE day shortly after the preceding events, word was received from the Taoist temple where Chia Ging had been living that he had died of an overdose of an elixir that he had prepared himself. Chia Gen was immediately sent for, but as he would not be able to return for ten days or half a month, Yu-shih did what she could with the funeral arrangements. She also asked her stepmother, Yu Lao-niang,[1] to come and help her with the affairs of the inner apartments, since Phoenix was still indisposed and unable to take charge as she did at the time of Chin-shih's death.

By a previous marriage Yu Lao-niang had two daughters known as Er-chieh and San-chieh.[2] They were both quite beautiful but very different in character, for while the first was pliable and complaisant, the second was stubborn and strong-willed. They, with their mother, were frequent visitors at the Ningkuofu, and there was gossip about their relationships with Chia Gen and Chia Jung. Chia Lien had heard about them and often envied Chia Gen and his

1 "Lao-niang" means "maternal grandmother."
2 "Second sister" and "third sister," respectively, Yu-shih being the first.

son. The funeral gave him the opportunity to meet them. He soon found out that Er-chieh was the more approachable of the two and decided to concentrate his attentions on her. He would find excuses to call on Yu Lao-niang and thus manage to exchange glances and sometimes a few whispered words with her.

Chia Lien's interest in Er-chieh was not lost on Chia Jung. One day while the two were riding together on an errand, Chia Lien spoke glowingly of Er-chieh, of her beauty and sweetness, of her dignified demeanor and gentle speech. "Everything about her commands love and respect," he concluded. "Everyone speaks well of your Shen-shen,[3] but in my opinion, she doesn't begin to measure up to your Er-yi."[4]

Thereupon, Chia Jung said, "Since Shu-shu likes her so much, how about letting me be your matchmaker and get her for your second chamber?"

"Are you serious or only joking?" Chia Lien asked, smiling broadly.

"Of course I am serious."

"That would be wonderful," Chia Lien said. "But I am afraid that your Shen-shen would not consent to it. Then your Lao-niang may not be willing. Still another thing is that I understand she is already engaged."

"The engagement doesn't mean anything," Chia Jung said. "She was promised to a Chang family years ago, one of those prenatal engagements. Since then, the Chang family has declined, and my Lao-niang has remarried. It is now more than ten years since the Changs have been heard from. My Lao-niang has often regretted the engagement and expressed the wish to break it off. It is only a matter of finding a more suitable match. The Chang family, being very poor now, can easily be bought off. As to my Lao-

[3] "Wife of a paternal uncle younger than one's father."

[4] "Second maternal aunt." It is hoped that readers will agree that in such contexts as this the use of Chinese forms of address and of reference are justifiable. The alternatives would be "your Aunt Phoenix" and "your Aunt Er-chieh."

niang, I am sure that she would be more than willing. The same thing is true of my father. The only difficulty is, of course, that Shen-shen may object."

Chia Lien was so pleased with the prospect that he did nothing but grin. After a while, Chia Jung continued, "If Shu-shu has the courage, I am sure things can be arranged. It would involve some extra expense, that's all." When asked to elaborate, he said, "Shu-shu need not say anything to Shen-shen. I shall speak to my father and my Lao-niang. Once their consent is secured, Shu-shu can buy a house near by, hire a few maids and servants, and then arrange for a quiet wedding. If Shu-shu takes care to get only maids and servants whom he can trust, the secret can be kept indefinitely from the family. Shen-shen will be the last to know in any case. If after six months or a year, the secret should get out, Shu-shu can always say that he has done this because he wants to insure a male heir. Shen-shen will have to accept the situation once the rice is cooked."

Desire makes one blind, as the saying goes. Chia Lien was so dazzled by the prospects held out by Chia Jung that he failed completely to see the difficulties in the way. He forgot for the moment how Phoenix was all eyes and ears, how impossible it was to keep anything from her, and how she always managed to have things her way. He forgot that there was a period of state mourning to be observed as well as that for his own uncle. He forgot that it was illegal to take a concubine without the knowledge and consent of one's wife. Nor did he stop to question Chia Jung's motives, which were far from disinterested. For Chia Jung, too, had designs on Er-chieh and he knew his father's feelings about her. He could not hope to gain his ends as long as he could see her only in the Ningkuofu, but if Chia Lien were to marry her and keep her in a secret nest, he would have a better chance, since Chia Lien would have to spend most of his time in the Yungkuofu with Phoenix.

Chia Lien readily consented to Chia Jung's scheme. Things went off as Chia Jung had expected; Yu Lao-niang gave her consent all too eagerly, and Chia Gen saw no objections. Yu-shih had her misgivings but she was used to giving in to her husband's wishes and so did not press the point. As for Chang Hua, Er-chieh's betrothed, he was in no position to resist the pressure that was brought upon him.

Chia Lien then bought a house in a back street about two li from the Yungkuofu and had it completely furnished. He also bought two bondmaids and hired two older servants for the house, for he was afraid that it might arouse speculation if he assigned servants from the Yungkuofu. When all was ready, Yu Lao-niang and San-chieh were first installed in the new house, and then on the first auspicious day, Er-chieh was brought over from the Ningkuofu in a sedan, and the wedding ceremony was secretly performed.

Chia Lien spent as much time as he could with his new wife. He always managed to give some excuse to Phoenix for his absences. He did his best to please Er-chieh. He bade the servants to address her as if she were his chief spouse, confided to her the affairs of the Yungkuofu, told her of Phoenix's illness, and promised to make her his proper wife in the event of the former's death.

Thus two months went by. Chia Ging's funeral was now over, and one day Chia Gen decided to call on Yu Lao-niang and thus have an opportunity to see San-chieh. This he did that evening, after having ascertained that Chia Lien was not there. At first, he was entertained by Yu Lao-niang and the two sisters, but later, Er-chieh excused herself and went back to her own room, for she was afraid that Chia Lien might return unexpectedly and she wished to avoid embarrassment.

After a while, Chia Lien did return. When informed by the servants that Chia Gen was at the house, he only smiled and said nothing. He went to Er-chieh's room and chatted with her as if there was nothing unusual in the air. Er-chieh, however, felt constrained to speak of the situation. So when the amorous Chia Lien fondled her and declared that she was far superior in beauty to Phoenix, she said, "You are being very kind. But even if I were more beautiful than she, you will have to admit that I am at a disadvantage because of my past."

"What past? I do not understand what you mean," Chia Lien said.

"There is no use pretending that you do not know," Er-chieh said. "I am grateful to you for overlooking it. What has been done cannot be undone, and I feel that I can depend on you. But what about my sister? Things cannot go on as they are."

"You can most certainly depend on me," Chia Lien assured her. "I am not the kind that is jealous of the past and I am sure that since you are now mine, Gen Ta-ko will give me no cause to be jealous in the future. As for your sister, I propose that we bring her and Ta-ko together. Then he can come here without any feeling of embarrassment. What do you think?"

"You mean well, of course, but I am afraid it will not do," Er-chieh answered. "In the first place, you never know how my sister will react. Then, you mustn't forget that Ta-yeh is married to our eldest sister."

"There is no harm in trying," Chia Lien said; he had been drinking and felt no inhibitions. "I'll go now and see what I can do."

Chia Gen was obviously uneasy at Chia Lien's sudden appearance, but the latter insisted that his dear brother should feel free to come, that he owed his happiness to him, and that if Chia Gen should act otherwise, he would himself feel obliged to foreswear the place. Having thus put Chia Gen at his ease, he poured two cups of wine, gave one to Chia Gen and offered the other to San-chieh, saying, "Drink these cups of double happiness, Ta-ko and San Mei-mei, so that we can congratulate you."

At this, San-chieh jumped up and cried, shaking her finger at Chia Lien, "I will have none of your impudence. It is best not to pierce the screen of a shadow show. You are very much mistaken if you think you can treat us like two courtesans just because you have money. You have, with your honeyed words and false promises, tricked my sister into compromising herself, getting herself into a situation where she cannot openly face the world because of that jealous shrew of yours. But you cannot deceive me. If you both behave yourselves, well and good. If not, I'll show you what I am capable of. I'll make life miserable for you both and, if necessary, match my life against your much-vaunted Feng Nai-nai. You want me to drink? I shall do so gladly, for it is nothing to me."

Thereupon, she poured out a cup herself, drank half of it, and, pulling Chia Lien toward her, she offered the rest to him, saying, "I have never let your brother drink from my cup but I'll let you have the pleasure."

This outburst and unmaidenly conduct was so totally unexpected that Chia Lien and Chia Gen were completely taken aback and did not know what to do. They tried to escape from the scene, but San-chieh would not let them. She drank cup after cup and heaped on them more abuse, torrent after torrent. Then finally tiring of it, she left them and went back to her own room.

After this, she made things rather uncomfortable for Chia Lien and Chia Gen. She made all kinds of demands on them and complained about everything. Upon the slightest provocation she would send for Chia Lien, Chia Gen, and sometimes Chia Jung and berate them, calling them impostors and cheats and other opprobrious names.

This went on for some time until Chia Gen realized that San-chieh, though beautiful as a rose, was too prickly for him. He finally gave up hope of ever getting her for himself. He told Chia Lien to marry her off as soon as he could. The latter consulted Er-chieh and decided that they would speak seriously to San-chieh.

San-chieh guessed their intention. She wept touchingly and said to Er-chieh, "I know that Chieh-chieh has something of importance to say to me. I know, too, that things cannot go on like this. Chieh-chieh has now a home, and so has Mother. It is their intention that I, too, should find a home. It is true that a girl must marry some time or other, but it is the most important event in her life and must not be entered upon without careful consideration. I have acted in a very unmaidenly manner because I found it necessary to protect myself by this subterfuge. Even now, I cannot assume false modesty. I must speak plainly: unless I can be betrothed to the man I really want, I would rather remain unmarried all my life."

Chia Lien said, "It shall be as you wish. Just name your man and we will try to get him for you."

"There is no need to name him," San-chieh said. "Chieh-chieh knows whom I mean."

"Who is this man then?" Chia Lien asked his second wife, but she could not think of the man San-chieh had in mind.

Just then, one of Chia Lien's confidential servants came in and told him that Chia Sheh wanted him immediately. So he hurried off, without learning the name of San-chieh's choice.

The next day when he returned, Er-chieh said to him, "You need not worry yourself about this matter. My sister is a stubborn girl. She has already made her choice, and nothing will ever make her change her mind. As the man happens to be away, you might as well put the matter out of your mind and wait until he comes back."

"Who is this man?" Chia Lien asked. "I would very much like to see what he is like."

"It is a long story," Er-chieh answered. "Five years ago at the birthday of my maternal grandmother, a theater party was given at the house by amateurs. Among the actors was a female impersonator by the name of Liu Hsiang-lien. It seems she fell in love with him, though she never had a chance to speak to him."

"Is it he?" Chia Lien exclaimed. "I should say that she has good taste. I know him. He is very handsome but he has never shown any interest in women. He is a good friend of Pao-yu, who can perhaps tell us where he is if anyone can. Some time ago, he gave a thrashing to Hsueh Lao-ta and left the city because he felt embarrassed to see us. His whereabouts are uncertain; it may be years before he is found."

"Then it will have to be years," Er-chieh said. "There is no thwarting that girl of ours. It must be as she says."

San-chieh entered and said, "Brother-in-law must know once for all what sort of a person I am. I am not one of those who say one thing and mean another. I never change my mind once it is made up. I shall marry no one except Liu Hsiang-lien. I shall wait for him all my life if necessary." Then she took a jade hairpin and broke it in two, saying, "If I do not mean what I say, let me be like this pin."

Chia Lien made inquiries but failed to find any lead to Liu Hsiang-lien's whereabouts. In the meantime, San-chieh underwent a complete change. She became quiet and maidenly in her demeanor and gave up rouge and powder and gay clothes. True to her word, she was going to wait for the man of her choice all her life if necessary.

CHAPTER THIRTY

In which San-chieh gives her life to prove her true love
And Hsiang-lien abjures the Red Dust because of his remorse

A FEW days later, Chia Lien set out for Ping-an-chow on a mission for his father. Three days out of the Capital, he encountered a caravan of travelers and found to his surprise Hsueh Pan and Liu Hsiang-lien among them. Greetings over, they repaired to an inn, and there Chia Lien said to them, "After the quarrel between you two, we tried to bring you together and effect a reconciliation but we were unable to do so because Brother Liu left the city soon after that. I am glad to see that you have made peace without us. How did it happen?"

"It was owing to a very unusual circumstance," Hsueh Pan answered. "I went with one of my managers to Feng-tien to buy merchandise. On our return trip, we were attacked by bandits, and just as we were having the worst of the fight, Brother Liu appeared, drove away the bandits, and saved our lives. He would not take anything for his help, so we became sworn brothers and have been traveling together. He has an aunt living not far from here. He is going to visit her for a while and then join me at the Capital. I am to find a house for him as soon as I get there, for he plans to get married and settle down."

"I am glad to hear all this," Chia Lien said. "I wish I had known it before; it would have saved me a lot of unnecessary worry. And speaking of marriage, I think I have exactly the right person for Brother Liu." Then he went on and told his friends about his own marriage to Er-chieh and proposed that Liu Hsiang-lien marry San-chieh. He said nothing, of course, of the fact that San-chieh had chosen him herself.

Hsueh Pan was delighted with the proposal and urged Liu Hsiang-lien to agree to it. The actor said, "I always wanted to find a really beautiful girl myself but I can hardly refuse the good offices of you two."

"You don't have to comply for our sakes," Chia Lien said. "There is no use of my boasting about my sister-in-law, but I am sure that when you see her you will thank me and agree with me that she has unmatched beauty."

Hsiang-lien was overjoyed by this assurance. He said, "I shall be back at the Capital in less than a month. How about arranging for a formal engagement then?"

"Let's make it definite now," Chia Lien said. "I have no doubt you will keep your word, but you are a man of uncertain movements. If you should suddenly decide to go off on one of your long journeys, it may be years before we find you again. You can't keep a girl in suspense like that. So I suggest that you make it definite by giving me a token of some kind."

Hsiang-lien said, "You can depend on my word. But I come from a poor family and am, moreover, away from home. How am I to manage a suitable present?"

Hsueh Pan offered to help, but Chia Lien said, "I do not mean the usual present of jewels and gold and silver. What I have in mind is something from Brother Hsiang-lien's person. It does not have to be anything valuable."

"In that case, I'll give you this for a token," Hsiang-lien said, unbuckling the sword he was carrying and handing it to Chia Lien. "It has been in my family for generations, and I have never parted with it."

Thus, the engagement between Liu Hsiang-lien and San-chieh was sealed, and the travelers went on their separate ways.

On his return to the Capital, Chia Lien went straight to Er-chieh and told her and San-chieh of his meeting with Liu Hsiang-lien and the engagement. He gave San-chieh the sword, which she took and found, upon inspection, to consist of a pair in the same sheath. On one sword was engraved the characters "yuan" and on the other, "yang," which together make up the name of the mandarin duck, the symbol of conjugal happiness. San-chieh was overjoyed. She took the sword to her room, hung it on the wall, and gazed at it as she congratulated herself that she was at last to get the man of her own choice.

In the Eighth Month, Hsiang-lien arrived at the Capital. Soon after that, he went to see Pao-yu. In the course of their conversation, he asked about Chia Lien's secret marriage.

"I know little about it," Pao-yu said. "I only heard about it from Ming-yen. By the way, Ming-yen told me that Brother Lien was asking about you before he left. I wonder why?"

Hsiang-lien told him, whereupon Pao-yu heartily congratulated him, saying, "She has rare beauty, a most worthy match for you."

Nevertheless, Hsiang-lien seemed troubled. He said, "What I cannot understand is why they should choose me. Surely, if she is as beautiful as you say, they should be able to arrange a match for her with a family much richer and better connected than mine. Moreover, Brother Lien is not an especially close friend of mine. It seems strange that he should seek me out, to say nothing of the fact that it is most unusual for the girl's family to take the initiative. I have been having my misgivings about that matter and regretting the fact that I gave my sword as a token. I thought I would speak to you and find out more about the girl and her family."

"Why do you let yourself be troubled?" Pao-yu said.

"You said that you wanted a beautiful maiden. You have her now. What else should trouble you?"

"You must know something about the family, since you vouch for the girl's beauty," Hsiang-lien said.

"Of course I know them. They are stepsisters of Gen Ta-sao. I saw them at the funeral."

Liu Hsiang-lien stamped his foot and said, "I do not like this. This engagement will never do. In that East Mansion of yours the only clean and decent things are perhaps the pair of lions in front of the gate. I have no wish to be made a cuckold."

Pao-yu winced, and Liu Hsiang-lien said hastily, "Forgive me. I am agitated and did not know what I was saying. You must tell me frankly what her character is like."

Pao-yu forced a smile and said, "If you know things so well, what is the use of asking me? Maybe I, too, am not innocent."

"Please do not take it to heart," Hsiang-lien said, bowing low in apology. "I did not realize what I was saying."

"Don't mention it again," Pao-yu said. "If you do, it will then seem that you really meant offense."

After the interview with Pao-yu, Liu Hsiang-lien decided to break the engagement. He went to see Chia Lien in his secret home. When he was introduced to Yu Lao-niang, he addressed her as a friend's mother instead of as his future mother-in-law. Chia Lien was puzzled. Then Hsiang-lien said, after tea was served, "I have some very embarrassing news to impart. I found on returning home that my aunt had made an attachment for me while I was away. If I were to obey you, Brother Lien, it would be disobeying my aunt. If my engagement token had been gold or silver, I would not think of asking its return but, since it is a sword that has been in the family for generations, I dare not part with it and would beg you to give it back to me."

Chia Lien said, "Think what you are saying! A promise is a promise. An engagement is not something to be taken lightly, and I am afraid that you cannot break your own word."

"That is true," Hsiang-lien said, "but under the circumstances there is nothing else to do. You must give me my sword. I shall abide by whatever penalties you may see fit to impose."

Chia Lien was going to say something, but Hsiang-lien suggested that it would be better if they went to the outer room to talk the matter over.

San-chieh, who was in the next room, was happy when she heard that Hsiang-lien had come. Then she heard Hsiang-lien's request. She knew that he must have heard scandalous things against her. If she let him and Chia Lien retire to the outer apartment and discuss the matter, Chia Lien probably could do nothing to change Liu Hsiang-lien's mind. If they could come to an open dispute, it would only cause her public humiliation. In an instant, she made up her mind. She rushed into the room and said, "Do not go yet, for here I am with your sword." In her left hand was the sheath, and in her right, which was behind her back, was one of the swords. She handed the sheath to Hsiang-lien. As Hsiang-lien extended his hand to receive it, she pressed the keen edge of the sword to her throat.

Too late did those in the room rush forward to prevent it. They were paralyzed by the flash of the sword. They saw her swing it toward her throat. When they recovered from the shock, San-chieh had already fallen dead.

> The crumbled peach blossoms cover the earth
> with red;
> The jade mountain crashes and falls, never to rise
> again.

Yu Lao-niang cried and cursed Hsiang-lien and said that he must pay with his own life. Chia Lien seized him, intending to hand him over to the gendarmery. But Er-chieh was more sensible. She said, pacifying her mother, "He did not force her in any way. It would do no good to hand him over to the authorities. That would only bring us public disgrace. It is better to let him go."

Chia Lien released Liu Hsiang-lien, but the latter did not try to get away. He said, wiping away his tears, "I did not know that she was such a resolute and chaste woman. Woe is me that I have lost such a wife."

He stayed and saw San-chieh laid in her coffin. He then left the house, wandering aimlessly, thinking of the courage and chastity of San-chieh and her beauty, now that he had seen her. As he was wandering toward the deserted regions outside the city, he seemed to hear the swish of silk and the tinkling of jade and gold ornaments. He saw a vision of San-chieh, with the sword in one hand and a book in the other. She said to him, "I have waited five years for you, but your heart is as cold as your face. So I have died to atone for my love for you. The Goddess of Disillusionment has appointed me to revise the records of the various spirits with debts of love. But I do not want to leave you without a final parting word, for I shall never see you again."

With this, she vanished before he could speak to her. He burst into lamentations and cried until he was faint. Suddenly he awoke and found himself lying in a ruined temple with a lame Taoist priest sitting by, catching fleas from his tattered coat. He saluted the priest and asked what place he was in and who he was. The latter answered, "I know not what place this is or who I am. I only know that I am here until I am somewhere else." These simple words struck Hsiang-lien with sudden illumination. He cut off his hair with his sword and followed the priest to we know not where.

CHAPTER THIRTY-ONE

In which Phoenix overwhelms her rival with apparent kindness
And Er-chieh undoubtedly perishes by some diabolical scheme

It is said that the only way to keep people from knowing one's secrets is to have none at all, and so in due course of time, Phoenix learned of the secret marriage between Chia Lien and Er-chieh. Hsing-er, one of Chia Lien's confidential servants, was responsible for the discovery. One day as he was talking to another servant about their "new Nai-nai," Phoenix overheard him and immediately summoned him to her.

"Your master and you have been up to some trick," she hinted darkly. "Now tell me what you know without concealing anything." Hsing-er was frightened out of his wits by the unexpected question and kowtowed repeatedly, while Phoenix continued, "I know that this matter is not your fault or of your instigation. But you should have come and informed me. Now tell me everything, and I shall pardon you. Otherwise, you had better feel your neck and see if you have more than one head to spare."

Hsing-er said, trying to appear innocent, "What does Nai-nai refer to?"

Phoenix was furious. "Strike the wretch for lying!" she commanded. Wang-er, one of her favorite servants, came up to carry out the command, but Phoenix stopped him, saying, "Let him strike himself. Your turn will come next."

Hsing-er obeyed and, drawing back first one hand as far as he could and then the other, he struck himself vigorously on his cheeks until Phoenix told him to stop.

"I suppose you know nothing concerning a certain new Nai-nai?" Phoenix asked again, more explicitly.

Realizing that there was no use in concealing the matter any further, Hsing-er kowtowed and said, "I'll tell everything if Nai-nai will have mercy on me. I couldn't help it. The master said that he would kill me if I told Nai-nai."

"Hurry!" Phoenix prompted.

Hsing-er began, still kneeling on the floor, "One day the master was riding together with Jung-ko to the other mansion from the Temple. They were talking about Gen Ta Nai-nai's two sisters, and Jung-ko said that he would try to get the second Yi Nai-nai—"

Phoenix interrupted him with an oath and said, "Shameless wretch, which Yi Nai-nai do you mean? Where does this Yi Nai-nai of yours come from?"

Hsing-er kowtowed and was at a loss as to what to say. Phoenix urged him, and he continued, "The master was much pleased with the proposal of Jung-ko. I don't know how it happened, but somehow the match was arranged."

"Of course, you don't know how it happened. But go on."

"Then Jung-ko rented a house—"

"A house? Where is the house?"

"It is right behind our mansion, not far from here," Hsing-er said.

Phoenix turned to Patience and said, "We were like two corpses while all this went on!"

Hsing-er continued, "Then Gen Ta-yeh gave the Changs some money, and that silenced the Changs—"

"The Changs?" Phoenix was surprised at the unexpected turn in Hsing-er's recital. "Where do the Changs come in?"

"Ah," Hsing-er said, "Nai-nai does not know that the other Er Nai-nai—" Then suddenly realizing that he was using the forbidden form of address in referring to Er-chieh, he quickly slapped himself, causing Phoenix and the others to laugh. "The second sister of Gen Ta Nai-nai," Hsing-er went on, "was originally betrothed to a family by the name of Chang. But they are now poor and were induced to return the engagement papers when Gen Ta-yeh gave them some money."

Hsing-er went on and told Phoenix about the house, the servants, the suicide of San-chieh, and the fact that Yu-shih was at the house a few days after the wedding. After extracting from Hsing-er all he knew, Phoenix told him to be off. Hsing-er kowtowed and retreated out into the yard, though he did not leave immediately, as Phoenix might have more questions for him.

"Come back!" Phoenix commanded.

Hsing-er bowed reverently and waited.

"What are you hurrying off for?" Phoenix said. "Are you going to your new Nai-nai and tell her what has happened? From now on, you are not to go over there again. You should be ready to answer my summons whenever I want you. I'll break your legs if you are late by a single minute. Now you can go." The servant obeyed, but Phoenix called him back again and said, "I suppose you'll now run to Er-yeh and tell him everything."

"I wouldn't dare to do that even if I had a thousand heads," the servant answered.

"If you say a word about this, you had better beware of your skin," Phoenix said, as she dismissed Hsing-er for the last time. Then she turned to Wang-er, who had come forward to wait for his turn. But she only said, "You can go now but you shall answer for it if this leaks out."

Chia Lien was on another trip to Ping-an-chow, which occupied nearly two months. Phoenix, in the meantime, conceived a plan for the destruction of her rival. One day, accompanied by Patience, Feng-er, Chou Jui's wife, and Wang-er's wife, she set out to call on Er-chieh. The latter greeted her as "elder sister" and begged her forgiveness for not having gone out to meet her. Ushering her into the room, she made Phoenix sit in the chair of honor and then, kneeling on the cushion that one of the maids had brought, she kowtowed to her to acknowledge her superior position. She tried to ingratiate herself with Phoenix, explaining to her that everything had been arranged for her by her mother and Yu-shih.

Phoenix also tried to put Er-chieh at ease. "In a way, I am to blame that things happened the way they did," she said graciously. "Having Er-yeh's interest at heart, I couldn't help occasionally counseling him against 'sleeping with willows and lying with flowers,' both because it is injurious to his health and because it causes anxiety to Lao Tai-tai and others of the older generation. You will understand these silly worries well, I am sure, since you are also a woman. But it seems that Er-yeh has misunderstood me and thinks that I am jealous. Nothing is further from the truth. In fact, I have often suggested to him that it would be a blessing to us all if he took to himself a second wife, so that she might bear us a son whom we can look to in the future. It is a great humiliation and an injustice to me for Er-yeh to make this matter secret, as if I were a jealous woman who could not tolerate another member in the household."

Phoenix's manner was sincere, and everyone who knew her marveled at her sweet reasonableness. She continued, "I heard about it only the other day and I hastened to come here to call on Mei-mei and to ask Mei-mei to come back home with me. If you live here outside and I inside, how can I be happy? People will talk. It will reflect not only upon me but upon you as well. Of even greater importance is Er-yeh's own reputation. I implore you to come with me. You will live as I do, eat the same food, and wear the same clothes. When Er-yeh comes back, he will see that I am not the jealous woman he thinks. If you will not take pity upon me and come with me, I shall come to live with you here and be your maidservant. But you must put in a good word for me here and there, so that Er-yeh will not be unkind to me."

As she spoke of the wrong the world had done to her,

the abuses she had suffered, she began to weep. Er-chieh, who was easily swayed, became convinced of her sincerity and reproached herself for having believed the ill reports she had heard. She went with Phoenix into the Takuanyuan and was installed in a room near Li Huan's apartment. She was introduced to the young ladies of the Garden, who were as surprised by Phoenix's extraordinary tolerance as they were delighted by the beauty and charm of Er-chieh.

Phoenix dismissed Er-chieh's maids and gave her Shan-er, one of her own maids. She assembled the maids in the Takuanyuan and told them they were to be responsible for Er-chieh and that they would all answer for it if she should run away. This precaution was unnecessary, for Er-chieh was not the type of woman who would think of doing such a thing. She was wafted hither and thither by every wind of circumstance. The turn of events pleased her, for Phoenix was always kind to her when they met, and the young ladies of the Takuanyuan were, of course, very courteous and considerate of her.

However, after three or four days, she began to notice a change in the maid Shan-er; the girl had become disobedient and insolent. One day, finding herself short of oil for her hair, Er-chieh asked the maid to go to Phoenix for some. But the maid said to her, "Er Nai-nai,[1] you should be a little more thoughtful than that. Ta Nai-nai[2] is a very busy person, and we should not bother her with such trifles. I would not be so particular if I were you. You must remember the compromising position you have gotten yourself into. In the hands of another woman not as kind and generous as our Ta Nai-nai, you would have been discarded, left out to suffer. Where would you be then?"

This humiliated Er-chieh, and yet she did not dare complain for fear that Phoenix and others would think that she was faultfinding and inconsiderate. Gradually Shan-er became worse and worse, until she would not even bring Er-chieh's dinner on time. When she did bring it, the food

[1] "Second mistress."
[2] "Principal mistress."

was generally cold and consisted of leftovers hardly fit to eat. Once or twice, Er-chieh summoned up enough courage to speak to her but she soon abandoned this, as each time she did so, the maid would become wildly abusive. Every few days, Phoenix came to see her. On these occasions, she was full of honeyed words, calling Er-chieh her "dear Mei-mei," asking solicitously how she was getting along, and saying that she must let her know if any of the servants showed any lack of courtesy and thoughtfulness. Turning to the servants, she would say, "I know you always take advantage of those who are kind and fear only those who are severe with you. If I should ever hear a single complaint from Er Nai-nai about you, I shall have your skins!" This forestalled any intention Er-chieh may have had to complain about the conduct of Shan-er or others.

In the meantime, Phoenix had located Chang Hua, the first betrothed of Er-chieh. He turned out to be a worthless wretch who spent his time around gambling dens. He was instigated to bring a suit against Chia Lien, charging him with marrying in a period of family and state mourning, forcing Chang Hua to break his betrothal, and several other crimes that Chia Lien was technically guilty of. Then Phoenix went to the Ningkuofu and there made a terrible scene, railing at Yu-shih and Chia Jung and threatening to tell the Matriarch what they had done to lead Chia Lien into such criminal offenses. Chia Jung begged and implored until Phoenix relented.

Next, Phoenix introduced Er-chieh to the Matriarch, saying that she herself had secured the second wife for Chia Lien with the assistance of Yu-shih. The Matriarch was greatly pleased and praised her for having in mind the welfare of her husband and the importance of continuing the family line. With the knowledge of the Matriarch, Er-chieh was moved into the rooms that Phoenix had prepared for her. The Matriarch was pleased with Er-chieh, too, for she was such a beautiful and modest girl.

Phoenix's plan was to make everything appear as if she were not jealous and, at the same time, to get rid of Er-chieh in some way. To further this end, she gave more money to Chang Hua, bidding him to insist on having his betrothed back. Then she went to the Matriarch and told her that, because of an oversight on the part of Yu-shih, Chia Lien had married someone who was already betrothed and that the former fiancé was bringing suit to recover her. The Matriarch scolded Yu-shih for her carelessness and told Phoenix to pacify Chang Hua as best she could.

Ostensibly Phoenix obeyed but actually she encouraged Chang Hua to press the suit. Finally, Chia Gen decided that the matter had gone far enough. It was out of the question for the Chias to give up Er-chieh. He summoned Chang Hua and told him that if he valued his own skin he had better drop the suit. Chang Hua was willing but he was, on the other hand, spurred on by Phoenix. Chia Gen solved the problem for him by giving him a hundred taels on his promise that he would leave the Capital.

Upon his return from Ping-an-chow, Chia Lien went over to his new house and felt uneasy when he learned that Phoenix had been on the scene and had taken Er-chieh away with her. He was embarrassed on meeting Phoenix, but the latter promptly put him at his ease by saying that she was glad he had secured a second wife who might bear them a son and only reproached him for thinking that she would object to it. She would say to Er-chieh, "I am very sorry that people talk so much about Mei-mei. Even Lao Tai-tai and Tai-tai now know your story. I wish I knew what I could do to stop such evil gossip." Secretly she would encourage the maids to make things as miserable for Er-chieh as possible.

Presently she found an accomplice in Chiu-tung, a maid whom Chia Sheh had given to Chia Lien for having successfully concluded his mission at Ping-an-chow. Because she had been given to Chia Lien by Chia Sheh, the maid felt her position superior to that of Er-chieh. She did not give much thought to Phoenix and Patience, much less the unfortunate Er-chieh. She was not to be trampled upon by a woman who entered the house through adultery, she would say in Er-chieh's hearing. Phoenix egged her on. She would take Chiu-tung aside and say to her, "You are young and reckless. You must know that she is Er-yeh's favorite. Even I dare not claim equality with her. It is foolhardy for you to offend her."

As expected, this inflamed Chiu-tung and made her heap more abuse upon Er-chieh, who languished under the relentless persecution and became prey to a consuming illness. The only thing that sustained her was the hope of giving birth to a son, who would give her some security. She was in fact with child, but a doctor who was summoned made a wrong diagnosis, and his drastic remedy caused a miscarriage.

Chia Lien was sorrow-stricken and would have had the doctor arrested and punished if the latter had not fled on learning of his mistake. Phoenix seemed to be even more sorrow-stricken than Chia Lien. The best doctors must be called in, so that dear poor Mei-mei could recover and bear them another son.

A fortuneteller was consulted; he said that the patient's illness was caused by the crossing of her star with that of someone born under the sign of the Rabbit. This brought forth another outburst from Chiu-tung, who happened to be the only person around Er-chieh born under that sign.

"She and I are like river water and well water," she shouted. "Why should my star conflict with hers? She used to see and meet all sorts of people and never suffered anything because of it. Why should she be so susceptible now? I would like to ask whose child that was, anyway? She can fool only the master. What is a child? Given time, anyone can bear one, and a thoroughbred at that."

She went to Madame Hsing and complained that Chia Lien and Er-chieh did not treat her kindly. Madame Hsing sent for Chia Lien and scolded him, saying that it was unfilial of him to treat unkindly someone that his father had given him. Chiu-tung, thus encouraged, was more insolent than ever. She stood outside of Er-chieh's window and hurled at her insult after insult.

That night, Er-chieh resolved to end her miserable life. She had heard that gold would cause death. She struggled to her feet, found a piece of gold in the jewelry cabinet, and swallowed it. As she was unattended, it was not until late the next morning that her death was discovered.

CHAPTER THIRTY-TWO

In which Sha Ta-chieh's ignorance proves to be a source of her blessings
And Bright Design's beauty becomes the cause of her downfall

YU Er-chieh's funeral was an extremely simple one. After a few brief services held in the Pear Fragrance Court, she was buried beside the tomb of San-chieh, as the Matriarch deemed that she had no rightful place in the Chia family cemetery. Chia Lien had to attend to all the details himself, for Phoenix would not lift a finger to help him. Besides her unwillingness to do anything for her former rival, she was in fact beginning to find herself involved in plans for the New Year festivities.

The poetry club had remained inactive while Li Huan, Quest Spring, and Precious Virtue relieved Phoenix of some of her duties during her illness; it was revived in the spring and was renamed the Peach Flower Club. Before many meetings were held, however, a message from Chia Cheng announced that he was about to return to the Capital from his provincial post. This made it necessary for Pao-yu to brush up on his studies and copy off enough calligraphic exercises to satisfy his father that he had not been idle during his absence.

Chia Cheng returned in time for the Matriarch's eightieth birthday on the third of the Eighth Month. The occasion was celebrated with great elaborateness, surpassed only by the visit of the Imperial Concubine. The festivities lasted a period of eight days, beginning with banquets for the Imperial Princes and ending with offerings by the stewards and servants of the two mansions. Phoenix was again in charge, and everything went well under her capable supervision.

Now there was in the Matriarch's apartment a maid named Sha Ta-chieh, or Sister Stupid. She had big feet and large features. She was completely guileless, if not simple-minded, and often said things that made the Matriarch laugh. For this reason, she was treated with special consideration and allowed more liberty than the other maids. She often went into the Garden to play when she had nothing to do.

On one of these excursions shortly after the preceding events, Sister Stupid came upon an embroidered purse while looking for crickets behind some rocks. Instead of the usual decorations of birds and flowers or figures in conventional costumes, it had on one side two human figures completely naked and locked together as if engaged in a wrestling match. The maid was fascinated by her find and was thinking of showing it to the Matriarch, when Madame Hsing happened to pass by.

The latter's feelings would be easily imagined when the maid showed her the purse. But if she felt mortified, how much more so Madame Wang must have felt when she learned of the discovery of such an object in the Takuanyuan, since the affairs of the Yungkuofu were her responsibility rather than Madame Hsing's.

Phoenix was chatting with Patience in her apartment, when Madame Wang was suddenly announced. Madame Wang's face was grave. She curtly dismissed Patience as soon as she entered the room and then, taking the embroidered purse from her sleeve, threw it to Phoenix, saying, "Look at that!"

Phoenix was shocked when she saw the "spring picture" on it. "Where did Tai-tai get this?" she asked.

"Where did I get it?" Madame Wang said, her voice shaking a little. "Are you asking me? I have always thought that you were a careful person, but apparently you have your lapses. How could you be so careless as to leave such a thing around? One of Lao Tai-tai's maids found it and, if your Tai-tai had not encountered her, she would have taken it to show Lao Tai-tai!"

Phoenix was taken aback by the accusation. "What makes Tai-tai think that this belongs to me?" she asked. Her face, too, became grave.

"Who else could it be?" Madame Wang said. "In the inner compounds you and Lien-er are the only young married couple. The older maidservants couldn't have this sort of thing, and the young ones would have no way of coming by it. It must be that worthless Lien-er who got hold of it somehow and gave it to you. Candidly, such things are to be expected of young people nowadays. What disturbs me is that you should be so careless. What if one of your sisters had come upon it? Worse still, one of the maids might have found it and taken it outside. Just imagine what a scandal that would be!"

"Tai-tai's line of reasoning is, of course, correct," Phoenix said, kneeling before Madame Wang, "and I should not presume to contradict Tai-tai. But the fact is that I never had such a thing in my possession. Just reflect, Tai-tai . . . Even if I did have such a thing, I would not think of carrying it around with me, especially into the Garden. We sisters often tease one another and tug at each other in fun. The chance of its being seen by my sisters and the maids is so obvious that I could not possibly have risked it, no matter how careless I am."

Phoenix went on to point out that, although of the immediate members of the Yungkuofu she was the most likely object of suspicion, there were other frequent visitors to the Takuanyuan, such as the concubines of Chia Sheh and Chia Gen, who were about her age and just as likely to have such a thing.

When she finished, Madame Wang said, "Please get up. I should have known that you could not have been responsible but in my great agitation I did not think. The question is what are we to do about it?"

"The most important thing is to keep the matter quiet," Phoenix said, "so it does not reach Lao Tai-tai. We should confide only to some of our most trusted servants and have them search the Garden under some pretext. This, too, might be a good time to discharge some of the undesirable elements among the servants, both to guard against future incidents and as an economy measure. What does Tai-tai think?"

"You are right, of course," Madame Wang answered. "But I would not think of depriving your sisters of the maids. As it is, each of them has only two or three fairly presentable ones. Difficult as things are, we have not come to this point yet. I would much rather make some personal sacrifice than to deprive them. But you go ahead with the search you suggested."

Soon Chou Jui's wife, together with four other pei-fang of Madame Wang and Phoenix, arrived, simultaneously with Wang Shan-pao's wife, Madame Hsing's pei-fang. It was she who had brought the purse and who was now sent by her mistress to learn what was being done about it. Not wishing to use her own servants only, Madame Wang turned to her and said, "Tell your Tai-tai that I should like to have your help in this matter if she could spare you."

Now Wang Shan-pao's wife had always borne a grudge against the more favored maids in the Garden, because none of them paid much attention to her. She was eager at this chance to show her importance and to settle scores with those who had been particularly curt with her. "I should not be saying anything," she volunteered, "but the truth is that some of the maids need a little discipline. They act as if they were mistresses and not servants. They are unbearably insolent. They always have their way because everyone is afraid to say anything, lest it be twisted around and made to appear that the young ladies themselves were being criticized. Tai-tai wouldn't know these things, since she does not go into the Garden very often."

"I can well imagine," Madame Wang said, nodding in agreement. "It is only to be expected that the personal maids of the young ladies would be a bit spoiled."

"That is true," Wang Shan-pao's wife agreed, "but some of them go beyond the bounds of decency. I have in mind Ching-wen [Bright Design] in Pao-yu's room. She is quite pretty, but the trouble is she knows it too well. She dresses herself like a Princess Hsi Shih and acts like one. She has a quick temper and a sharp tongue and is apt to scold and carry on in the most outrageous manner on the slightest provocation."

This description of Bright Design suddenly reminded Madame Wang of a maid she had noticed. She turned to Phoenix and asked, "The last time I accompanied Lao Tai-tai to the Garden, I noticed a girl with a willowy waist and eyes somewhat like your Lin Mei-mei's. She was berating a little ya-tou. I did not like her at all but I did not say anything, because I did not want any unpleasantness before Lao Tai-tai. I have wanted to find out who she was but have not gotten around to it. She seems to fit the description of Ching-wen."

"Ching-wen is the prettiest among the maids and she is a bit sharp," Phoenix answered. "Tai-tai's description fits her all right. However, I do not recall the incident and would not presume to identify her."

"That's easily settled," Wang Shan-pao's wife said. "All Tai-tai has to do is to summon her and see for herself."

"Hsi-jen and Sheh-yueh are the ones I generally see when I visit Pao-yu's room," Madame Wang said. "They are all nice, plain, simple girls. I did not realize that Pao-yu is open to the influence of a girl like Ching-wen. I have always hated the type. She mustn't be allowed to corrupt Pao-yu." Then turning to one of her maids, she said, "Go and get one of Pao-yu's maids. I want Hsi-jen and Sheh-yueh to stay with Pao-yu, so bring Ching-wen. Say nothing of why I want her."

Bright Design was not feeling well that day and had just waked up from a nap when Madame Wang's maid came to ask for her. She had always been afraid of Madame Wang and always tried to make herself inconspicuous when the latter visited Pao-yu. She was surprised to be sent for but she had done nothing and had no particular misgivings, especially since she had not taken trouble to make herself up at the time. But one can always find fault when he is looking for it. To Madame Wang, who immediately recognized her as the maid she had in mind, the plainness of her dress and the absence of make-up appeared studied rather than natural, and this aroused her anger. "What a picture you make!" she said with a sneer. "A veritable Hsi Shih Indisposed! What do you affect these poses for? You may think I know nothing about you, but I do, and I shall take care of you soon enough. How is Pao-yu today?"

The poor maid knew immediately that someone had spoken against her and that her only defense was to show that she was not close to Pao-yu. She knelt and replied, "I do not go into Pao-yu's room as a rule and cannot say just how he is. Hsi-jen and Sheh-yueh are the ones who wait on him. Tai-tai should ask them."

"You should be slapped for giving me that absurd answer," Madame Wang said. "Don't you have eyes and ears? Are you dead that you know nothing of what goes on? What are you for if you can't even answer a simple question like that?"

Bright Design answered, "I was one of Lao Tai-tai's maids. When Pao-yu moved into the Garden and Lao Tai-tai assigned me to his court, I told Lao Tai-tai that I was clumsy and would not prove satisfactory, but Lao Tai-tai said, 'I don't want you to attend to Pao-yu's personal needs. Your job is to serve on the night watch in the outer rooms. You don't have to be clever to do that.' So I had to go.

Pao-yu rarely asks for me, but when he does, I go and answer what I am asked, and that is all. When I have nothing to do, I sew things for Lao Tai-tai. As to Pao-yu's personal needs, there are the nurses and older servants and his personal maids, such as Pervading Fragrance, Musk Moon, and Autumn Sky. That's why I am unable to answer any questions about Pao-yu. However, I shall be more attentive in the future if Tai-tai wishes me to."

"Don't trouble yourself about that," Madame Wang said, "for the farther you keep away from Pao-yu, the better it suits me. But since you were assigned to Pao-yu by Lao Tai-tai I shall have to speak to her before I get rid of you. Now you can go and try not to act like a siren! I have no use for girls like you."

That evening, after the Matriarch had gone to bed, the search party proceeded to the Garden. They began with the servants on the night watch but found nothing more incriminating than a few candles and a jar or two of oil for lamps, which someone had hidden away with the idea of taking them home later. Such petty thievery was nothing unusual and was more or less to be expected in a large household like the Yungkuofu, but Wang Shan-pao's wife pounced on them as if she had uncovered a great crime. She insisted that these should be taken as evidence and reported to Madame Wang for disposal the following day.

Then they went to the Peony Court, where Pao-yu was commiserating with Bright Design. He was mystified by the appearance of Phoenix with a large retinue of senior help and was even puzzled when they went directly into the maids' room. When he asked Phoenix what it meant, the latter answered, "Some valuable object has been stolen and no one would admit to it. It has been decided to search all the maids' rooms."

She sat down and had some tea while Wang Shan-pao's wife went on with the search. After inspecting the objects lying around in the rooms, she ordered the maids each to open their chests; this they all did promptly, with Pervading Fragrance setting the example. But Bright Design was not there to open hers and, just as Wang Shan-pao's wife was asking whose it was and why it had not been opened, Bright Design stalked in and, without a word, opened the chest and dumped its contents on the floor. At this, Wang Shan-pao's wife said, her face flushed, "You needn't get angry over it, Ku-niang. We have come here not because we want to but because Tai-tai has ordered us. If you do not wish to be searched, all you have to do is to say so. We'll then pass you by and report it to Tai-tai. You don't have to behave like this."

This only further inflamed Bright Design. She said, pointing her finger at Wang Shan-pao's wife, "So you are here by Tai-tai's orders. What of it? I am here by Lao Tai-tai's orders. I know all Tai-tai's servants but I do not think I ever have had the pleasure of meeting you, who seem so favored and important."

Wang Shan-pao's wife was about to say something, but Phoenix said to her, "It is beneath your dignity, Ma-ma, to argue with them. You had better go on with your search, for there are other compounds, and if we tarry here too long, the news might get around." Wang Shan-pao's wife held back her anger and looked over Bright Design's things carefully; finding nothing incriminating, she so reported to Phoenix.

As they left the Peony Court, Phoenix said to Wang Shan-pao's wife, "I have a suggestion that I hope you will agree to. It is that we should search only our own people and not Hsueh Ku-niang's maids. That would be quite improper."

"That goes without saying," Wang Shan-pao's wife agreed.

Next, they visited Black Jade's compound and there in Purple Cuckoo's room they found some mementos that Pao-yu had given her. Wang Shan-pao's wife thought she had here something incriminating, but Phoenix soon disabused her of the notion.

In the meantime, Quest Spring heard of the search and was ready for the women when they arrived. She asked the group what they had come for, and Phoenix said, "It is about some article that has been missing. The outside compounds have been searched without success. It has been suggested that the girls in the Garden be searched also, not because they are under suspicion but because this is the only way to clear them."

"You need not be so polite about it," Quest Spring said, laughing. "You might as well come right out and say that my maids are all under suspicion and that I am a receiver of stolen articles. So start your search with my things." So saying, she commanded her maids to open all her chests and parcels for Phoenix to inspect.

"Mei-mei mustn't take offense at me," Phoenix said, smiling placatingly. "I am doing this only because Tai-tai has commanded me to."

Then as Patience and others helped Folio to lock up the chests, Quest Spring said, "Be sure to look over the things before locking up, for I have complete custody of my maids' things except their immediate personal effects. If they have stolen anything, you will find it among my things, not in their rooms. For this reason, I cannot permit their rooms to be searched. I am a strict mistress, I know everything about them and everything they possess, and I am completely responsible for them. You can repeat what I have said to Tai-tai. I shall take all the consequences for disobeying her orders."

Phoenix said, "Since the maids' things are all here in your custody, there is no need of searching through them."

"No need of searching through them," Quest Spring said, "when I have opened up everything for you to see! I insist that you go through them, for I would not permit another search and I do not want you to say later that I shielded my maids."

"All right," Phoenix said, laughing, "we have gone through everything and found nothing." Then turning to her assistants, she asked, "You have, haven't you?"

"Yes, we have," they answered, falling in with the fiction.

But Wang Shan-pao's wife, being tactless, chose this moment to indulge in a crude joke. She had heard about Quest Spring, how she was not one to trifle with, but she thought that was only because others did not know how to handle her. From the fact that Quest Spring had addressed all her remarks to Phoenix, she drew the conclusion that the young lady was angry at Phoenix and that she herself and the other servants were not the subject of her displeasure. So she went up to Quest Spring and, pulling up the flap of her coat, said, "Look! We have even searched Ku-niang's person. There is—"

But before she could finish, she had received a resounding slap from Quest Spring. "Who are you that you dare to touch me?" she said angrily to Wang Shan-pao's wife. "Because of your age and the fact that you have served Tai-tai for many years, I pay you the respect of addressing you as Ma-ma and treat you with courtesy. But this does not mean that you can become familiar. I have tried to overlook your presumptuous ways and your officiousness, but now it has come to laying hands on me. Perhaps you think that you can deal with me as you do your own Ku-niang. You are wrong." Then unbuttoning her coat, she turned to Phoenix and said, "If you must search my person, do it yourself, instead of letting one of the servants lay hands on me."

Phoenix and Patience hastened to button up Quest Spring's coat, saying, at the same time, to Wang Shan-pao's wife, "Ma-ma, you must have been drinking to forget yourself like this. You had better leave the room before you make another blunder." Finally, with many apologies, Phoenix and Patience persuaded Quest Spring to go to bed, after which they went to Li Huan's and Compassion Spring's, where they managed to search the maids' rooms without disturbing their mistresses.

When the party arrived at Welcome Spring's, the latter had already gone to bed, and the maids were preparing to do the same, so it was some time before the knocking was answered. Now, Chess was the granddaughter of Wang Shan-pao's wife, and Phoenix was curious to see if her things would be searched as thoroughly as the other maids'. The search party started with the other maids' belongings and found nothing. When it came to Chess, Wang Shan-pao's wife made a perfunctory search and said, "There is nothing here."

But as she was about to close the chest, Chou Jui's wife said, "It is only fair that we look through her things as carefully as everyone else's." She rummaged through the chest and came up with a pair of man's shoes and a letter from the maid's cousin that indicated that the two had met secretly in the Garden only a few days before.

This unexpected discovery filled Wang Shan-pao's wife with shame. She slapped her own face and cursed herself, saying, "You old wretch who's lived beyond your time. What have you done to bring this upon yourself? Why didn't you mind your own business?"

Though the search turned up nothing incriminating against Bright Design, she was banished together with Chess. She had not been well at the time. The disgrace aggravated her illness, and she who was so proud and sensitive died not long afterward.

CHAPTER THIRTY-THREE

In which Hsueh Pan is married to a Lioness of Ho-tung
And Welcome Spring is mated to a Wolf of Chung-shan

ONE day Pao-yu, in accordance with his parents' wishes, went to Chia Sheh's compound to meet Sun Shao-tsu, Welcome Spring's fiancé. The choice was Chia Sheh's. Both the Matriarch and Chia Cheng were opposed to the match, for the Suns were a newly arrived family and Sun Shao-tsu's grandfather had attached himself to Chia Tai-shan only because the latter was in a position to help him out of a difficulty of some kind. But since marriage is the primary concern of one's parents, they did not press their point, and the engagement was finally sealed. Sun Shao-tsu's visit was the final step in its consummation.

Pao-yu did not like Sun Shao-tsu. His reaction to Welcome Spring's engagement was typical of one who refuses to face realities. He could not see why beautiful maidens should marry and become slaves of men who would take them for granted, when they could just as well remain carefree and do nothing but play games and write verses.

That night, Pao-yu slept fitfully and was plagued by nightmares. He would wake up calling for Bright Design or mumble incoherently. The next day, he had no appetite and developed a fever. This was, of course, the result of recent events, the search of the Garden, the expulsion of Chess and others, the departure of Welcome Spring, and, above all, the humiliation and death of Bright Design.

When the physician was summoned, he ordered Pao-yu confined to his room for a hundred days. After a month or so, he recovered sufficiently to fret under the confinement and tried to coax the Matriarch to let him go out, but to no avail. So it happened that he missed the wedding of Hsueh Pan and also that of Welcome Spring, both of which took place during this period.

Now Hsueh Pan's bride, named Cassia, was the only child of a Hsia family. The Hsias were as rich as the Hsuehs and, like them, had held a commission as purchasing agents for the Palace for generations. Cassia was quite pretty but she was badly spoiled by her widowed mother. She was selfish, suspicious, and quarrelsome and mean to those in her power. When thwarted in the slightest degree, she would fly into a temper, cry, and curse as freely as any common scold.

Now that she was married, she made up her mind that she would not play the modest and obedient wife or daughter-in-law. She must show that she was her own mistress, and this she must do from the first, before any wrong ideas were formed about her. She could not have adopted a better plan. Hsueh Pan, being one of those who "tires of the old and dotes on the new," was eager to please his bride and readily gave in to her when differences arose. Thus, in the first month of their marriage the give-and-take was about equally shared; by the second month, Hsueh Pan began to take more and give less.

Hsueh Pan was a living example not only of the saying just quoted but also of the other common saying, "To covet the land of Shu after grabbing the region of Lung." After having gratified his passion for Cassia, he began to turn his attention to her maid Cherry, who was by no means unattractive. The maid was willing enough but, knowing her mistress well, was afraid to encourage him.

At the moment, however, Cassia was more interested in

turning Hsueh Pan against Lotus, though the latter had been exemplary in her conduct and had given no ground for jealousy. In her tortuous, scheming mind Cassia saw an opportunity to use Cherry as a tool against Lotus. Thus, she did nothing to stop Hsueh Pan's none too subtle flirtations with her maid.

One evening, Hsueh Pan pinched Cherry's hand as she handed him a cup of tea. The maid pretended to object and withdrew her hand. In the process, the cup was dropped and crashed upon the ground. To cover his confusion, Hsueh Pan accused the maid of carelessness. She retorted that he was to blame.

"Don't be so obvious," Cassia merely said. "I am not blind to what you have been up to." Hsueh Pan grinned as the maid left the room, blushing.

Later at bedtime, Cassia made a pretense of not caring where he spent the night. "Go where your heart is," she said to him with a playful push. "I don't want to see you starve your heart out." Hsueh Pan only grinned again. Cassia continued, "Do what you want so long as it is not behind my back."

To show his gratitude, Hsueh Pan performed his conjugal duty to the best of his ability that night. The next day, he did not go out at all, hoping for an opportunity to gratify his desire. In the afternoon, Cassia deliberately left him alone with Cherry in the room. Then having given them enough time for the preliminaries, she called a little maid and said to her, "Go tell Lotus that I left my handkerchief in my room. Have her get it for me but let it appear that the suggestion came from you."

The maid did as she was bid and said to Lotus, "Nainai left her handkerchief in her room. I am sure she would be pleased if you got it for her."

Lotus took the suggestion eagerly; for her mistress had been finding fault with her, and she wanted to do everything she could to appease her. So it happened that she walked into her mistress' room just as Cherry was on the point of yielding to Hsueh Pan, who had not bothered to close the door. She withdrew quickly, her face burning with shame.

Hsueh Pan was unruffled by the intrusion, for he had the tacit consent of his wife; but Cherry was disturbed. She had said many unkind things about Lotus and did not want to give the latter a chance to retaliate. So she pushed him away and rushed out of the room crying rape.

Hsueh Pan's anger can be well imagined. He poured upon Lotus a stream of oaths and imprecations. That evening, Lotus added too much hot water to his bath. He insisted she did it deliberately to scald him and he beat her, a thing he had never done before, quick-tempered though he was; for Lotus had always been treated more like a daughter than a bondmaid.

Having no further reason to tantalize Hsueh Pan, Cassia arranged for him to spend the night in Cherry's room for a period of time and for Lotus to come and sleep in her room to attend to her needs. These proved to be many, for she would wake the poor girl seven or eight times a night to bring tea, to massage her legs, and so on, making sure that the maid would not have a good night's sleep. She found fault with everything Lotus did, declaring that the girl was deliberately trying to provoke her and to drive her to her death so that she, Lotus, could monopolize Hsueh Pan. Cassia began to complain about an ache in the region of her heart and limbs. These alleged ailments persisted and defied medical diagnosis.

Then one day as one of the maids ripped open her pillow to change the stuffing, she found in it a paper effigy with the day and hour of Cassia's birth written on it and with five needles thrust through the heart and the limb joints. Hsueh Yi-ma was at a loss as to what to do; Hsueh Pan ordered the servants and maids to be flogged until the guilty one confessed.

"There is no use in making the innocent suffer," Cassia said. "It is probably Cherry, who wants to take my place."

Hsueh Pan said, "It couldn't be she; she has not been in your room recently."

"Who else could it be then, unless you think I have been experimenting with black magic on myself?"

"Lotus should know," Hsueh Pan said. "She has been waiting on you these days."

"There is no use questioning anyone," Cassia said. "No one will admit it. I think it is best to forget about it, to pretend that it never happened. What does it matter if I die? It will give you a chance to marry someone better to your liking. For I know in my heart that you all want me out of the way!" She began to cry bitterly.

The effect of these words was not lost on Hsueh Pan. Lacking anything handier, he pulled off the door latch and began to beat Lotus with it, until his mother stopped him, saying, "You mustn't jump to conclusions. The girl has been with us many years and has always been faithful. She couldn't have done that."

Thereupon, Cassia, to edge Hsueh Pan on, cried even louder, saying, "First you take my own maid away by force and make me take Lotus into my room. You won't let me question Cherry because she is hot in your favors. Now you pretend to strike Lotus. I know what's in your mind! You want to drive me to my death, so that you can marry someone more beautiful and better connected than I."

Hsueh Yi-ma was furious at the shameless way in which her daughter-in-law carried on and her absurd accusations and insinuations; she was even more furious at her son for allowing his wife to behave like this. She had no way of knowing who was responsible for the black magic. Truly, just as "even the wisest mandarin cannot clear up family muddles," so "even the most discerning parents are helpless in disputes between son and wife."

In her anger and helplessness she shouted to Hsueh Pan, "What have I done in a previous incarnation to deserve a son like you? Even a dog in heat is not so shameless as you. How could you do such a thing as to make your wife complain about her maid being taken away and raped. How can you face people after this? What makes you think that Lotus is guilty? I know you; you are always ready to abandon the old for the new. Since you are tired of Lotus, I'll have her sold if that will bring peace." Then turning to the servants, she commanded, "Now, one of you go and get the broker, and we'll be rid of this thorn in the flesh and tack in the eye. Only then can we have peace."

Hsueh Pan bowed his head in silence at his mother's outburst, but Cassia would not be silenced. She said, crying still louder, "If you want to sell her, go ahead and do it. You don't have to make insinuations with your references to a thorn in the flesh and a tack in the eye. To whom is she a thorn in the flesh and a tack in the eye? If I were the jealous kind as you insinuate, I would not have allowed him to have my maid."

Hsueh Pan stamped his feet and said helplessly to Cassia, "Stop! Stop! Don't make us a laughingstock any more than you have to!"

Cassia only spoke louder, saying, "I have nothing to be ashamed of! Why should I, when it is your darling favorite who is trying to accomplish my death? Perhaps you really want to sell me and put her in my place? Who doesn't know that the Hsuehs have money and influence and can buy their way into anything? Why not go ahead and get rid of me? What are you waiting for? But let me ask you this. If I am not good enough for you, why did you wear your heels out running to our house in the first place?"

Thus she raved on, and Hsueh Yi-ma and her son would have been treated to more of the same sort if Precious Virtue had not finally come out and urged them to leave the shrew alone.

Hsueh Yi-ma's declared intention to sell Lotus was, of course, only a threat uttered in a moment of unthinking passion. In a family like the Hsuehs, as Precious Virtue pointed out, one may send a bondmaid back to her people or give her in marriage to a man of suitable position, but to sell one was unheard of. So Hsueh Yi-ma agreed to let Lotus stay with her daughter, thus removing one cause of friction.

Lotus had never been strong, being a victim of menstrual

disorders. The suffering and humiliation she went through now aggravated her condition and caused a complete stoppage. She lost interest in food and grew thinner day by day. Nothing the physicians prescribed helped to improve her condition.

Cassia continued to make scenes. Once or twice, Hsueh Pan, fortifying his courage with wine, tried to put her in her place, but when he threatened to beat her, she would turn her back to him and dare him to go ahead; when he threatened to kill her, she would stretch out her neck and dare him to cut off her head. So in the end, his threats only made him smaller and more contemptible in Cassia's eyes.

Next, Cassia turned her attention to Cherry. The latter, however, was every bit her mistress' match. She not only talked back but did so in more effective language. When Cassia was provoked to strike her, she would, though she did not strike back, scream until all the neighbors could hear, roll on the ground, threaten to commit suicide, "looking for knives and scissors by day and ropes and cords by night."

Between the two, there was never any peace in the Hsueh household. Hsueh Pan would steal out of the house when things became unbearable, but for Hsueh Yi-ma and Precious Virtue there was no such convenient escape. They could only shut themselves in their rooms and weep. Nor could they keep their trials a secret, for Cassia's scandalous conduct soon became common knowledge in the two Chia mansions, spreading even to Pao-yu and causing everyone to sigh and shake his head.

By this time, Pao-yu's hundred-day confinement was over, and he had paid Cassia the customary visit. On that occasion, she conducted herself decorously enough, and if he had heard nothing about her, he would have thought her just as lovely as his sisters in the Takuanyuan. He wondered greatly how the monster she was reported to be could be masked by such a beautiful exterior.

One day while Pao-yu was at Madame Wang's, Welcome Spring's nurse came to her with her mistress' greetings. She spoke of Sun Shao-tsu's tyrannies and oppressions and concluded, saying, "All our Ku-niang can do is to weep in secret. She would like Tai-tai to send for her, so that she may have a respite for a few days."

"I have been thinking of doing that for the past few days," Madame Wang said, "but I have not gotten around to it for one reason or another. We'll send someone to get her tomorrow, since that happens to be a lucky day."

Welcome Spring came to visit the Yungkuofu the next day. She told Madame Wang and other members of the family of her troubles and grievances: how her husband was addicted to wine and gambling, how he had affairs with practically all the maids and some of the servants' wives. "I remonstrated with him a few times, but he only cursed me, saying that I must have been soaked in vinegar to be so jealous. He also mentioned that Lao-yeh owes him five thousand taels. So, when aroused, he points at me and says, 'Don't put on airs like a lady. Your father gave you to me in payment for what he owes me, so you are nothing but a purchased slave. If you don't behave yourself, I'll give you a beating and banish you to the maids' quarters.'" She began to weep as she unfolded her story, and soon everyone present was weeping, too.

Madame Wang tried to comfort her, saying, "You'll have to make the best you can of it, my child. Your uncle tried to dissuade Ta Lao-yeh from accepting the proposal, but he would not listen. It must be your fate."

"I do not see why I should be so ill-fated," Welcome Spring said, crying. "Mother left the world when I was only a child. The only happy years I knew were those I spent on this side. I never thought my life would end like this."

When asked where she would like to stay during her visit, she said that she would like to have her old room, adding, "Next to my brothers and sisters, it has always been second in my thoughts. I may never have another chance to spend a few happy hours there."

"Don't say such nonsense," Madame Wang chided her. "Quarrels between young husband and wife are not uncommon. You should not be so resigned." She immediately ordered the Brocade Chamber to be made ready. She also told Pao-yu not to mention anything to the Matriarch, so as not to make her unhappy.

Welcome Spring stayed for three days in happy reunion with the other young ladies and the maids. Only then did she go to the other side, where she spent two days with Madame Hsing, by which time the Sun family had sent someone to fetch her. She would have liked to stay longer but she dared not, lest it cause her husband to fly into another rage.

PART II

CHAPTER THIRTY-FOUR

In which Black Jade despairs when there is yet hope
And takes heart again when all is lost

PAO-YU had not attended school now for two or three years, partly because of his frequent spells of illness and partly because Chia Cheng was frequently away at some provincial post, and the Matriarch was ever ready to humor him. But Pao-yu was now seventeen and must prepare himself in earnest for the Examinations. Consequently, after consulting with the Matriarch and Madame Wang, Chia Cheng decided to send him back to the family school. He himself took Pao-yu to Chia Tai-ju and impressed upon the latter that he must be strict with his son and make him carry on his studies.

The Peony Court was quiet without Pao-yu. Pervading Fragrance was sitting with her embroidery one day, absorbed in thought. The absence of Pao-yu was a blessing in a way. If he had been at school all this time, the maids would have been less involved with him, and there would have been fewer complications. Bright Design would not have been disgraced and hastened to her death. Then her thoughts turned to herself. She, after all, would only be a concubine to Pao-yu. Her future depended largely on the character of Pao-yu's wife. If this future mistress were kind and generous, Pervading Fragrance could expect a life of happiness. If not, her fate might be like that of Yu Er-chieh or Lotus.

Who would Pao-yu's wife be? From the conversations of the Matriarch and Madame Wang, it seemed that Black Jade would be the eventual choice. What sort of mistress would she make? At this, her heart began to beat faster, and her face became flushed. She would go see Black Jade and sound her out.

Black Jade was cordial. She dropped the book she was reading and asked Pervading Fragrance to sit down. After Purple Cuckoo brought tea, they sat and talked about various things. Soon their conversation turned to Lotus and Yu Er-chieh. Pervading Fragrance said, "Poor Lotus deserves a better mistress. How unkind fate has been to her! I have been told that her mistress is even worse than *she* is." Here she held up two fingers to indicate Phoenix,[1] as she did not want the other maids to hear the name.

Just then, an old maidservant came in with a jar of preserved lichee from Precious Virtue. The old woman kept looking at Black Jade and then said, "No wonder our Tai-tai is always saying that this Ku-niang and Pao-yu would make a perfect pair. I have never seen a young lady quite as beautiful."

After her visitors left, Black Jade, too, became lost in thought. Pao-yu seemed to love her above everyone else; she felt certain of that. But the Matriarch and Madame Wang had not indicated their preference for his future wife. She wished that her parents had decided the matter for her before they died. But then they might have betrothed her to some other family, and she might not have known Pao-yu at all. Now there was at least hope.

She fell asleep thinking about these things and dreamed that Chia Yu-tsun had come to take her home to be married. As she wondered what it meant, Madame Wang and others suddenly appeared to congratulate her, telling her that her father—for it seemed in her dream that her father

[1] Chia Lien, her husband, being Er-yeh or "young master Number Two.

was still living—had remarried and that her stepmother had betrothed her to one of her relatives. Black Jade protested that it could not be true, but they only smiled and said that she would soon find out herself.

Then she was in the Matriarch's apartment. Here at least, she thought, was someone who would heed her appeal. She knelt before her grandmother and told her that she did not want to leave her, that she wanted to stay with her all her life. The Matriarch appeared indifferent; she said that she was powerless to prevent it and that a girl had to marry sooner or later. Black Jade could not expect to stay in the Yungkuofu all her life. "Then let me stay as your bondmaid," the girl pleaded. "I shall serve you faithfully and earn my keep and not be a burden to you. But do not let them take me away."

The Matriarch was deaf to her entreaties. She said to one of her maids, "Take Ku-niang back to her own apartment; she is wearing me out."

Realizing the futility of any further entreaties, Black Jade left the Matriarch. She deplored her fate and declared to herself that all the former kindness of her relatives had been false. She thought she would kill herself. Then it occurred to her that she had not seen Pao-yu anywhere around. He might be able to do something to help her.

No sooner did this thought occur to her than Pao-yu suddenly appeared. But he, too, seemed indifferent. He said, grinning all over, "Congratulations, Mei-mei!"

In her desperation she forgot her modesty. She took Pao-yu's hand and said reproachfully to him, "Now I know that you have been false. How could you say a thing like that if you ever loved me?"

"I have not been false," Pao-yu answered. "But what can I do if your parents want to give you to someone else?"

"But I do not want to go," Black Jade insisted helplessly.

"In that case you can continue to stay here," Pao-yu said. "You were originally betrothed to me. That's why you came here to live in the first place."

Then it seemed to Black Jade that she was indeed betrothed to Pao-yu long ago. She was happy now that she had suddenly realized it. She said to Pao-yu, "I have made up my mind that I would rather die than leave here, but tell me, do you want me to stay or do you want me to go?"

"Of course I want you to stay," Pao-yu answered. "If you do not believe me, I'll show you my heart." So saying, he suddenly produced a sharp knife from nowhere and plunged it into his breast.

Black Jade was terrified; she put her hand on the opening to stop the gushing blood and cried, "How could you do that? You should kill me first!"

"Don't be afraid," Pao-yu said. "I'll show my heart to you." He thrust his hand into the opening and began to probe around, as Black Jade cried and tried to stop him. Then Pao-yu exclaimed, "Oh, I have lost my heart! I shall die!" So saying, his eyes turned upward and he fell back with a thud.

As Black Jade burst out crying, she heard Purple Cuckoo's voice calling to her and bidding her to wake up. The dream was so vivid that she was still sobbing and her eyes were wet. She got up, undressed, and went back to bed but for a long time, she could not fall asleep. And she coughed most of the night. The next morning, when Purple Cuckoo took the jar out to clean it, she uttered an involuntary cry, for she found specks of blood in it. When Black Jade asked her what was wrong, she was afraid to tell the truth and merely said she almost dropped the jar. But Black Jade was not deceived; she thought she recognized the salty taste in her throat. When Purple Cuckoo reentered the room, she noticed that she had been crying. Black Jade was certain that she had spit blood; she realized for the first time that she was seriously ill.

Soon everyone in the Garden knew of her illness. Quest Spring had sent one of her maids to invite Black Jade to join her and River Mist at Compassion Spring's to look at the painting she was making of the Takuanyuan, and she was therefore the first to know about it. She immediately went to see Black Jade and later informed the Matriarch.

When Pervading Fragrance went to the Bamboo Retreat and learned from Purple Cuckoo of Black Jade's nightmare, she told the latter that Pao-yu had awakened that night with a severe pain in his chest.

A few days later, the Matriarch had occasion to speak with Chia Cheng about Pao-yu's progress in his studies. As usual, Chia Cheng deprecated his son's accomplishments, whereas the Matriarch tried to magnify them. "You are too impatient," she said to her son. "You should remember the saying that one mouthful of food will not make a fat baby. By the way, I think it is time to arrange for his engagement. I want you to keep your ears open and get a nice girl for him. It doesn't matter whether she comes from a family related to us or not, whether rich or poor. The important thing is that the girl be sweet-natured and not too homely."

Thus, the Matriarch was still quite open-minded about Pao-yu's future wife; she had thought of it only in general terms, not with reference to any specific candidate. She had made such casual remarks as "they make a nice-looking pair" about Pao-yu and Black Jade but then she had made similar observations with reference to Precious Virtue and others.

One of Chia Cheng's secretaries suggested the daughter of a certain Chang family, distantly related to Madame Hsing by marriage. When the Matriarch asked the latter about it, she learned that the girl was an only child and that the parents expected their future son-in-law to live with them. This was out of the question, of course, for as the Matriarch pointed out, Pao-yu had to be looked after. He was not one to manage the affairs for some other family.

During the discussion of this proposal, Phoenix suggested Precious Virtue as the most suitable candidate. She remarked, "Why look elsewhere when we have a Heaven-ordained match right in our midst?" Asked to elaborate, she said, "Has Lao Tai-tai forgotten the precious jade and the golden locket and what has been prophesied about them? Our families are already related; the marriage would add yet another bond between us."

The Matriarch was pleased with the suggestion and told Madame Wang and Phoenix to sound out Hsueh Yi-ma when they had the opportunity.

But in the meantime, Snow Duck had heard about the proposal from Folio, Quest Spring's chief maid. She took Purple Cuckoo aside and told her about it. They were overheard by Black Jade, who was so overcome with despair that she resolved to neglect her illness and thus bring an early end to her unhappy life. Alarmed by the rapid deterioration of her mistress' condition, Purple Cuckoo went to inform the Matriarch of it.

Snow Duck was left alone with her half-conscious mistress. She was beginning to feel frightened and wished that Purple Cuckoo would come back soon, when Folio came in on an errand. Thinking that Black Jade was unconscious, she asked Folio if she were sure that what she said about the proposal was true.

"It was true, all right," Folio said, "but it fell through because Lao Tai-tai raised objections. I have been told that she had someone picked out for Pao-yu right along but did not say anything about it. The girl is related to our family and lives right here in the Garden. Lao Tai-tai likes the idea of adding another bond to the existing one."

"In that case, this one is dying for nothing!" Snow Duck exclaimed, pointing to her mistress.

"What do you mean?" Folio asked.

"You wouldn't know, of course, but our Ku-niang apparently heard me tell Pervading Fragrance about the proposal. Since then, she became worse every day, until she is now near death."

"Then let us speak quietly. She may hear us now."

"She won't hear us. She is unconscious. I am afraid that it won't be long now."

At this point, Purple Cuckoo returned and scolded them, saying, "You two should not talk here. Are you afraid that she won't die soon enough? Go outside if you must talk."

But Black Jade was not unconscious. She felt a great relief when she heard that the proposal had fallen through. When she heard that the prospective bride lived right in the Garden and that her union with Pao-yu would add another bond to the two families, she was sure that it must be herself. She felt and looked so much better by the time the Matriarch, Madame Wang, Phoenix, and others arrived that Phoenix said to Purple Cuckoo, "Why did you frighten us like this? Your Ku-niang's condition is not half so serious as you said."

"But she was not like this when I left her," the maid said. "She looked terrible then. Otherwise I would not have dared to disturb Lao Tai-tai. It is strange that she should have changed so much for the better in such a short time."

The Matriarch said, "Don't scold her. She is inexperienced. It is better to be on the safe side."

Black Jade's sudden illness and recovery soon became general knowledge and everyone was a little mystified. The Matriarch guessed the true cause when she learned all the circumstances. One day as she was chatting with Madame Wang, Madame Hsing, and Phoenix, she said to them, "Pao-yu and Lin Ya-tou have been together since their childhood. I have always thought of them as children, and it never occurred to me that there could be anything between them. But I am beginning to think that Lin Ya-tou's sudden spells of illness may have something to do with the way they feel toward each other. It is probably unwise for them both to live in the Garden. What do you all think?"

"Lao Tai-tai must be right," Madame Wang said. "But it might cause gossip if one of them is suddenly moved out of the Garden. It would seem that marriage is the best solution."

The Matriarch was silent for a moment before she said, "Lin Ya-tou has her good qualities but she has a perverse streak in her. Moreover, she is sickly, and I am afraid she may not live long. I am inclined to think that Pao Ya-tou is the most suitable."

"That's what we all think," Madame Wang agreed. "But

Lin Ya-tou must also be taken care of. She is now old enough to think of such things. She may have a sentiment for Pao-yu, as Lao Tai-tai suggests. If that is the case, his engagement to Pao Ya-tou might present a delicate situation."

"Her engagement will have to come after Pao-yu's," the Matriarch said. "She is a couple of years younger. But you are probably right about her feelings. We must keep the news from her."

Upon this, Phoenix turned to the maids and said, "Do you all hear what Lao Tai-tai has just said? Not a word of Pao-yu's engagement anywhere. If it becomes known, you will all be held responsible."

And so it happened that the Matriarch definitely decided on Precious Virtue just as Black Jade became certain that she had been chosen as Pao-yu's wife and was beginning to take heart again.

CHAPTER THIRTY-FIVE

In which the unseasonable blossoming of the begonia proves to be an evil omen
And the sudden disappearance of Pao-yu's jade is followed by the loss of his reason

ONE day Black Jade heard an excited chatter in the Takuanyuan. Purple Cuckoo was sent out to investigate and brought back the report that the begonia trees in the Peony Court had suddenly burst into bloom. The day before, Pao-yu had remarked that he had seen some buds on the branches, but no one had paid any attention to him, as it was nowhere near the begonia season. Now there was no mistake about it; the trees were covered with a mass of bright flowers for all to see. Purple Cuckoo was told that the Peony Court was being tidied up in anticipation of the Matriarch's coming.

The Matriarch was already there when Black Jade arrived at Pao-yu's compound, as were Madame Wang and Madame Hsing. The Matriarch tried to minimize the unnaturalness of the phenomenon before them. "The begonia generally blooms in the spring," she said, "but it has been known to bloom in warm spells in the autumn. Though we are now in the Eleventh Moon, it is just as warm as in the Tenth, which again is not unlike the Third Moon, the season for begonias."

Madame Wang tried to fall in with the Matriarch's interpretation, and Li Huan suggested that it might be a sign of some happy event in Pao-yu's life. Quest Spring, however, was not deceived by these optimistic interpretations. She said nothing but thought to herself, "This cannot portend anything good, for what follows the way of Heaven prospers and what goes against it perishes. The unnatural phenomenon we are witnessing must be a warning that the family fortune is on the decline."

Black Jade was pleased with what Li Huan said, for Pao-yu's happy event would also be hers, she thought.

Now Chia Sheh and Chia Cheng also arrived on the scene. The former said that some malignant spirit must be behind the strange phenomenon and that the trees should be cut down. Chia Cheng, however, took the Confucian view that the best way to render the evil spirits powerless is to ignore them. The Matriarch was displeased with these unhappy suggestions. She said, "Say no more of portents and evil omens. If it portends good, you can all share it; if it portends evil, let me bear it all."

In changing his clothes to receive the Matriarch, Pao-yu had forgotten to put on his jade. When Pervading Fragrance noticed it and asked what he had done with it, he said he must have left it on the k'ang. The maid looked for it but could not find it. Pao-yu suggested that Musk Moon or some other maid might have hidden the jade as a joke, but they all denied it. Thereupon, Pervading Fragrance made a thorough search of the Peony Court and then every court and compound where Pao-yu had been on that day, but all in vain. After a few days, all hope of recovering the jade was given up. Everyone now knew of the loss except the Matriarch, for no one wanted to distress her unnecessarily.

Pao-yu seemed listless and preoccupied after the loss, but Madame Wang thought this was only natural since he had worn the jade all his life. Besides, she had other things to occupy her thoughts. Her brother had been appointed to a high post in one of the ministries and was on his way back to the Capital. She looked forward eagerly to the reunion. Then the Imperial Concubine suddenly died, and for a month or so, Madame Wang and the Matriarch had to be in attendance at the funeral.

During this time, a gradual but noticeable change had come over Pao-yu. He looked normal enough but acted like one whose soul had left him. He followed the suggestions of Pervading Fragrance; otherwise he did nothing but eat and sleep or stare vacantly into space. The maid realized that he was not merely depressed at the loss of his jade but was really very sick. She went to Black Jade and hinted that perhaps she could divert Pao-yu and cheer him up, but Black Jade refused, believing that she would soon be married to Pao-yu and in the meantime must avoid gossip. Precious Virtue could hardly be expected to visit him, since she had been told of her coming engagement to him. Hsueh Yi-ma went to see him occasionally but she, too, was preoccupied because Hsueh Pan was at the time in prison on a charge of murder and she was busy arranging for his defense.

After the funeral of the Imperial Concubine, the Matriarch went to the Peony Court to see Pao-yu. She was relieved to find him up and about and looking well but presently she noticed that he was merely following the promptings of Pervading Fragrance. The Matriarch said, "When I first came in, I saw nothing amiss but now I observe that he is very sick indeed. Tell me, how long has he been this way?"

Realizing that the truth could no longer be withheld, Madame Wang told the Matriarch about the loss of the jade. At once, the Matriarch became greatly alarmed and reproached Madame Wang for not having told her earlier. She declared that the jade was Pao-yu's life and must be recovered at any cost. She sent for Chia Cheng and, as he was not home, she gave orders immediately to post a reward of ten thousand taels. She decided to take Pao-yu to her own apartment, saying, "I did not like the strange behavior of the begonia trees. The jade kept the evil spirits from doing any harm, but without it Pao-yu is no longer safe here. That's why I want him taken to my apartment."

"Lao Tai-tai is right," Madame Wang agreed. "Lao Tai-tai's good angels will protect Pao-yu."

"It is not that," the Matriarch said, "but I have many volumes of Buddhist scriptures in my apartment. I'll have them read and keep the evil spirits away. Ask Pao-yu if he doesn't think so."

But Pao-yu only grinned.

It was a dismal New Year at the Yungkuofu. The festivities were halfhearted and perfunctory, owing to the recent death of the Imperial Concubine and Pao-yu's illness. To make things even more depressing, news of the death of Wang Tzu-teng came two days after the Feast of Lanterns. Madame Wang grieved deeply for the loss of her brother and fell ill herself as a consequence.

In the following month, Chia Cheng was appointed Imperial Commissioner of Revenues for the province of Kiangsi. He was not pleased with the new honor, as one might expect. First, he was without the kind of administrative experience needed for the post. Then, the Matriarch was aged and Pao-yu seriously ill. He was thinking about these things when he received a summons from the Matriarch.

Chia Cheng knew that the Matriarch had something important to impart when he saw that Madame Wang was also in the room, in spite of her illness.

"You are going away very soon," the Matriarch said to him. "There is something I would like to see settled before you go, but I don't know whether you will obey my wishes."

Chia Cheng stood up and said, "What is Lao Tai-tai saying! How would her son dare disobey anything Lao Tai-tai commands?"

The Matriarch continued, "I am now eighty-one years old. You have been appointed to a distant provincial post and you cannot decline the appointment because your elder brother is at home to wait upon me. After you are gone, I shall have only Pao-yu to cheer me. Now he is very sick and shows no signs of improvement. Yesterday I sent Lai

Ta's wife to consult a fortuneteller who said that Pao-yu will get well only if he marries someone with the gold destiny. I know you do not believe in such things but I thought that under the circumstances you might be willing to forget your prejudices. Now tell me, do you want Pao-yu to get well or don't you?"

Chia Cheng answered, "How could Lao Tai-tai ask such a question? For though your son cannot hope to be as solicitous and loving of his son as Lao Tai-tai is of her grandson, yet he is not without parental feelings. Your son may have been somewhat hard with Pao-yu, but that's because he has not tried to be worthy; it is like attempting to make a piece of iron into steel. But if Lao Tai-tai wishes him to get married, how could there be any possible objection? Your son has been concerned with Pao-yu's illness, too, but he has not asked to see him because Lao Tai-tai does not wish it. Would Lao Tai-tai permit her son to see him now?"

At this, the Matriarch bade Pervading Fragrance bring Pao-yu into the room. He inquired after Chia Cheng's health as Pervading Fragrance prompted but otherwise showed no interest in his surroundings. He was thin and emaciated, and his eyes were vacant; it was evident that he did not have full possession of his senses. Chia Cheng was grieved to see his son's condition and bade Pervading Fragrance take him back to his room and let him rest. Then he said to the Matriarch, "Lao Tai-tai knows best what to do to save Pao-yu and must do as she wishes. But has it been made clear to Yi Tai-tai?"

"Yi Tai-tai gave her consent long ago," Madame Wang said, "but we have not broached the subject of an early wedding because of the misfortune that has befallen Pan-er."

"That is an obstacle," Chia Cheng said. "It is hardly proper for a girl to marry while her elder brother is in prison. Moreover, there is the mourning for Her Highness to consider. Though weddings have not been forbidden, Pao-yu still ought to observe the rules governing the mourning for an elder sister, which means nine months. Again, the date for my departure has been set by the Board of Rites. How can matters be arranged in the few days still left?"

But the Matriarch had made up her mind. Everything must be done before Chia Cheng's departure, for it might be a year or two before he returned. So she said to Chia Cheng, "I can manage everything if you want to save Pao-yu's life. We can send Kuo-er to see Pan-er and get his consent; I am sure he will agree to this for Pao-yu's sake. As to the mourning period Pao-yu must observe, that does present an obstacle. But then this need not be a real wedding after all. It can be done quietly, so that it will seem more like a propitiatory service than a wedding ceremony. Pao Ya-tou is a sensible girl and will not mind. After Pao-yu recovers and is out of mourning, we can have a real wedding."

Chia Cheng's sense of propriety was outraged by the irregularity of the procedure outlined by the Matriarch, but he kept his feelings to himself. He said, "Doubtless Lao Tai-tai's judgment is right. But we must be sure to keep the matter secret so as to avoid criticism." He left the Matriarch's presence full of misgivings and melancholy reflections. The series of recent events would not occur in a family whose fortune was in the ascendancy. And now this irregular wedding. But owing to his impending departure, he had no time to see to things himself; the arrangements must be left to the Matriarch, Madame Wang, and Phoenix.

Pao-yu did not hear a word of the discussion, for he fell into a heavy sleep as soon as he returned to the inner room. Pervading Fragrance, however, heard everything. She was happy at the turn of events, for she was sure that Precious Virtue would be a good mistress. But what about Pao-yu? How would he react when he learned the truth? The Matriarch and Madame Wang knew something of the regard Pao-yu and Black Jade felt for each other but they did not know the whole story. Precious Virtue vividly recalled that summer day when Pao-yu mistook her for Black Jade and the things he said to her. If Pao-yu felt so strongly about Black Jade, would not the knowledge of the approaching marriage make him worse instead of better?

With these thoughts in mind, she went to Madame Wang and confided to her all she knew. She also suggested that the Matriarch and Phoenix should be told, so that measures could be taken to safeguard Pao-yu. Madame Wang agreed, and Phoenix proposed a scheme to resolve the dilemma. First, the engagement was to be kept secret, so that Black Jade would not hear of it; then, Pao-yu was to be told that he was engaged to Black Jade and would soon be married to her.

CHAPTER THIRTY-SIX

In which Pao-yu appears happy at his approaching wedding
And Black Jade is brokenhearted because of her tragic fate

ONE morning after breakfast, Black Jade decided to visit the Matriarch and present her compliments. On her way she found that she had forgotten to take a handkerchief and she sent Purple Cuckoo to get one. As she approached the hillside where she had once buried flowers with Pao-yu, she found Sister Stupid crying by herself. Black Jade stopped and asked the maid why she was crying, and the latter said, "Now Lin Ku-niang, you be the judge of this and see if my Chieh-chieh was right in slapping me."

"Who is your Chieh-chieh?" Black Jade asked.

"I mean Chen-chu in Lao Tai-tai's room. I was talking with Hsi-jen Chieh-chieh about the marriage and I said, 'We have been calling her Pao Ku-niang; it will be some time before we get used to calling her Pao Nai-nai.' And just for that Chen-chu slapped me, saying that I had disobeyed orders. They didn't tell me that I mustn't say anything about it, even to those who already know."

Black Jade took the girl to a quiet spot and soon got from her the full story, except the part where Pao-yu was to think that she was to be his wife. The news struck her like a thunderbolt; she felt as if her heart were filled with a mixture of oil, soy, sugar, and vinegar, the exact taste of which she could not discern. She left the maid, bidding her say no more of the matter to anyone if she did not want to get slapped again, and started back toward the Bamboo Retreat. A little distance away she turned back again, without knowing exactly what she was doing. It was then that Purple Cuckoo came back with the handkerchief. She had seen her mistress start back toward the Bamboo Retreat and then turn around, wandering aimlessly with unsteady steps. She also caught a glimpse of Sister Stupid walking away. When she caught up with Black Jade, she saw that her face was pale and her eyes fixed in a vacant stare. Realizing that something was wrong, she urged her mistress to go back to her room, but Black Jade did not seem to hear; she only said, "I must ask Pao-yu."

When they arrived at the Matriarch's, the latter was taking a nap, and most of the maids were playing in the yard. Only Pervading Fragrance was with Pao-yu. He was sitting on the bed with his fixed grin and showed no sign of having noticed Black Jade. Nor did Black Jade seem to know where she was. She sat down opposite Pao-yu and grinned back at him. Suddenly she asked, "Why are you sick, Pao-yu?"

And Pao-yu answered, "I am sick because of Lin Meimei."

Pervading Fragrance and Purple Cuckoo were shocked to hear such an outspoken profession and tried to steer them to some other subject. There was no need for their anxiety; for after this exchange, the two lovers fell silent again. Pervading Fragrance, knowing that Black Jade was sick as well as Pao-yu, whispered to Purple Cuckoo that she should take her mistress back to the Bamboo Retreat. "Ku-niang has only recently recovered and must rest," she said. "I'll send Autumn Sky to go with you, in case you need help."

Black Jade stood up when Purple Cuckoo went to her and took her hand. When the maid said to her, "It is time for you to go home and have a rest," she repeated after her mechanically, "Yes, it is time for me to go home and have a rest." But she walked out of the room without assistance; she seemed, in fact, unwontedly vigorous.

Purple Cuckoo uttered a sigh of relief when they at last reached the Bamboo Retreat, saying, "*Amitofo!* at last we are home." But just then Black Jade bent forward and vomited a quantity of blood; the two maids barely had time to catch her and prevent her from falling. They helped her into her room and put her to bed.

After a while, Black Jade regained consciousness and, seeing the tearful faces of her maids, asked why they were crying.

"Ku-niang did not seem well after she returned from Lao Tai-tai's," Purple Cuckoo said. "We were frightened."

"Don't be silly," Black Jade said to them. "I won't die so easily." But as the encounter with Sister Stupid and the story she told came back to her with all its details, she only wished that she could die as quickly as possible and thus pay the debt of love that she must have owed in a former life.

On being informed by Autumn Sky, the Matriarch came to see her, with Madame Wang and Phoenix. She found her deathly pale and her breathing barely noticeable. Black Jade opened her eyes slowly when the Matriarch called to her and said, "Lao Tai-tai, you have loved and cared for me in vain."

At this, the Matriarch's heart ached but she tried to comfort her granddaughter, saying, "Don't be afraid, my child. Take care of yourself and you will be well soon." Black Jade smiled faintly and closed her eyes again.

In the days following, she grew steadily weaker. Purple Cuckoo tried to hearten her by assuring her that what she suspected or heard could not be true, but she only smiled and said nothing. She coughed continually and vomited blood more and more frequently. Purple Cuckoo kept a faithful watch over her and went two or three times a day to report her condition to the Matriarch. But the Matriarch was occupied with preparations for Pao-yu's wedding. She had the doctor visit Black Jade regularly but she herself did not come. Nor did others in the Yungkuofu, for they too were busy because of the approaching wedding. Black Jade could not help noticing this and feeling a little sad when she recalled how solicitous they used to be in the past.

One day, realizing that she had not long to live, she said to Purple Cuckoo, "Mei-mei, you are the only one who knows the secret of my heart. Ever since you came to me from Lao Tai-tai, I have always looked upon you as my own sister." The effort exhausted her, and she had to stop for breath. Purple Cuckoo began to cry. After a long while, Black Jade spoke again. "I feel uncomfortable lying down all day. Come and help me to sit up."

Purple Cuckoo said that she must not exert herself but, when she saw that her mistress was determined to sit up, she helped her to do so. She put cushions behind her and supported her with her arms. Then Black Jade called to Snow Duck and said to her, "Bring me my book of poems." The maid brought the manuscript book and put it by her side. Black Jade nodded and then looked in the direction of a box on the shelf. She seemed irritated because the maid could not read her thoughts, but she could not tell her what she wanted because she was seized by a fit of coughing. When Purple Cuckoo held a handkerchief to her mouth, she brushed it aside impatiently and finally managed to say, "Not that—the one with the writing on it." Purple Cuckoo realized then that she wanted the handkerchief Pao-yu had sent her and on which she had written some stanzas. She had Snow Duck get it from the box and handed it to Black Jade, who tried to tear it up but was too weak to do so. Purple Cuckoo guessed the reason for the action but, lest she aggravate Black Jade's grief, merely said, "Don't be angry. It will only make you feel worse."

Black Jade then asked for a fire, and Purple Cuckoo, thinking that she was cold, suggested that she lie down and put on more covers, as the smoke from a fire might make her cough. Black Jade shook her head. Snow Duck went out and made a fire in the charcoal burner, brought it in, and set it in the center of the room. Black Jade motioned her to bring the burner nearer. Then watching for a moment when the two maids were not at her side, she took the book and the handkerchief, leaned forward, and with a supreme effort threw both into the fire.

Purple Cuckoo was frightened by the condition of her mistress. It was too late to disturb the Matriarch, and it might turn out to be another false alarm; yet what if Black Jade should die during the night? The maid was torn with indecision and was glad when daylight came at last. Black Jade seemed a little better but after breakfast, she began to cough violently again. Purple Cuckoo decided that she must inform the Matriarch of the crisis. Bidding Snow Duck and others to look after her mistress, she went to the Matriarch's. There she found only a few older servants and some little maids.

"Where is Lao Tai-tai?" she asked them. They said that they did not know. She went into Pao-yu's room but then realized that he could not be there, as he must have moved to his wedding chambers. She asked the maids about it, but they only returned evasive answers. "How cruel these people are!" Purple Cuckoo thought to herself. She was indignant at their utter indifference. She returned to the Bamboo Retreat, weeping all the way. At the gate she saw two little maids waiting anxiously for her and knew immediately that Black Jade must have taken a turn for the worse.

Black Jade's face was flushed, which Purple Cuckoo knew was a bad sign. She went for Black Jade's old nurse, but the latter cried and was no help at all. Then she thought of Li Huan; being a widow, she would not be at the wedding. On hearing the sad tidings from the frantic maid, Li Huan immediately set out for the Bamboo Retreat. She thought of Black Jade's rare beauty and her many accomplishments and reflected on the irony and cruelty of fate. She knew, of course, of the plan conceived by Phoenix and therefore had not come to see Black Jade, for she could not bring herself to pretend that she knew nothing. But now she must go and have a parting word with her.

There was no sound when she entered the gate; she thought that maybe she was too late. She wondered if they had the afterlife things ready. Hurrying into the sitting room, she met Purple Cuckoo coming out from the inner chamber. The latter only pointed to the inner room, being too overcome by grief and weeping to speak.

Inside Li Huan found that Black Jade was already too weak to speak. Li Huan called to her gently. She opened her eyes slowly and seemed to recognize her visitor but otherwise she showed no sign of life, her breathing being barely perceptible.

Turning around, Li Huan did not find Purple Cuckoo as she had expected, so she went to the other room. There she found the maid weeping and sobbing as before. "Silly maid," she said. "This is no time for weeping. You must get your mistress's clothes ready and put them on her. You do not want her to go away as she is, do you?"

At this, Purple Cuckoo sobbed more inconsolably than ever. Li Huan began to weep, too, but she had greater self-control than the maid. So, patting her gently on the shoulder, she said, "Don't cry, my child. You must hurry up and get her things ready. There is not much time left."

Just then, Patience came in with Lin Chih-hsiao's wife. When asked what had brought them, Patience answered, "Er Nai-nai is concerned over how things are here and sent me to find out. But since Ta Nai-nai is here, there is nothing to worry about. I shall tell her that she need only think of affairs over there." Li Huan nodded, and Patience went in to see Black Jade.

Li Huan then said to Lin Chih-hsiao's wife, "You can go and see that the afterlife things of Lin Ku-niang are ready. Come back and let me know." Lin Chih-hsiao's wife agreed but did not go.

"What else do you want?" Li Huan asked.

"Er Nai-nai has consulted Lao Tai-tai, and they want

to have Purple Cuckoo over there," Lin Chih-hsiao's wife answered. "They think that would reassure Pao-yu."

At this, Purple Cuckoo could no longer contain her anger and indignation. "Lin Nai-nai will please retire," she said sarcastically. "Wait until this one here is dead before you take her maid away. They need not be so——"

Then regaining her self-control, she went on in a milder tone, "I have been in constant attendance at the sickbed; I am not fit for the wedding chambers. Besides, Lin Kuniang has her moments of consciousness and always asks for me."

Li Huan said, "It seems that Lin Ku-niang and this maid were destined for each other. She brought Snow Duck from the south, but it is this one whom she loves. I am afraid that we cannot separate them."

Lin Chih-hsiao's wife was cut to the quick by Purple Cuckoo's rudeness but she did not retaliate because the maid was in such a pitiful state. Now she said, "I do not mind what she has just said to me, but what am I to say to Lao Tai-tai and Er Nai-nai? I cannot repeat what she said."

Just then, Patience came out from the sickroom and, after learning what the discussion was about, suggested that Snow Duck might be sent instead.

CHAPTER THIRTY-SEVEN

In which Precious Virtue is married according to predestination
And Black Jade dies in fulfillment of an ancient debt

SNOW Duck did not relish her assignment, but what could a bondmaid do except obey? As she sat in her room in the compound allotted by Chia Cheng to Pao-yu and Precious Virtue, she thought about her mistress and what she had meant to the bridegroom and wondered if Pao-yu was really sick of mind and did not know what was happening or was only pretending so as to evade Black Jade. If it was only a pretense, what could he say when he met her, as he was bound to do sooner or later? With these thoughts in mind, she went into Pao-yu's room.

Pao-yu looked better than he had for some time. He was still confused and incoherent but he seemed happy. Not knowing the secret, Snow Duck hated him for his heartlessness and left him without speaking. Pao-yu, on the other hand, was impatient for the wedding hour. "Lin Mei-mei is only coming from the Bamboo Retreat," he said to Pervading Fragrance. "Why should it take so long?"

The maid answered, suppressing an inclination to laugh, "She is waiting for the appointed hour. She cannot come any sooner."

The hour finally arrived. As the sedan entered the courtyard, a small orchestra played the customary wedding music. It was a dismal affair for a family like that of the Yungkuofu, though for an ordinary family it would have been considered quite adequate. The bride wore a red veil and was assisted from the sedan by the bridesmaid. And who do you think this was? It was no other than Snow Duck. Pao-yu was surprised that it was not Purple Cuckoo but then he thought to himself, "Ah, of course. Snow Duck is the maid Lin Mei-mei brought from the south, while Purple Cuckoo was originally Lao Tai-tai's maid. It is only fitting that on an occasion like this Snow Duck should be at her side."

Then came the crucial moment for the unveiling of the bride. The Matriarch and others present all watched tensely for what would happen when Pao-yu found that the bride was not Black Jade.

Pao-yu approached his bride awkwardly and said, "Meimei is well now? I have not seen you for so many, many days. What is the use of wearing that thing?" He was about to take off the veil. The Matriarch and the others all held their breath. But he stopped and mused aloud, "Lin Meimei is very sensitive. I must not offend her." He waited for a moment but could not bear the suspense. He went to Precious Virtue and took off her veil. As he did so, Snow Duck hastily withdrew; and Oriole, Precious Virtue's maid, came forward to take her place.

Pao-yu could not believe his eyes, for the bride looked so much like Precious Virtue. He rubbed his eyes and looked again. There was no doubt about it. It was Precious Virtue. She was dressed in her wedding costume, in which she looked unusually beautiful. Pao-yu stood staring. He turned around and was surprised to see Oriole. He was bewildered and thought that he must be dreaming. The attendants took from him the lamp he was holding and made him sit down. While he stared vacantly with a puzzled air, seemingly unconscious of his surroundings, Phoenix and Yushih led Precious Virtue into the inner room. Then the Matriarch told Pervading Fragrance to put Pao-yu to bed.

Pao-yu asked his maid, "Where am I? Am I dreaming?"

"Do not say such silly things. This is your wedding day. Why do you think that you are dreaming? Lao-yeh is outside. Don't let him hear you say such silly things."

"But who is that beautiful maiden sitting there?" Pao-yu persisted, pointing to Precious Virtue.

The maid put her hand to her mouth to hide her laughter. She said, "That is, of course, the newly married Er Nai-nai."

Pao-yu said, "You are mistaken. Who is Er Nai-nai?"

"Pao Ku-niang, of course."

"Where is Lin Ku-niang then? What has become of her?"

"It was Lao-yeh's decision that you should marry Pao Ku-niang. Don't talk any more about Lin Ku-niang."

Pao-yu was not satisfied. "But I saw it was Lin Ku-niang a little while ago. There was Snow Duck, too. Are you all joking with me?"

Phoenix came forward to him and said, "Hush! Pao Ku-niang is in the inner room. You will offend her if you say anything more. Lao Tai-tai will not let you offend her."

The next day witnessed Chia Cheng's departure from the Capital. With the exception of Pao-yu, who was excused because of his illness, the younger generation all accompanied him ten li beyond the Capital to bid him farewell. For the farewell at home, Pao-yu had been carefully rehearsed in advance, so that Chia Cheng did not notice the sudden relapse that his son had suffered. He told Pao-yu to apply himself and asked Madame Wang to make sure that Pao-yu attended the next Provincial Examination for the degree of "Elevated Man."

After Chia Cheng left, Pao-yu grew steadily worse. On the Ninth Day, the Matriarch managed to send him to Hsueh Yi-ma's house to keep up appearances. Precious Virtue was resigned, though she said to herself that her mother had been too hasty in consenting to the unusual wedding. Hsueh Yi-ma regretted it, too, when she saw Pao-yu at the Ninth Day visit—but what can one do after the rice is already cooked?

One day Pao-yu had a comparatively clear moment. He took Pervading Fragrance aside and said to her, weeping, "Please tell me how Pao Chieh-chieh came to be here. I remembered that Lao-yeh betrothed Lin Mei-mei to me and that I was being married to her. How does it happen that Pao Chieh-chieh came and usurped her place? I want to clear the matter up but I am afraid to offend Pao Chieh-chieh. Lin Mei-mei must be crying herself to death now."

Pervading Fragrance did not dare tell him the truth. She evaded the question by saying that Black Jade was not well. "I'll go and see her," Pao-yu said. He tried to get up but he had been so ill and had fasted so long that he did not have the strength. He fell back and wept. "I do not have long to live. But I want you to tell Lao Tai-tai my wish. I am sure that Lin Mei-mei will die, too, when I die. So tell Lao Tai-tai to put us both in the same room. We can be cared for together in the same place. If we recover, well and good. If not, we can at least die together. We have been together for these many years. Pray, for the love there has been between us, tell Lao Tai-tai this is my last wish."

Precious Virtue happened to return at this moment. She heard Pao-yu and said to him, "Do not utter such gloomy words. You are just beginning to recover and should take care of yourself, instead of entertaining such thoughts. Even if you want to die, Heaven will not let you, for Lao Tai-tai loves you and it would break her heart if you should die. Then there is Tai-tai herself. They are all looking forward to your recovery and to your gaining a name. Besides, though I am ill-fated, I do not believe that it will turn out for me as you think. For these three reasons I am afraid that Heaven will not let you die, even if you wish it."

Precious Virtue decided to resort to a drastic remedy. She added, to Pervading Fragrance's horror, "You need not think of Lin Mei-mei any more, for she died a few days ago while you were unconscious!"

Pao-yu sat up and cried, "Is it true?"

"Of course it is true," Precious Virtue said. "Do you think I would say such a terrible thing of anyone if it were not?

Lao Tai-tai and Tai-tai did not tell you because they did not want to cause you additional suffering."

Pao-yu cried unrestrainedly until he fell back, exhausted and unconscious.

The death of Black Jade coincided with the wedding hour of Pao-yu and Precious Virtue. Shortly after Snow Duck was taken to the wedding chambers, Black Jade had regained consciousness. During this lucid moment, which was not unlike the afterglow of the setting sun, she took Purple Cuckoo's hand and said to her with an effort, "My hour is here. You have served me for many years, and I had hoped that we should be together the rest of our lives . . . but I am afraid . . ."

The effort exhausted her and she fell back, panting. She still held Purple Cuckoo's hand and continued after a while, "Mei-mei, I have only one wish. I have no attachment here. After my death, tell them to send my body back to the south—"

She stopped again, and her eyes closed slowly. Purple Cuckoo felt her mistress' hand tighten over hers. Knowing this was a sign of the approaching end, she sent for Li Huan, who had gone back to her own apartment for a brief rest. When the latter returned with Quest Spring, Black Jade's hands were already cold and her eyes dull. They suppressed their sobs and hastened to dress her. Suddenly Black Jade cried, "Pao-yu, Pao-yu, how—" Those were her last words.

Above their own lamentations, Li Huan, Purple Cuckoo, and Quest Spring thought they heard the soft notes of an ethereal music in the sky. They went out to see what it was, but all they could hear was the rustling of the wind through the bamboos and all they could see was the shadow of the moon creeping down the western wall.

Word of Black Jade's death had been kept from Pao-yu. Even the Matriarch was not informed of it until a few days afterward; there was enough to grieve her without the knowledge of the death of her granddaughter. So when Precious Virtue thus broke the news to Pao-yu without warning, the indiscretion astounded everyone. But in her own mind Precious Virtue was convinced that it was best to tell him. The shock, she reasoned, might well be good for him, since his illness was largely mental. She proved to be right, for Pao-yu improved steadily after he regained consciousness and, with the aid of the doctor's prescription, was able to get about after a few days. Some months later, after Pao-yu's period of mourning for Cardinal Spring was over, a feast was held to complete the wedding, and Pao-yu and Precious Virtue became husband and wife in fact as well as in name.

CHAPTER THIRTY-EIGHT

In which the Takuanyuan becomes a prowling ground for malign spirits
And the Ningkuo and Yungkuo mansions come to their inevitable downfall

COMPARED to its condition when the poetry club flourished, the Takuanyuan was now almost uninhabited. Pao-yu lived in a compound near Madame Wang's apartment and was not allowed by the Matriarch to visit the Takuanyuan except on rare occasions, for though Black Jade's remains had been removed and were now resting in a convent, the Bamboo Retreat was still there and might revive his sorrow.

Precious Harp went to live with Hsueh Yi-ma after her cousin's marriage. River Mist had returned to her family —who were once more in the Capital—and was about to be married. During recent months, she had visited the Yungkuofu twice, once when Pao-yu was married and once when he "rounded the chamber." In the meantime, Welcome Spring had married, and as a result, the Brocade Chamber was closed, and Mountain Wreath went to live with Madame Hsing. The Li sisters were living with their own family and visited the Yungkuofu infrequently. There remained in the Garden only Li Huan, Quest Spring, and Compassion Spring.

One evening around the Festival of the Harvest Moon,

Phoenix was passing near the Takuanyuan and decided to visit Quest Spring. As there was a bright moon in the sky, she dismissed the lantern carrier and entered the Garden with only two maids. Overhearing some of the maids on watch quarreling in one of the courtyards, she sent one of her maids to investigate and continued on her way with the other. A sudden gust of wind wailed through the Garden groves, causing the night birds to fly up and circle over the agitated trees. Phoenix felt a chill down her back. She sent the remaining maid to fetch her silver squirrel vest and take it to the Autumn Study.

After the maid left, Phoenix began to feel apprehensive and hastened her steps. Near the Autumn Study she seemed to see someone moving in the dark. She asked who it was but received no answer. Then she suddenly heard someone saying behind her, "Have you forgotten me, Shen-shen? Has Shen-shen forgotten what I told her some years ago about perpetuating the family school and ancestral burial ground?" Phoenix realized with a shudder that it was Chin-shih. She spat to cast off the evil influences and started running. She stumbled and fell. When she recovered herself, it seemed as if she had been dreaming. The two maids now returned together. Phoenix hurried home with them, pretending that she had been to the Autumn Study and found that Quest Spring had retired.

A few days later, Yu-shih also had occasion to pass through the Garden and fell ill the next day. She was delirious at times and would jabber about demons and ghosts. It was evident that she had encountered some malign spirits in the Garden. A fortuneteller was consulted. He prophesied that the evil spirits would bring more illness to the Ningkuofu. The prophecy came true. Chia Gen, Chia Jung, and the latter's wife all fell ill, one after the other. Some Taoist priests were called in and by charms and incantations cleared the Garden of the evil spirits. The superstitious fears were thus dispelled, and people again dared visit the Garden, though at night, few who lived there ventured out of their courtyards alone.

Chia Cheng's post in the provinces required more administrative shrewdness and ability than he had and, as a result, he was betrayed by his underlings and earned for himself the notoriety of an unusually avaricious official, though he never received bribes or touched anything that was not his. He would have liked to resign the post but, for lack of a valid excuse, was forced to serve out his term and await the Emperor's pleasure.

While at his post, he received a letter from one of the higher provincial officials proposing marriage between his son and Quest Spring. Chia Cheng wrote to the Matriarch and asked for her decision. The latter realized that Chia Cheng must be favorably disposed toward the proposal, since he had taken the trouble to consult her. She therefore consented. There was a general feeling of regret and sorrow in the Yungkuofu at the marriage of Quest Spring in such a distant place, but one must be resigned to one's destiny; when the ancient one in the moon has made the tie, nothing is gained by trying to break it. Quest Spring was sent to Chia Cheng at his post and was married to the son of the frontier official in due time.

Pao-yu was, more than others, affected by the departure of Quest Spring; to him it was as if she had been exiled. He had seen his elder cousin Welcome Spring married. He had heard that the Sun family was notorious for their miserliness and their cruel exactions upon the daughters-in-law, and he had observed Welcome Spring's unhappiness when she returned to visit the Yungkuofu. He had also heard that River Mist's husband was not strong, though he was handsome and gifted and kind to her. Now Quest Spring must leave for the frontier province to be married. He was saddened and began to show signs of a relapse.

After Chia Cheng returned from his post, he had an audience with the Emperor, who seemed displeased. Chia Cheng had been attacked by the viceroy in a memorial to the Throne, charging him with incompetence and failure to check the malfeasance of his subordinates. He waited outside after his audience for intimations of the Emperor's decision and was relieved when his friends among the cabinet ministers told him that his dismissal from the office was considered an adequate punishment for his incompetence, as the Emperor realized that Chia Cheng was ignorant of the corruption of those under him and had not benefited from their illegal exactions.

There were charges, however, made by the censors against Chia Gen and Chia Sheh that could not be glossed over. Chia Gen, it appeared, had been guilty of corrupting the sons of many of the eminent families in the Capital. The Ningkuofu, Chia Cheng learned, had been a favorite gambling resort for these unworthy sons. Of an even more serious nature was the charge that Chia Gen had compelled the daughter of a respectable family to become a concubine, causing her to commit suicide. This case involved several judicial departments of the Capital, as the censors discovered that the first betrothed of the girl in question had brought suit at the time and that justice had been subverted by Chia Gen's bribery. This, of course, was the Yu Er-chieh episode.

The charges against Chia Sheh were that he had entered into conspiracies with provincial officials for the purpose of tampering with lawsuits and corrupting justice. An even more serious charge was the death of a certain owner of some rare antique fans, for which Chia Sheh was the indirect cause.

The result of these charges by the censors was that, while Chia Cheng was entertaining his friends upon the occasion of his return, the Yungkuo and Ningkuo mansions were suddenly surrounded by Imperial Guards. Chia Sheh and Chia Gen were arrested and their properties confiscated. The confusion caused by the ruthless and insolent guards was indescribable. Every courtyard was visited, trunks and chests opened, and valuables seized. Happily, Prince Peace of the North arrived with another decree from the Emperor enjoining the guards from indiscriminate seizure of the properties of both Chia Cheng and Chia Sheh. The search was placed under the personal supervision of the Prince, who, being a good friend of the Yungkuofu and of Pao-yu, showed leniency wherever it was possible. But unfortunately he did not arrive in time to prevent the uncovering of evidence of the usurious loans made by Phoenix.

The Emperor, in whose mind the memory of the late Imperial Concubine Chia was still fresh, was inclined toward clemency. After reviewing the evidence of the various charges against the Ningkuo and Yungkuo mansions, he summoned Chia Cheng to the Palace and announced his decisions through the Prince. Chia Sheh, it seemed, was a relative of the provincial official with whom he had been observed in frequent communication, the nature of which seemed to have been strictly private—at least the censors were not able to present any concrete evidence to the contrary. As to the charge in connection with the fans, these were, after all, curios, not to be compared with real property. The death of the owner of the fans was caused rather by his own eccentricity than by active persecution from Chia Sheh. His Majesty also discovered that there were extenuating circumstances in the charges against Chia Gen. Consequently, the sentences were lenient; they were exiled to the frontier, where they were to serve the interests of the Emperor as atonement for their misdemeanors. Chia Cheng, whose reputation for probity was not unknown to the Emperor and who was absent from home at the time these incidents occurred, was completely absolved. Both his title and his property were restored to him.

The Imperial magnanimity was as unexpected as the first signs of Imperial disfavor. The Matriarch, who was deeply stricken when she was surrounded by her children and grandchildren weeping and crying piteously, had thought that she might never see her two sons again. She had prayed to Heaven that she would gladly suffer for the sins of her children, and she felt that her prayers were answered when Chia Cheng came back to her.

Chia Cheng looked into the family affairs and found that for years the income from rentals and other sources had been far below the expenditures and that there were numerous debts to be met. He reprimanded Chia Lien for having let things go on like this, yet he had no way of remedying the situation. Chia Lien continued to manage affairs in much the same way. One of the first things he did after he was enjoined by Chia Cheng to adopt measures of economy was to sell some land to cover the various expenditures that Chia Sheh and Chia Gen would need during their exile.

Phoenix had been ill for some time, though she tried to conceal it, as she hated to relinquish her hold on things. She fainted when she heard that her apartment had been visited, for she knew that the notes would be discovered. She thought that the Matriarch would no longer love her and that her husband would reproach her. She despaired and waited for the end. But the Matriarch came to see her soon after the departure of Chia Sheh and Chia Gen and seemed to love her as before. Her hopes were revived and she began to recover.

When the New Year came around, the recent misfortunes were too close for the two mansions to enter lightheartedly into the festivities. But on the twenty-first, the birthday of Precious Virtue, the Matriarch prepared a feast in her honor. She felt deeply for Precious Virtue, who during the first year of her marriage had not seen a happy day. She contributed some of her own money toward the expenses of the feast and sent for River Mist, who was at the time living with her own family, and Welcome Spring and the Li sisters. Welcome Spring had not come or sent word when the Yungkuofu was in disgrace. She tearfully told the Matriarch and others that her husband's family at first would not let her have anything more to do with her own people, but when they learned that Chia Cheng had inherited the title and that the Yungkuofu was still in Imperial favor, they allowed her to visit her family again.

The Matriarch's effort to make everyone feel cheerful was only a partial success, for Madame Hsing and Yu-shih were sad because of the exile of their husbands. Phoenix tried to be entertaining but she, too, did not quite succeed.

CHAPTER THIRTY-NINE

In which the Matriarch returns to Heaven after a long life
And Phoenix attains eternal rest from her self-imposed labors

SINCE the shock she received at the time of the seizure of the Chia mansions, the Matriarch had not been well. She had now reached the advanced age of eighty-three, an age when a slight indisposition often brings on the end. One day after the doctor had warned Madame Wang and others, the Matriarch's children and grandchildren all gathered in her room. The Matriarch seemed to have rallied and asked for tea. Madame Hsing brought her a cup of ginseng extract, but the Matriarch insisted that she must have tea. This was brought to her. She drank the tea and expressed a wish to sit up. Chia Cheng and the others said, "Lao Tai-tai can command us as she wishes. She need not exert herself."

But the Matriarch said, "I feel much better after the tea. I want to sit up so that I can talk with you with greater ease." After she was assisted to a sitting position, she continued, "It is now more than sixty years since I came into your family. I have enjoyed many blessings during this time. From your Lao-yeh down to the sons and grandsons, everyone is on the whole worthy . . . and Pao-yu . . . I have loved him . . ." She stopped, and her eyes searched the room. Madame Wang understood her wish and pushed Pao-yu forward. The Matriarch drew her hand from under the coverlet and placed it on Pao-yu's head. She said, "My son, you must vindicate yourself . . ." Pao-yu's eyes were filled with tears, but he did not dare weep. The Matriarch then said, "I want to see one of my great-grandsons. After that, I shall rest in peace. Where is Lan-er?" Li Huan pushed Chia Lan forward. The Matriarch relinquished Pao-yu and put her hand over Chia Lan and said, "You must be good to your mother. You must accomplish something so that she can be proud of you . . . And where is Feng Ya-tou?"

Phoenix was standing behind her. She answered as she came in front of the bed, "Here I am."

The Matriarch said, "My child, you have been too clever. You should invoke blessings by kind and pious deeds. I have not been very pious myself and have not fasted or said my prayers as much as I should. How about the copies of the *Diamond Sutra* that I wished to have copied last year? Have they all been given away?"

Her mind turned to those who were not present in the room. She said, "Our Ta Lao-yeh and Gen-er are in exile . . . But where is Yun Ya-tou? Why doesn't the heartless creature come to see me?" The others knew why River Mist had not come but they did not tell her. It was better that she did not know that River Mist's husband had contracted an incurable illness and was not expected to live. Nor did they tell her about the death of Welcome Spring, who had withered in the hostile atmosphere of the despicable Sun family and had died shortly before.

The Matriarch then looked at Precious Virtue and sighed without giving utterance to her thoughts. She closed her eyes for a moment, opened them again slowly, and glanced over the room. Then she closed them again for the last time, with a smile on her face.

Although Phoenix was two generations removed from the Matriarch, she was nevertheless asked to take charge of the funeral because of her capable management of Chin-shih's funeral several years earlier. Phoenix was not eager to assume the responsibility, for she realized the difficulties she would encounter; however, she could not refuse the request of Madame Wang and Madame Hsing.

On making a survey, she found that her task would be even more difficult than she had feared. She had at her disposal only twenty-one male servants and nineteen female servants. Besides these, there were only about thirty young and inexperienced maids. This was not half as many as were available for the funeral of Chin-shih, and the funeral of the Matriarch was many times more important. There was a very limited amount of money to draw upon, and there were not enough chairs, tables, dishes, and other utensils for the use of the banquets and other funeral ceremonies.

Chia Cheng, who was governed by the teachings of the Confucian canons, gave little thought to the funeral. For him the sincerity of mourning meant more than lavish expenditures. He abandoned himself to mourning and left the funeral arrangements to others. Whenever he was consulted about a particular detail, he would shift the responsibility onto Madame Hsing, who as the wife of the first son of the Matriarch was rightfully the chief mourner. And Madame Hsing had her reasons to incline toward economy. She did not wish to make further inroads upon the family's dwindling resources.

Thus, Phoenix was left in a very difficult position. She was blamed whenever anything went wrong and yet she was not supplied the means for the bare necessities. She was especially distressed by the reproaches of Faith, who had begged her to see that the Matriarch's funeral was appropriate to her position and virtue. "Lao Tai-tai was never extravagant in her life," she had said. "I do not understand what Lao-yeh meant about the sincerity of mourning and the teachings of the sages but I know that Lao Tai-tai used to love Nai-nai and myself and was kinder to us than the rest, and that I for one will be ashamed to face her in afterlife if her funeral is skimped. So I implore Nai-nai to spare no expense. Lao Tai-tai provided for this herself."

The Matriarch, in fact, had made provisions for the future. Shortly after the misfortune that befell the family, she had taken stock of her resources, her personal savings over a long and prudent life, and distributed what she had in appropriate portions to Chia Sheh, Chia Cheng, and others, and set aside a certain sum for her own funeral. Phoenix was distressed by Faith's suspicion that she was responsible for the undue economies, yet she could not accuse Madame Hsing, her mother-in-law. She worked indefatigably, night and day. She had to wheedle, threat, exhort in turn to win any response from the servants and maids. When she ventured to steal a minute's rest, inevitably something happened, and she would hear insinuations that she had become uncommonly fond of her beauty sleep. The night before the funeral, when the Matriarch's remains were to be taken to the Iron Sill Temple, she broke down and was unable to leave her room, although on that day she was needed most.

On the same night, Faith committed suicide. While others were busy with the preparations for the next day, she had retired into the inner room of the Matriarch. No one noticed her absence. She thought of the past and meditated upon her uncertain future and decided to follow her mistress to the grave. When her body was discovered hanging from the beam the next morning, everyone was profoundly affected by her loyalty and resolution. Chia Cheng ordered that she should be buried as a granddaughter of the Matriarch and allowed Pao-yu, who was more deeply affected than anyone else, to do honors to her as an elder sister.

During the services for the Matriarch at the Temple, bandits invaded the Takuanyuan. Fortunately there was among the few manservants remaining in the mansion a certain Pao Yung, a man of great courage and strength, who rallied his cowardly fellows and routed the robbers before they did much damage. During the raid, however, some of the bandits had seen Exquisite Jade, the nun who lived in a convent in a remote corner of the Takuanyuan, and had been greatly impressed by her beauty. They returned later and carried her off beyond the frontiers of the Empire. The fate of the nun, who was so fastidious in her habits and so jealous of her purity, was unknown, but one could easily imagine the horror and the irony that such a fragile flower should fall into such foul hands.

The fright caused by the bandits' raid aggravated Phoenix's illness, and little hope was entertained for her recovery when the members of the Yungkuofu returned from the Temple and saw her critical condition. A few days before her death, she received an unexpected visit from Liu Lao-lao, whom she found hale and hearty as on the occasion of her first visit. She was touched at the contrast between time's treatment of her and of Liu Lao-lao, for the latter had grown fat on the crumbs from the Chias' table and was now in comfortable circumstances, while the Yungkuofu had declined and she herself was dying, with few to care.

Her last days were filled with painful experiences. She who had been the center of activity and the object of the most flattering solicitations now lay dying with only Patience to comfort her. Her husband, whom she had in the past held under her thumb, was not only neglectful but openly contemptuous. Chiu-tung, Chia Lien's concubine, ignored her as if she had already died, and they both seemed to be waiting for the end. She was haunted by Yu Er-chieh, whom she had persecuted to death, and Kin-kuo and her betrothed, whose fates she had sealed when she, at the height of her power and prestige, reached out her hand from the Water Moon Convent and broke their engagement. She dreamed of Chin-shih, who assured her that her sufferings were almost over and that they would soon be reunited in another sphere.

Although it naturally added to the gloomy atmosphere, her death came as no shock to the Yungkuofu, for she had been ill for so long. Chia Lien was now filled with self-reproach and mourned for her. Patience, who was more stricken than anyone else, took care of Phoenix's daughter, and it was through her stratagem and the help of Liu Lao-lao that the daughter was saved from being sold into concubinage by the plot of one of her maternal uncles and the connivance of Madame Hsing herself, during Chia Lien's absence from the Capital. Patience became, eventually, Chia Lien's wife. But all these things did not happen until later. In the meantime, let us return to Pao-yu.

CHAPTER FORTY

In which Pao-yu abjures the Red Dust when the Red Dust seems rosiest
And Pervading Fragrance is married when she has the least intention to marry

PAO-YU was not insensible to the vicissitudes of his family, although he could hardly be expected to be of much comfort or assistance to the other members of the Yungkuofu in the demented condition in which he found himself after the loss of his jade. His studies were, of course, neglected, not only because he was mentally unfit for the exertion, but also because Chia Cheng had no time to think about him.

As pressures gradually eased, however, Chia Cheng realized that he must look into the progress of his son and prepare him for the Examinations to be held in the fall. He summoned Pao-yu and instructed him to review his studies and write some essays to illustrate what progress he had made. But before Pao-yu had time to resume his studies, an incident occurred that rendered the project impossible.

Pao-yu had heard of a certain Chen Pao-yu,[1] the son of a friend of Chia Cheng, whose birthday was the same as his own. To have someone with the same birthday and of the same age and name was remarkable enough, but

[1] "Chen" is a homophone for "true," as "Chia" is for "false." See the couplet on p. 7.

in this case, the coincidence went further: Chen Pao-yu was reputed to look exactly like Chia Pao-yu; so much so, indeed, that when two maidservants from the Chen family visited the Yungkuofu some years earlier, they declared that had they seen Pao-yu in their own house, they would have taken him for their own young master. Pao-yu had often wondered about this counterpart of his and wished to meet him. Now the opportunity came. The Chen family had come to live in the Capital, and one day Chen Pao-yu's father called at the Yungkuofu with his son.

Pao-yu found that the reports of the resemblance were not exaggerated. Had they worn the same clothes, they would have taken one for the other's reflection in a mirror. Pao-yu was delighted. Here, he thought, was someone like himself, one who could understand him, with whom he could talk, on whose sympathy he could count. His disappointment was profound. For though in looks Chen Pao-yu was exactly like him, in ideas and conversation they were as unlike as water and fire. Chen Pao-yu's aspirations and sense of values were, it appeared, those of a youth destined to be the envy of all parents and to be held up as a shining example for all other youths. When Pao-yu ventured to confide to him some of his own thoughts, Chen Pao-yu gave him no encouragement but counseled him, instead, to give his thoughts to the Examinations, the only road whereby one could fulfill one's duty to one's parents, one's ancestors, and one's Prince.

Pao-yu returned to his own apartment in utter weariness and despondency. He went to sleep without comment. When Precious Virtue and Pervading Fragrance questioned him, they received more than ordinarily incoherent answers, accompanied by inane and disconcerting grins. They thought Pao-yu might be having another of the spells to which they had grown accustomed and that he would recover in a few days, as he had recovered on previous occasions. But Pao-yu grew steadily worse, until one day the doctor who had been treating him refused to prescribe.

As all hope was given up, and Chia Lien, enjoined by

Chia Cheng, was about to prepare his afterlife things, a Buddhist monk suddenly appeared and said that for ten thousand taels he would restore the jade and save Pao-yu. Before they recovered from the surprise of this announcement, which was, as the reader will recall, reminiscent of another monk who appeared at a critical moment in Pao-yu's life, the monk invaded the inner apartments and went directly to Pao-yu's room. He approached Pao-yu and whispered in his ear that he had come to restore the jade to him. At these words, Pao-yu opened his eyes and took the jade from the monk. He looked at it appreciatively and then said, "We have been separated for a long time."

The monk was ushered into the outer guest hall where he insisted on his ten thousand taels and said that he would take the jade away if the silver was not forthcoming immediately. His clamorous demands reached the hearing of Pao-yu, who had regained full possession of himself in the meantime, and he came out, after overcoming the objections of Madame Wang and others, to speak to the monk. They seemed to be uncommonly congenial and chatted and laughed together like old friends. Their conversation, however, was unintelligible to those who heard them, though the words "The Green Meadows Peak" and "The Land of the Great Void" could be made out. Finally, the monk went away without demanding his ten thousand taels.

When Madame Wang asked Pao-yu if he had inquired about the monk's residence, Pao-yu answered, "The place where he lives is far if you think it is far and near if you think it is near."

The significance of these enigmatic words did not escape Precious Virtue. She said to him, "Come to your senses! Lao-yeh and Tai-tai have only you and expect you to bring honor to them."

"I, too, am speaking of honors," Pao-yu answered. "Have you not heard the saying that when one son abjures the Red Dust, seven generations of his ancestors are elevated to Paradise?"

Madame Wang, also, was saddened by Pao-yu's words,

for his hint of forsaking the world was clear. "What has come to our family!" she sighed. "Our fourth daughter has been talking about becoming a nun, and now this one is saying that he wishes to be a monk." And she began to weep.

"Do not cry," Pao-yu said, smiling. "I was only joking. Tai-tai must not take it to heart."

But he was not joking. During his conversation with the monk, everything had come to him clearly revealed. He began to recall, though vaguely, his former life, to remember and comprehend the dream in which he was entertained by the Goddess of Disillusionment, and to see clearly his own destiny. He kept these thoughts to himself, for he did not wish to distress Madame Wang and the others. If he inadvertently betrayed himself, he would disarm suspicion with inane laughter.

There was at least one person in the Yungkuofu who did not seem to be distressed by Pao-yu's ill-concealed desire to enter the gate of Buddha; this was Compassion Spring. She had always been of a solitary disposition and never seemed to delight in the festivities that once enlivened the Takuanyuan. Her only intimate had been Exquisite Jade, the nun. She had never had the courage, however, to express her aspirations, for she knew that a family like her own would not permit one of its daughters to enter the convent. But after the reverses of the family and the ill fate that befell so many of its members, she grew more disillusioned than ever, and her disillusionment gave her the necessary courage. At first, Madame Hsing and Madame Wang did not take her seriously, but when she reiterated her determination and threatened to commit suicide if her wish was not granted, they were forced to let her invest herself as a Taoist priestess, with the promise of ultimate freedom to do as she pleased. Purple Cuckoo, Black Jade's maid, begged to accompany Compassion Spring and won the consent of Madame Wang. This took place during the absence of Chia Cheng, who had, shortly after the recovery of Pao-yu's jade, set forth with the remains of the Matriarch, Phoenix, Black Jade, and Faith for Chinling, where the Chias' ancestral burial grounds were.

Now the Examinations were approaching. Chia Lan's industry surprised no one, as he had always been noted for his faithful application to his studies. But Pao-yu's sudden change was a wonder to Precious Virtue and Pervading Fragrance. He secluded himself in a quiet room in which he had only the books needed in preparing for the ordeal. He would read and write all day and sometimes study far into the night. Precious Virtue and the others were pleased, thinking that at last he had come to his senses.

On the morning of the opening day of the Examinations, Pao-yu and Chia Lan went to take leave of Madame Wang, who said, "This is the first time that you two will have been away from home overnight. You must take good care of yourselves and return as soon as you finish your papers, so as not to cause undue anxiety to those at home."

Pao-yu knelt before his mother and kowtowed three times, saying, "I shall never be able to repay Tai-tai's kindness to me but I shall try my best at the Examinations and earn the degree. Perhaps this will make Tai-tai happy and in a way atone for my past unworthiness."

He then bowed to Li Huan and assured her that Chia Lan would succeed. To Precious Virtue he also bowed solemnly and said, "Chieh-chieh, I am going now. You can wait with Tai-tai for the good tidings."

Pao-yu's solemn behavior was attributed by those present to the fact that he had never left home alone, but Precious Virtue had a presentiment that she would never see him again.

The last day of the Examinations found Madame Wang waiting eagerly for the return of Pao-yu and Chia Lan. At midday they had not yet appeared. Servants were dispatched to make inquiries at the Examination Hall but they, too, did not return. Toward evening, Chia Lan returned alone and, with tears in his eyes, said that Pao-yu had disappeared.

It developed that they had left the Examination Hall together, Pao-yu having waited for Chia Lan to finish his papers. But no sooner had they emerged from the gate than Pao-yu was suddenly missing. Chia Lan and the servants who had accompanied them to the Examinations searched everywhere and made inquiries of everyone around, but no one had seen him.

During the following days, the whole Capital was canvassed, and the aid of numerous friends was enlisted in the search, but still there was no trace of Pao-yu. The Yungkuofu was so upset that the Announcement Day came unnoticed. About the Fifth Watch, several maids ran into Madame Wang's room, where the ladies were keeping a vigil, and shouted, "Congratulations, Tai-tai, Nai-nai, and all!"

Madame Wang's immediate thought was that Pao-yu had been found. "But *where* is Pao-yu?" she asked. Neither the maids nor the servants answered.

Both Pao-yu and Chia Lan had passed the Examinations –Pao-yu in seventh place and Chia Lan in one hundred and thirteenth. Ming-yen, Pao-yu's page, threw some cheer into the midst of despair by arguing that an "Elevated Man" could not be lost, since his name would be heralded throughout the Empire, but Compassion Spring observed that he could be lost if he wished to be. Quest Spring, who had returned with her husband's family to the Capital during these hectic days, pointed out that there was every evidence that Pao-yu had disappeared of his own will and that there was no use in fretting over the inevitable.

One of the results of the success of Pao-yu and Chia Lan at the Examinations was the pardon granted by the Emperor to Chia Sheh and Chia Gen and the restoration of their titles and properties. His Majesty, in reviewing the list of successful candidates, noticed the names of Pao-yu and Chia Lan, both from Chinling. He inquired if they were related to the late Imperial Concubine and decreed the pardons after his ministers had presented the result of their investigations. He further decreed an official search for Pao-yu throughout the Empire.

Chia Cheng was returning from the south when the news of the recent events reached him. He was overjoyed when he learned that Pao-yu had received his degree, sad when he learned that he had disappeared, and somewhat cheered again when he learned that his brother had been pardoned. In the evening, he sat in the cabin of the canal boat to compose a letter to the family. He was looking reflectively into the moonlight as he began to write about Pao-yu. Suddenly he perceived someone with bare head and feet standing at the bow, his flaming red cape contrasting sharply with the snow-covered bank of the canal. The man knelt facing him and kowtowed four times. Chia Cheng hurried out to see who it was and found himself face to face with Pao-yu. "Is it not Pao-yu?" he asked.

But before Pao-yu could answer, a monk and a priest appeared and, each taking one of his arms, said, "Your worldly obligations have been fulfilled. Come without delay!" The three then jumped ashore and vanished.

When there was no longer any doubt that Pao-yu had disappeared forever, the first thought of Pervading Fragrance was that she would remain faithful to him for the rest of her life. She cried even more than Precious Virtue did, for she had known Pao-yu much longer, and her position depended upon him rather than upon her mistress. But unfortunately things do not always turn out as one wishes.

One day her brother came to see Madame Wang and told her that a certain Chiang family had asked for his sister in marriage. Madame Wang at once consented and gave him a generous sum for the dowry. Pervading Fragrance did not want to leave the Yungkuofu and yet she could not very well say that she wanted to be faithful to Pao-yu, for after all, she was only a handmaid in his apartment. What right had she to be "loyal"? Her modesty restrained her from speaking. She could only weep. The thought came to her that she must do nothing rash to cause her kind mistresses any pain or inconvenience. She would die in her brother's house. But once there, she saw how thoughtful her brother and sister-in-law were, how they had seen to everything and had made elaborate preparations for the wedding. No, she could not die in her brother's house. She must wait just a little longer, until after the wedding. Alas! the Chiang family was even more thoughtful in their preparations to receive her. Everyone addressed her as Nai-nai and was kind and courteous to her. How could she curse their house with death? It was impossible to do other than resign herself to what fate seemed to have thrust upon her.

A few days after the wedding, the bridegroom discovered a red handkerchief in her chest. He recognized it as his own, one that he had given to Pao-yu, and realized that he had not married just a maid of the Yungkuofu, but Pao-yu's own handmaid. He became even more solicitous and humble toward his bride. He showed her the green handkerchief that Pervading Fragrance had once embroidered for Pao-yu and that Pao-yu, in turn, had given him. This was, indeed, no other than Chiang Yu-han, or Chi-kuan, the actor whom Pao-yu had known.

With the return of Chia Sheh and Chia Gen from exile and the restoration of their properties, there was, needless to say, a new atmosphere of prosperity about the Ningkuo and Yungkuo mansions. The Emperor, after hearing the unique history of Pao-yu, expressed his regret that Pao-yu did not wish to serve at the Court and bestowed on him the title of "The Immortal of Literary Exquisiteness." In a way, Pao-yu did not completely disappear from the Chia family, for soon it became known that Precious Virtue would give birth to a child. In due course this turned out to be a son.

Now the only important character in the book still unaccounted for is Lotus. After Hsueh Pan was thrown into prison and later exiled to the frontier, Cassia, dissatisfied with her virtual widowhood, set about seducing Hsueh Kuo. In her blindness she did not see that Hsueh Pan's cousin was not only capable of disloyalty and treachery but he was himself happily engaged to Mountain Wreath and was shortly to be married to her. One day, as Cassia was making brazen advances to Hsueh Kuo and thought that she was about to achieve her end, the unwitting appearance of Lotus provided Hsueh Kuo with a chance to escape. In retaliation, Cassia tried to poison Lotus. But the latter was not destined to die thus; Cassia herself drank the poison by mistake and perished. Later, when Hsueh Pan returned home as a result of a general pardon, he took Lotus as his chief spouse. One would think that after such an unhappy life, fate might relent and allow her to live out her life with a measure of happiness. But that is not fate's way; Lotus died in childbirth within a year of her marriage.

ANCHOR BOOKS

FICTION

ARROW OF GOD—Chinua Achebe, intro. by K. W. J. Post, A698
THE COUNTRY OF THE POINTED FIRS AND OTHER STORIES—Sarah Orne Jewett, A26
A DIFFERENT DRUMMER—William Melvin Kelley, A678
DOWN SECOND AVENUE—Ezekiel Mphahlele, A792
DREAM OF THE RED CHAMBER—Tsao Hsueh-Chin; Chi-Chen Wang, trans., A159
ENVY AND OTHER WORKS—Yuri Olesha; Andrew R. MacAndrew, trans., A571
GOD'S BITS OF WOOD—Ousmane Sembene, A729
HALF-WAY TO THE MOON: New Writing From Russia—Patricia Blake and Max Hayward, eds., A483
A HERO OF OUR TIME—Mihail Lermontov; Vladimir Nabokov and Dmitri Nabokov, trans., A133
INFERNO, ALONE AND OTHER WRITINGS—August Strindberg; in new translations, Evert Sprinchorn, ed., A492c
A MAN OF THE PEOPLE—Chinua Achebe, A594
MOTHER EARTH AND OTHER STORIES—Boris Pilnyak; Vera T. Reck and Michael Green, trans. and eds., A625
19 NECROMANCERS FROM NOW: An Anthology of Original American Writing for the 70s—Ishmael Reed, A743
POCHO—José Antonio Villarreal, intro. by Dr. Ramon Ruiz, A744
POOR PEOPLE and A LITTLE HERO—Fyodor Dostoevsky; David Magarshack, trans., A619
REDBURN—Herman Melville, A118
RETURN TO LAUGHTER—Elenore Smith Bowen, Foreword by David Riesman, N36
THE SCARLET LETTER and YOUNG GOODMAN BROWN—Nathaniel Hawthorne, Alfred Kazin, ed., A732
THE SECRET AGENT—Joseph Conrad, A8
THE SHADOW-LINE AND TWO OTHER TALES—Joseph Conrad, intro. by Morton Dauwen Zabel, A178
SISSIE—John A. Williams, A710
THE TALE OF GENJI, I—Lady Murasaki; Arthur Waley, trans., A55
TEN GERMAN NOVELLAS—Harry Steinhauer, ed. and trans., A707
THREE SHORT NOVELS OF DOSTOEVSKY—Constance Garnett, trans.; Avraim Yarmolinsky, ed. and revised, A193
UNDER WESTERN EYES—Joseph Conrad, intro. by Morton Dauwen Zabel, A323
VICTORY—Joseph Conrad, A106
THE WANDERER (LE GRAND MEAULNES)—Henri Alain-Fournier; Françoise Delisle, trans., A14
WHAT MAISIE KNEW—Henry James, A43

ANCHOR BOOKS

CLASSICS AND MYTHOLOGY

THE AENEID OF VIRGIL–C. Day Lewis, trans., A20
FIVE COMEDIES OF ARISTOPHANES–Benjamin Bickley Rogers, trans.; Andrew Chiappe, ed., A57
FIVE STAGES OF GREEK RELIGION–Gilbert Murray, A51
FROM RITUAL TO ROMANCE: An Account of the Holy Grail from Ancient Ritual to Christian Symbol–Jessie L. Weston, A125
A HISTORY OF ROME–Moses Hadas, ed., A78
MIDDLE ENGLISH ANTHOLOGY–Ann S. Haskell, AO10
MYTHOLOGIES OF THE ANCIENT WORLD–Samuel Noah Kramer, ed., A229
THE ODYSSEY–Homer; Robert Fitzgerald, trans., A333
SOCRATES–A. E. Taylor, A9

ANCHOR BOOKS

DRAMA

AN ANTHOLOGY OF GERMAN EXPRESSIONIST DRAMA: A Prelude to the Absurd–Walter H. Sokel, ed., A365

AN APPROACH TO SHAKESPEARE, in two volumes–D. A. Traversi, A74a, b

THE BIRTH OF TRAGEDY AND THE GENEALOGY OF MORALS–Friedrich Nietzsche; Francis Golffing, trans., A81

BRECHT: THE MAN AND HIS WORK–Martin Esslin, revised edition, A245

BRAND–Henrik Ibsen; Michael Meyer, trans., intro. by W. H. Auden, A215a

THE CLASSIC THEATRE: Volume I: Six Italian Plays–Eric Bentley, ed., A155a

THE CLASSIC THEATRE: Volume II: Five German Plays–Eric Bentley, ed., A155b

THE CLASSIC THEATRE: Volume III: Six Spanish Plays–Eric Bentley, ed., A155c

THE CLASSIC THEATRE: Volume IV: Six French Plays–Eric Bentley, ed., A155d

COMEDY–Henri Bergson; George Meredith, A87

A COMPANION TO SHAKESPEARE STUDIES–H. Granville-Barker and G. B. Harrison, ed., A191

FIVE COMEDIES OF ARISTOPHANES–Benjamin Bickley Rogers, trans.; Andrew Chiappe, ed., A57

FIVE PLAYS OF STRINDBERG–Elizabeth Sprigge, trans., A219

GHOSTS AND THREE OTHER PLAYS–Henrik Ibsen; Michael Meyer, trans., A215e

GOETHE'S FAUST–Walter Kaufmann, trans., bilingual edition, A328

HAMLET AND OEDIPUS–Ernest Jones, A31

HEDDA GABLER AND THREE OTHER PLAYS–Henrik Ibsen; Michael Meyer, trans., A215c

INFERNO, ALONE AND OTHER WRITINGS–August Strindberg, new translations, Evert Sprinchorn, ed., A492c

MIDDLE ENGLISH ANTHOLOGY–Ann S. Haskell, AO10

THE MODERN THEATRE, Volume 1, Eric Bentley, ed., A48a

THE MODERN THEATRE, Volume 2, Eric Bentley, ed., A48b

THE MODERN THEATRE, Volume 3, Eric Bentley, ed., A48c

THE MODERN THEATRE, Volume 5, Eric Bentley, ed., A48e

THE PEOPLED WOUND, The Work of Harold Pinter–Martin Esslin, A739

PEER GYNT–Henrik Ibsen; Michael Meyer, trans., A215d

REFLECTIONS: Essays on the Modern Theatre–Martin Esslin, A771

SHAKESPEARE OUR CONTEMPORARY–Jan Kott; Boleslaw Taborski, trans., A499

SIX PLAYS OF STRINDBERG–Elizabeth Sprigge, trans., A54

THEATRE EXPERIMENT: An Anthology of American Plays–Michael Benedikt, ed., A636
THE THEATRE OF THE ABSURD–Martin Esslin, revised edition, A279
TRAGEDY AND PHILOSOPHY–Walter Kaufmann, A689

ANCHOR BOOKS

HISTORY

AFRICA AND THE VICTORIANS—Ronald Robinson and John Gallagher, with Alice Denny, AO4
AGAINST THE WORLD: Attitudes of White South Africa—Douglas Brown, A671
THE AGE OF COURTS AND KINGS: Manners and Morals 1588–1715—Philippe Erlanger, A691
THE AGE OF GEORGE III—R. J. White, A706
AGRARIAN PROBLEMS AND PEASANT MOVEMENTS IN LATIN AMERICA—Rodolfo Stavenhagen, ed., A718
THE ANCIENT CITY—Fustel de Coulanges, A76
ANTIWORLDS AND "THE FIFTH AGE"—Andrei Voznesensky; Patricia Blake and Max Hayward, eds., bilingual edition, A595
THE ARAB WORLD TODAY—Morroe Berger, A406
BACK OF HISTORY, The Story of Our Origins—William Howells, revised edition, N34
BASIC WRITINGS ON POLITICS AND PHILOSOPHY—Karl Marx and Friedrich Engels; Lewis S. Feuer, ed., A185
THE BIBLE FOR STUDENTS OF LITERATURE AND ART—G. B. Harrison, ed., A394
THE BIBLICAL ARCHAEOLOGIST READER, Volume III—Edward F. Campbell, Jr. and David Noel Freedman, eds., A250c
BIRTH OF CIVILIZATION IN THE NEAR EAST—Henri Frankfort, A89
THE BOOK OF THE COURTIER—Baldesar Castiglione; Charles S. Singleton, trans., Edgar de N. Mayhew, ill. ed., A186
BRATSK STATION AND OTHER NEW POEMS, Yevgeny Yevtushenko—Tina Tupikina Glaessner, Geoffrey Dutton and Igor Mezhakoff-Koriakin, trans., intro. by Rosh Ireland, A558
CHOU EN-LAI—Kai-Yu Hsu, A652
CRISIS IN EUROPE: 1580–1660—Trevor Aston, ed., intro. by Christopher Hill, A575
DARWIN, MARX, WAGNER: Critique of a Heritage—Jacques Barzun, revised second edition, A127
THE DEAD SEA SCRIPTURES—Theodore Gaster, trans., revised and enlarged, A378
DEMOCRACY VERSUS EMPIRE: The Jamaica Riots of 1865 and the Governor Eyre Controversy—Bernard Semmel, A703
DISCOVERIES AND OPINIONS OF GALILEO—Stillman Drake, trans., A94
THE DISCOVERY OF INDIA—Jawaharlal Nehru; Robert I. Crane, ed., abridged, A200
EAGLES IN COBWEBS: Nationalism and Communism in the Balkans—Paul Lendvai, A687
EARLY MAN IN THE NEW WORLD—Kenneth MacGowan and Joseph A. Hester, Jr., revised edition, N22
THE EASTERN ORTHODOX CHURCH—Ernest Benz, A332
1848: The Revolution of the Intellectuals—Lewis Namier, A385

9Ab

JOHN CALVIN: Selections from His Writings–John Dillenberger, ed., A751

JOURNEYS TO ENGLAND AND IRELAND–Alexis de Tocqueville; J. P. Mayer, ed., A611

KARL MARX ON COLONIALISM AND MODERNIZATION–Shlomo Avineri, ed., A688

THE LAND TO THOSE WHO WORK IT: Algeria's Experiment in Worker Management–Thomas L. Blair, A734

LATIN AMERICAN POLITICS: Studies of the Contemporary Scene–Robert D. Tomasek, ed., new revised and updated edition, A498

LIFE IN MEXICO: The Letters of Fanny Calderón de la Barca with New Material from the Author's Private Journals–Howard J. Fisher and Marion Hall Fisher, eds., AO16

A MAN OF THE PEOPLE–Chinua Achebe, A594

MAO TSE-TUNG ON REVOLUTION AND WAR–Mostafa Rehai, ed., A730

MARX IN THE MID-TWENTIETH CENTURY: A Yugoslav Philosopher Reconsiders Karl Marx's Writings–Gajo Petrović, A584

THE MIND OF THE EUROPEAN ROMANTICS–H. G. Schenk, A655

MONT-SAINT-MICHEL AND CHARTRES–Henry Adams, A166

MOTHER EARTH AND OTHER STORIES–Boris Pilnyak; Vera T. Reck and Michael Green, trans. and eds., A625

MYTHOLOGIES OF THE ANCIENT WORLD–Samuel Noah Kramer, ed., A229

THE NAZI REVOLUTION 1933–35: Prelude to Calamity–Eliot Barculo Wheaton, A690

NEW DIRECTIONS IN BIBLICAL ARCHAEOLOGY–David Noel Freedman and Jonas C. Greenfield, eds., A753

A NEW HISTORY OF THE COLD WAR–John Lukacs, third edition, expanded, of A History of the Cold War, A533

NOBODY WANTED WAR: Misperception in Vietnam and Other Wars–Ralph K. White, A612

OBSTACLES TO DEVELOPMENT IN LATIN AMERICA–Celso Furtado, A747

THE OLD REGIME AND THE FRENCH REVOLUTION–Alexis de Tocqueville; Stuart Gilbert, trans., A60

THE PACIFIC ISLANDS–Douglas L. Oliver, revised edition, N14

THE PATH TO DICTATORSHIP, 1918–1933: Ten Essays by German Scholars–John Conway, trans.; intro. by Fritz Stern, A547

THE PHILOSOPHY OF HISTORY IN OUR TIME–Hans Meyerhoff, ed., A164

THE POLITICS OF CULTURAL DESPAIR–Fritz Stern, A436

POOR PEOPLE and A LITTLE HERO–Fyodor Dostoevsky; David Magarshack, trans., A619

QUEEN ELIZABETH I–J. E. Neale, A105

RECOLLECTIONS–Alexis de Tocqueville; J. P. Mayer and A. P. Kerr, eds., A749

THE RECORDS OF MEDIEVAL EUROPE–Carolly Erickson, ed., A770

THE RELIGIONS OF MANKIND–Hans-Joachim Schoeps; Richard and Clara Winston, trans., A621
REVOLUTIONARY RUSSIA–Richard Pipes, ed., A685
RETURN TO LAUGHTER–Elenore Smith Bowen, Foreword by David Riesman, N36
THE RUSSIAN REVOLUTION: The Overthrow of Tzarism and the Triumph of the Soviets–Leon Trotsky: F. W. Dupee, ed., selected from The History of the Russian Revolution, Max Eastman, trans., A170
SCIENCE AND CIVIC LIFE IN THE ITALIAN RENAISSANCE–Eugenio Garin; Peter Munz, trans., A647
THE SEVENTEENTH-CENTURY BACKGROUND–Basil Willey, A19
A SHORT HISTORY OF SCIENCE: Origins and Results of the Scientific Revolution–Herbert Butterfield and Others, A180
SOCIALIST THOUGHT–Albert Fried and Ronald Sanders, eds., A384
SOCIETY AND DEMOCRACY IN GERMANY–Ralf Dahrendorf, A684
SOCRATES–A. E. Taylor, A9
THE SOUTHEAST ASIAN WORLD–Keith Buchanan, A639
THE SPLENDID CENTURY: Life in the France of Louis XIV–W. H. Lewis, A122
STUDIES OF LATIN AMERICAN SOCIETIES–T. Lynn Smith, A702
THE THIRTY YEARS WAR–C. V. Wedgwood, A249
THREE SHORT NOVELS OF DOSTOEVSKY–Constance Garnett, trans.; Avrahm Yarmolinsky, ed. and revised, A193
THREE WAYS OF THOUGHT IN ANCIENT CHINA–Arthur Waley, A75
TODAY'S LATIN AMERICA–Robert J. Alexander, second edition, revised, A327
TO THE FINLAND STATION: A Study in the Writing and Acting of History–Edmund Wilson, A6
THE TOWN LABOURER: The New Civilization 1760–1832–J. L. and Barbara Hammond, Preface by Asa Briggs, A632
THE TRIUMPH OF THE MIDDLE CLASSES–Charles Morazé, A633
VIETNAM: THE ORIGINS OF REVOLUTION–John T. McAlister, Jr., A761
THE VILLAGE OF VIRIATINO: An Ethnographic Study of a Russian Village from Before the Revolution to the Present–Sula Benet, trans. and ed., A758
THE WANING OF THE MIDDLE AGES–J. Huizanga, A42
WHITE MAN, LISTEN!–Richard Wright, A414
WRITINGS OF THE YOUNG MARX ON PHILOSOPHY AND SOCIETY–Loyd D. Easton and Kurt H. Guddat, trans. and ed., A583
A YEAR IS EIGHT MONTHS: Czechoslovakia 1968–Journalist M, A750